Brought up in Ayrshire, Alice Renton worked at a variety of jobs before moving, after her marriage, to Canada. On returning home two years later, she settled in Sussex with her husband; they have five children, all now adults. Her husband, Tim Renton, who is also a writer, was an MP for many years. Alice splits her time between Sussex and London, with holidays largely spent in her native Scotland.

As well as running a tree nursery and consultancy business, Alice Renton has written two non-fiction books, *VICTORIA, the Biography of a Pigeon* and *TYRANT OR VICTIM? A History of the British Governess*. Her first novel, *WINTER BUTTERFLY*, is also available from Review.

Acclaim for Alice Renton's writing:

'*Winter Butterfly* is a real achievement: wonderful characters, beautiful descriptions... kept me turning the pages like a maniac... the physical details round the dialogue give it the most vivid focus'   John Wells

'An ingenious and entertaining story of family deceptions'   *Family Circle*

'A genuine page-turner... a sharp, witty, beautifully written story that will keep you absorbed for many pleasurable hours'   *Sussex Express and County Herald*

Also by Alice Renton

Winter Butterfly

Maiden Speech

Alice Renton

Copyright © 1997 Alice Renton

The right of Alice Renton to be identified as the Author of the Work has been asserted by her in accordance with the Copyright, Designs and Patents Act 1988.

First published in 1997
by HEADLINE BOOK PUBLISHING

First published in paperback in 1998
by HEADLINE BOOK PUBLISHING

A REVIEW paperback

10 9 8 7 6 5 4 3 2 1

All rights reserved. No part of this publication may be reproduced, stored in a retrieval system, or transmitted, in any form or by any means without the prior written permission of the publisher, nor be otherwise circulated in any form of binding or cover other than that in which it is published and without a similar condition being imposed on the subsequent purchaser.

All characters in this publication are fictitious and any resemblance to real persons, living or dead, is purely coincidental.

ISBN 0 7472 5480 X

Printed and bound in Great Britain by
Clays Ltd, St Ives plc.

HEADLINE BOOK PUBLISHING
A division of Hodder Headline PLC
338 Euston Road
London NW1 3BH

For Stephen Phillips and Margaret Chellingworth
with my love,
confident that they will forgive me

Chapter 1

Peter and Susanna Westerham, walking past the closed double doors into the hall, heard another prolonged eruption of applause. They collected their coats from the row of hooks under a sign saying MANAGEMENT CANNOT BE HELD RESPONSIBLE FOR ANY LOSS OR DAMAGE.

'Not even damage to egos, I suppose,' said Peter.

They let themselves out into the street, and walked through the damp darkness of the car park in silence.

'I'll drive this time,' he said.

Susanna passed the car key over the roof, and got into the passenger seat.

Before starting the engine Peter stroked her cheek with the back of his fingers.

'Cheer up,' he said. 'Don't look so tragic.'

'It's pitch dark. How can you see what I look like?'

'I can feel you looking tragic,' said Peter, starting the engine.

'It was the hat, wasn't it?' said Susanna.

'No, of course it wasn't. It had nothing to do with the hat. It was my speech. Or their speeches. Certainly not the hat.'

He reversed and turned the car.

'It was the hat,' said Susanna. 'I don't know why I wore it. I had this idea that Conservative women wear hats. First sign of political naïveté, I suppose. Not a hat among the whole lot of them. Not even a blue rinse or a string of pearls, that I could see.'

'How lucky you didn't dye your hair blue for the occasion, then,' said Peter.

'Do you think they were typical, that crowd?'

'Well, if they were, I will never get a seat.'

'You will, Pete, of course you will.'

She looked at the hat which lay on her knee like an abandoned kitten. She had borrowed it from her mother, whose taste in hats was medieval. It was velvet, and floppy. Susanna had no hat of her own.

'Yes,' she said again, looking at it, 'it was definitely the hat. I can't blame Ma. She said not to wear it.'

'You're trying to distract me, aren't you?' said Peter, squeezing his wife's hand. 'You needn't worry, I'm not seriously disappointed, because I didn't really feel I was going to get it. I wonder how the voting went. I tried to find out, but they weren't telling.'

'Your speech was brilliant,' said Susanna. 'I know a lot of them voted for you, because of the way they didn't mind catching my eye.'

'Not enough, alas. Oh, well, it's all good experience. There will be others.'

'And better ones, far better ones. Nearer home. Nicer people.'

'Safer seats,' said Pete.

'You'll be glad you didn't get this one.'

'I'm glad already. Stuffy lot.'

'I thought so too,' said Susanna. 'Obsessed with law and order. Sorry, loranorder. And by-passes. Nothing beyond their own back yards. The one who got it, didn't he look smug when you and the other guy were congratulating him?'

'He's been on a lot of shortlists, so I guess he reckoned he deserved this one. And he's been an MP before, so he had quite a lot going for him.'

'I couldn't stand him,' said Susanna, 'the way he kept banging on about "the House" while we were all waiting in that depressing room. Why couldn't he call it the House of Commons, like anyone else? And that patronising way he kissed his wife when they called him in. If you ever get selected, I forbid you to kiss me in front of people.'

Peter steered the car to the side of the road and put an arm round Susanna's shoulders. Pulling her towards him, as far as the seatbelt would allow, he kissed her mouth gently, affectionately.

'I'll kiss you whenever I want to. Thank you for your loyalty. I mean it, love. Don't make a face. Let's go and have a decent meal somewhere near the hotel, and drown our sorrows.'

They drove on through the characterless streets of the Midlands town that they would now never know any better. Earlier in the day they had tried to convince themselves that it had a certain charm. Now it did not matter to them that it had not.

To this extent, the Westerhams were in agreement, thinking as one, as the loving couple they were. But, under the act that they were each putting on to cheer the other, lay a fundamental difference of thinking: Peter Westerham was deeply disappointed at being turned down by the selection committee; Susanna Westerham was just as deeply relieved.

Fifteen years' practice as a country solicitor in Kent had been enough to convince Peter Westerham that there should be more to life. It was not that he did not enjoy his work, or was not successful at it. But having been young when he joined the partnership, he would in eight years' time be the senior partner, at the age of forty-eight. The thought of having nowhere further to go depressed him. He had been for some years a member of the local District Council, and it was while brooding on this in the waking watches of a summer night, wondering whether the County Council might be a rather more interesting challenge, that the idea of parliament had struck him. It was at night again, two weeks later that he had woken up suddenly and certain that this was what he wanted to do.

He had nudged Susanna till she grunted, and said, 'Sukie, listen. I thought I might try and be an MP.'

'O.K,' she said, 'good idea. Now shut up. I'm asleep.'

In the morning, Susanna was downstairs before Peter. She let two large breedless dogs out of the kitchen and walked after them away from the stone farmhouse, through the garden to the gate of a paddock where a large sandy-coloured pony with a black eel-stripe down its back stood dozing in the sunlight. Susanna let herself into the field and walked up to the mare, whose huge stomach swung like a hammock between the black legs.

She put an arm under the pony's head and slapped her gently on the chest, leaning her cheek against the new summer coat on the neck and savouring the wet morning smell of horse.

'You're in no hurry, are you, old lady?' she said, watching the gentle rise and fall of the great belly.

When she got back to the kitchen some minutes later Peter was thinking of making coffee. Susanna stood for a moment watching his back as he bent to peer at the controls of the electric percolator. She smiled and waited. After a few seconds he said, 'Oh, what's the point?' and reached for a jar of instant granules.

Susanna moved quietly forward and, putting her arms round him from behind, hugged him, leaning her cheek against his back, rather as she had recently hugged the pony.

'I'll make real coffee for you,' she said, 'but in the old jug. It's easier. No foal yet.'

'No foal?' said Peter. 'I forget, which pony is it?'

'Skye, the old mare. It'll be her fifth. It should be any day now, but she'll never do it if she thinks I'm watching. Very Victorian and prudish, is Skye. She insists on privacy, and a dark moonless night.'

'It must be her Presbyterian upbringing,' said Peter.

Susanna was moving about, collecting marmalade, honey, filling the kettle, putting slices of bread in the toaster. She turned to see Peter opening one of the letters that had been delivered that morning. Then she suddenly remembered.

'Pete, you didn't mean that, did you, what you said in the night, about being an MP?'

'Yes, I did, actually,' said Peter, looking up. 'What do you think?'

Susanna paused, absorbing this totally unexpected reply.

'Do you think you would enjoy it?' she said, curiously.

'Well, it's like Council work, on a larger scale, and rather more important, so quite a lot more exciting. Yes, I think I would enjoy it.'

'Don't you need a sense of mission? Or vocation? Or frustration, or something?' said Susanna, looking over her shoulder at him from where she stood by the toaster.

'Oh, I think I could find some missions,' he said, sitting down at the table. 'Housing, environmental isshoos, racism, that sort of thing. Legal training is quite useful, and it's one thing you can easily go on doing at the same time as being in parliament.'

Susanna said nothing until she was sitting down and buttering a slice of toast.

'Which party?' she said then.

'Which party?' Peter looked surprised. 'Conservative, obviously. I've always voted Conservative, as you know. It would have to be Conservative.'

'I am always impressed by people who know where they stand, politically speaking,' said Susanna. 'I haven't the conviction.'

Peter looked at her quizzically, unsure how to take this, but she did not elaborate.

'I see myself as a Conservative, a pro-European Conservative, liberal, left of centre, socially responsible.'

'I don't know that that's the public perception of the party,' said Susanna.

'Well, perhaps I can help to make it so,' said Peter. 'Seriously, though, would you mind, if I tried to get a seat?'

'Why does that matter? You must do what you feel like doing. It could be interesting, if you're really sure it's what you want,' said Susanna, screwing on the lid of the marmalade unnecessarily tight. She knew him too well to believe that this was something that had just occurred to him, and was sure that he was not so much asking her as telling her. She was speaking mainly to cover her surprise and mild horror at what she was hearing.

'I would need your help a bit,' said Peter.

'Well, I would try to . . . um . . . yes, if you needed help, of course, whenever I had time. But I should tell you that I am planning to get our own stallion, and take some visiting mares. I will be fairly busy in the long term.'

'That's a new idea, isn't it?' said her husband. 'What are you planning?'

Susanna launched into explanations of how she saw her small stud developing. There were twenty acres of grazing land attached to Restings farmhouse, and she rented another seven. She had started breeding Highland ponies when their children were young, as a job she could do from home, using Restings as her stud name. The sturdy Scottish breed had a great popularity in the south of England, and she had made a small but steady income, producing carefully broken four-year-olds for adult riding. Now the travel costs and lack of adequate stallions in the region made it desirable to bring some new blood from Scotland.

'Then I can have him standing here, and take visiting mares, which means more work, but more money and more fun, too. There is a nice sounding three-year-old, newly registered, with just the blood lines I want. He has bad splints, so he can't be shown, but he is offered on loan for a few years. I am thinking of going up to Perthshire to negotiate next week. I wouldn't get him till next year, though.'

Since their children had left home for boarding school Susanna had expanded her small business successfully, and Peter had been impressed by her careful planning.

'Do you think you and Rachel will still be able to manage, or will you need extra help?' he asked.

'No problem at the moment,' said Susanna.

Peter Westerham's decision caused some surprise in his family. His twin son and daughter, Mark and Emma, both deep into their A levels, were interested but inclined to be dismissive.

'It's just a notion,' Mark had said to his sister. 'We're not really that sort of family. I can't see Dad as an MP, can you? He'll grow out of it.'

But he had been wrong.

Far more concerned was the twins' elder sister, Leonora. When she heard that he had made an application to go on the Conservative Central Office candidates' list, she descended on Restings like a blonde fury, and harangued Peter angrily.

'You can't do this to me! How can I tell my friends that my father is a Tory MP?'

Leonora, at twenty-two, had just left university. Much of her time there had been spent protesting. It had saddened Peter and Susanna to see her excellent first year results being followed by two further years of sitting in trees, camping outside perimeter fences, and blowing hunting horns around most of the greener areas of the country. Her blind adoration of a lean and earnest young man with an endemic and carefully reasoned anger against all authority and most pleasures, had nearly brought an end to her education. She had, however, achieved a third class degree in English and Social Studies and left without disgrace, unlike her boyfriend, who, to her parents' disappointment, was still operative in her life.

'I shall probably not manage to become an MP,' said Peter, 'so the problem is unlikely to arise.'

'I think you must be out of your mind even to consider it,' said his daughter, 'and I do think you should think of your family. God, the *shame* of it . . .'

Peter looked at her with despairing affection. It seemed such a short time since she had sat on his knee and told him that if she couldn't marry him, her father, she was never, ever, ever going to marry anyone.

The interviews, weekend sessions and other formalities Peter had to go through had made little impact on the Westerham family's life until one week end, when two of their three children were at home, he announced over lunch:

'You see sitting before you, as from today, a newly approved member of the Conservative official parliamentary candidates' list. Potential is of course a word that should be inserted there. I have yet to find a constituency willing to adopt me.'

'What does all that mean?' said Emma, her short-cropped blonde head turning from one parent to the other.

'It means,' said Peter, 'that I have been judged pure in thought, word and deed by the Conservative powers-that-be and I am on The List. Which means, in theory, at least, that when I apply for interviews I won't be discarded right away.'

'Hey, Dad, you're so cool, you never told us,' said Mark. Unlike his twin, he had dark hair, but the wide-set eyes in his round face had the same intensity as his sister's. They both had a curious way of watching without blinking, which strangers could find disconcerting. In looks both resembled their father, not particularly short, but rather square in build, and with the same quick, warm smiles. As twins they were by no means inseparable, but they had a deeper understanding of each other than normal siblings.

'Did you know, Mum?' said Emma.

'Of course I knew. Dad told me yesterday. He only heard yesterday.'

'I mean, do you approve, Mum?'

'If Dad really wants to do it, of course I approve,' said Susanna. 'Rather him than me, though. He'll have to be in London an awful lot, when he gets in.'

'When he gets in. I like your confidence,' said Peter.

'Of course you'll get in,' said Emma. 'They'll be lucky to have you. Couldn't it be the Green Party, though?'

'Bo-o-ring,' said Mark. 'Ouch.'

His twin aimed another kick at his shins.

'Mind the glasses,' begged his mother. 'Do you want to come and see my new foal? I haven't given him a name yet.'

'What about Restings Tory?' said Mark.

'Restings Lobby Fodder,' said Emma, 'or Restings Sleaze.'

'Oh, Lord, you can guess the level of jokes here in future,' said their father.

'My ponies are not politically inclined,' said their mother, rising from the table.

'You go and count its little hooves with Mum, Em,' said Mark. 'Dad, I want you to discuss my future with me in a fatherly way. Newcastle have turned me down, as you know, silly sods, but I've got a conditional offer from Durham.'

Mark's school life had not been consistently blameless, but he had so far had none of the rebellious tendencies that his parents had been confidently expecting in an adolescent son. Peter was touched and grateful to be consulted now, and did not realise how much Mark relied on his approval and advice.

He poured some more coffee for them both.

If Susanna gave the appearance of not being much concerned about the proposed change of direction in her husband's life, this appearance was misleading. She was intensely interested, and extremely apprehensive. But it was not in her nature to interfere in the way her relations or friends led their lives, and she never gave advice unless pressed. She did not think her views on politics or the political life would impress Peter, and if she said what she really thought about his plans the fun that he appeared to be having might be inhibited. Susanna believed in people having fun. It was a trait she had inherited from her mother. And it was to her mother that she voiced something of her fears.

Rachel Willoughby had lived for some years in the wing of Restings farmhouse. When her daughter and son-in-law had invited her to share their home she had taken some time in deciding whether to accept, unsure as to what it might do to them all. After a brief marriage she had spent much of her life, if not alone, never in any relationship that meant much to her. She had developed a carapace of amused detachment, and an ability to be happy in her own company. Nevertheless, when offered a share in the pretty farmhouse, she had found the temptation hard to resist. But her fear of destroying the comfortable relationship that existed between her daughter and son-in-law and herself was greater than her need for their company. She had, in the end, agreed to move in, and it was probably her assiduous awareness of the dangers of house sharing between generations that had been the main reason for the success of the arrangement. She put up barriers, ostensibly for her own sake, but covertly for theirs.

'I must have my own front door,' she had said. 'And my own telephone. I don't want anyone monitoring my comings and goings, suspicious though they may be. Just because I am old, I do not necessarily have to behave.'

Having established her own separateness, she made a point of never 'dropping in' or borrowing. That her relatives from the other end of the house regularly dropped in, and borrowed, gave her nothing but pleasure. She paid her way in kind: having worked with horses when she was young, she was of more use to Susanna with the pony stud than any of the girls who had previously been employed. Her love of her grandchildren and of the dogs had also given Susanna and Peter an extra element of freedom.

Susanna knocked on the window of her mother's kitchen as she passed, and went in through the door. With her hands clasped round a mug of coffee, she broke Peter's news.

'I think he knows what he is doing, Ma, but I am not sure he is aware of what it may do to him. Or to us.'

'Go on,' said Rachel Willoughby. She was standing at the window, peering at a sheet of paper through glasses that were wedded to her neck with a piece of string and held together by a safety pin on one side and a paper clip on the other. For fifty of her sixty-two years she had had perfect eyesight, and now deeply resented the outlay on 'magnifiers' that she bought at the local chemist.

'Well, he's not going to be here much, for a start, if he becomes an MP,' said Susanna, 'and I don't think we are either of us going to like that.'

'It's irrevocable, is it? This leaflet appears to say that I have been invited to visit an island in the Caribbean without paying a penny on condition that I pledge my life to reading three Mills & Boons a year. It sounds rather a good deal. It is fascinating, what comes through one's letterbox.'

'Nothing's irrevocable,' said Susanna, 'and he hasn't even got a constituency yet, but he's determined to do it. I haven't seen him so enthused for a long time. There's a recycling bin for junk mail by the bottle bank in Wraybury.'

'In that case, I should deal with the problem when it arises,' said her mother. 'The initial rush of enthusiasm is never easily quelled. I would advise you to hold your fire until the first doubts set in. I always feel I should read this stuff before I throw it out. It seems only fair. I suspect this is a sign of an empty mind. All will change when my computer arrives.'

She dropped the highly coloured leaflet into a wastepaper basket and turned to look at her daughter. Susanna often thought when watching her mother that if she managed to age as well as Rachel she had little to worry about. They were remarkably alike, both of reasonably tall and slim build. Their photographs, as Rachel said caustically, were 'like an advertisement – Before and After, Before being preferable'.

'I hope I am wrong,' said Susanna. 'He really seems to want to do it. It's selfish of me to mind, I suppose, because I have all I want, with the stud, and home, and the odd bit of supply teaching . . . while he just doesn't feel stretched enough. Yes, I am being selfish. But . . . somehow . . . frightened.'

'Boat-rocking, isn't it?' said her mother sympathetically. 'I understand how you feel. You never know, though. It might be fun.'

'It might be fun,' repeated Susanna, without conviction.

Peter sensed the holding back in Susanna, and needed to find out if it was real. So after the failure to emerge triumphant from the shortlist for the Midlands constituency, the ex-MP having been so obviously preferred, Peter decided to speak to her again. Talk was not something lacking between them. They talked a great deal. But Susanna, he found, always had a tiresome tendency to shy away from serious discussion unless positively cornered.

This detached attitude had been one of her great attractions for him when they had first known each other. As Susanna Willoughby, the pretty, diffident, bicycling undergraduate whose punctured front tyre had brought them together, she had entranced Peter Westerham with her distinctive reticence in giving her opinion. In this she differed from many of her contemporaries. She was also reluctant to give advice, but it was after the slow discovery that her opinions and advice, once obtained, were not only excellent but were becoming essential to his happiness that Peter decided to ask her to marry him. He was, of course, also deeply in love with her, and had remained so. The bicycle tyre, in the event, was mended competently by Susanna, the necessary spoons having been found by Peter.

Now he found her adjusting a stiff latch on one of the field gates.

'Sukie,' he said, 'will you have a serious session with me?'

'Now?' she said. 'On a sunny day like this?'

'The sunnier the better. Sit down, and we'll lean against the gate.'

She sat beside him, and pursing her lips turned on him a look of extreme concentration.

'Before the next selection hassle,' said Peter, his elbows on his knees and his hands dangling, 'I want to know what you really feel about this parliament business. The Hertfordshire seat is coming up soon, and I'm on the preliminary list of ten, and then Lincolnshire.'

'I suppose I want to know what you really feel first,' said Susanna.

She looked at the clean, blunt profile beside her. The only noticeable changes since she had first known and loved it were a slight thickening in the neck and a sprinkling of grey in front of the ears. She was aware that there were inner changes, too, a restlessness that had been apparent for some time and that she would be foolish to ignore.

'Well,' he said, nibbling a stalk of grass, 'I really feel I need a change, just at this stage of my life. It may be something to do with seeing the children moving on. I feel a need to achieve, to feel I am using myself effectively. I believe I could be a good MP. I think that I have the brain and the energy and . . . Oh, I don't know, Sukie . . . I just have a great urge to see if I can get there. and if I get there, to see if I can do something.'

'And you definitely see yourself as a Conservative?' said Susanna, the sun warm on her closed eyelids as she rested her head against the rails of the gate.

'I think so. A leftish Conservative, yes.'

They sat in silence for a while, Susanna picking the petals off a buttercup and examining the spiky remainder.

'Would we have to move,' she asked, 'if you get a seat?'

'I hope not. I am sure not. Usually a flat or a cottage in the constituency is enough, they say.'

'I would find the idea of moving very difficult.'

'I know, Sukie, and the one thing I am determined not to do is to make you give all this up. I know how you love it.'

'These spring mornings,' said Susanna, looking round her at the sparkling lushness of the new grass, 'when the foals are young and the buttercup petals stick to their noses . . . heaven must be like this.'

She shrugged. 'You know what, Pete, when you want something the way you want this, you *have* to go for it. Otherwise you will always feel discontented.'

'It is a sort of itch,' he said, nodding. 'I find myself thinking about it all the time. It's not important, like you and the kids are, but I just desperately need a new challenge.'

'You don't have to say it all over again. I understand.'

'I thought you did, Sukie. Thank you. That's all I wanted.'

It was a very long time later that he remembered that though Susanna had given her encouragement, she had not actually given her opinion, either of his plans or his politics.

Susanna, meanwhile, had made up her mind that she would give him all the support he wanted in getting a seat to fight, and that she would do it with all the enthusiasm she could muster. It did not stop her hoping that he would fail.

Peter did fail to get beyond the final ten for the seat in

Hertfordshire but to his amazement, after what had seemed an unsuccessful interview, found himself once again on a shortlist of three, this time for the Lincolnshire seat.

He telephoned the news from his office, where he had been rung by the constituency agent. His voice was quick with excitement. Susanna congratulated him warmly, and then made herself a mug of tea. She put in twice her normal dose of sugar, and went outside. She stood gazing over the stone wall that separated the garden from the rise and fall of the open fields that made their view, hardly seeing the variously coloured ponies grazing in the distance.

Turning, she saw her mother attacking the long green growth of a laburnum bush behind the hedge that separated their gardens. She joined her, and started picking up the twigs that were scattered about, as she repeated what Peter had said.

'He's so pleased. But, oh dear, Ma, can you imagine it? Lincolnshire! It's so flat, you could see the North Pole. But for the curvature of the earth,' she added, remembering to whom she was talking.

'No,' said her mother, scratching her head with her secateurs, 'that is not reasonable. I suspect part of Eastern Scotland and probably the Shetland Isles and Spitzbergen would be in the way. I may be wrong about Spitzbergen.'

'Don't be difficult. Could you see me in Lincolnshire?'

'Now, that's a different matter . . .' Rachel looked pensively at her daughter.

'Oh, Ma, can you be serious?'

'With a little notice,' said Rachel, resuming her snipping. 'Well, he may not get selected.'

'Or he may,' said Susanna. 'I feel rather fatalistic about it all. It's going to happen sooner or later, and I dread his getting something miles away, or in some inner city. That would be London, I suppose, because most other inner cities would be Labour.'

'I imagine,' said her mother, 'that a London constituency would be the easiest to manage from here in Kent.'

'That's true,' said Susanna, 'but even so, when would he ever get home? I just don't know how we would manage being apart.'

'It would be convenient, wouldn't it,' said Rachel, looking with interest at a pod of laburnum seed, 'if someone poisoned one of the local MPs, and a seat became free near here.'

'Ma! You are not to think of it.'

'All right,' said her mother placidly. 'I was only trying to be helpful.'

Without the need for poison or any other form of violence, a local seat did become vacant, a short time after Peter, accompanied to the north of Lincolnshire by Susanna without a hat, had once again just missed selection. An elderly and little known backwoods peer succumbed unexpectedly to a heart attack and, since he was childless, his nephew, who had won the seat of Kentish Weald at the previous election, was wafted despite himself to the House of Lords. A bye-election was to be called imminently.

'It's the perfect seat for you, isn't it?' said Susanna. 'Right next door to home. And you wouldn't have to nurse it for years, with the bye-election so soon.'

'My dear girl,' said Peter gloomily, 'everyone will be after it. Huge Tory majority, near London – it's a triple-plum seat. I have about as much hope as a goldfish in a tank of piranhas.'

'But look at your experience, Pete. You've been on other shortlists. And you're local.'

'But this seat's a far cry from the ones I've been shortlisted for so far, love,' he said. 'The big boys weren't interested in those, or I would never have got on the shortlists. But Kentish Weald, they'll have four hundred or more people trying to get it. They'll want someone who has fought an election before. And they'll want someone well known. They can pick and choose, in a seat like that.'

'Well, damn it,' said Susanna, 'you belong here, you know the place. They should choose you and not some carpetbagger from London and points north.'

'Oh, we'll have a try,' said Peter. 'I've sent my name in already, to tell the truth. It's all experience. But there is no point in being hopeful, honestly.'

'Do you see this? Bloody cheek.'

Major-General Sir Rupert Hascombe threw his folded copy of *The Times* with an expert flick of the wrist so that it slid across the carpet in front of the fireplace of his drawing room towards his wife in the opposite armchair.

'I did. I thought you would be annoyed.' Lady Hascombe continued to prick and pull at her tapestry, leaving the offending paper lying at her feet.

'Well,' said Hascombe, 'it states as a fact that Robert Maybrick will be the next MP for Kentish Weald. You'd think we had no say in the matter at all, and that it was all being decided by Central Office, advised by the press.'

'Well, isn't it, really?' said his wife. 'I mean, you've had more than one telephone call about it already.'

She selected a strand of wool carefully from an overflowing bagful, holding it up to the lamp on the table beside her to check the colour.

'They can telephone as much as they like, but the selection is made here, in Wraybury, and not in London. That wretched man Peacock has been at me too. I expect he has telephoned everyone on the executive, with his greasy voice. If he thinks that I will fall for his sort of fawning suck-uppery he can think again. "With your experience, Sir Rupert, you will understand why Central Office is counting on us not to let the Prime Minister down."'

'We look on the poor man as our constituency agent, because we pay him,' said Lady Hascombe. 'But he is nurtured and trained by the party, isn't he, so the strong tea of Central Office runs freely in his veins. And if Central Office wants to place an ex-minister, it's in Peacock's own interests to do his best. They have the jobs. Could brambles have yellow leaves, do you think? I've run out of green. Can you remember, do they turn yellow in autumn?'

'This Maybrick fellow may be an ex-minister,' said Sir Rupert, 'but he wouldn't have lost his seat at the last election if he were any good, would he? Anyway, we don't want other people's cast-offs here. And we are quite capable of selecting our own candidate without London interfering. We get their approved list, and there is some sense in sticking to that, I suppose, but after that it is up to us.'

'What you really mean,' said his wife, threading a golden strand, 'is that choosing a candidate is the one bit of fun you people on the local executive committee get in twenty years, and you're not going to let Central Office spoil it.'

'So right, as always, Floss,' said Hascombe, nodding. 'I was coerced into being on the executive committee, and it has never exactly been a frolic. In fact, it's been pretty much of a pain. But now, power! Power at last! And I've made sure poor old Mrs Fittall is on the selection panel. She's one of the most assiduous fund-raisers in the constituency. She's brewed enough elderflower wine to make a personal Euro lake, and jumble is her middle name. She deserves her moment of glory, and she'll give 'em hell at the interviews.'

'Who else is selecting?'

'All the usual lot, with Peacock, for the first rounds, and then when we get down to the three finalists the whole crowd comes and votes. That's the whole paid-up membership, if they turn up. And you'd be surprised how many have suddenly remembered to send in their subscriptions.'

'What fun. I shall come to that one,' said Lady Hascombe.

'Not if you haven't paid your dues, you won't. Fully paid-up members only.'

'Rupert! You wouldn't do that to me!'

'Oh yes, I would,' said her husband triumphantly. 'No preferential treatment for the committee members' wives or anyone else. All right, calm down. I always pay yours when I pay mine, you hopelessly spoilt child.'

Florence Hascombe made a face at him, and bent her grey head over her smile.

'I'm going to get a decent MP this time if it's the last thing I do,' said Peacock the Conservative agent. He was unusually talkative this evening, thought his wife, a sign that he was in a good mood. She must avoid saying anything that would break it. Mrs Peacock was particularly sensitive to her husband's moods. She had had twenty years of marriage to assess them and their effect on their home life.

Brushing a wispy strand of her pale hair behind her ear, she said, 'Yes, dear, I'm sure you will.'

'This time I'm going to the top. I don't expect any trouble from the selection panel. The chairman will do as I say, and the rest will take the lead from him, with a little careful manipulation on my part. I expect an overwhelming vote for Robert Maybrick right from the start. If we swing it, Central Office will be happy, and when I apply for the area agent's job they'll remember, you mark my words.'

'Will they make Mr Maybrick a minister again, then, when he gets elected?' asked his wife.

'Bound to,' said the agent. 'He's young, he's bright, and he's a personal friend of the PM. All he needs is a seat.'

'And you're going to give him that, dear. I am sure he will be very grateful.'

'That's right, he will,' said Peacock. 'And it all helps.'

He was smiling to himself, and his normally peeved expression disappeared as he contemplated a rosy future in the flickering flames of the coal fire. His sharp features, which his secretary had once likened to those of a ferret – 'quite a nice-looking ferret, mind you' – softened in the glow, and in the shadow you could see how he had once been quite good-looking, when he still had a full head of hair.

He was positively pleasant in this mood, thought Mrs Peacock. And as long as she could keep him talking about himself and his prospects he would stay in it. She wondered, as she often had before, whether, perhaps, their life together would have been different if she had been able to contribute in some way to his career. Unobtrusively, of course. He would not have liked her to have any of the credit for his success. But of course if he had been successful, he might have been different anyway. He used to be different, when he was younger. But then, she had been different too, and pretty, in a pale sort of way. And slim. She tried hiding her thickening waist with floppy cardigans now, but you couldn't really blame him for losing interest. Men were not like women, in that way. He had been very affectionate once, though. Very affectionate. She could remember, one summer holiday, in Wales, not long after they were married, by that river, they had sat on that grassy bank and he . . .

'Did you?' said her husband, almost shouting.

'Oh dear, what? Did I what, dear?'

'Did you put the kettle on – are you asleep?' His wife irritated him beyond belief when she drifted off with that silly expression on her face.

'Yes – no – I'll get your tea now. I'm so sorry.'

And Sylvia Peacock bustled out of the room.

Chapter 2

Peter was driving, Susanna was reading the *Wealden Echo*.
'The selection process hasn't exactly made the headlines,' she said, 'but it's on the front page.'

'What's the headline, then?' said Peter. 'I need to know about the local concerns.'

'A nice bit of alliteration: Frisky Feline Foils Firemen,' said Susanna.

'Cat up a tree? I don't believe it.'

'You're right not to believe it. It's "cat down a drainpipe". It takes up the top half of the front page, with a photograph.'

'So where is the candidate selection?'

'Further down. Shall I read it?'

'Well, just give me the essence.'

For a minute Susanna read in silence. Then, she said:

'It's headed: LOCALS OUSTED IN TORY SELECTION RUMPUS, question mark. The Tory agent says four hundred and forty people have applied for the candidacy, with what he calls some strong locals among them. I hope you feel strong. But the gossip is that Tory Central Office will insist on one of their protégés being adopted. Can they do that, Pete?'

Peter shrugged.

'Anyhow,' Susanna went on, 'the agent, who seems to be called Peacock, denies this, says Kentish Weald will choose its own candidate, blah blah, and then it lists the other candidates chosen so far. The Lib Dem is called Horton, he's chairman of the local water company. No Labour candidate chosen yet. That's about it. See letters page. Shall I see letters page?'

'If you like,' said Peter.

Susanna turned pages, and found the letters.

'They're all about veal calves, and council things . . . oh, here we are. Hang on . . . yes, a splendid letter about the so-called rumpus, saying the vote for the Tory candidate will be rigged, and they'll have a Londoner foisted on them who won't know a weald from a wold, or care. What's wrong with the men and women of Kent, he thunders? Name and address withheld.'

'You see what I mean,' said Peter. 'Everyone knows that the locals don't get a look-in for a seat like this. Oh, well.'

'Then there's a list,' said Susanna, 'of ex-MPs who are likely to have applied.'

'There you are, then. I haven't a hope.'

When they arrived home at Restings Farm he went straight to the table in the porch for the mail. Restings had no letterbox. The postman would open the porch door, shout 'Morning' and throw in a bundle of mixed mail for both ends of the house. His mother-in-law had sorted it into piles. On top of his pile lay a letter marked Kentish Weald Conservative Association.

'Open it, open it!' said Susanna.

Peter swallowed.

'It's certainly come quickly,' he said. 'That's hopeful. Let's have a mug of tea in our hands and take it calmly.'

'Twaddle. You're anything but calm. Come into the kitchen,' said Susanna.

They found their elder daughter sitting at the kitchen table, reading a newspaper over folded arms. As they entered she lifted her head and shook back the long straight fair hair that hung down to the table. They were used to the casualness of manner towards her parents that had appeared during her student days. The treasured freedom of action acquired then was in conflict with her visceral need to be welcomed at home. Her parents recognised this, and tried hard not to be irritated by her unannounced arrivals, reminding each other regularly that the important thing was that she came.

'Didn't I tell you I was coming?' said Leonora languidly, seeing their surprise. 'I thought I had. There was nothing on this weekend, so I thought you'd like to feed me.'

Sitting side by side at the other end of the flowered tablecloth, Peter and Susanna read the letter together.

'What's the excitement?' said Leonora.

Susanna put an arm round her husband and kissed him on the cheek.

'They want to interview Dad for the Kentish Weald seat. He's on the preliminary list of eighteen interviewees. Well done, love. You were wrong!'

Leonora made a snorting noise, and bent over the paper again.

'They can't have interviewed over four hundred people already, can they?' said Susanna.

'No, of course not,' said Peter. 'They just sift the list and interview about twenty. I guess they have had to include one or two locals, to avoid the flak, and I just happen to be one of them.'

'Don't be so self-denigrating,' said Susanna. 'You're in there with a chance. Interview next Friday. Are you free?'

'Of course I'm free, idiot. How can I not be free?'

'Am I to come?' said Susanna.

Peter looked at the letter again.

'"At this stage we do not require that spouses of applicants should attend interview, though applicants may be questioned on family interests." That answers your question, I'm afraid, and I guess "spouses" covers daughters, too, Leo,' he added mischievously, 'in case you thought of asking.'

'Oh, Dad, for God's sake. The whole thing disgusts me,' said Leonora forcefully. 'You are just demonstrating an absolute lack of values, to want to get involved in a totally corrupt system. Capitalism is the—' She could not recall the quotation she had in mind. 'Anyway, why should I want to listen to you telling a lot of lies just to get a nomination?'

'I don't tell lies, you irreverent chick,' said Peter, offended.

'Then you'll never make an MP,' said his daughter, with satisfaction.

'Cynic,' said Susanna lightly. 'He will make a wonderful MP. Just because he *would* never lie.'

'A cynic, mother, as you know, is what an idealist calls a realist. Politics is the art of the possible, the end justifies the means and so on – all those expressions were coined to give politicians excuses for the things they do.'

Peter looked ostentatiously at his watch and left the room. Leonora relaxed visibly.

'And I wish he wouldn't call me Leo. Mum, doesn't it worry you at all, what he's doing?'

'Does it worry you, darling?' said Susanna.

'Yes. I wish he wouldn't.'

'How do the other two feel?'

'The twins?' Leonora shrugged. 'I don't suppose they have even thought about it.'

She took a cigarette from a packet in her pocket and lit it.

Her mother sighed inwardly and pushed a saucer towards her.

'Tell me why it worries you, Leo – Leonora,' she said. 'I don't want to offend you, but is it just because you feel your friends will laugh at you?'

'Johnnie and I have had a row, if that's what you mean.'

'Ah,' said Susanna. 'I see.'

She looked compassionately at her daughter, who tried to look unconcerned. Susanna thought she was expecting another question.

'I'm sorry,' she said. 'Was it about Dad?'

'Partly.' Leonora was near tears. 'I don't want to talk about it, actually.'

'No, of course. But otherwise, what do you really think about

Dad trying to get into politics? Do you think it would suit him?' Susanna was making conversation, now. 'Everyone needs a new challenge every now and then, and Dad is just at that age when—'

'Mum, I think it's horrible,' Leonora interrupted. 'It really worries me. How can you take it so calmly? Doesn't it worry you? Do you want Dad to change? I can't believe you can go into that rat-race without becoming one of the rats. I mean, politicians . . . he hasn't got the mind of a politician, so his whole way of thinking, his attitudes, his values will all change.'

'You weren't being very kind about his values a few minutes ago,' said Susanna.

'O.K., O.K., I know. I was angry. Actually Dad is so straightforward, and sort of old-fashioned-honourable, and I hate the thought that he will have to forget all that.'

'Leo, surely that is simplistic, and perhaps even a bit childish?'

Susanna had turned towards the sink, and started as Leonora's fist hit the table and she shouted:

'*I am not a child!* What do you both think I am? Leo, a teddy bear or something?'

'I'm sorry,' said Susanna, meaning it. 'I should not have said that.'

'*He* always treats me like a child,' her voice was high and full of pain, 'as if I had no feelings at all. And do you think he cares what he has done to me? I stood up for him. I argued for him when Johnnie attacked him, but do you think Dad cares about me and Johnnie – what he's done to *my* life? He won't even notice, because he's so wrapped up in this bloody political thing.'

She blew her nose loudly into a handkerchief. Susanna, passing behind her, squeezed her shoulder gently. She let a few minutes elapse before speaking again, stacking the dishwasher and allowing Leonora time to recover herself.

'You have a very sad view of politicians,' she said.

'Well, I do, yes,' said her daughter, sniffing. 'You only have to have read the newspapers for the last few years for that.'

'And a very rosy view of the press!'

'They can't all be wrong,' said Leonora glumly.

'The press has attacked politicians since printing was first invented,' said her mother. 'It's what journalists are there for. And they do it to whatever party is in power. Anyway, surely it is better to have people like Dad, as you've just described him, going into politics, than the wrong kind of people? Another thing, darling, is that he is so excited about it. That may sound a bit juvenile, but the thought of it is what makes him jump out of bed in the morning. Would you take that from him?'

'But you're worried too, Mum, aren't you?' said Leonora, looking up at her. 'I can tell.'

'I have worries, yes, but I can't define them quite as easily as you do. There's that telephone. I had better get it, because I think Dad's in the garden.'

And again Susanna managed to avoid saying what she thought. She spoke again to Peter, however.

'Pete, I don't think you should tease Leo. And we must remember to call her Leonora.'

'Was I teasing her?'

'You know you were. She really is distressed about this political thing, and beneath all that tiresomeness she is just as fond of you as ever.'

'I know that,' said Peter, 'but goodness she can be smug and irritating sometimes. As if she hadn't wasted two years on the silliest kind of politics herself.'

'I think she needs a bit of extra understanding at the moment. I gather all is not well between her and Johnnie.'

'Well, thank goodness for that,' said Peter, unsympathetically. He blamed the young self-styled anarchist for trying to alienate their daughter from her parents.

'Yes, well.' Susanna paused. 'But it may be hurting. Be patient with her.'

After the first round of interviews, the list of applicants for the Conservative candidacy was reduced from eighteen to nine. Maybrick, the ex-minister, was still there, and so was Peter Westerham. The others were a predictable mix of businessmen and ex-MPs. Of the only two women, one was local, the chair of the health authority.

'An interesting lot of interviewees,' said Cyril Eversley, chairman of Kentish Weald Conservative Association, holding court at the bar of the Conservative Club in Wraybury, the market town in the centre of the constituency. He liked to drop in every now and then at the club. 'Approachability, it's called,' he explained to his wife. 'It's good to be seen around.'

He usually came straight off the commuter train from London, and asked one of the station taxis to give him half an hour and then pick him up. Then he walked to the club. He always went home by taxi, because 'a fellow likes a drink on the way home, and there is no point in taking risks with the police.' In fact a fellow had lost his licence some eighteen months earlier, and a fellow's wife had made it clear that she was not going to fetch and carry for him.

'A very interesting lot,' he repeated, 'and it has been a testing business sifting out the wheat from the chaff, I can tell you. But we've had some real brain-power trailed in front of us at the selection meetings. Fascinating. Shows the healthy state of the party, when so much talent wants to get into politics.'

'Can you give us a hint, Cyril? Robert Maybrick is one of them, isn't he? And that other fellow the *Echo* talked about?'

Eversley was surrounded by a group of regulars, who, if their faithfulness to the club bar was an indication of their Tory fervour, were ardent Conservatives indeed. The chairman laid a finger against his nose. He relished the sense of importance the attention of his drinking companions gave him.

'That would be telling,' he said. 'We have taken a vow of secrecy until we get down to the last three. But I can tell you this, Central Office has its eye on us here in Kentish Weald, and they're sending us some of the potential party leaders of the future. Kentish Weald will be on the map in no mean way after the next election. You see if I'm not right.'

'When will you have chosen the last three?'

'Quite soon, quite soon.' Eversley could not precisely remember the date of the next stage. 'We have to maintain radio silence, you know, because of the press interest. The hounds are sniffing around, and I have some experience in these things. Tell a friend, and the friend tells another, and in no time it's public knowledge. Well, all right then, David, I'll have a quick one, thank you very much, just to be sociable, and then I must be off. A lot of paperwork in this business, you know. Central Office wants its reports sharpish.'

He raised his refilled glass to the group around him.

'It amazes me,' said Lady Hascombe, licking an envelope and sealing it up, 'that out of four-hundred-odd people who want to stand for Kentish Weald, you should end up selecting your candidate from nine people without a single quality between the lot of them.'

'I didn't exactly say that,' said her husband. 'Who have you been writing to?'

'Paying bills,' said his wife. 'You owe me a fortune. I am not sure I can afford you much longer. Yuppies, yahoos and long yawns, was the expression you used about your interviewees, I think. I was merely translating it.'

Rupert Hascombe was sitting back to front on an upright chair watching his wife as she worked.

'Well,' he said, 'it was the most boring two days I have ever spent, listening to eighteen speeches all on more or less the same subject. Mrs Fittall slept through most of both the afternoons, lucky woman. But when she did ask a question, it was a corker. One eager chap claimed that he was local, a native of Sussex. She opened an eye, and said, '"Where from?" "West Hoathly," he said. "That's not how they pronounce it there," said Ellie Fittall, and shut her eyes again. That fixed *him*.'

Florence Hascombe laughed and lifting her chin peered down at a flimsy bit of paper through the glasses on the end of her nose.

'She sounds useful,' she said. 'Who would you choose, if it was all up to you?'

'Not either of the ex-MPs, I can tell you that,' said Hascombe. 'One is pretty harmless, but colourless, too, He said nothing of any interest at all. I can't even remember his name. And the other is just a bit too interesting – a Genghis Khan foot soldier. Geoffrey Lyne, he's called, a stuffed blackshirt.'

'What on earth can we have bought from a warehouse in Hastings? What about the ex-minister, Rupert? Robert Maybrick? What's he like?'

'Awful,' said Hascombe. 'Even if Peacock were not pushing him so hard I wouldn't want him. He's far too pleased with himself – every question he is asked he uses so crudely to give himself a boost. "I have some experience of this, of course, from my time in the Foreign Office", or "Well, I happen to know the Prime Minister's view on that, from a chat I had with him last week" – that sort of thing, all the time. There is not an ounce of modesty in the man. But has he bothered to find out anything about this constituency? Not a hope. Surrey, Sussex, Kent, he wouldn't know the difference. Arrogant, confident he will get it. Can't stand him. But at least he's better than the other one, Lyne.'

'They sound delightful,' said his wife. 'You haven't told me who you *would* choose.'

'The yuppies are out. One is a Lloyds broker, and the other turned up in a dirty great Range Rover straight out of the showroom with new tyres and this year's registration. We can't have poor Madge Hollywell, the health authority chairman. She'd make a bloody good MP, and she's local, but after the hospital fiasco she'd lose us a lot of votes, I'm afraid. There are two perfectly decent lawyers, one of them local, called Westerham, with a sense of humour.'

'They don't sound very exciting, I admit,' said Florence Hascombe. 'Was there really no one more interesting on the first longlist?'

'There may have been,' said her husband, 'but honestly, Flo, getting a motley band like us to agree on a shortlist of eighteen and then to reduce it to nine is a miracle in itself. For instance, Mrs Fittall insists they be married, and not divorced, Tom Wright insists they be English-born and male and white and over thirty, someone else insists they be under forty and preferably female, and so it goes on. The real laughs will be agreeing on the final three. After that, thank God, it's out of our hands.'

Leonard Peacock, Conservative Party agent for the Kentish Weald division, sat back in his swivel chair and crossed his legs. The chair belonged in fact to Lelia, his part-time secretary in the small outer office. He had borrowed it that morning and moved it into his own office before the arrival of the area agent because he felt that it gave him more of an air of authority than his usual static one. The area agent could sit in that. Lelia, next door, was now perched on an elderly wooden chair that Peacock had taken from an abandoned insurance office down the corridor, and was complaining audibly about what it was doing to her back. Ever since Peacock had tried and failed to persuade Lelia 'to be nice to him' one evening when they had been working late, she had become more demanding and less respectful. He would have to define their relative positions again more clearly.

Peacock lit a cigarette to calm his nerves. He was apprehensive about the descent from on high of Ronald Brinkman. He did not know him well. Brinkman was one of the most senior agents in the party, very experienced and said to be highly regarded at Central Office as an efficient hatchet man. He was approaching retirement. They said that he planned to stay until after the next general election, and after that Peacock wanted his job. If he was to get Brinkman's blessing, a lot depended on this morning's meeting.

Brinkman arrived five minutes before Peacock expected him. Lelia's window overlooked the street, but instead of giving her boss her normal warning of a visitor's arrival, she got her revenge for the chair by showing him straight in.

Peacock, who had been ready and waiting all morning, felt unprepared. He had not had time to flap away the pall of smoke that hung around him. He had planned to be caught in the middle of a telephone call, so that Brinkman would have time while waiting to register his brisk efficiency in dealing with a problem.

'Oh, ah, yes . . . Good morning . . . good to see you, Ronald. I, er, hope you didn't have too bad a drive?' he said, flustered. He had also planned to say Ronnie, right away, as he had heard others do, but somehow it had not come out.

'Morning, Leonard. No, there's never much traffic at this time of the morning,' said Brinkman, laying his briefcase on the side table, and sitting down. Peacock's half proffered hand sank again to his side. He already felt wrongfooted. Of course Brinkman would have had an easy drive down the motorway in mid-morning. He must get back to his plan for the meeting.

'Lelia,' he said, stepping to the open door, 'will you be so good as to bring us some coffee?'

'Yes, Mister Peacock,' said his secretary very deliberately. Peacock had asked her, just on this occasion, to drop her normal familiar 'Len'.

'Or would you rather have tea?' he asked his visitor.

'It is immaterial. Whatever she's making,' said Brinkman. 'I haven't got a lot of time, Leonard, so perhaps we can get down to business.'

The telephone rang. It went on ringing, because Lelia, Peacock realised, was down the passage filling the kettle. He knew she would not hurry back.

'Excuse me,' he said, 'I think I had better get that. I'll tell them to ring back.'

He went into her office, fearing that it might be his wife asking if he would be in for supper, or a similarly unimpressive matter. It was a reporter from the *Wealden Echo*.

'Not at this moment, I am in the middle of a meeting,' Peacock said. 'Yes, of course. I'll ring you back later.'

'The press,' he said airily, back in his own office. Brinkman had not moved. He sat with his arms folded, looking patient.

'That is partly what I have come to talk to you about,' he said. 'Handling the press. This bye-election is attracting a lot of publicity, as they always do, and we want a minimum of flak about how the show is run. For a start, I hope my visit here today will not be mentioned.'

'Not mentioned? No, of course not,' said Peacock, a cold frisson running through him. His mind ranged wildly over the people to whom he had mentioned it.

'It is very important,' said Brinkman, his thin nostrils twitching like a pair of sensitive antennae, 'that there should be no suggestion that we at Smith Square are having any hand in the selection procedure. As you know, local Associations are entirely autonomous, and have a completely free hand an selecting candidates. It is part of the essential democracy of the party.'

'Yes, of course, I know all that, Ronald.'

'Good,' said Brinkman coldly. 'I just wanted to make sure. So you will deal firmly with any rumours to the contrary.'

'Of course.'

'Now, then – ah, thank you so much. No, no sugar.' He took his coffee cup from Lelia, who smiled at him winsomely.

'Sugar for you, *Mister* Peacock?' she asked, not so winsome.

He nodded. She knew he always took two spoonfuls in his coffee.

They both watched her expressive buttocks stretching the possibilities of her skintight skirt as she left the room.

'Right,' said Brinkman, after the door closed, 'now, your shortlist. I am sorry to see that you failed to interview some of the names I gave you.'

Peacock tried hard not to sound apologetic.

'They were not your front runners, so I thought it better not to be pressing too hard at that stage.'

'Mm. That may be wise, tactically. Who are your panel, incidentally? Just ten of them, is it?'

Peacock pulled a sheet of paper towards him.

'The constituency chairman, of course. You know him, don't you, Cyril Eversley?'

'We know him. Is he still hitting the bottle?'

'Better, I think,' said Peacock. 'At least, he's not driving, which makes it safer. The press missed his conviction, I'm glad to say, as it all happened up in Warwickshire. We were lucky there.'

'You can control him, I suppose?'

'No problem. Eats out of my hand,' said Peacock, smirking.

'Then?' Brinkman did not smile.

'Then there's the Association Secretary. She'll co-operate pretty well. And two farmers. They're all right.'

'Never trust farmers. Too weatherbeaten. You can't always tell what they are thinking. Keep an eye on them. After that?'

'Sir Rupert Hascombe. Ex-army, landed gentry, you know the type.'

'He sounds all right,' said Brinkman.

'Ye-es,' said Peacock doubtfully. 'I hope so. There's another ex-army one, Major Wright, Right as they come, actually, in political terms. Everyone who isn't Tory is a commie, with him. Then an old bidd— old lady called Fittall who's been there forever. I didn't want her, but she represents the ordinary branch members, so it looks good, I suppose. Not a very nicely spoken lady, I'm afraid, with rather a sharp tongue.'

'Stupid old cow' was how he had described Mrs Fittall to Mrs Peacock, after the sharp tongue had called him 'a twerp' in his own office.

'Will she listen to you?'

'Oh, I can handle her,' said Peacock. 'And the last three have all been very active in the constituency over the last few years.'

'That sounds all right,' said Brinkman, 'but keep them on a tight rein. Sometimes it goes to their heads, and they get original ideas. "Spotting a winner before he's known", and that sort of thing. Remind them of their responsibility, duty to the party, all that stuff. This is the list, Leonard, of the three finalists we want. Read it, and then swallow it, now.'

Peacock took the piece of paper from the area agent, and read the three names. He then tore it in small pieces. Brinkman was looking at him intently, and for a horrified moment Peacock wondered if he was really meant to swallow it, a sort of virility test, then rejected the thought. He rolled the pieces between his hands and dropped them in the wastepaper bin.

He was playing for time, because one of the names surprised

him. He guessed this might be his moment to shine, demonstrating the local knowledge that Central Office seemed in this instance to lack.

'Robert Maybrick, yes, obviously,' he said, 'and I imagined you would want Geoffrey Lyne. He is known here, of course – when he was an MP he spoke at our supper club. But Madge Hollywell? Surely not! She is still on the list, but only just, because she's local. She is not at all popular round here. You know she's chairman of the health authority? And after the hospital closed, they all blamed her, and—'

'I know all that, Peacock,' Brinkman interrupted with irritation. 'It's my business to know. That's why she's there, in the final three. It is party policy now to have a woman on the final shortlist. If there's a good one, we'll have her. If there isn't, we'll have a bad one. This one isn't bad, but she won't win, for the reasons you give. We all know the mess she got into over the hospital. That makes sure that one of the two that we do want gets it. Got it?'

He spoke as if to a child, with an encouraging smile.

'Oh,' said Peacock, impressed.

'Right. We would prefer Maybrick, because he should walk straight into a government job, but we would be quite satisfied to get Lyne back. He has ministerial potential. In fact, Maybrick will almost certainly get Kiddingstone, so it might be better if Lyne made it here. One or the other, anyway.'

Peacock made a mental note that Maybrick must win. He knew the value to his career prospects of being agent to a definite minister rather than a potential one.

Brinkman looked at his watch.

'Have you got that quite clear then, Leonard? You make sure that when the membership that we can't control roll in for the big final selection meeting, they'll have to choose one of the two candidates we want.'

'No problem. Leave it to me,' said Peacock importantly.

Brinkman spoke once again, meaningfully.

'And again, Leonard, this conversation has not happened.'

As he passed through the outer office he paused for a moment by Lelia.

'You need a decent chair, young lady,' he said, patting her shoulder, 'with all the work you're going to have to do over the next few weeks.'

When he had gone, Peacock decided to defer the problem of Lelia and her feelings and to deal instead with the more nagging worry of the area agent's strictures about the press. This decision proved to be a tactical error. He was about to call the Association chairman when the telephone rang. Lelia, still sulking, did not trouble to find out who was on the line but put the caller straight through. It was, again, the reporter from the local paper, Kieran Mitchell.

'Mr Peacock, we go to press tomorrow, so I wanted to have another word with you about the selection procedure for the Tory bye-election candidate? You mentioned that Tory Central Office was taking a keen interest in the process, and you were expecting them down to consult. When is that happening?'

'Did I say that?' said Peacock, his face reddening. 'I think you must have misunderstood me. Er . . . of course Central Office takes an interest, but not till we send them the result, you know. As a Conservative Association we are, of course, totally autonomous, and we have a completely free hand in selecting our candidate.'

'So there would be no question of Central Office trying to influence the selection procedure?'

'None at all, absolutely not. I will telephone them when it is all over, and you too, of course, my dear. You shall have an exclusive, if you're a good girl.'

Nothing like keeping the local press on side, thought Peacock. He knew all about that.

'So, to sum up,' said the girl, 'the selection of the Tory candidate will be entirely decided locally?'

'That's right, Kirsten.' Rather a pretty little thing she was, he remembered. 'And you'll be the first to know. Come along to the club and I'll give you a drink.'

'Thank you, Mr Peacock. I might take you up on that. Can I just ask one more question? You had a visitor this morning. Would that have been someone from Central Office, by any chance?'

Peacock felt as if he had been kicked in the stomach. He paused, just too long.

'A visitor? This morning? Er . . . I had one visitor, yes. How do you know?'

'I'm in the call box opposite your office, so I saw the big black car, and the gentleman with the briefcase. Was he from Central Office, possibly?'

'That was a private visit . . . a local businessman, and none of your business,' said Peacock furiously.

'Funny,' said Kieran, 'it was a London number plate.'

'Look here, Kirsten, you—'

'Kieran,' said the girl. 'Must dash. Thanks a lot, Mr Peacock.'

By the time Peacock got to the outer office window to glare down at the telephone box it was empty.

Kieran Mitchell, crouching behind a parked car and peering through its windows, saw him standing there and nodded with satisfaction.

Chapter 3

Susanna's supposition about Leonora's lovelife proved to be well-founded. Within a week she was home again, hunching her way miserably about the house. She spent long periods of a weekend in her bedroom, tearing down the posters and impedimenta of her girlhood, and passionately reducing the room to a cell. Asking if she could use some white emulsion she found in an outhouse, she erased her past with long, messy strokes.

Her grandmother found her in the corner of a field by the stables stoking with dry twigs a roaring bonfire that needed no such help, in view of the amount of basketwork, wooden beads and ethnic cotton that had already fed it. Rachel watched for a few minutes and then sat down on the ground. Soon Leonora joined her.

In silence they maintained vigil while the flames reduced themselves to nothing, and the sultry embers sank into a lava of dispirited ash.

'It does you good to have a clear-out every now and then,' said Rachel, with deliberate triteness.

'It helps. I feel much better. Cathartic, I suppose,' said Leonora. 'Funny.'

'Stopping things is always much harder than starting them.'

'Yes. That's why you put it off, I think. You need a reason.'

'Was it your reason, or his?' said Rachel.

Suddenly Leonora was defensive.

'It was Dad's fault. He's totally wrapped up in himself, and fff— sorry Gran – to hell with everyone else. He is so *insensitive*. Johnnie always said lawyers were parasites, and politicians were worse.'

Rachel noted the past tense.

'Some and some,' she said, all anodyne.

'I was living a lie, he said, between my family and him.'

'Speaking as a member of your family, Leonora, I am relieved you chose us.'

Leonora snapped a twig viciously into small bits and threw them towards the fire.

'I don't suppose Dad will even notice, far less be grateful.'

'In fairness, he didn't really know Johnnie, did he? Only you did,' said Rachel.

'He didn't try, did he? It was awful when I brought him home, Dad was awful and Johnnie was awful. I couldn't bear it. And Johnnie couldn't understand anything about Restings.'

'Funny,' said Rachel blandly, 'how we all love Restings.'

'Trouble is, I loved him too.'

Gently the tears began to roll, and Leonora leant her head on her grandmother's shoulder.

After a short while, she said: 'You're very good, Gran, at just understanding without saying anything.'

'Well,' said Rachel, 'I was just about to say that this grass is damp. I think I am getting piles. What about some of the hard stuff to round off the day?'

'Just what I need, Gran. It's cold. And it's starting to rain, feel it?' said Leonora. 'God, I'm glad I don't have to go down to Newbury. That's what we would have been doing, this weekend. I hated all that mud.'

And they went in to Rachel's end of the house as the garden receded into darkness.

The telephone rang with startling loudness and jerked Cyril Eversley out of his reverie. He had had a long day, mainly spent in other offices than his own. On his return he had been met at the station by his wife and driven straight to a supper party at which he considered their host had been conspicuously stingy with his drink. Now, home at last, he was what he referred to as 'winding down'. His wife had gone up to bed some time earlier, saying pleadingly, 'You'll come soon, won't you, dear?' Then, putting her head round the sitting-room door again a few minutes later to say, 'Cyril, don't you think you've . . . ?' had withdrawn, shaking it, in response to his glare.

The result was that he filled his whisky glass once more, to prove that he was a man in his own house. Then he had fallen to thinking of the glory that would be his as chairman when the Association adopted, and the constituency subsequently elected, a man with cabinet potential. Indeed, Peacock had assured him that he had it from the horse's mouth that Maybrick was likely to go straight into the cabinet immediately after the bye-election. Images floated through his mind of himself walking through tall wrought-iron gates into Downing Street, giving a casual nod to the policeman who swung them open on seeing him. Well, perhaps not Downing Street at this stage, but certainly into the House of Commons he would walk, a respected figure of the party hierarchy; offering guests a drink on the terrace, perhaps. He was just raising a casual hand to the Chancellor of the Exchequer when the telephone came to life.

His hand jerked, and whisky flew out of his glass onto his trousers. He flapped drops over the carpet and then reached for the receiver.

'Yes? Staplewood 972 2202. Sorry, 972 2022. Who's that?'

'Is that Mr Eversley?' said a girl's voice.

'Cyril Eversley speaking,' he said.

'Oh, Mr Eversley, I am so glad to have found you. I do hope you won't mind my ringing you so late.'

'Not at all, my dear, what can I do for you?'

It was a pretty woman, he thought, at least a pretty voice, so presumably . . . She almost sounded in distress.

'Mr Eversley, you don't know me, but my name is Kieran, Kieran Mitchell. I would be so grateful for a minute to talk to you, if you are not too busy.'

'Talk away, my dear.' He felt comfortable and expansive. She sounded young, and in a flutter.

'Well, you see,' said the girl, 'I work for the *Wealden Echo*. I am fairly new there, and I am trying to do a piece about the selection of the new Conservative candidate, which has to go to my editor tomorrow. I was talking to Mr Peacock, the agent, today, and I have been very careless and mislaid my notes – it's so silly of me, I would telephone him, but of course his office is closed, now.'

Poor child, she seemed quite upset.

'Tell me the problem, my dear, and let's see if I can help,' said Eversley.

'Well, I gather that Conservative Central Office is paying a great compliment to the constituency by asking the committee to select Robert Maybrick as candidate. I mean, it would be a great honour to Kentish Weald to have him as our MP, wouldn't it?'

'Well, of course, it would,' said Eversley, 'but the selection is not made yet, my dear. It is a very democratic process.'

'Oh, yes, Mr Eversley. I don't know much about politics, but I know it is all very democratic. Were you there, this afternoon, Mr Eversley, at Mr Peacock's meeting with the gentleman from Central Office?'

Damn Peacock, thought Eversley, why had he not told him this? The Association chairman not present at such a meeting – it was iniquitous. It put him in a humiliating position.

'The meeting . . .' he said, hesitating.

'Yes, at the Association office,' prompted Kieran.

'Well, you know, I am a very busy man, and I cannot be everywhere at once. I was at a different meeting this afternoon.'

'You wouldn't know, then, if Mr Maybrick's application was discussed?' asked the girl.

'Oh, I get a full report of these meetings, don't worry.'

This was embarrassing.

'So Mr Peacock will have passed on to you Central Office's request to you for Mr Maybrick to be included in the final shortlist. Will it be you who relays this to the selection committee, or is that Mr Peacock's job?'

'No, that is not Mr Peacock's job,' said Eversley. 'I am the Association chairman, not Peacock. I shall pass on the request to the committee myself.'

He felt deeply upset that Peacock should have put him in this position, which amounted to an undermining of his authority.

'I am sure that the Kentish Weald Association has a very good relationship with Central Office, Mr Eversley?'

'Of course, excellent, excellent.'

'Thank you so much, Mr Eversley,' said Kieran, 'You have confirmed everything I gathered from talking to Mr Peacock. I do try very hard to be accurate. Thank you so much for your help.'

Eversley felt mildly uncomfortable as he put the receiver down. He was blurrily aware that talking to the press had been discouraged by Peacock, but the child was very friendly, and had lost her notes. He had, as she said, only confirmed what Peacock had already told her. There could be no harm in that. And it was as well to have a friendly relationship with the press. In any case, Peacock had caused the situation by keeping his chairman in the dark. It had made him feel an absolute fool. He must speak to the agent sometime about their relative positions. Sometime. He did not find Peacock easy to talk to.

His whisky glass seemed to be empty.

'You are sure of all this, Kieran?' said the editor, tapping his pencil against his teeth.

'Quite sure.' Kieran Mitchell had also assured him of the anger that her story would cause, and the editor knew that anger sold papers.

'Very well,' he said, making up his mind. 'We will move the attempted arson onto page two. I'd like some photographs. Get one of Maybrick, then ring round all the likely venues and find out where the final selection meeting is. It has to be pretty soon, because they can't keep the shortlisted candidates on the hook for too long. There'll be a hall booked somewhere.'

The second selection meeting took place in the Association Office; nine candidates from whom three were to be chosen.

There was no doubt that Robert Maybrick's ten-minute speech to the committee was an accomplished performance. It left the committee impressed and dazzled. When he showed himself to be considerably less knowledgeable on constituency matters they were easily convinced by his excuses.

'I am, as you know, much involved in policy making in the party, so I have not had time to make myself as familiar as I should have liked with local Kent problems. Should you do me the honour of selecting me I will make this good, very thoroughly and without any delay.'

By contrast, most of the other candidates seemed relatively amateur, and Peacock knew that it would need no intervention on his part for Maybrick to be shortlisted, despite the mutterings of one or two committee members.

The ex-MP Geoffrey Lyne's speech was also witty and polished, and he had the committee laughing from the start. His views, all derisive, on the European Union, raised keen interest in his listeners.

The discussion after all the applicants had gone home was not especially good-tempered. Everyone was tired, and most felt that others had hogged the questioning. More than one committee member, led by Sir Rupert Hascombe, mentioned the rumoured interference by Central Office, which Peacock strenuously denied.

'Who do they think they are, telling us what to do?' said Ellie Fittall indignantly.

Hascombe, who had observed that her eyes had been shut through most of the speeches, winked at her approvingly.

'Mrs Fittall, the choice is in our hands,' said Eversley soothingly. 'Central Office has no vote in this, and you do.'

'Let's get on and vote, then,' she replied. 'It's after seven o'clock and I want to get home. It's the snooker on tonight, and I like to have me supper first. It'll be baked beans, the speed we're going. You can cross off Madge Hollywell, for a start. She wouldn't win this seat even if she was the only name on the ballot paper. Not with her record locally. They'll never forgive her for the hospital.'

'She was very good on questions. It's a shame,' said someone.

Peacock decided the time had come for a little expert manipulation.

'Through the chairman, if I may,' he said unctuously, 'I think we might face a lot of trouble if we don't field a local candidate in the final three. You'll all have seen the *Echo* last week. Well, Mrs Hollywell has the stature to make a challenge for the candidature.'

'You mean she's big. That's true. She's certainly a big girl,' said Major Wright, and laughed heartily at his joke.

'I don't think that's funny,' said Mrs Drayton, the doctor's wife. 'Madge Hollywell would make an excellent MP, and remarks about her appearance are quite unnecessary.'

'You are quite right, Mrs Drayton,' said the Association secretary, 'but even if it was unfair, she carried the can for the hospital closing, and people would just laugh if we put her on the list.'

'Well, have the other fellow, Westerham, he's local,' said Hascombe. 'Knows what's going on round here. Made a good joke, too. He'd do.'

The discussion moved on.

There was a strong move in favour of Geoffrey Lyne coming from several members of the committee, though Ellie Fittall muttered 'Carpetbagger' each time his name was mentioned. Finally, it was her threat to go home unless they voted soon that concentrated everyone's minds, and the papers with the candidates' names were circulated. Maybrick emerged as the front runner, with Geoffrey Lyne and Peter Westerham neck-and-neck behind him.

Peacock went home satisfied. He had failed to get Mrs Hollywell into place, but in the end it wouldn't matter. Westerham was not well known, and his chances of collecting more than a handful of votes were minimal.

Central Office would be pleased.

'We've got Maybrick of course, in the last three,' said Rupert Hascombe to his wife, after chewing on lasagne that had waited too long in the oven, 'and a local solicitor, called Westerham, who's the outsider (there's a contradiction in terms for you), and that ghastly man Lyne. He's a fascist, and has a good line in jokes, so probably half the membership will fall for him. If he's adopted, I'm emigrating.'

'He might still not win the election,' said Florence Hascombe.

'My dear love,' said Hascombe, 'whoever gets the Conservative nomination here wins the seat. He has got to be stopped at this stage or we've had it. We've got to make sure of Maybrick, as the lesser of two evils.'

'Well, how do you propose to do that?'

'I think we will ask Eversley here to supper,' said Hascombe, 'and his wife. And see what a little base flattery will do.'

The banner headline in the *Wealden Echo* the following morning was such that Mrs Peacock, after a glance, put on her hat and coat and went out, determined not to reappear until her husband had left for his office. The words were just what her husband wanted to see, but they had appeared, disastrously, a week too early.

MAYBRICK IS TORY CHOICE, they read, and the rest was worse.

LOCAL VIEWS IGNORED

As predicted by the *Echo* last week, prominent Tory ex-minister Robert Maybrick was last night put in the pole position to win the Kentish Wealden seat at the coming bye-election. A high level visit to the constituency put paid to the hopes of Kent candidates as Tory Central Office imposed its will on the local organization.

The *Echo* last week exposed the plot to exclude applicants from the Kentish Weald area from the selection procedure. Tory sources are keeping mum about the identities of the other successful finalists, but the *Echo* can reveal that they all carry the official Central Office stamp of approval.

The article continued with interviews with members of the public. 'I think it's diabolical,' said Mrs A.W., who did not wish her name to be revealed. 'There are plenty of local boys who would make better MPs than that lot up in London.'

On the leader page the insult to Kentish blood was described in more high-flown terms than by Mrs A.W. but the sentiments were basically the same.

Peacock, when he had read it all, swore effusively and telephoned Eversley.

'Smith Square will crucify us,' he said, 'when they hear about this.'

'Now look, Leonard,' said Eversley, 'I want to explain . . .'

This was the moment when Peacock realised that the fault might not be entirely his.

'You spoke to that girl,' he said.

'Yes, but, you see, she only asked me to confirm what you had already told her.'

'Little bitch,' said Peacock. 'She was hiding outside the office, and she saw Ronald Brinkman arrive. She guessed the rest. It was pure speculation, and you had to go and confirm it all. Didn't I tell you not to talk to the press?'

'She said – she said you had talked to her, and she, well, she said she had lost her notes. How was I to know?'

'How indeed?' said Peacock wearily. 'And that bloody paper goes to bed on Tuesday. We hadn't even finished the selection when they printed it.'

He sighed. Eversley's uncomplicated mind was something he counted on for his own purposes. A chairman he could manipulate was the best kind of chairman, but it also had its downside.

'Please God it doesn't get into the nationals,' he prayed.

Whether it did or not, Central Office heard. Brinkman did not come down again, but telephoned.

'Go on, tell me,' he said, without preliminaries.

Peacock, feeling no temptation this time to call him Ronnie, said without hesitation: 'It was Eversley. They rang him late at night, and he had been drinking, I imagine.'

'I thought you said you had him under control.'

'I have now, after that, I promise. He won't say a word to anyone without consulting me first.'

'Make sure of that.' Was it Peacock's imagination; was the hint of menace he seemed to hear only in his mind? 'Remember, we want Lyne. Next time we speak I expect you to tell me we have got him.'

'Or Maybrick,' said Peacock boldly.

'Or Maybrick. That's all.'

And the line went dead.

'How did they know about Maybrick being in the last three? Was it just guesswork?' said Susanna Westerham, when Peter came home from his office in Tunbridge Wells that evening. He found her in the sitting room, where she was perched on the windowseat mending a headcollar. She was forcing the needle through the leather with a thicker leather pad strapped to the palm of her hand.

'I read it in the paper before you knew yourself,' she said, 'before you telephoned me. And why, I should like to know, do they only mention Maybrick, and not you and Geoffrey Lyne? You'd think the whole thing was over.'

'Well, it is, bar the shouting,' said Peter.

'You should do the shouting, if they don't give you a fair hearing on Thursday,' said Susanna.

'Oh, they will, but they'll vote for Maybrick. And even if they don't, they'll vote for Lyne, who's pretty well known, after all.'

Susanna, working away with her head down, wished disloyally that she could be sure he was right in this prognosis. He sat down opposite her, at the other end of the seat. 'Why choose someone well known?' said Susanna, reaching out and taking hold of his hand to make amends for her thoughts. 'It would be far more interesting for them to have a handsome, debonair—'

'Intelligent, witty,' nodded Peter.

'Sexy, loveable unknown quantity like you, who would think of new ideas instead of just rehashing old policies.'

'And put up the backs of half the party with them.'

'Do you think you would do that?' said Susanna, seriously.

'Well, I'm not trying to get into politics just to be lobby fodder. I'm not stupid enough to think I can change the world, but I would try to improve it round the edges, and that means treading on toes, I guess. Telling the truth is not always popular, and that is what I will do, I promise you, if I ever get there.'

He picked up his briefcase, and got up to leave the room. He turned at the door.

'Sukie, tell me, what's got into Leo these days? What is she sulking about?'

'I don't think she's sulking,' said Susanna, shaking the finished headcollar into shape, and picking small bits of twine from the seat. 'I told you she had broken up with Johnnie, and I suppose she is still getting over it.'

'She's well rid of Johnnie,' said Peter unsympathetically. 'But I can hardly get her to say a polite word to me. She's not blaming me, is she, for goodness sake? Spoiling her left-wing image, or something?'

'I guess it's more complicated than that. Perhaps you need to spend some time with her, and talk a bit.'

'Well, that's not easy,' said Peter. 'If she's here she seems to leave the room whenever I come in. And quite honestly, Sukie, until this selection business is over I'm just too busy to pander to adolescent drama queens.'

'Pete, that isn't fair.' Susanna stood up and faced him. 'You're hurt, aren't you, because she won't go along with what you are doing?'

It was true. Peter did feel hurt because his elder daughter so obviously disapproved of his plans. He was used to her unstinting love and admiration, which had only been withdrawn, he felt, while she was preoccupied with what he termed her unsuitable boyfriend. That this alienation should continue after the break-up did not seem fair.

'Of course I'm not hurt,' he said irritably. 'I don't care what she thinks. I just wish she would be more – well, less prima-donna-ish. It's childish and boring. And you can tell her I said so.'

He moved again towards the door, when guilt struck him.

'But thanks for all *your* encouragement, love,' he said. 'I couldn't do without it. You seem a lot more enthusiastic than you were. Is it a bit of an act?'

'I'm a rotten actor,' said Susanna. 'Peter, tell me something. On the map, the nearest point of Kentish Weald constituency is just ten miles from here. If they asked you to move, so as to be in the constituency, what would you say?'

'We are not moving, Sukie,' said Peter emphatically and annoyed. 'I promised you that. Do none of you have any faith in me any more? This is our home, and that's not going to change. Anyway, it's not going to get to that, don't worry. I'm going to have a bath before supper.'

A few minutes later Susanna, having gone out into the garden and into the house again via the other door, was watching her mother peering through a pair of reading spectacles that she was holding on her nose with her left hand at the user's manual for her computer.

Rachel sensed the disquiet in her daughter before she even spoke.

'Your glasses are broken, Ma,' said Susanna. 'Why are your glasses always broken?'

'Because I haven't got a paperclip. Have you got a paperclip?' said Rachel, turning a page.

'Not on me.'

'Well then, neither have I. When I have, they won't be broken any longer. What's the matter?' She turned in her chair, lowering the glasses, and looked at her daughter.

'Nothing, I just came to see you.'

'A drink then. Gin and tonic? Wine?'

'A glass of wine would be lovely,' said Susanna. They sat opposite each other in comfortable, sagging armchairs. Rachel looked at Susanna and Susanna looked at the wood fire that blazed in the hearth despite a warm evening.

'Ma,' she said, 'you're burning that box you made.'

'Yes,' said Rachel. 'I have given up woodwork. It was a case of wouldn't work, as far as I was concerned. I now know that I have no genius for construction. Better to recognise these things than to go on fooling oneself. I destroy quite well, though.'

'Do you think you have a genius for computing?' said her daughter, turning to the blank but demanding grey screen that dominated the room from its table in the corner.

'That remains to be seen. The phraseology is daunting. Is Peter home?'

'Yes,' said Susanna. 'He's having a bath, You know the final selection for Kentish Weald is on Thursday? No, Ma, the two events are *not* connected.'

'I am reassured,' said her mother. 'Yes, I read that. Do you think he's going to win it?'

'I don't know, Ma. Anything's possible. He wants it so much that he is hardly even allowing himself to hope.'

'And you?' Rachel asked.

'What can I say?' Susanna shook her head slowly. 'He wants it. I want him to be happy. If he doesn't get this one, the next chance is way down in the West Country. We'd have to go down there at weekends. I rather like Devon, actually.'

Her mother watched her as she sank into silence, gazing at the dwindling flames. She saw the distress in her face, but made no comment.

Eventually Susanna said: 'I have a very strong feeling that he may win this one, against all the odds. So I am preparing myself for that. And I certainly won't let him down if he does. Better here than Devon.'

She drained her glass, as if she were making a pledge.

'Will you come over to supper, one evening?'

'Yes, but not tonight. I'm going to work on my layout options.'

She kissed her daughter affectionately, and shut the door behind her. She stood looking into the smoking ashes of her failed carpentry effort and thinking about their conversation. She felt an ache of worry. The solid happiness of Susanna and Peter's marriage was central to her own life. They had always sailed their little ship with such unruffled calm and confidence, and she sometimes felt that only she, watching from the cliff-top of her own experience, was aware of the clouds that always lay just beyond a seemingly perfect horizon. Now, she thought, Susanna too seemed to be sniffing the wind.

Many years earlier, when Rachel's marriage had come to an end, she had been so entirely taken by surprise that for a long time afterwards she had blamed herself for being unnoticing of changes that must have been taking place in Hugh, her husband. It was only as her experience of life increased that she had realised that often the most fundamental changes in people's attitudes can occur without any visible outward sign of the turmoil within.

There was no comparison, of course, with what was happening here, in the next generation, but she could only feel reassured that such changes as were taking place in the Westerham menage were apparent for all to see. Susanna was getting due warning.

Rachel suddenly felt an old, remembered need for Hugh's presence and advice.

Mr and Mrs Cyril Eversley arrived on the dot of eight o'clock at the front door of Little Marden Hall, a touch nervous, but expecting to enjoy themselves. It was an attractive house, Queen Anne with balanced Georgian additions, too comfortable-looking to be grand, but impressive enough. The Eversleys had never been invited there before, and were not disposed to be offended about that. The invitation for tonight was surely a forerunner of many such invitations in the future, to this house and others of importance. They confidently expected a whirl of social activity to be theirs in the happy aftermath of the bye-election, when they could hope to be on first-name terms with senior politicians and other national figures.

Mrs Eversley's hopes went even further. Her dream was to read her husband's name in the New Year Honours list. 'Eversley, Cyril P., for political services'. Mr Cyril Eversley, OBE! Not CBE – that was too much to hope for, so she mustn't think of it. Even an OBE would set them apart from their acquaintances. She wondered whether when their names were linked together, as when she applied for tickets for the annual civic dinner, she could use it then. Mr &

Mrs Cyril Eversley OBE. She gave a little shiver of delight at the thought. Actually, even an MBE would be nice.

They had dressed with some care, interpreting the 'come as you are, don't dress up' as implying that there was no question of full evening dress. Maureen Eversley's purchase two days earlier during a rushed shopping trip to London was perhaps a little on the slinky side, but it was flattering and she had found it impossible to resist. It would be useful, anyway, in their exciting future. Cyril Eversley wore a dark suit, unbuttoned, as it was getting just a touch narrow across the back, and a tie almost identical to one worn by Jeremy Paxman.

They were surprised when the door was opened, not only by Sir Rupert Hascombe himself, but Sir Rupert in a sweater and tired corduroy trousers.

He was all affability, helping Mrs Eversley off with her lace shawl and saying such nice things about her dress that she glowed with pleasure.

'You will have to forgive me for being unchanged. I have only just come in and ... er ... well, you know how it is. Come into the drawing room and I'll just let Florence know you've arrived.'

Leaving his guests admiring the view from the long drawing-room windows, he burst through the green baize door and into the kitchen. His wife was stirring something on the Aga and the big pine table was laid with a colourful and welcoming array of glass and china on a cheerful check tablecloth.

'My God, Flo, they're here, not just early but dressed up to the nines. What on earth are we to do? We can't feed them in here. They're expecting a dinner party!'

'Don't panic,' said Florence, starting to move fast as she talked. 'Give them a drink, show them the library. Tell them we didn't invite anyone else, because— because we wanted to get to know them, or our other guests dropped out, or something. I'm sure you can combine charm with inventiveness. I'll have everything into the dining room in five minutes. Can't do silver, I'm afraid, because it hasn't been cleaned for months. And I'll get out of my trousers. It'll be fine, don't worry.'

When Florence Hascombe walked into the drawing room eight minutes later to greet her guests it would have been impossible to guess at the frantic flurry of activity she had just been through. She apologised unfussily for not being there when they arrived. She was calm, elegantly dressed and as charming as a good hostess can be who is determined to make everyone feel at ease. Rupert Hascombe smiled his admiring gratitude, and led the way into the dining room as if he ate there every night. There was nothing like candlelight, he thought, for concealing household deficiencies, like shabby curtains and imperfectly dusted furniture.

They drank excellent white Australian Chardonnay with good, bubbling hot food, which Florence Hascombe described as 'ancienne cuisine'.

'My family prefer large helpings and lots of potatoes,' she said, 'so we haven't really adapted to current cooking fashions. I always think restaurants that serve everything in tiny helpings in little lakes of pink sauce are a bit of a con, don't you?'

Maureen Eversley wondered why she had felt nervous. Lady Hascombe at home was not a bit as she had expected and, secretly, feared. In fact, she was quite ordinary, and very easy to get on with.

'I would be so pleased to have the recipe for your fish pie,' she said.

'*Oh*, how flattering,' said Florence. 'You shall have it with pleasure. Remind me before you leave.'

When the meal was over, they sat in the library, and after a while Sir Rupert asked Eversley how he thought the meeting of the membership would go on the following evening.

'Well,' said Eversley, drawing importantly on his cigar, 'it is all a matter of numbers, of course.'

'Of course,' said Hascombe, nodding solemnly.

'How many turn up, and how many will vote. For each one, I mean. All numbers, that's the inneresting thing.'

Mrs Eversley looked anxiously at him. She knew that tone of voice. He had had a glass of whisky before dinner, a fair share of the wine, a glass of brandy, and now the whisky glass in his hand was nearly empty. She dearly wished that she had managed to dissuade him from the glass he had had to steady his nerves before leaving home.

'What order will they speak in, the three contestants?' said Florence Hascombe.

'Well, I wanted albaphet – alphabetical order, but Peacock says they are to draw lots. To tell the truth,' Eversley leaned forward confidingly, 'my idea was best, because we really want Maybrick to speak last. Speaking last he'll leave a lasting impression, if you'll forgive the pun. But Peacock says we can't get away with it. Y'know Central Office wants Maybrick to get it?'

'Oh, really?' said both Hascombes together, their faces expressing innocent and fascinated interest.

'Yes,' said Eversley, leaning back in his chair. 'It looks like we'll have a ve'y distinguished Member of Parliament here in Kentish Weald. I think they'll vote the way we want, though, either way. Geoffrey Lyne'll have a big following, too, of course. Among the more radical members of the er . . . membership. We are a broad church, in the Tory Party, as I have often said.'

'Yes, indeed,' said his host, earnestly. 'Can I fill up your glass?'

'Well, just a small one,' said the chairman, avoiding his wife's eye, 'for the road, as they say. My wife drives, very graciously, when we go out, y'know.'

'Some orange juice would be nice,' said Mrs Eversley, to Sir Rupert's offer.

When he was seated again, Hascombe said, leaning forward with his elbows on his knees, 'You are held in a lot of respect, I know, in the constituency, Mr Eversley.'

'Oh, well, I dunno about that, but I do my best, I do my best,' said Eversley, smiling. 'I look on this as a public service, y'know. Like to do my duty. Very inneresting, too.'

'You must be thinking about the meeting on Thursday. I imagine the members will expect you to say a few words about the election before the candidates come in, wouldn't you?'

'Do you really think so?' said the chairman. 'I think Peacock was expecting to explain the – the form, acshally, and I was just to congratchlate the winner at the end. Watcha think?'

'Well,' said Hascombe, 'it's not my business, but I think that, as chairman, you should start the meeting. Then you can make clear that everyone understands that it is our duty in a seat with such a natural Conservative majority to return a candidate who will be really useful to the government. Then ask them to decide for themselves which one that would be. You can't mention any names, of course, but they will know you mean Maybrick. I think they would listen to you, and you would do it very well.'

'You think I should do that?'

'Well,' said Hascombe, 'I think that would increase Maybrick's chances, and that would, of course, please the powers that be.'

'Yes,' said Eversley, 've'y well. Yes. F'you really think so. Thank you for your advice, Rupert. Always listen to good advice. Yes, dear, it is late.'

Both the Eversleys left elated and satisfied, but this did not prevent the chairman from sleeping all the way home.

After they had gone, the Hascombes washed up the dishes together.

'You're thoughtful, Floss,' said he.

'Yes. I am wondering whether your plan won't have the opposite effect from what you hope.'

'How do you mean?'

'Well, after all the aggro in the *Echo*,' said Florence, 'the membership may be offended at being told implicitly to vote for Maybrick. Eversley may go bumbling in and do more harm than good.'

'I know it's a risk,' said Rupert, 'but you know what a right-wing lot they are in this constituency. Hangers and floggers to a man, and if I don't do something to stop Geoffrey Lyne I'll never speak to myself again. I think there are enough suggestible people out there to do as their chairman says. People like a little help in making decisions. Remember, it will be only the real party devotees who will come, and it will just remind them that Maybrick would be a feather in the constituency cap.'

'Well, I hope you are right,' said Florence. 'The trouble is, if you're not, and the members think they are being pushed towards Maybrick, he'll get them all voting for Lyne.'

'Please God not.'

'Poor man, your chairman,' she said, as they went upstairs. 'I don't think he knew he was being manipulated.'

'I don't think he would have noticed if I had hung a sign round my neck saying "manipulator at work". He's not very bright, as you probably gathered.'

'No. But I liked him,' said his wife. 'And I thought she was rather a dear. I must remember to send her the fish pie recipe. I tend to feel that Mrs Eversley will be doing the driving for the rest of her days, don't you? Indeed, I rather hope so.'

Chapter 4

Susanna, her eyes still closed, reached out a sleepy hand to touch Peter. She groped about on his side of the bed, but found only cold sheet. She pressed a button on the small radio clock on her bedside table, and saw that it was just after 5 a.m. She guessed where he was.

A little while later, the bedroom door opened quietly, and she said, 'It's all right, I'm awake.'

'I'm sorry, love, did I wake you? I couldn't sleep, so I thought I would just put the finishing touches to my speech for tonight.'

He slid back into bed.

'I thought you did that last night,' said Susanna sleepily, her head on his shoulder, and her arm across his chest.

'I thought I had gone on too much about Conservative principles, so I've axed most of that bit and I put back the bit about pre-school education.'

'Pete, darling, relax. I am sure it's perfect. Try to sleep a bit now.'

He did, eventually. It was Susanna who stayed awake, careful not to rock the bed, till the diminished voice of James Naughtie told her that the previous night's vote in the House of Commons had been won by the government with the help of the Ulster Unionists. She supposed she would soon mind much more about that sort of thing. It was hard to imagine.

The Westerham twins were sitting at the window table of a Covent Garden coffee bar, their regular haunt now that the exams were over. Neither was seriously nervous about failure, but rather about the level of success.

'When they first said two Bs and a C, I said great, no problem, but now . . .'

Emma gazed mournfully into her coffee cup. The thump of rock music from the flashing machine behind her almost drowned her words.

'Stop moaning, Em, you'll be all right. You always feel like this before you hear.'

'Dad really wants me to get to Bristol, and—'

'Oh, cool it, Em. You're being boring. Dad is so busy thinking about his own exams, you know, interviews and stuff, that he'll just be glad you get anywhere. You know they're choosing their candidate this week?'

Mark's attempt to steer his twin's thinking worked.

'Are you going down?' she said.

'This evening? Ye-e-eh,' he said. 'Got to encourage them. Think of all the sports days and school plays they came to.'

'I'll come too,' said Emma. 'They were all right, weren't they? They never seriously embarrassed us, like some parents. Not till now, anyway. Mark, don't you think he might have talked to us a bit before he started all this? I mean, it's going to affect us all.'

Mark said nothing, dipping a lump of sugar in his coffee. She flicked a toothpick at him.

'Are you listening? I wish he wasn't doing it.'

'So does Leo – you should hear her,' said Mark, flicking it back. 'She'll get over it, I think what's really bugging her is that Dad doesn't appreciate her mighty sacrifice.'

'Johnnie wasn't doing her any good,' said Emma judicially. 'I think Dad was a welcome excuse, in a way. She's behaving as if Johnnie chucked her, but we all know it was the other way round.'

'Well, like I said,' said Mark, 'she just wants a bit of appreciation, and Dad can't see it.'

'Time for divine intervention, do you think?'

'No, baby. Mistake. Heavenly Twins keep out. Let them sort it out themselves.'

Cyril Eversley telephoned Peacock. The agent reeled in horror at his suggestion that the assembled members of the Association should get a pep talk from their chairman at the start of the selection meeting.

'A, there isn't time,' he said. 'It will be a long enough evening in any case. B, people are pretty annoyed already at the suggestions of interference from Central Office, however much we have denied it, and they will think you are putting on the pressure. C . . .' he paused. C, he had been going to say, was that Eversley would somehow manage to make an almighty balls-up of it, but there must be a more tactful way of stopping him.

The hesitation was all that Cyril Eversley needed. He was still elated by his enjoyment of the previous evening, when he had felt treated as a chairman should be treated. Peacock was, after all, just a paid agent.

'Now look, Leonard,' he said, 'this is an important occasion. I have been talking to some prominent people, and the feeling is that it is the chairman's job to address the meeting at the beginning as well as at the end, and that is what I propose to do.'

There was an unusual determination in his tone, and Peacock felt that on this particularly busy day he did not have time to argue.

'All right,' he said, rather to Eversley's surprise. 'I will do a draft for you. Lelia can type it out, and bring it down to the hall. I'm going down there now to sort out the chairs, so if you come in about lunchtime you can see what you think of it.'

The chairman agreed with relief. He was not entirely clear in his mind what it was he had agreed with Hascombe that he should say, and he had the wit to see that he might get it seriously wrong.

Peacock rang off.

'I want you to bang something out on the computer, Lelia, please,' he said.

'Bang it yourself,' his secretary replied without hesitation. 'You've given me more than I can do before this evening as it is. And you can take it down to the hall yourself. All those voting papers have got to be done again, for a start, because the printing ink leaked and they're all streaky. Look at that.'

'Oh, ff—' started Peacock.

'And no bad language, thank you,' Lelia tossed her head, 'or I'm leaving. Now. You know today's my half day, and I'm going to be late away as it is. Someone will have to give me a hand folding the slips for the seats, or they won't get done.'

Peacock knew she would finish her jobs before she went, but he also knew better than to trade on it. Lelia seemed to have lost all respect for him since that evening when he had, well, got a bit carried away. The annoying thing was that he found her even more distracting now than he had before, and he could swear her skirts were getting even shorter. Perhaps she was not so frigid after all. His approach had been wrong.

'I'll ring my wife and tell her to come in,' he said. 'She can fold the slips, and she can answer the telephone, too, and that sort of thing. Fetch and carry for you. Would that help you, Lelia?'

She assented, mollified.

'I may not be able to get back, because there's a lot to do down there, but I know you can manage the office. Thank God I can trust you, Lelia.'

'Nice to be appreciated,' she said.

Cheered, Peacock reached for his typewriter. The office would be quiet, anyway, because all the action would be down at the hall. Now to deal with his chairman's oratorical problems.

Peter Westerham was dressed, having changed his tie twice and back again, and was putting finishing touches to the finishing touches to his speech. The twins were downstairs with him, plying him with cups of coffee, drinks, potato crisps and Maltesers, all of which he refused. He had eaten very little all day, though he maintained that he was not nervous, and as he couldn't possibly win, why should he be?

Susanna stood in front of the looking glass in her bedroom. More or less satisfied, and seeing that there was still a full half hour until they needed to leave, she went round to see her mother.

'Do you think this will do?' she said.

'No, not really,' said Rachel Willoughby, looking at her with her head on one side. Susanna was wearing a slim middy-length deep blue skirt, and a blouse with a small flowered pattern open over a lighter blue T-shirt. A broad belt emphasised her small waist, and her feet were neatly shod in flat-heeled slip-on shoes.

'Oh, dear, why?' Susanna sighed. 'I thought it struck just the right note. It's too hot to wear a suit, and a cotton dress might look as if I wasn't trying.'

'You look charming, very pretty indeed, and entirely suitably dressed. That must be a mistake. I think you should wear skintight jeans, a tight, low-necked, ribbed sweater and huge dangling earrings. Oh yes, and Doctor Foster boats.'

'Doc Marten,' said Susanna, giggling.

'If you want to stop Peter getting into parliament, you are going to have to work at it, my child. Dressing like the perfect Tory wife is not the way to go about it. On the other hand, with careful choice of the right clothes you could pull it off today.'

'Get thee behind me, Mother,' said Susanna. 'No, not literally – what are you doing?'

'I am going to give you a punk haircut,' said Rachel, snapping her scissors.

'Ma, be serious,' said Susanna, giggling. 'I am supporting Pete. I told you that.'

She leant against the windowsill and folded her arms. With her face silhouetted against the light, her mother could not see her expression as she talked, but she heard the forced cheerfulness in her voice.

'I was a bit worried, at the start – as you know, of course. You are quite a hard person to hide things from. But now I am used to the idea, I'm beginning to think it could be quite, well, interesting. Don't you too, secretly? The idea of him being in parliament? And I am sure that if Pete and I can do it together it will work, and it can even bring us closer, if that were needed, which it isn't. Think; I have never really shared any of his work with him – I mean, a solicitor's wife doesn't live in the office, unless she's a lawyer too. But this political thing, it is something we can actually share. I think I could quite enjoy it, in a way, as long as I can still run my business, and as long as I don't actually have to make speeches. You don't think I would have to make speeches, do you? Oh Lord, I hope they don't ask that.'

'You could make speeches, if you had to,' said Rachel. 'Anyone can, if they have to. If they believe in what they are saying.'

She had listened more carefully to her daughter than she appeared to. Her face showed nothing of what she was thinking.

'If Peter wins this, and gets elected,' she went on, 'I'll buy you a joke book for Christmas. That's one problem solved.'

'About my making speeches?'

'No, about Christmas.'

'Not if he doesn't get it,' said Susanna. 'You'll have to think of something else. That's him blowing the horn. It's far too early, but I'd better go. He's so nervous, poor love. He needs his hand holding.'

'Will you telephone,' said Rachel, 'and let me know how it goes?'

'Are you sure you won't come, Ma? You can't be in the hall, not being a member, but you can be supportive with the twins in the hotel bar.'

'Certainly not,' said her mother. 'I can't imagine anything more dreadful. I shall stay here and moan at the harbour bar instead. And by the time you get back I will have a spreadsheet to show you. I have yet to find out what I should spread on it. Almost everything nowadays is carcinogenic.'

'Well, I'm off,' said Susanna. 'Wish him luck.'

Rachel watched from the window of her small bathroom as the family car drove away, taking care not to be seen. There were lines of concern between her eyebrows. She knew her daughter very well, and she was aware of how she must have worked at thinking herself into this new attitude.

'I wish you both luck, my darlings,' she said quietly, 'but, oh dear, you will need more than luck.'

Peacock was near panic. The Rainbow Hall was a long wide room, semi-attached to the back of the biggest hotel in Wraybury. It had been built to accommodate weddings, dinners, rock concerts and other activities that might have discommoded hotel residents had they taken place in the main dining room. It was big enough to seat two hundred people comfortably, but almost every seat was already taken, and Peacock could see others still arriving. It was only ten to seven.

Kieran Mitchell, sitting watching from her car outside, felt great satisfaction at seeing in such a positive visual fashion the result of her efforts. The hall would be packed. Her articles in the *Wealden Echo* had aroused unusual interest in the Tory selection, and her editor, though no Tory, was pleased. Interest sold papers.

Sylvia Peacock, who had been sent down to the hall by Lelia with a box full of printed slips during the afternoon, caught sight of her husband. He was actually standing still. Each time until now that she had tried to approach him he had waved her away, saying he was busy. She had laid the slips neatly on every seat, and done the same with the voting papers. Now she saw an opportunity to divest herself of the fax she had brought with her. Lelia had given it to her in an envelope, saying languidly, 'You'd better get down to the hall. He might be interested in that.' But so far any attempt to pass it to her husband had met with the same sort of reaction as she got now.

'Go away. Stop pestering me. I'm busy. If you want to be useful, go and beg some more chairs from the hotel management. Don't come back without them.'

And he turned back to his position beside the chairman greeting members of the Association as they came through the door. There were quite a few faces that he had never consciously seen before, so every name had to be checked against the computerised printouts of paid-up members.

'Fairly brings them out of the woodwork, doesn't it?' said Major Wright, who had been acting as an usher, with other members of the executive. 'Never seen half these people out canvassing. Who are they all? The outlying branches, I suppose. There's that Widdecomb fellow. Didn't know he could keep upright without a bar stool under him. Thought he lived in the club.'

'If they are fully paid-up members they have the right to vote,' said Peacock piously. He was secretly delighted at the high turnout, because the voting figures would indicate to Central Office that the constituency Association was livelier and in better shape than was actually the fact.

There were now about twenty people waiting for chairs, and there was a groan of annoyance from them when Sylvia Peacock arrived back to say the fire regulations would allow no more seating.

'That's bad management,' a voice said. 'They should have booked a bigger hall, for goodness sake. How long are we going to have to stand for?'

Peacock's calm deserted him, though he tried not to show it. It was seven o'clock, the advertised starting time: not enough seats and one of his principals still not there. It didn't matter how hard you tried . . .

'No, I'm busy. Go and sit down. That can wait, whatever it is.' Angrily he pushed aside his wife, who was once again trying to put an envelope in his hand, and addressed the chairman. 'I'll go and see if Maybrick has arrived.'

'The other two are here?' asked Eversley anxiously.

'They were both early,' said the agent. 'I've got them in the small lounge just inside the hotel, with their wives. You had better come and meet them.'

They left the treasurer on the door, with instructions to keep a special look-out for journalists trying to get in.

'Especially female ones,' said Peacock, viciously.

Peter and Susanna were sitting side by side on an over-stuffed sofa, facing Geoffrey Lyne and his wife. Mrs Lyne was tall and dressed in a well cut silk suit, with an understated chic simplicity that at once made Susanna feel inadequate. She had got it all wrong.

'No, you look perfect,' Peter had whispered, when she muttered 'Sorry – I should have dressed up more,' into his ear. Susanna never fussed about her clothes normally, and she was grateful to Peter for not looking surprised at what she said, and for saying the right reassuring thing, without qualification.

The Lynes were friendly, talkative and apparently as relaxed as if they were all meeting for a casual drink. The Westerhams tried to appear as comfortable as their opponents looked, but knew they were failing. Peter's hand constantly strayed to the pocket that held his notes.

When the chairman and agent came in, they all got to their feet.

'No, no, do sit down,' said Eversley, shaking hands all round. 'I am Cyril Eversley, chairman, for my sins, of the Association. I must apologise for keeping you waiting, but it's all going swimmingly out there – a splendid turnout, I'm glad to say. The only problem is that Mr Maybrick seems to be delayed. We think perhaps his train . . . do you think, Leonard?'

'He was coming by car,' said Peacock, witheringly. Eversley talked too much.

'What are you planning? Do we toss up for who goes first? Or fight for it?' said Lyne, smiling.

'You draw lots,' said Peacock, unsmiling. He explained briefly the planned procedure of speeches and questions.

'Splendid,' said Lyne, genially. 'Very well planned.'

Peter nodded dumbly, and Susanna realised that she was sweating. It was a warm night. Thank goodness she wasn't wearing a silk suit. Mrs Lyne, however, looked cool and calm.

'Now,' said Eversley, in case Peacock appeared to be taking control, 'if Maybrick, Mr Maybrick I should say, doesn't arrive in time, I think we will have to start without him. I hope you don't mind? We'll draw the lots now, shall we, and see how it goes?'

Peter and Lyne each took one of the proffered cards.

'I seem to be third,' said Lyne cheerfully.

'Second,' said Peter.

'Well, Mr Westerham,' said Peacock, 'I sincerely hope that Mr

Maybrick will arrive in time to take his place, but if not, have you any objection to going first?'

'No, of course not,' said Peter, having every objection. To go first was the worst thing that could happen to him.

The audience was already restless as the result of the delay and Peacock knew a bored meeting could be a dangerous one.

The few words that Eversley addressed to the assembled membership from the platform some minutes later were, in Peacock's view, and as he had dreaded, not nearly few enough. Eversley had left the notes that Peacock had drafted for him in the gents in the hotel, and discovered this when it was too late to do anything about it. His momentary panic was dispelled by seeing Rupert Hascombe in the audience. Now he remembered his advice.

After some rambling sentences about distinguished candidates and loyalty to the party, the chairman tried to conclude: 'There has been some talk, the press, you know, suggesting that we are not free to choose, that pressure has been put upon us, which is nonsense, of course, it is completely democratic and you each have a vote, you know. That is not to say that we don't have a very strong candidate, two, three very strong candidates, that is, and . . .'

Shit, mouthed Peacock.

'And you will choose, I am sure, the best man for the party and for Kentish—'

'Why are there no women?' someone called.

'Oh, well—' said Eversley, thrown. 'There were some ladies whom we interviewed, some very excellent and charming ladies, indeed, but, er, in the end, we thought, er . . .'

He glanced at Peacock, who sensed disaster and stood up.

'With the chairman's permission I would like to make clear,' he said, 'that the procedure laid down by Conservative Central Office has been followed precisely.'

There was an audible murmur of dissatisfaction from the hall, and a voice called, 'Isn't that the problem?' Another said, 'It's already after time. I move that we get going.'

Since there was still no sign of Maybrick, Peter and Susanna were the first to walk up the side steps and on to the platform. Bright lights shone in their eyes as they faced the audience. Susanna felt unaccountably nervous, a problem she had not had before. Smiling determinedly, she felt that she was grinning like a skeleton. She barely heard the chairman's introduction, and even when he said, 'Mrs Susanna Westerham, who breeds donkeys, I believe', she failed to react.

As Peter began to speak, though, she found herself thinking normally again. She heard the almost imperceptible quiver in his voice, noticed the slight flutter in the papers he held, and tried to will courage and confidence into him. She made an effort to concentrate on his words and soon found herself listening with interest. It was obvious that he had done his homework pretty thoroughly.

When he had finished, stopping neatly on fourteen and a half minutes, the chairman invited questions from the floor, 'addressed to the candidate or his lady wife'.

'I think my interest in family values,' Peter replied to the first, 'can be judged by the fact that I have been happily married for twenty-three years, that I have three children who are constantly at home, and that my wife is here beside me. I believe in the family, and I am lucky enough to have a wonderful and supportive one.'

Susanna thought about this while Peter, more confident now, enlarged under questioning on his belief in the European Union and his revulsion to capital punishment. The supportive family was a bit of a myth, she reflected. She, his wife, was reluctant, the twins were slightly sceptical and Leonora was plain angry. As for Rachel, hard to tell.

Only two questions were addressed to Susanna, easy general ones about their home life and interests. Just enough to demonstrate what my voice sounds like, she thought with relief, answering carefully.

'One more question only, please,' said Eversley, in response to a whisper from Peacock.

'Mr Westerham,' said a woman, 'you live down Westbury way, I understand. If you were chosen, would you be prepared to move into the area?'

'Good evening,' said Peter. 'Yes, I have lived with my family for seventeen years just ten miles outside the constituency boundary, in a house that has become our home. I know the whole of the surrounding area very well, and the furthest end of the constituency is only fifty minutes' drive from our house. But of course, if you were to do me the honour of choosing me as your parliamentary candidate we would, if asked, be prepared to move to a house in the constituency.'

Susanna swung her head sharply to look at Peter, and then she smiled, to try to hide her abrupt reaction. She would not let him down in public, and in any case, perhaps she had misheard him. Uncomfortably though, she knew she hadn't. How could he have said they would move from Restings, so soon after his promise to her?

As they returned to the small lounge, and the Lynes took their place on the platform, Susanna felt like challenging Peter right away.

Instead, she said, 'What happens if Maybrick has had an accident, or if he just doesn't turn up?'

'I don't know.' Peter was sitting with his elbows on his knees, his hands linked and drooping, his head low. He had deflated like a spent balloon now that he was no longer on show. 'But I do know that Geoffrey Lyne looked extraordinarily pleased when the agent told us just now that Maybrick still hadn't arrived. So I assume that if he doesn't turn up, it is just a walkover for Lyne.'

'Pete,' her own feelings thrust aside, Susanna reached for his hand, 'you mustn't think like that. You spoke brilliantly.'

'Oh, Susanna,' he flung himself back on the sofa, 'you heard the reaction from half the hall when I said I was anti-hanging. And on Europe. He'll give them the answers they want. If only Maybrick would come; then at least those votes might be split between the two of them, and then, well, then I might have a fighting chance.'

Susanna watched him. She too had sensed the disapproval at Peter's answers to some of the more palpably right-wing questions. Dimly in the distance they heard a burst of applause.

'Pete,' she said consolingly, 'how could you have answered differently? You have to say what you believe – you have to tell the truth as you see it.'

'I should have been less definite,' said Peter, shaking his head. 'I could have phrased it all differently.'

Susanna watched him, frowning.

'Why don't we go and have a drink?' she said. 'We don't have to sit here like condemned prisoners. Or we could just scarper, go home and telephone to say we've changed our minds, and they can keep their rotten constituency.'

Peter laughed, and put his arm round her.

'That's the spirit, my Sukie. I love you. What would I do without you? I should have said before, you were terrific. When they asked you whether you would play a part in the constituency you sounded sensible and enthusiastic. Mentioning your business, and the family needs, was wise, too.'

'Wisdom wasn't in it,' said Susanna. 'I was just protecting myself, I'm afraid. There's no way I'd be available for everything that came up. What about that drink? My throat is like pumice stone. We could go to the bar in the hotel and tell the twins how it's going. They must be longing to hear.'

'I don't think we can,' said Peter. 'We've just got to tough it out. In any case, if Maybrick doesn't make it, it could all end much sooner than we expect, and then we can drink ourselves silly. Listen, love, after this, I won't keep trying for every seat that comes up; only if something really good becomes available locally. Otherwise we will just get on with our lives, and think of something else to do.'

She squeezed his hand, and said nothing.

Once Lyne was on the platform, Peacock felt more relaxed. He picked up the envelope that Reese, the treasurer, had pressed into his hand some time earlier.

'Your wife said you should see it. It's a fax, I think,' he had said.

Peacock opened it under cover of the table.

Rupert and Florence Hascombe were sitting very near the back of the hall. He kept up a disapproving running commentary into her right ear throughout Lyne's speech, causing her sometimes to laugh quietly, sometimes to say Sshhhh.

'I can't think why they don't ask the different candidates the same questions,' he whispered now, 'so that they can at least compare their answers.'

'Well, they've both been asked about Europe.'

'But by different people, in different ways,' said Hascombe.

'At least it shows that one is for, basically, and one is against,' said his wife.

'Lyne is known as a Euro-sceptic already, anyway.'

'Why don't you ask a question, then, Rupert?'

'Members of the selection panel are not meant to, not tonight. Anyway, I am keeping my powder dry.'

Lady Hascombe looked at her husband suspiciously.

'A loose cannon with dry powder can be a dangerous thing,' she whispered.

A man rose in front of them.

'Point of order, Mr Chairman.'

'Yes?' said Eversley from the platform, peering down the hall, his hand shielding his eyes from the lights. 'Is that Major Wright? I think you have asked a question already, Major Wright. We have to let someone else have a chance.'

'That's my point of order. If I can only ask one question, how can I find out how Mr Lyne would reply to the same question as I asked Mr Westerham? Unless someone else asks it, that is?'

'There you are!' said Rupert Hascombe to his wife.

There was a ripple of 'Hear, hear' round the hall.

Eversley turned anxiously to Peacock for his view, but Peacock had disappeared from his chair. He was talking agitatedly into a wall telephone in the passage just outside, his finger in his other ear.

Floundering, Eversley said: 'Well, you see, we made certain rules, and I really ... well I do see what you mean. If it is the same question, yes, all right, Major Wright, you may ask the same question of Mr Lyne.'

'Thank you, sir. Mr Lyne, what are your views on capital punishment?'

'I am happy to give them to you, sir,' said Lyne. 'I am not only a firm believer in the deterrent value of the death penalty, but if elected as your member of parliament I would intend to bring in a private member's bill . . .'

When Lyne had finally finished his long and specific answer there was a burst of fervent applause from a large section of the audience, and as it died away there was heard a rising hiss of disapproval from others among them.

'What's that?' said Ellie Fittall, waking from an apparent snooze in the front row. 'Is something happening, at last?'

Rupert Hascombe was sitting upright and bristling.

'My God, if we get that man, I am leaving the country, I swear it.'

'I don't know how you're going to stop him,' said his neighbour.

'I'll think of something,' said Hascombe. 'I may need your support, if you feel like me. Even Maybrick *must* be an improvement on that.'

Meanwhile, on the platform, Mrs Lyne, cool and calm, was telling the audience, in response to a question, that there was nothing she enjoyed more that attending constituency functions and chairing committees, and how much she hoped there would be scope for that, if her husband should be selected.

Another point of order was raised from the floor.

'As Major Wright was allowed to ask the same question again, can I ask my question again? And of Mr Maybrick, as well?'

This threw Eversley into further mental turmoil, from which he was saved by Peacock reappearing on the platform beside him.

The agent was looking grim and shaken. He answered curtly, and his answer was repeated louder and verbatim by the chairman to the audience.

'No. The rules are made, and we can't change them now.'

A chorus of dissent rose from the hall. Several people jumped to their feet, and Eversley sat down again, unsure what to do.

'Call them to order,' hissed Peacock. 'Say you have an important announcement.'

'But I haven't,' said Eversley.

'Yes, you have. Here, I've written it down. It's about Maybrick. He's not coming. You'll have to calm them down.'

Eversley stood up again, paper in hand.

'Order, please. Order.'

Angry discussion in the hall drowned his voice. Peacock banged on the table.

Lyne leant forward and touched Eversley on the arm. He was unable to see what was written on the paper in the chairman's hand.

'I think it might be sensible,' he said, 'if my wife and I left the platform till you get things sorted out.'

'Yes, yes, of course, you're right, thank you,' said Eversley. 'We won't be long. Just a technical hitch, you know. Thank you. Excellent.'

The hall quietened as the Lynes went down the steps and out through the side door.

'Order,' said the chairman once again. The hum of talk in the hall subsided reluctantly. 'I have an announcement to make, which may surprise you. I must say, it surprises me. I had no idea this might happen. It is a message we have, from Central Office, to say – er, I'll read it out, if I may – that yesterday evening Mr John Maybrick was selected as prospective parliamentary candidate for the constituency of Kiddingstone, and is therefore not eligible to be considered for Kentish Weald. Mr Maybrick wishes every success to the lucky candidate who may be selected for Kent—'

The rest of his words were drowned in a rising rumble of surprise and indignation from the hall. A dozen people stood up.

'Bloody bad manners, that's all I can say,' shouted one man cholerically.

'This is a disaster,' said Rupert Hascombe grimly to his wife.

'Order, order,' said the chairman helplessly. 'Order . . .'

'Why didn't they have the courtesy to let us know this morning?' called another voice. 'We could have seen another of the shortlisted candidates.'

Peacock spoke urgently. 'Tell them, for goodness' sake, that we have to choose from the other two. NOW. Get it going again. Take charge, can't you?'

Eversley swallowed. He was sweating profusely. He raised his voice to a shout.

'Order, please. Order. I have no doubt Central Office will have an explanation for the delay in—'

'Get on with it,' hissed Peacock through his teeth. His head was metaphorically in his hands. Things had gone about as badly as they could. He had yet to realise that he was to blame for this fiasco, but he had no doubt that Eversley had the ability to make the situation even worse.

'May I remind you,' said Eversley, 'that we have heard tonight two excellent speakers, one a well known, er, public figure and the other a splendid, er, local gentleman. We owe it to them now to proceed, and to make our selection, as they are waiting nearby. You have heard them both and er, asked them many questions, so . . .'

'Voting papers,' said Peacock.

'Oh, yes, you will find, on your chairs, the voting—'

'Point of order, Mr Chairman.'

A tall figure had risen at the back of the hall.

'I can't see. Who is it?' said the chairman, shading his eyes with his hand from the overhead light.

'Sir Rupert Hascombe,' said Peacock gritting his teeth. He did not trust the man.

'Oh yes, indeed, Sir Rupert Hascombe. Yes, Sir Rupert?'

'Just a point, Mr Chairman, before we vote.' Hascombe's voice was strong and clear, and even Ellie Fittall listened. 'Would I be right in saying that Mr Geoffrey Lyne would be Central Office's other preferred candidate? I am sure that as loyal members of the party we would want to take account of Central Office's wishes.'

Eversley was hugely relieved by this apparently friendly helping hand, and answered with alacrity.

'Thank you, Sir Rupert, for that contribution. Of course the choice is entirely ours, but if we can be helpful in our—'

His words were drowned by the growing murmur of anger from the crowd before him. Someone sitting halfway down the hall turned and shouted at Hascombe.

'I'll choose my own candidate, thank you very much. I don't need instructions from Central Office. Not after that muddle.'

'That's right, he's quite right. It's a secret ballot, isn't it?' called another member.

Rupert Hascombe sat down again, well satisfied. He nudged his wife.

'One shot, at the right moment, and right on target. How's that?'

'Glad to have you on my side, sir,' said Lady Hascombe. 'Do you want to borrow my pen?'

The vote split, almost equally, between the two remaining candidates. But not quite. Peter Westerham was announced to have won the Conservative nomination by a clear majority. No figures were mentioned but a very substantial number of people remained seated while others rose and cheered the result.

As the hall emptied, Rupert Hascombe patted the chairman on the back.

'Well done,' he said. 'You did that extremely well. Couldn't have done better myself.'

Eversley thanked him, and went home happy.

'How many was it?' asked Mrs Peacock later.

'Two,' snarled her husband. 'That's clear, isn't it?'

Sylvia Peacock did not ask any more questions. Over many years she had learned to recognise the pinched look about the narrow nostrils that indicated that Leonard Peacock was on the borderline between rage and violence.

Peacock had been so angry after the count that he had not even congratulated the winner. The icy handshake from the loser remained in his mind like a nail protruding uncomfortably on the inside of a coffin.

Chapter 5

On the way home, Peter and Susanna followed the twins' car. Peter drove. They talked in bursts interspersed with long silences.

'I still can't believe it . . . to have the impossible happen like that,' said Peter. 'And Lyne's face – did you see him? He couldn't believe it either. I almost felt sorry for him. Almost.'

Susanna sat and thought about Lyne's face. At the time she had been so near the tears of released strain and mixed emotions that she had been busy hiding her own face.

'Evidently they were fed up with Maybrick not turning up,' said Peter, 'and somehow that worked in my favour.'

'Who is this man Hascombe?' said Susanna. 'Someone said he swung it in some way.'

'I've no idea. We'll find out in time.'

Their changed situation had left them both feeling slightly stunned.

'Peter,' Susanna said, as they neared home. 'The thing you said, when you were asked about moving house. I thought you weren't going to say that?'

'Sukie, don't be silly – it was no risk. There's no way they would ask us to move, not for the sake of ten miles. The chairman said that to me, anyway, before we left. I knew it was quite safe to say it. You know I wouldn't let you down over that.'

'Mmmm,' said Susanna.

'What is it? I mean that,' said Peter, taking his eyes from the road to look at her. He took her hand and held it on his thigh.

'Oh, I know you wouldn't want to move from Restings,' Susanna said, looking straight ahead. 'But isn't suggesting that you *would* move rather the sort of thing politicians are supposed to do?'

He didn't answer for a moment.

'Sukie, I think that's a bit childish, isn't it? We are not moving, and that's what matters.'

'Yes,' said Susanna. She was thinking about Leonora, and remembering another conversation some weeks earlier, when she had suggested to her daughter that *she* was being 'a bit childish'.

The subject had been much the same; the fear that Peter's attitudes might change.

'Go on,' said Emma.

'What happened then?' said Mark. 'Go on, ball by ball. We want to hear it all.'

'Well,' said Susanna, 'we all sat and stared at each other in the waiting room.'

'No, we didn't,' said Peter, 'we talked – made conversation.'

'Did we?' said Susanna.

They were sitting at home, eating spaghetti. Rachel Willoughby had been asked to join the party and sat with a glass of wine in her hand at the end of the big pine table. She had eaten already. She looked from her son-in-law to her daughter and wondered. They both seemed elated, and she could not help smiling at their pleasure.

'Anyway,' said Peter, 'the agent came in. Sour-looking man, called Peacock. He told us Maybrick had been selected for another seat. So we all gasped—'

'And Lyne and his wife looked absolutely delighted,' said Susanna, 'because they knew that they were bound to win, then. They tried to cover it up by saying how pleased they were for the Maybricks, because they know them as friends. But I felt really annoyed at the way they seemed to be brushing Dad's chances aside.'

'You are over-sensitive,' said Peter. 'Anyway, the agent said that they were voting on the two of us and went away again, leaving us and the Lynes staring at each other.'

'That must have been quite a tense few minutes,' said Rachel.

'Minutes?' said Susanna. 'It seemed to go on for hours. Can you imagine, Ma? We had to try to behave normally and politely. "And will you be going away in August, Mrs Westerham?" How could I say, "Yes, if you win tonight. If we do, probably not"? Everything we talked about seemed hypothetical. It was a very odd time.'

'Go on,' said Emma.

'It was over half an hour, in fact,' said Peter. 'Then the chairman and agent came in together, and the chairman said, "Will you come with me, Mr and Mrs Westerham?"'

'We thought we were being quietly sent home, honestly we did,' said Susanna.

'But we weren't,' said Peter. 'As soon as we were through the door he hissed in our ears that I had won. Peacock, the agent, meanwhile, was telling the Lynes that they had lost. I went back into the room to shake hands with Geoffrey Lyne, and he could hardly speak, poor fellow. Then we were being taken up onto the platform and I was introduced as the new prospective parliamentary candidate for Kentish Weald!'

'Oh, Dad,' said Emma. Her eyes were fixed on her father, wide and unblinking. It was hard to tell what she was thinking.

'Did they cheer and let thousands of balloons rise to the ceiling, with women screaming and fainting?' said Mark.

'It's not *quite* like that in England, I'm afraid,' said Peter, 'but they clapped politely, most of them.'

'Most of them?' said Rachel.

'What were you twins doing while this was going on?' Rachel asked.

'Giving interviews to the press, telling them our political views. They lapped it up,' said Mark.

'What press?' said Peter.

'The *Wealden Echo*, actually. She wasn't much older than me, but she has an expense account. She bought us a beer. I wouldn't mind being a hack.'

'Don't worry,' said Emma, reassuringly, 'we gave her her money's worth. There's nothing she doesn't know about Dad's toothbrushing habits.'

The telephone rang. Mark went to answer it. When he came back into the room he sat down again and drained his wine glass.

'Who was that?' said his mother.

'Leonora.'

'Did you tell her?' said Emma. 'Does she want to speak to Dad?' She wished at once that she had not spoken.

'She was in a bit of a rush, I think.' Mark was avoiding meeting any eyes as he spoke. 'She said she knew he would win. She sort of said well done.'

Mark's voice was very flat. His words came like a sudden shower out of a blue sky. Susanna spoke quickly to stop their dampening effect. This was hardly the moment for Leonora's disapproval.

'Dearest Pete,' she said, 'it's time to drink your health. To you – Peter – Dad – and to your success. Raise your glasses, ladies and gents!'

'Confusion to your enemies, Pete,' said Rachel, holding up hers.

And they drank with all the enthusiasm they could muster.

'You have an explanation?' Ronald Brinkman's voice down the telephone carried no inflection.

'The chairman, I'm afraid. The one circumstance beyond my control,' said Peacock. He had made notes on a bit of paper which lay in front of him on his desk, in case he should dry up while talking to the area agent. It was easy to plan what you were going to say, and then find that it slipped from your mind when the pressure was on.

'The chairman? Cyril Eversley? The one who you said, and I quote, "eats out of your hand"?'

'You know he drinks,' said Peacock swallowing.

'Out of your hand?'

'He – he –' Peacock looked desperately at his notes, but Brinkman was going on.

'I telephoned Mr Eversley this morning,' the area agent's voice was smooth and modulated, 'to congratulate him, as is normal, on selecting an excellent candidate, and to invite him to a strategy meeting next week on the bye-election. We talked about the unfortunate publicity and he told me that a reporter from one of the local papers had had an interview with you about my visit last week. But you told me, Leonard,' he sounded politely puzzled now, 'that it was he who, and I quote, had had a pint or two and talked to the press. What did he have to talk to the press about, Leonard? I thought my visit was entirely confidential. He was not to know I had been down, was he?'

'No, no,' said Peacock, sweating. 'That's not true – not an interview, just a telephone call. She'd seen your car, and I denied it, of course, and then she—'

'Leonard, you have made the most almighty balls-up of the candidate selection.'

The conversational tone in Brinkman's voice made his words additionally menacing to Peacock. Plain anger would have been easier to bear.

'You have ensured maximum exposure in the press, and the result was everything we most try to avoid. Well done. And the final outcome is that we've still got one of our top men to place, and you have handed a prime seat to a nonentity of a candidate with suspect views.' The tone changed. 'Has he at least got a good wife?'

'A good wife?' said Peacock stupidly, smarting under the onslaught. His notes were no good to him now.

'Yes, Leonard,' with sneering patience, 'a good wife. One who'll do all the expected duties. I hope you haven't landed us with some free-thinking career woman as well.'

'Oh, no,' said Peacock, grasping at the straw. 'She'll be all right when I've licked her into shape. Nice little thing. She'll do as she's told.'

'Mm,' said Brinkman, clearly unimpressed. 'Well, now I suggest that you get some brains onto your campaign committee. The Chief Whip is going to announce the bye-election date today. It will be the second Thursday in July. Write that down, will you, Leonard, to make sure there is no misunderstanding?'

The silken tone was back again.

As Peacock replaced the receiver, the paper with his notes on it fluttered off his desk and fell into his metal wastebin. He kicked it across the room, followed it and kicked it again, several times.

Lelia put her head round the door, and said: 'Do you mind? I'm trying to work in here.'

The *Wealden Echo*, when it came out the following week, made clear that all credit for saving Kentish Weald from outsiders was due to the paper's campaign for the selection of a man 'with Kent mud on his boots'. Eloquent in triumph, Kieran Mitchell had taken pleasure in stressing that Conservative Central Office had been snubbed and Peacock humiliated in the selection of a local candidate. Ellie Fittall was quoted as saying, '"A Sussex pig won't be druv", and that goes for Kent pigs too.'

'You would think they had fended off an invasion of Viking cannibals,' said Rachel. 'I never realised we were in such danger.'

A photograph of a man and a woman bearing no resemblance to Peter and Susanna occupied the next section of the front page, with the caption 'Peter and Susan Westerham celebrate their victory'. The garden shed also in the photograph suggested a link with the next article: 'IS OUR SHED HAUNTED? Couple's smashed flowerpots mystery.'

'There are just so many mistakes in these articles, quite apart from the photograph,' said Emma indignantly. 'They've called Mum Susan, Dad's age is a year out, when I last counted you had three children, not two, we don't live very near Tenterden, and Dad's not the junior partner, he's one of the senior ones. And they don't say anywhere how brilliant you are. I don't know why I bothered to talk to that girl.'

'The words "accuracy" and "press" are seldom linked together,' said Susanna. 'There's more than that, if it matters: He's been a district councillor for seven years, not six, and his boots are spotless and mud-free. I gave them their annual summer wash last week, very kindly, when I was doing my own, and he hasn't worn them since.'

'There is no detail so trivial that the press cannot get it wrong,' said Peter. 'Do you want to come to my adoption meeting? That really can be a family affair – you can all come, if you like.'

'Yes, we'll come and embarrass you,' said Mark. 'What do you think, Emma, black leather, studs and safety pins? Or shall we do the twin cross-dressers?'

'If you come,' said Peter, 'you'll behave.'

Leonora did not come to the adoption meeting, which went smoothly enough, with nearly a hundred Association members turning up at the Conservative Club, some to salute their candidate, others to look at him with curiosity. But she came down from London the following evening, and hitched from Wraybury station. She had come, she said, to collect some clothes. She took little part in the talk at supper, and managed to avoid communicating with Peter.

'I'll need a lift to the station in the morning,' she said to Susanna later.

'Dad has to go to the council offices and lodge his nomination papers tomorrow, leave his deposit with the electoral returning officer and that sort of thing. I think it would give him real pleasure if you went with him, then he could drop you after for a train.'

'Mu-u-um,' said Leonora, in exactly the tone she would have used a few years earlier if she had been asked to tuck her shirt in.

'I know how you feel, darling, but he needs our approval so much in this. He needs to feel we are all behind him.'

'But I'm not.'

'Leo – we all have to pretend a bit, sometimes, for each other. Will you? He'd be so pleased, though he might not show it.'

'*Please* call me Leonora.'

'Oh hell,' said Susanna, 'I hoped you hadn't noticed. It slipped out from habit. I will try, I promise.'

'Mum, I cannot sanction what Dad is doing by taking part in this charade. Sorry.'

So Susanna dropped the subject. And she managed not to smile the following morning when it became apparent that Leonora was not going to get to Wraybury except by accepting a lift from Peter.

That evening he said coldly to Susanna: 'I guess Leonora didn't plan to come with me this morning.'

'Did she say that?' said Susanna.

'Not in so many words. I wish she would stop being so bad-tempered with me. She should grow up.'

'I told you, she's going through a bad patch, that's all. Apart from your politics thing, she's not enjoying her job, and she's feeling spare generally. And she's started smoking again. I don't think she regrets Johnnie, and if one can believe the twins, she definitely dumped him, rather than the other way round. But she is obviously not too happy. I guess that's why she has been in touch a lot lately.'

'Well, I'm glad it's not just me that's upsetting her,' said Peter, bitterly. 'It was like driving a sack of potatoes, for all the talk I got out of her in the car. Thoroughly unfriendly. She came into the council chamber, though.'

'She did?' said Susanna, surprised. Could Leonora have been listening to her after all?

'Yes, and not just from curiosity, but with the clear intention of making trouble, as far as I could make out. She kept well away from me while they were checking the nomination papers, and started openly fraternising with the other candidates. I didn't really mind that, but then when I tried to say goodbye to her, she turned away, making it quite clear in front of everyone that she was snubbing me.'

'That was naughty,' said Susanna. 'Pete, don't take it too seriously. You will have to speak gently with her about Johnnie sometime, I think, just to sort it all out.'

'If she apologises to me I will, but I am not crawling to a spoilt brat.'

His tone persuaded Susanna that the moment had come to change the subject. She was saddened by the rift between Peter and Leonora and felt some sympathy with each of them. But Peter was being surprisingly and uncharacteristically hard on his daughter.

'How many candidates are there?' she said. 'I imagined it was just you and Labour and Lib Dem.'

'There's a whole gaggle of us – you name it: there's the Green candidate, a Natural Law candidate – those are the people who levitate – a Monster Raving Loony candidate, Referendum candidate, Anti-motorway candidate—'

'What motorway?' said Susanna, mystified.

'Any motorway, as far as I can make out. There are one or two more, I think. You get the lot, sane, mad and madder, at a bye-election. The electoral returning officer was already looking a bit shredded, I thought. I could only think of all the zany votes I'm going to lose.'

'Who is your real opposition?'

'Oh, the Lib Dem, without a doubt. He got nearly fifteen thousand votes last time, and he's well known. Our best hope is that this drought goes on. He's a director of the water board, so a hosepipe ban next week is just what we need.'

'You are getting quite devious, Pete,' said Susanna, laughing. 'Actually, we could do with some rain – we have never had more than a sprinkling this summer and we're getting really short of grass. The mares need it for their foals' milk.'

'Let's get the election over first, shall we?'

Susanna had not been looking forward to canvassing, but by the end of the second week she was finding it easier than she had expected.

'But it does seem so arrogant,' she said to Rachel, 'telling people how they should vote. I don't blame at all the ones who simply say, "It's a secret ballot, thank you," and shut the door.'

It was a golden summer evening. Rachel and Susanna were leading a mare with her foal round in a large circle, Rachel holding the youngster by the light foal 'slip' headcollar on its small head. The training session was going smoothly, so they could talk.

'How do you know what to say?' said Rachel. 'I wouldn't have thought political chat was your strength, if it's not rude to say so.'

'It's not, obviously. Look out!'

'Steady, little fellow,' Rachel was stroking and calming the bouncing foal, 'we don't want to go ahead of your mum.'

'Try holding the slip with your left hand,' said Susanna, 'and putting your right hand on his other shoulder – it sometimes works. That's it. It's an act, canvassing, a performance, and you know how I used to enjoy acting at school. Each doorstep is another little stage, and each audience is an unknown quantity. I'm getting better at finding out quickly if they are with us or against us – and then I suppose I try to leave them smiling if possible, whichever way they are going to vote. I feel a bit of a fraud, though, Ma, as I get more and more expert. I've developed standard replies to different remarks, and they come trotting out so glibly. So if you have an argument, it can be quite fun, but after, I find myself thinking, do I really believe what I am saying?'

'Do you?' said Rachel, curiously.

'I suppose so. I try to.'

She led the mare through a gate and into the field where two other mares with foals were grazing. She slipped the headcollar off and the pony's head dropped instantly to graze. The foal, released, kicked its heels up and galloped madly round in a circle.

They stood watching them all for a few minutes, leaning on the gate.

'Ma, it's very good of you to keep an eye on the ponies while this is going on. I don't know how I could help Pete otherwise.'

'No hassle, as Mark says,' said Rachel. 'A pony makes a nice change from a mouse, and I would get square-eyed if I didn't get away from my VDU occasionally. It is all too compulsive.'

'What are you going to do with all this knowledge?' said Susanna. 'Start a business?'

'Something will turn up,' said Rachel. 'At the moment I am creating the vacuum, confident that it will be filled. I am not yet prepared to worry about what it will be filled with. Not, at least, till I can merge text without looking at the instruction book. After that I'm going to get myself a power haircut. Don't you think that would suit my new image?'

'No, I want you to go on looking like a proper mother.'

'Spoilsport, that's what you are. Susanna . . .'

'Yes,' said her daughter, tucking her arm comfortably through Rachel's as they walked back towards the house. They separated at the flagged path, to walk in single file.

'Susanna,' said Rachel, from behind.

Susanna turned.

'That is your "reluctantly going to give you some advice" voice, isn't it?'

'Yes. Susanna, talking about mothers, do keep in touch with Leonora. She isn't happy.'

'Ma, even I can tell that. It seems to be partly about Pete, and partly about breaking up with Johnnie. She doesn't seem to want to talk about it, apart from being aggressive about Pete wanting to be an MP. It is really sad to see her stand-off with him, when she has always been so close to him. I wish he had time to talk to her properly. Though I'm not finding her easy, either.'

'Keeping in communication is what matters. Write to her, then. About anything,' said Rachel. 'Letters are very comforting things, often much better than telephone calls.'

'Sukie,' said Peter, walking into the kitchen early the following morning, 'we have a minor problem. We have two cabinet ministers coming down to jolly us along.'

'How dramatic! Which ones?'

'The Home Secretary, no less, and the new transport minister.'

'What are you going to do with them?' she asked.

'They are each coming for a morning,' said Peter. 'They'll do a bit of canvassing with me, just for the press, then there are two lunchtime meetings organised on the two industrial estates. The Home Secretary will speak at the first, tomorrow, and the other is on Thursday.'

'What's the problem, then?'

'The office. The chairman and Peacock have to be accompanying the ministers, and Peacock's sidekick at the office, sexy as she may be, is not really capable of fielding the telephone calls that come in non-stop. Most of the worthwhile people are organising canvassing parties, and we need someone intelligent in the office to answer the telephone and soothe the nerves of the electorate.'

'I think I am getting the message,' said Susanna. 'Quite honestly, my feet are crying out for a break. I'll do it, willingly.'

So she spent a day in the constituency office, fascinated by the range of calls she fielded. She advised on the whereabouts of polling stations, answered complaints about lack of leaflets, of canvassers, of government commitment, of advice. When stumped, she promised to refer to the agent 'as soon as he came in'.

Only once did she lose her cool, to a complaint about excessive television coverage of the bye-election, but she confined herself to saying, 'Why not just turn it off?'

'Pete,' she said later, 'I know Peacock is a surly so-and-so, but honestly, I would not be a political agent for all the caviare in Russia.'

'And I know what you would do for caviare,' said Peter, understandingly. 'Perhaps we should appreciate Peacock more. But I do find him a pain. I don't think he can forgive me for not being a cabinet minister.'

'Heavens,' said Susanna, 'you're not even an MP yet.'

During gaps between calls, however, Susanna found time to write a letter.
Dear Leonora . . .
She had not written chattily to her daughter since she had left college, but for once she found it easier to talk on paper than to her face.

> It was lovely to see you two weekends ago. It seems longer since you were here, and, rather like when one is in hospital, the real life that you represent seems in a different era, or certainly a different world from ours. We think, eat, talk nothing but the bye-election. Every day, from ten till five, and sometimes for two or three hours in the evening as well, we are out canvassing. I know you are not happy about what is going on, but it is happening, so there's no point in my pretending that I have much else to write about!
>
> In any case, I am writing to let off a bit of steam, and get the pressure out of my system.
>
> We have finished the third week of the campaign, and the gloss is wearing off a little. For one thing, I have a blister on my heel from running up and down just too many garden paths. For another, whatever it may have been doing in London, it has been raining here. I know I have been praying for rain (for purely agricultural reasons) but I wish it would do it at night, and stop by day, instead of the other way round. I cannot tell you how hard it is canvassing in the rain.
>
> I stumble blindly up a flagged front path to the door of a house, holding my umbrella in front of my face, vainly trying to shield a fistful of pamphlets inside the front of my coat. So how do I ring the bell? I daren't do it with the hand that has the papers in it, because if the rain gets on the window stickers, which have glue on them, they are impossible to separate later. The other hand is busy with the umbrella. Bright idea – hold the umbrella between my teeth, taking the weight of it on my shoulder. Then I press the bell. It doesn't work. I look up to see if there is a knocker, the umbrella tips back, a drip from the gutter hits me squarely on the nose. I locate a knocker and bang it, but there is no answer. I count slowly up to twenty

and then bend to put a 'Sorry you were out' card through the letterbox, which for some reason is at ankle height. They must have very small postmen round here. The flap is so stiff, that I am clearly going to have to hold it open with one hand while inserting the card with the other. So with the umbrella still gripped in my teeth, I sit on my heels to give me enough flat knee-space on which to balance the pile of papers while my hands are busy. All goes well, but suddenly the door is opened from inside. The householder gives a startled cry on seeing what must look like an enormous black shiny mushroom wobbling on the doorstep. Just as I am rising to my full height, with all the dignity I can assume, a fitful gust of wind catches the umbrella and jerks it backwards. The discomfort to my teeth is second only to the mental anguish I suffer as I realise I have forgotten the pile of assorted leaflets on my lap, some of which have slid into a puddle while the rest are being wafted on the wind back down the garden path. I smile bravely, however, and begin, '*Good* morning, I am calling on behalf of—' but the door has been closed again and, too late, I see the VOTE LIBERAL DEMOCRAT sticker in the window.

Have I your sympathy? It isn't like that all the time. Today it was dry, proper July weather again, and everything fresher and brighter for the wash. Please God it stays like this till polling day. I am told, though, that bad weather favours our party, which I suggest is one of those old wives' tales. Can I really believe that the Conservatives have all the umbrellas and cars?

We do so hope you may come to The Count on the night of the 19th. We can get tickets for close family, but we need to know fairly soon, as there is great demand, and each party is only allocated so many. Do come. It is a big night for Dad. The polls close at nine – we will be having supper at home, and the fun will start about ten.

Susanna hesitated before signing *much love, Mum*. Should she add more? She knew Leonora would not come, and she did not want to push her too hard: it would be like persuading a conscientious objector to enlist. In any case, she understood how her daughter felt. In spite of her doubts, she posted the letter; it was, at least, 'keeping in touch'.

She was surprised by a telephone call two days later from Leonora. She would love to come to the count, she said, and would get home in time for supper beforehand. What on earth, thought Susanna, is going on? A conversion on the Damascus road?

So the whole family, including Rachel, drove to Wraybury town hall on the evening of polling day. Susanna knew that, in theory at least, she and Peter were exhausted. Apart from the effort of the campaign, and the restless nights of canvassing dreams, there had been polling day itself. The Association treasurer had driven them round every polling station in the constituency, about fifty in all, as well as the supporting Tory committee rooms in nearby houses. At each they had been cheerful, interested, encouraging, grateful, handshaking, coffee-drinking, drink-refusing and rushing on. It had taken from eight in the morning till eight in the evening, but after hot baths and food the sense of exhilaration was so great that Susanna knew they could, if necessary, have started all over again.

'Great night for burglars,' said Peter, as he locked the front door.

Susanna was standing looking up to where the misty swathe of the Milky Way cut across the spangled sky.

'There are almost too many stars for comfort,' she said.

'Forget them,' said Peter. 'One will do, one good and lucky one.'

'The important thing is not to get star-struck,' she replied. 'Or starry-eyed.'

'I am planning to be a star turn, actually.'

'How startling,' said Susanna, giggling.

They got into the car, and held hands as they drove, feeling closer than they had had time to feel for some weeks.

Chapter 6

The town hall of Wraybury was a noble Georgian building that had been doomed in the sixties, considered bad for the progressive image of the town. In the seventies there had been protests against its demolition and its elegantly curved balustraded stone entrance steps had been the site of a 'sit-in', which Ellie Fittall claimed was the cause of the anal discomfort from which she still suffered. In the eighties the handsome edifice had been finally saved for posterity by the intervention of heritage bodies, but was now little more than a façade. It was far too small to house, but did something to conceal, the inelegant sprawl of modern flat-roofed council offices lying out behind it.

'Where are the cheering crowds?' said Mark, looking round as they approached the entrance steps.

'Here we are,' said a voice.

Turning, they saw a tall, elderly couple following behind them.

'Good evening,' said Peter, smiling in recognition, 'Susanna, I don't think you have met Sir Rupert and Lady Hascombe.'

'Good evening, Mrs Westerham. Rupert Hascombe. We haven't yet had the pleasure of meeting you. It's nice to put a face to a name. My wife, Florence. And this is the family?'

'Yes,' said Susanna. 'May I introduce my mother, Mrs Willoughby? And our son Mark, and his sister Emma, and . . . Leonora? There's another one, somewhere.'

The swinging door indicated that Leonora had gone on up the steps into the town hall.

'I look forward to meeting her too,' said Florence Hascombe. 'Have you enjoyed the campaign, or are you merely exhausted?'

Talking, they all went in together.

The square, marble-floored entrance hall was full of people. Seats had been set in groups, and two large television screens had been erected, one at either side, so that the count could be watched by those without the privilege of tickets for the council chamber. Peter recognised some of the Conservatives clustering round one screen, while the Labour and Liberal Democrat supporters had their camps near the other, with the other parties scattered between the two.

The bar was open and operating in an adjoining room, and most people had drinks in their hands.

On the television screens a team of journalistic commentators, wagging their heads and talking earnestly, were inaudible amid the chatter and laughter.

After introducing his family and communing for some few minutes with the Tory supporters, Peter said to the twins: 'Only those of us with passes can actually go into the chamber, but you get a good view, I gather, from upstairs. Let's go and suss it out.'

They climbed the stone staircase, where bearded and moustached faces gazed self-importantly down on them from huge mediocre portraits. A recurring item in each was the heavy mayoral chain that adorned the proud chests.

The hall where the count was held was the main council chamber of the old town hall. The wealth of the fathers of Wraybury in the nineteenth century had found expression in the lavish decoration and the balustraded balconies from which the burghers could watch, if not easily hear, the deliberations of their masters.

Down on the parquet floor below, the Westerham family saw lines of trestle tables stretching the length of the great room. In front of the platform at the far end, another long table was stacked with large, battered, black tin boxes of voting slips. Looking at them, Peter suddenly felt a surge of excitement, a gut feeling that belonged to schooldays: the open goal, or the last stretch of a cross-country run when you knew that you still had the reserves to overtake the leaders. This rush of adrenalin, this heart-gripping excitement was something he missed and hankered after. It was extraordinary that Susanna could not understand this, for all her sympathetic attitudes. It was not a dissatisfaction with his marriage, it was a need for something new, for the unexpected to happen for once – she should see that. It was all very well for her, satisfied with her ponies, her occasional teaching, her home and her comfortable view of the future. He needed something more.

He looked at her standing close by. She was pointing at something happening down below and laughing with Mark.

He took a mental tug at himself. She was here, wasn't she? She had been out on the streets and lanes every day of the campaign, full of apparent enthusiasm and commitment. She showed every sign that she was coming round to it.

'We'd better go down again,' said Peter. 'They'll be starting at any moment. Coming, Susanna? The twins can watch from here.'

'We'll go and find Leo and bring her up,' said Mark.

Peter and Susanna were welcomed in the chamber by faces they knew: Ellie Fittall, Major Knight and several others, all cheerful and chatty. Though no drinks were allowed in the chamber itself, it was apparent that Cyril Eversley had already visited the bar more than once.

'You'll be all right, old man,' he said confidingly to Peter, grasping him by the elbow. 'No problem. No problem.'

They walked round, talking to the counting team who, with nothing yet to do, were looking at the candidates with interest. The others were there, wearing huge rosettes with the colours of their party. The Monster Raving Loony candidate, a tall gangling young man in a sou'wester, had a purple rhododendron flower in his button hole.

'I love it,' said Susanna to him. 'Is it silk?'

'Silk?' he replied. 'I picked it this morning from my rose bush.'

Susanna smiled dutifully.

The candidates, each with a spouse or attendant girl- or boyfriend, shook hands as they met. Most were excessively friendly, cracking strained jokes, and only the Conservative and Liberal Democrat hangers on, the henchmen of the serious contenders, were noticeably cool to each other. The agents of the different parties circled anxiously.

A hush spread as the returning officer made an inaudible announcement, and several boxes of voting slips were poured out onto the tables. The counting clerks, now armed with rubber thimbles, fell to with professional dexterity.

The hall was now very quiet, with only the sound of rustling paper and the low murmurs of the watchers.

'It's all so . . . manual,' whispered Susanna to Peter.

'What did you expect, robots? Machines?'

'What I mean is, it must have been done like this, in such a basic way, ever since voting started, whenever that was.'

'Well, this way, everyone can see there is no cheating.'

'I wonder why an X,' said Susanna, 'and not a tick, when you vote? An X is so negative.'

'Could be something to do with the way people used to make their mark with a cross if they couldn't write, perhaps. I don't know,' said Peter.

'Do you think they do it like this America? It seems so very amateur and British.'

The twins found Leonora sitting on a stool at the bar. She was talking to a good-looking young man and they seemed to be having no communication problems.

'These are my siblings,' she said, slightly reluctantly, 'Mark, Emma.'

'Hi,' said her companion. 'I'm Andrew. You none of you look alike.'

'We were all foundlings,' said Mark conversationally. 'They started with Leo and thought they could do a bit better, so they went hunting again and they happened to find us in the same plastic bag, a sort of job lot – two for the price of one as it were—'

'Oh, shut up,' said Leonora.

'Your sister said you were twins,' said Andrew, grinning.

'Yes,' said Emma smiling up at him, 'but male and female twins are never identical. They don't need to look alike any more than any brother and sister. They are two eggs, you see, not one split one, and they don't share a—'

'Oh God,' said Leonora, 'spare us the gynaecological details, can't you? I'll buy you a drink if you'll go away.'

'No, let me,' said Andrew, turning to the bar. Then, as an afterthought, 'But I don't mean you need go away.'

'Hello there,' said another voice. 'Are you the Westerhams? Jolly good. I thought you must be. I've met your parents, in the course of duty, so it's nice to see the offspring.'

Standing beside them was a rather stout young man in a blazer.

'I'd like to introduce myself,' he said. 'I'm Terry Lowther, chairman of the Kentish Weald YCs.'

Vibes whipped round the three Westerhams.

'Wicees? What's that?' said Emma.

'YCs? Don't you know?' said Lowther. 'You *have* got a lot to learn. Young Conservatives, of course.'

He smiled at Leonora.

'My goodness,' she said, 'they *are* starting them young nowadays! And you must be quite an old one, if you're the chairman.'

'What do you do, apart from just be young?' asked Mark, fixing him with his wide-eyed stare.

'That's quite a full-time job of course, nowadays,' said Emma.

'Well,' said Terry Lowther, feeling that he was being bounced lightly between these disconcerting people, 'we represent the party to the, er, younger generation, we attend the party conference as their representatives, and we have branches in virtually every constituency in the country, with regular meetings.'

'Fascinating,' said Leonora, shaking her head in wonder. 'But what do you actually do? Do tell us. We really want to know.'

'Yes, really,' said Emma, bright-eyed and eager. 'It's so interesting. And when you grow up, do you automatically become real Conservatives?'

'There's nothing unreal about us, I assure you.' The young man laughed uneasily. 'We are a very vital part of the political scene. I addressed the conference last year at Blackpool.'

'Oh, really,' said Leonora, 'how absolutely thrilling. On what?'

'Oh,' said Lowther airily, 'on national and European issues, as it happens.'

'An issue, an issue, we all fall down,' said Mark, falling off his bar stool.

'Oh – what's that? I'm all wet!' Leonora squealed.

Andrew, holding four brimming glasses of beer between his hands, had turned from the bar to rejoin them and was quaking with laughter, so that cold beer was slopping around him.

'Do you mind?' said the Young Conservative chairman icily, flicking lager off the sleeve of his blazer.

'Ss-ssorry,' said Andrew. 'Really sorry. If you could all be quiet for a minute I might get these on to a table while there's still something left in them.'

Terry Lowther was staring at him.

'You're – you're – ' he stuttered.

'Andrew Manning,' said Andrew, stretching out his hand.

Terry did not take it.

'But you're one of the candidates,' he said.

'That's right. I am the Green Party candidate. Seen relaxing before the count.'

'It's not before the count,' said the YC chairman coldly. 'The count has started. Shouldn't you be in there, encouraging your supporters? If you have any, that is.'

'Ooh, below the belt,' said Emma.

'Not very good form, I should say,' said Mark.

There was a stir among the crowd in the hall. The video screen that could be seen through the door had lit up, and the counting tables were visible on it.

'I'm going upstairs to watch,' said Mark, 'Coming Leo? Emma? They don't mind you taking drinks up to the gallery.'

'Yes, let's,' said Leonora. 'Do you mind, Andrew, if we do? Thanks, though. See you later, I expect. Good luck!'

And the three Westerhams left the two young men side by side.

Rachel was sitting nearby and watching, amused by the obvious antipathy between the two. She was sharing a table with the Hascombes, and they were all keeping an eye on the video screens.

'Can you fill me in?' she said. 'Who are those two young men whom my grandchildren have just left?'

'The plump one is the local YC chairman,' said Florence Hascombe, 'and the other, the one he is glaring at, is the Green Party candidate. I suspect your elder granddaughter is the cause of the confrontation, don't you?'

'How very entertaining,' said Rachel. 'I had not understood the political angle in that little scene. What fun.'

'I've got it!' said Rupert Hascombe, 'I have suddenly realised who you are.'

'Is my cover blown?' said Rachel, feigning alarm. 'I'll come clean.

I am, or was, an under cover agent for *Pravda*, women's section.'

'No, you are not, you are Rachel Gurney.'

'Good heavens,' said Rachel. She had expected only to be reminded that she was a candidate's mother-in-law. 'And who are you, or perhaps I should say, who were you, as we seem to be talking of the distant past?'

'I am Linda Hascombe's brother. Can you have forgotten? I once worshipped the ground you trod on.'

'Linda! Of course I remember her.'

'Rachel Gurney was at school with Linda,' said Rupert, turning to his wife, 'and Linda used to bring her home at weekends.'

'At least twice, as I remember,' said Rachel, laughing, 'and I do remember a younger brother, but I had forgotten your name. Rupert Hascombe, of course! We are talking about nineteen forty-six? Forty-seven? Something like that. I'm sure I enjoyed your infant passion at the time.'

'No, Rachel Gurney,' said Rupert, raising his glass to her, 'you were as cold as a marble statue, and you shone like a star at ping-pong. Your backhand is engraven on my heart. Do you ever see Linda?'

'Not for so long, sadly. We were thick as thieves then, and we did everything together. She . . . she was my bridesmaid.'

'You married Hugh Willoughby. Of course.' Hascombe hesitated, nearly went on, but changed his mind.

'Yes,' said Rachel. She glanced up at the video screen, on which very little activity could be seen. 'Oh look, things are hotting up out there. I think I must go upstairs again. I want to see naked democracy at work, red in tooth and claw.'

'We'll join you later,' said Hascombe, standing up.

'Good luck to your son-in-law,' said his wife.

They watched Rachel's narrow back as she went out into the hall. Florence looked at Rupert.

'Are my antennae over-sensitive, or would angels have feared to tread there?'

'No, you're right,' said her husband, frowning. 'There is a story. Finish your drink, though. We should go into the hall and show willing. I'll tell you about it later.'

Rachel did not go upstairs immediately. She went out into the market square at the side of the town hall. A breath of fresh air was what she needed, she decided. She strolled round the outside pavement of the square, her hands in her pockets.

Unexpectedly, she felt shaken by the revelation that Rupert Hascombe had known her in the past. No, to be honest, it was his mention of Hugh. It was not that she did not herself occasionally still think of Hugh, but she did it in the way that one turns the pages of an old album, looking backwards, flicking, not relating. What Rupert Hascombe had done was disconcerting: he had gone back to a part of her life that she seldom revisited, dropped her into it, as it were, and then led her forward into the memory of Hugh. She was not used to coming upon it from that angle, which she supposed was why she had beaten such a foolish retreat. She had been momentarily whipped back to her final schooldays, and then into the summer intoxication of her growing affair with the young soldier, newly released from the army.

Finding that they thought the same things funny had been magical, while finding that he loved her had been a dream from which daily she had expected to awaken. Now, standing staring sightlessly at Wraybury town hall, on a strangely still night, she revisited difficult territory; the breathless joy of their wedding day, the cold scent of arum lilies, the feeling of Hugh's hand holding hers, of his low voice making the vows that he was so painfully soon to break. Hugh's vows, then and later, had been their problem, she thought ruefully, seeing him in her mind face downwards upon a chilly marble floor, arms outspread, already far away from her. She had tried to pray on both occasions, in those very different churches, and both times found that her heart had been far too full of emotion to concentrate on what she should say.

It was odd, she thought, staring up at the golden ball and pinnacle that rather incongruously surmounted the small tower above the roof of the town hall, very odd, that Hugh could still take her by surprise, after all this time. One needed a warning of these things.

When he had first told her what he was going to do, what he had virtually already done, she had not argued. Why not? It had been her life too, and yet something inherent in her, something she must have acquired in the womb, prevented her from trying to stop him. She had made silly jokes, when her heart was bursting.

'Don't get any bad habits, will you?'

She had always trusted him, and now she trusted him somehow to change his mind, but he never had. Or not until it was too late.

Rachel gave a slight shiver, but not from cold. It was a warm night, and as she walked back towards the town hall she saw a woman standing on the steps, a small woman in a cardigan who smiled at Rachel as she approached,

'Gets hot in there, doesn't it? I came out for a breather too. You the mother of the bride, then?'

Rachel stared for a second at the bright eyes in the softly crinkled face. Were they uncommonly perceptive?

'Oh,' she said. 'Yes, in a way. If they win, that is.'

'Never you worry, love,' said Ellie Fittall, 'they'll win, unless the sky falls tonight. This is what they call the Tory heartland.'

She introduced herself, adding, 'I'm one of them grass roots they go on about:'

Rachel smiled and felt herself warming to the old lady.

'You going in?' she said. 'May I come with you?'

And they walked up the steps together.

'Did you know he was the Green candidate, Leo?' said Mark, as they hung over the balcony, watching the scene in the hall below.

'Andrew? Of course I did,' said Leonora. 'I've met him before.'

'Where?' said the twins together.

'When he was depositing his deposit, in Wraybury. I was there with Dad.'

'Ah-ha,' said Emma, grinning, 'I wondered why you were so willing to come tonight. He's gorgeous.'

'Consorting with the enemy,' said Mark, 'is a punishable offence in political circles.'

'Oh, shut up,' said Leonora. 'I was only being polite.'

'You're right about Rachel Willoughby,' said Rupert Hascombe to his wife as they watched from the opposite balcony. 'I really did put my flat foot in it. I didn't mean any harm, but she shut up like a clam, as you noticed.'

'It was as soon as you mentioned her husband. Is she still married?' said Florence.

'No, she's a widow.'

'Most people aren't especially sensitive about that, though. I wonder what happened.'

'I'll tell you what happened,' said her husband. 'I only wish I had remembered it sooner, because it's obviously a sensitive spot. She was quite a friend of Linda's, though I only met her a few times. She was very pretty, and a couple of years older than me.'

'You drooled a bit, did you?' said Florence.

'It didn't get me far. Seventeen-year-old girls are about five years older than fifteen-year-old boys. And there were rather a lot of droolers around her; but she got married, when she was nineteenish, to the most unlikely drooler of them all. She fell head-over-heels for this fellow Willoughby. Funny, quiet chap. Ex-army, and I think he'd been in prison in Germany. It seemed a bit of a waste, but it was all perfectly happy, as far as I know. They had a child – our candidate's wife, I suppose. And then one day, when they had been married – I don't know, a few years, Willoughby suddenly upped and told her that he had got religion – got it seriously. He had been accepted into a community of monks, and that was it. Goodbye.'

'Just like that? Do you mean she had no idea, no warning?'

'Evidently not,' said Hascombe. 'You'd think you would notice that sort of thing coming on, wouldn't you? Find a hair shirt in his sock drawer or something.'

'Poor girl. And with a child, too,' said Florence.

'Yes. He left her with a bit of money, I suppose, but she had to drag it up by herself. I think it – or she, rather – was only about three when he left. Quite rough for the wife, in her twenties. It wasn't exactly de rigueur to be a single parent in those days.'

'And she never married again?'

'Presumably not, as she's still called Willoughby,' said Rupert. 'She took it very hard, I remember, and disappeared for a bit. I don't think she divorced him. I don't know. Actually, I don't think he was more than forty when he died.'

'What a sad story,' said Florence. 'I gathered that she lives with the Westerhams. That can't be the easiest set-up, I would have thought, a mother-in-law on the premises. I wonder if it works.'

'I imagine she'd be pretty tactful,' said Hascombe. 'I can't see her as a cartoon mother-in-law.'

'That's because you knew her as a pretty girl,' said his wife.

'I ignore your remarks, Floss, as beneath my dignity. Do you see the Natural Law candidate down there? If you watch closely you might see him hover in the air. They practise levitation, or so the *Echo* said last week. Oh, hell, here's Peacock coming along. At least we don't have to avoid him. He no longer sucks up to me, he just hates me. No, I'm wrong. Here he comes.'

'Be polite,' said Florence Hascombe quickly.

'Am I ever not?' said Hascombe, wide-eyed.

Peacock looked irritable.

'Evening, Lady Hascombe,' he said. 'Evening. Have you seen the chairman? I suppose he's in the bar.'

'I don't think so,' said Hascombe.

'You know what now?' said Peacock. 'I have had the YC chairman complaining to me. Evidently those young Westerhams have been fraternising openly with the Green candidate, and they insulted Lowther in front of him. You'd think their father would have taught them how to behave before he brought them along here.'

Peacock never lost an opportunity to remind Rupert Hascombe that the wrong man had been selected for Kentish Weald, and that he blamed Hascombe for it.

'I thought they were rather a pleasant bunch, just like their parents,' said Hascombe breezily.

'Teenagers have no place at a count,' said Peacock.

'Even though they are old enough to vote?'

Peacock glared at him, and moved on.

'There you are: I was polite,' said Hascombe.

'Oh, that's what it's called,' said his wife.

* * *

From the balcony, the bird's eye view of the long lines of voting slips made it clear that one of the candidates was already well ahead of the others.

Susanna, moving behind the counting clerks with Peter, felt a strange embarrassment to see him so obviously winning. Watching seemed a form of gloating.

She caught sight of their children above and went up to join them.

'Come slumming, have you?' said Mark.

'Much more fun up here,' said his mother. 'We have to keep quiet down near the tables.'

'Could you see who's winning? Is that long line Dad's?' said Emma excitedly, infected by the atmosphere.

'Yes,' said Susanna. 'I don't think there can be any surprises now.'

'Whose is that tiny line? Just two piles?' said Leonora.

'It's either the Anti-motorway party or the Natural Law. The Monster Raving Loony is ahead of them both – the fringe parties are all jostling along at the bottom. Only Lib Dem and the Green have got many – you see those two reasonably long lines. The Green is doing rather well, actually. I think he'll come third.'

Mark looked sharply at Leonora, who was leaning over the rail beside him. He was expecting her to be looking studiously unconcerned. But instead he saw a tight little smile on her lips; a not entirely pleasant look that surprised him. Strange. He turned again to his mother.

'Is it nearly finished?' he said. 'It's after midnight.'

'No stamina,' said Susanna. 'Only a few more boxes, as far as I can see.'

The contents of the last boxes were tumbled out in front of the clerks. Peter looked up at the gallery and Susanna went downstairs again.

The end came quite quickly. When the final slips were counted and bundled the clerks sat back, stretching their arms and fingers, talking and laughing together. The tension round the tables subsided and all attention was on the little knot of agents and candidates gathered round the returning officer at the end table.

'What are they doing?' said Susanna to Rupert Hascombe, who had also now come down into the chamber.

'They are bickering over the spoiled papers and the returning officer is deciding which ones he will allow. The agents do a bit of horse-trading between them.'

A hush fell again as the party emerged on the platform. There was a slight jostling for the central positions. Susanna was standing at the back of the room by Hascombe.

'Nervous?' he asked kindly.

'I don't think so,' she said.

'How do you like the idea of being an MP's wife?'

'It will be a new experience,' she replied. 'Very exciting.'

Despite her cheerful voice, it was obvious that her words were forced. Hascombe glanced at her, and noticed the tautness of her expression. She did not look at him. He raised his eyebrows, but did not continue.

The results were read out in the order of the names on the voting slips. Each was greeted with cheers and whistles from the party supporters in the chamber and from the packed galleries above.

'The fringier the party the more noise they make!' giggled Emma.

'Shut up,' said Mark, scribbling down the figures.

The Loony candidate's three hundred votes were hailed with blasts on a hunting horn and cracker-like explosions, which made the returning officer frown with annoyance. But the television cameras were on him and he did not pause.

The seventeen-thousand-odd votes for the Liberal Democrat candidate won a huge roar of approval, and Peter's twenty-one thousand an even louder one. The Green candidate had polled eight thousand, easily beating all the remaining candidates, which caused shouts of delight from the Green supporters.

'Well done, Dad! Brilliant!' said Emma, hugging her sister. 'Isn't that brilliant?'

'But not a surprise,' said Leonora, looking bored.

'Let's go down,' said Mark. 'They must let us in now – we're the MP's family.'

'Wow, Dad's an MP! It's just hit me!' said Emma, as they raced for the staircase.

Susanna, standing alone at the back of the hall, had the same feeling. She could see Peter moving about on the platform, shaking hands, congratulating and receiving congratulations. He was smiling broadly. Photographers were gathering, allowed into the chamber on their press passes, though other people were still excluded.

'Mr Westerham, Mr Westerham,' they called, 'turn this way, please. Again!'

The clatter of camera shutters sounded above the chatter of the supporters who surrounded him.

Susanna had never actually considered how she would feel at the moment of Peter's election. If she had, she would have hoped to be elated, proud of Peter, swept along by the excitement. Instead, watching them all, she felt isolated, as if he were being rushed away from her at speed, and she was swamped by a great wave of dismay and loneliness. She stood staring at the platform, with the sensation of observing the scene from a great distance. Peter suddenly, irrevocably, seemed to have become public property.

'Hi, Mum,' said Mark, rushing up to her, grabbing her round the waist. 'Isn't this cool? How do you feel?'

'How do *you* feel? Did you have a good view?' said Susanna, turning, moving her mouth into a smile. 'I'm so glad you got in – are you all here?'

'We seduced the man at the door,' said Emma. 'I think he was one of yours. I don't see why everyone can't come in now.'

'I suppose till they've cleared the boxes they can't,' said Susanna. 'Let's go and see Dad.'

As they went forward they heard him call, 'Where's my wife? Susanna?'

He spotted them and beckoned them up to the platform.

There was no sign of Leonora, but the rest of the family was photographed from every angle and in every kind of grouping. They smiled, turned this way and that, and did what they were told.

'Well done, my darling,' said Susanna, when after some time she had a chance to give Peter a kiss that was not simply responding to the requests of the photographers. 'You got a *huge* vote.'

'Pretty good, isn't it?' said Peter, radiant and distant. 'I never thought we'd do as well. A tremendous effort on everyone's part. We must go and see the others – they'll all be out there waiting for us.'

'Mind you don't touch Cyril Eversley,' said Susanna. 'He might fall over.'

The other candidates left fairly soon, the Green candidate dangerously chaired down the steps by his friends, who had taken advantage of the extended licence. He winked at Leonora and the twins as they passed. Mark noticed that Leonora watched the party till they disappeared through the swing doors, again with that strange expression on her face. Her mind seemed to be absent.

It was an hour before Peter was free of his delighted party workers, who were euphoric in their pleasure. The bar had closed, but they had taken the precaution of filling their glasses beforehand. Eversley claimed to speak for them all as he toasted 'Our new, wunnerful Member of Parliament, Pe-peter Westerhouse and his lovely lady wife.'

At one-thirty in the morning the Westerhams finally left the town hall and found their car. Rachel Willoughby joined them on the steps.

'Were you all right, Ma?' said Susanna. 'I hardly saw you from beginning to end.'

'Very much all right. I had a lovely time. Everyone was very friendly, especially the Natural Law people. Do you think I am too old to leave the ground? I also made friends with a splendid lady called Fittall, who seems to be an ardent supporter of you both. I disillusioned her, rather than have her disappointed later. Shall I come with you, Leonora?'

'You'd better drive our car, I think,' said Peter to Susanna. 'Have you had a drink?'

'Only a soft one, recently,' she said.

'You'd better drive, love.'

The twins chattered in the back and Peter laughed with them. The elation was glowing from him.

It was late when they got home, but Susanna had a bath before going to bed. As she lay in the steaming water with her eyes half closed, tears leaked down her face. She was tired, of course; they had had a long day, she told herself in a motherly way; but she was aware that her weakness came not from tiredness but from . . . well, not fear . . . surely that was too dramatic a word . . . extreme apprehension, anyway. She tried to analyse the feeling, and to dispel it by thinking of Peter's pleasure, but all the time she was invaded by the thought that he did not know where they were heading, any more than she did. All she knew was that she liked where they had been.

But there was nothing to be gained by regretting the events of the day. Peter was high on success and she would not cast any shadow over his moment of triumph, even if she had to act the part of sharing it.

When Peter came into the bathroom she was wiping her face with a flannel.

'Bed's lovely,' he said. 'Do come.'

'I've never been to bed with an MP before,' she murmured as she slid in beside him.

'Come here,' he said, 'and feel the difference.'

Chapter 7

The telephone rang, crashing into their sleep. Susanna answered it, fumbling, with her eyes shut.

'Can I have a word with Mr Peter Westerham?' said a voice she did not recognise.

'Yes . . . is it . . . what time is it?' She reached blearily for her watch.

'I am afraid it is a little early, I'm sorry, but I would very much like—'

'Who is that?' Susanna said, having seen that it was six forty-five.

'This is the Today programme. We are wondering whether we could do an interview with Mr Westerham just after the eight o'clock news.'

'Hang on, you'd better speak to him.'

She covered the mouthpiece with her hand, and hissed at Peter, who was up on his elbow beside her.

'The Today programme! They want to interview you – I think it's that man, you know, whassisname, the one who interrupts all the time.'

Peter took the receiver. He agreed to be waiting by the telephone at eight o'clock.

Flopping back on the pillows, he reached a hand out to Susanna.

'God, I don't feel ready. I'd better get up and have some coffee or something. How did they get our number?'

'I think,' said Susanna, yawning hugely, 'we'll move the telephone round to your side of the bed in future.'

When the telephone rang again Susanna recognised that Peter would find it easier if she were out of earshot. She got out her bicycle and, with the dogs running alongside, went down to the village to collect their newspaper.

'Well now, you're an early bird,' said the elderly owner of the shop, 'I'm only just open. And I didn't think we'd see you on a bicycle any more, now that Mr Westerham is a member of parliament.'

'Heavens, Mrs Thomas, you're not going to start calling him Mr Westerham, are you?'

'Well, it's different now, isn't it? He's one of them now. It was on the news, early. I said to my husband, I said, we'll know who to go to, now, if we've got any problems.'

'Bad luck, Mrs Thomas,' said Susanna, putting a coin on the counter, 'he's not your MP. His constituency starts ten miles up the road. So you can just go on calling him Peter and complaining to someone else.'

'Don't you worry, dear, I was just pulling your leg. That's your change. I expect you'll have your picture in the papers now, with him being famous. We'll have to look out.'

As Susanna rode back she thought about what Mrs Thomas had said. Peter, it seemed, had become one of Them. Perhaps she had too.

The constituency was quiet for a few days, recovering from the effort of the election campaign. Peter spent time in the agent's office, and asked Susanna to come with him on his third visit.

'I gather some of the branches are hoping you will go to their fundraising events, and Leonard Peacock has a few dates to throw at you.'

'I would feel more co-operative with Leonard Peacock if he didn't call me "dear".'

'I noticed that – why don't you tell him not to?'

'Perhaps if I call him "ducky" he'll get the message,' said Susanna.

'We need him on our side, Sukie,' said Peter, 'so try to be friendly.'

'Of course I will. How do you get on with him?'

'He's a bit strange. Not very helpful, really. Just doing what he has to, like he did during the campaign, but not exactly forthcoming. We'll get used to each other, I expect. I wish he wouldn't make it quite so obvious that I am not his dream MP.'

'He's lucky to get you,' said Susanna. 'He might have got one of the other two.'

'He might have preferred that,' said Peter.

'Ignore him, then.'

'That's hard, when he runs everything in Kentish Weald division and throws files of paper at me every time I see him. Cyril Eversley's very friendly, though. I rather like him.'

In the constituency office Susanna found it difficult to keep her promise to Peter. Leonard Peacock knew only two ways of dealing with women, either ordering them about or flirting with them, and he could do neither with his MP's wife. So, not knowing how to talk to her, he tried being avuncular. It was not a success.

'You needn't feel nervous at the Bentridge branch ladies' committee lunch, dear,' he said. 'Just wear a pretty dress and draw the raffle. No need to say anything.'

'Just smile and look decorative, you mean,' said Susanna.

'That's right, dear. You are a very important part of Peter's equipment, if I may put it like that.'

Peter sensed Susanna seething and interrupted, asking questions about his advice surgery.

'I want to help, Pete,' Susanna said later, 'and I will, but that Peacock has got to take on board that I run a business: a small one, I grant you, but it comes first.'

'I think you made that fairly clear,' he said.

Peter went up to London to take his seat in the Commons on the Tuesday after the bye-election. He rang Susanna in the evening.

'I'm glad I told you not to come,' he said. 'There wouldn't have been much for you to see. I was marched up in front of the Speaker, gave him a little bow, and that was it. Then straight into orders for the day, just like the telly. Very dull.'

'And very exciting?'

'Yes, of course.' She could hear that he was smiling. 'They've given me a minder, a fellow called Jack Winthrop, who has a London seat. He has a minute majority, and he's obviously worried stiff about the General Election, when it comes. It makes me realise how lucky I am.'

'How does he mind you?' asked Susanna.

'Rather like a prefect when you first go to boarding school, actually. He showed me the library, and where the loos are, and where you loiter if you want to meet the press, and where you don't, if you don't. It's very like school, actually. You get your own locker. I expected to find someone's white mouse at the back of mine. You also get your own coat hanger, on a hook with your name written above it. And – your mother will love this – it has a little loop of pink ribbon attached, to hang your sword on.'

'I don't believe it – seriously?' said Susanna.

'Seriously. Perhaps I'll get hold of a sword – I bet Rupert Hascombe has one tucked away – and try it.'

'Where did you sit on those green benches?' said Susanna. 'How did you know where to go? I looked for you when there was a bit on the news this evening, but couldn't see you anywhere.'

'I sat very modestly, as a new boy should, at the very back, below the gangway. That's the other end from the Speaker.'

'I wonder how soon you will be brave enough to put your feet up on the back of the bench in front, like they all do, or is that for the sixth form only? You had better wear a peony or something in your button hole, or I'll never pick you out. The cameras move much too fast.'

'It's a wise woman who knows her own husband,' he said.

The end of the summer session of parliament came within two weeks of the bye-election. The Westerhams had rented a cottage in the Highlands, as they usually did, for most of August, but Peter joined them only for the first weekend.

'What about our fishing trip, Dad?' said Emma. 'You promised.'

'Twins, can I just defer the promise till next summer? I will be much more organised then.'

'Remember how quickly they grow up, nowadays,' said Mark. 'In no time they have left the nest and all you can do is lean on your zimmer and remember the promises you broke when they were young . . .'

'Which I can count on the fingers of one hand,' said Peter defensively.

'Oh, you're all right, Dad,' said Mark, punching his father. 'We just want you to know we care.'

Later, Susanna said, 'They really do care, you know, Pete. They have never had to share you with other people before. That's something we will all have to learn about.'

'Listen,' said Peter, 'parliament doesn't start again till late October. Apart from the odd constituency engagement, I can do things with them any weekend they care to be at home.'

The twins were starting at university that autumn, Emma at Newcastle and Mark at Durham. Susanna suspected that, as had happened with Leonora, they would be less interested in holidays with their parents after that.

Rachel never went on the family holiday. She always made clear that she needed a rest from her neighbours and liked to get the place to herself. If she took a holiday, she took it in winter, not when the country was at its best. Besides, the ponies, she said, were happier with someone they knew.

While the family was still in Scotland, she had invited Ellie Fittall to Restings for an afternoon. It had been meant as a kindly act, since she had discovered that Ellie's annual holiday with her sister in Worthing had been cancelled because of the latter's illness. The old lady had been entranced by the Restings garden, and had talked entertainingly of her childhood in a similar farmhouse in Sussex.

'Wasn't all tarted up like this, of course,' she said. 'There was plenty of muck around, because it was a real working farm, like. Me dad kept pigs, and the smell was something lovely.'

The visit had lasted longer than intended, and finished with a well matched and highly competitive game of Scrabble before Rachel had driven Ellie back to her flat in Wraybury.

'You've got a good vocabulary, Rachel, I'll say that for you,' had been the old lady's parting words.

During her third visit to Restings, it dawned on Rachel that Ellie was in no need of kindness, and the benefit of their friendship was mutual. Ellie was a seriously good companion and they saw eye to eye on most things.

'I had a telephone call from Susanna last night,' Rachel told her as she was driving her home.

'That's right, BT works on their consciences if they don't ring their mums,' said Ellie.

'I'd like to think that's all it was,' said Rachel. 'But she says they are coming home two days early.'

'Oh yes?' said Ellie inquiringly.

'She is blaming the weather, but . . .'

'What is it, then, if it's not the weather?'

'I don't know. Something's wrong.'

The holiday had not been a success. Susanna was quite open about it to Peter, and blamed herself.

'They all quarrelled, just as if they were nine or ten years old, bickered like small children. I have never known them all so bad-tempered, and somehow I couldn't break the pattern. Every time I suggested a plan they vetoed it, and if I didn't suggest anything they just went off down to the pub and came back separately. And it rained, which didn't help.'

'It is quite intolerable, at their age,' said Peter, 'and I shall tell them so.'

'Pete, no, you can't do that,' said Susanna, horrified.

But he did, and received the retort from Leonora that he was a fine one to talk, when he didn't even bother to stay with them. Even the normally equable Mark made it clear to his father that the blame, if there was blame, was to be shared among them all. The whole family was pervaded by an uncomfortable sense of shame and disappointment, which made them artificially nice to each other as they all prepared for their different terms to start. The twins left for their universities and Leonora went back to London and her job, leaving Peter and Susanna getting to know the ways of the constituency.

'That agent is a real pain, Ma,' Susanna said to her mother a few weeks later. 'I am no feminist, but Leonard Peacock's assumption that my time is at his disposal really irritates me. He hands me a list of engagements, and just looks amazed if I say that I am simply not very often free to drive to the far end of the constituency in mid-afternoon. "Oh yes, you keep ponies," he said to me once, as if they were stick insects or something. "I run a business, Mr Peacock," I said, as coldly as I could. "Yes, indeed. Very nice too," he said. How do you cope with a man like that?'

'A little wax figure and pins, I suggest,' said Rachel. 'It seldom works, but it uses up old candle ends.'

In November, shortly after the new parliamentary session started, Peter arranged seats in the public gallery for his family on the evening he was to make his maiden speech. He was not certain that they would all want to come and, though hoping for their loyal support, was careful not to press them.

'Are you nervous?' asked Emma the Sunday before, at lunch. She was home for a weekend, collecting books, tapes and any food she could lay her hands on.

'Not at all,' said her father, piling spaghetti on his plate. 'I've only rewritten it three times.'

'Do you mean you're going to read it out?' she said.

'No, you can't do that – I've got it all down to notes, which I pray I shall not have to look at.'

'So, are you going to make them all sit up and stare? Will we see it on the box?' said Mark when Peter telephoned him.

'Sit up and listen, I would hope, or else there is no point speaking at all, as I see it. You can come, you know, if you can be bothered, you and Emma.'

'Of course we're coming, me and Em,' said Mark. 'Can I bring some guys along, so we can organise a Mexican wave from the gallery?'

'No guys,' said Peter, 'just family. But you can all come, if you like.'

I think you had better count Leonora out,' said Susanna.

'Still sulking, is she? I haven't seen her for weeks.'

Peter's resentment at Leonora's desertion still bubbled. Her job as a researcher for a film company financed her small flat near Shepherd's Bush, but even at the height of her relationship with the anarchic Johnnie she had come home for odd weekends. Peter knew that her absence from home still related in some way to himself but he had given up bothering to wonder why.

'I expect she's busy,' said Susanna placidly.

Mark and Emma avoided each other's eyes.

'Would your mother like to come?' said Peter to Susanna.

'Granny says she is going to shout "Votes for women" and wave her umbrella,' said Emma.

'Why?' said Susanna.

'Because she says she was born too late to do it when it was relevant, and she has felt deprived ever since.'

Peter laughed. 'Your mother makes me almost as nervous as the twins do,' he said.

'She'd love to come, though,' said Susanna. 'We'll make sure she behaves. Is that all right?'

'I wouldn't be without her,' said Peter.

Peter had been speaking for nearly ten minutes, partly about his constituency, partly about his political beliefs. The House listened with polite semi-attention. But it was when the new MP mentioned the word Europe that his family, ranged along the second row of the visitors' gallery, became aware of a stirring of interest on the government benches, heads coming up, papers going down, muttered conversations ceasing, a coming alive that had not been evident before.

'Let us continue,' Peter concluded, 'ardently to strive for that "ever closer union" to which we pledged ourselves in 1975, so that we and future generations may see this great continent at last united in peace and co-operation.'

As he sat down, among the rumble of 'year, year, years' from both sides of the House came calls of 'don't overdo it' and 'one of those, are you?' from the Conservative back benches.

'Can we clap?' said Emma.

'I don't think we can make a sound up here without being thrown out,' said her mother.

'Who would throw us?' said Rachel, looking round.

'Those men with the gold chains round their necks aren't just ushers,' said Susanna. 'They are bouncers as well.'

'They look more like chairmen of county councils,' said Mark.

The Chamber was emptying, and another MP was speaking to an inattentive House. Peter remained in his seat down below. When the man sat down after ten minutes and the next member was called, Peter looked up to the gallery and nodded. Then he got to his feet and walked down the gangway between the green benches, under the little hanging microphones. The Westerham family filed out and met him in the lobby downstairs. In the high stone hall, watched over by huge statues of past prime ministers, Attlee and Churchill, Disraeli, Balfour and Lloyd George, they found themselves surrounded by living faces they recognised, well known television personalities milling about, talking and exchanging notes. Some people who they would have assumed to be deadly enemies in opposing parties joked and laughed together.

The Westerhams were fascinated, and disappointed when Peter said after a minute, 'This is the Members' Lobby – I'm afraid you can't hang around here. We'll go down and have a drink on the terrace. It isn't too cold.'

They passed along a passage lined with murals of scenes from British history into a far larger circular hall, with soaring stone columns surmounted by a domed ceiling sparkling with gold mosaic.

'Central Lobby,' said Peter. 'Anyone can come and meet their MP here. Very democratic.'

'Hey, Dad,' called Emma, 'have you ever noticed this?'

She was standing with her feet together in the centre of the pattern of the great tiled floor, looking up.

'What?' said Peter, walking over. 'Do you mean the chandelier? It would be hard not to notice it.'

'What I mean is, it's not in the middle.'

'How do you mean?'

'Stand here, and look up,' said Emma, delighted with her discovery.

They all stood in turn under the great chandelier and looked up to its roots in the domed ceiling.

'She's right. It's not central. It's about a foot out! What a miscalculation!' said Susanna.

'They shouldn't have paid the architect's bill,' said Mark.

'Who was the architect?' said Emma.

'Pugin – he did everything, the whole Palace of Westminster, right down to the wallpapers,' said Peter.

'Well,' said Emma, 'he'd have got his chandelier in the right place if they had taught him to start at the middle and work outwards.'

'Like in Bargello tapestry,' said Susanna, 'isn't that right, Ma?'

Rachel did not reply.

'You have a pregnant look, Granny,' said Emma.

'Yes,' said Rachel. 'I am about to give birth to a clerihew. How's this?

Sir Christopher Wren,
Made a minor slip now and then;
But when Pugin
Made a mistake it was a huge'n.'

'You are all idiots,' said Peter. 'No respect for the mother of parliaments. Come through this way and we'll go down to the terrace.'

As they leant over the parapet of the long terrace with drinks in their hands, watching the Thames, waving at the boats that went by, Susanna wished that they could hold this feeling of family closeness. The twins were enjoying themselves and Peter was on a high, the adrenalin still pumping through his system.

'You were brilliant, Dad, a real professional. They'll want you on Newsnight in no time.'

'How do you get your tongue round all those Honourables and Right Honourables, Dad, and how do you know who's which anyway?'

'What I can't get over is how none of the MPs have a name, just the Member for Ben Nevis, or whatever. How do you learn them, Dad?'

'Slowly and painfully,' said Peter laughing. 'I guess it will come naturally in time.'

'The Honourable Member for Kentish Weald has a nice ring to it,' said Rachel.

'Just Honourable? Aren't you Right Honourable, Dad?' said Emma.

'Not unless I become a privy councillor.'

'Only slightly honourable till then, is that it?' said Mark.

'Cynic,' said his grandmother.

'Was I all right, Sukie?' Peter said quietly.

'You were terrific, love. We were so proud.'

'Not all our side liked it, did you notice?'

'Who cares?' said Susanna. 'You said what you thought, and it was a great speech.'

A passing MP patted Peter's shoulder.

'Well done,' he said. 'Nice one. Now you've got that over, there'll be no holding you.'

'Thanks,' said Peter, standing up. He introduced his family.

'This is Jack Winthrop, who held my hand at the start. It was good of you to be there, Jack.'

'I wouldn't have missed it,' said Winthrop. 'You may get a bit of flak from the whips, though, nailing your colours to the mast like that.'

'You think so?' said Peter.

'More than likely,' said Winthrop. 'They like their new recruits to keep their options open. Not to worry. You stick to your guns and put a book in your pants. See you later.'

'What did he mean by that?' said Susanna.

'I'll let you know,' said Peter, 'when I find out.'

He was distracted, and tried to hide it, as they all dined together later in the Churchill Room restaurant.

'Do you always feed as well as this, Dad?' said Mark. 'I don't mind the nosh in this place at all.'

'No such luck,' said his father. 'Can't you tell when you're being treated? I normally eat in the café, but often I just have a sandwich in the train on the way home.'

The division bell rang for the ten o'clock vote, and his family watched half the diners leave their seats and make for the door.

'It's an amazing way to run a country,' said Mark.

'Seems to work, on the whole,' said his father. 'I must go and vote. See you very soon, and we'll have coffee outside.'

Some minutes later he was back, and apologising.

'I am so sorry. I have to go and see someone. If I take you up to Central Lobby, do you think you can find your way out? Thank you, all of you, for coming. Er – you'll remember how to find the car?'

'Who won the vote, Dad?' said Emma.

'The vote? Oh, us, of course. We have to.'

His mind was not with them, Susanna could tell, and she helped him to get away.

A few minutes later he was in the government whips' office.

'The chief wants to see you,' said one of the whips, sitting in a chair with his feet on one of the several desks that filled the big room.

'What about, do you know?' Peter tried to sound nonchalant.

'Well, I can guess, but I wouldn't want to steal his thunder,' said the whip, lighting a cigarette.

'When – now?'

'Nope. He's busy. Tomorrow at eleven o'clock, at Number Twelve.'

The following morning Peter walked along the short narrow street off Whitehall, passing the black doors whose numbers were famous the world over – Number Ten Downing Street, Number Eleven, to the last door, set at right angles to the other two, facing down the street, and much less famous: Number Twelve, office of the Parliamentary Secretary to the Treasury, otherwise and far better known as the Government Chief Whip.

As he dropped the knocker he identified the sick feeling that filled his stomach – the headmaster's study. This was ridiculous, and so was the schoolboy thought that crossed his mind that he had nothing to fear since he had done nothing amiss.

He was shown through a square ante-room lined with photographs of government chief whips who had occupied the office for the last hundred years. The early ones were of moustached Victorians, Whig, Tory and Liberal, formal and serious. The latter ones were more relaxed, often smiling. Few of them gave any sense of the enormous power wielded by the occupant of the chief whip's office in the government of the day.

Peter was left in the big L-shaped Whips' Room and stood at a window looking out onto St James's Park, dank and dreary in its winter garb. Again he was reminded of the window of that prep-school study, watching the rain dripping from the monkey puzzle tree outside.

A side door opened and the bulky figure of the Chief Whip appeared. He introduced himself as another man followed him into the room.

'I apologise for bringing you over here, Peter. I was going to be too busy this afternoon in the House to have the pleasure of meeting you there. Do you know Harry?'

The Deputy Chief Whip nodded, but said nothing. The Chief Whip moved towards a group of armchairs and sofas, then changed his mind. He pointed instead the long table running down the length of the room.

'Do sit down.'

He indicated a chair near the end and took another himself. The Deputy Chief Whip walked over to stand by the window.

'You had a good House for your maiden speech,' said the Chief Whip.

'Yes,' said Peter. 'It seemed to go all right, I think.'

His throat was strangely dry. He wished they would offer him some coffee – anything.

'Family enjoy it? Good, good. Always an exciting occasion for the family.'

'Yes,' said Peter guardedly. 'Thank you.'

The qualification that he was expecting to this preamble came quickly.

'A slightly unusual maiden, however,' said the Chief Whip. 'You seemed to be criticising the government more than is customary on such an occasion. Not that criticism is banned, don't get me wrong . . .'

His laugh was echoed hollowly by his deputy.

'. . . Oh, no. We thrive on that. But it is early days for you, Peter, I think. And on the whole it might be wiser not to take too firm a personal position on Europe, not while the whole situation is so fluid, if you get my meaning? I expect you will find an opportunity soon to water down what you said a bit. Never give hostages to fortune, is a good motto for any new MP to follow, I find.'

'I didn't say anything I don't think,' said Peter, irritated, trying not to sound defensive.

'No . . . No.' The big man looked at him steadily. 'I'm sure you didn't. I respect you for that. What do you think, Harry?'

The man at the window nodded. He was a dark silhouette against the light.

'We are interested in you, Peter,' the Chief Whip continued. 'You have parliamentary potential, clearly, and we would like to see that developed. So my general advice, for the time being, is not to get yourself allied to any particular faction at this stage. It leaves us all with our hands free when we are making decisions as time goes on. Do you see what I mean?'

'Yes,' said Peter. 'I think I see what you mean.'

He saw all too well, and a cold anger was rising in him.

'Right, then.'

The big man pushed his chair away and got to his feet.

'I see you have put yourself down for the select committee on housing. I hope you get it. That would be a good subject for you to concentrate on. Well, we mustn't keep you, Peter. We all have to get down to our constituencies for Friday, even Chief Whips. A cup of coffee before you go?'

'Thank you, no,' said Peter.

He went straight back to the office in the House of Commons that he shared with two other MPs. It was small and rather overheated. His allocation of space was about three square metres, apart from his not overlarge desk. He sat behind it, loosening his tie and running his fingers through his hair. His anger was seething in him.

The door opened and one of his colleagues came in. He too sat down and started piling papers into his briefcase.

'Going home?' he said. 'Share a taxi? I go past Waterloo. You all right?'

'I've just had the Mafia treatment in the whips' office,' said Peter. 'Chief Whip warned me off Europe. Told me to keep my nose clean if I ever want a job.'

'Sodding whips,' said the other. 'Don't let them get to you. They think the only way to disguise a split in the party is to plug it with poly-fools, which means backbenchers pledged to think what they're told to think, in the hope of one day being parliamentary under-secretary for Slip roads and Lay-bys. Don't fall for it, Peter. Come on, I'll drop you off. Listen, if you get late in the evenings, and you can't get home, you can always have a bed at my place. We keep a spare one made up, and by the time you get back to Kent after a late sitting you'll have to turn right round and come back. You're going to have to get a place in town, if you want to survive.'

'It's kind of you, but I'm managing, thanks,' said Peter. 'I'm still a practising solicitor, three mornings a week.'

As he sat in the train on the way home he found it impossible to concentrate on his papers. Now that he knew what he was up against a sense of depression came over him. Conform, or he was out – if he wanted to achieve he had to do it the whips' way. It was everything he had feared but had not allowed himself to worry about. He would have liked to talk it over with Susanna, but his pride could not face allowing her to see the gilt beginning to slide off the gingerbread.

Chapter 8

Peter's mail quadrupled in quantity, and Susanna's changed in character.

'Do I have to join an Area Women's Advisory Committee?' she said to Peter one evening, laying a letter in front of him. 'Who on earth would I advise, and on what?'

He looked at it.

'Of course you don't, unless you want to,' he said. 'Some people would love it. I bet you hated team games at school.'

'Quite right, I did.'

She opened an envelope addressed to Mrs Peter Westerham, House of Commons, that Peter had brought from London.

'And look, here's an invitation to join a Parliamentary Spouses Group. Me, a spouse! I never thought of myself as a spouse.'

She read the accompanying letter. Then she looked up at Peter.

'It may be meant kindly, but it assumes that I am going to be lonely and "find time hanging heavily on my hands". I should be so lucky!'

Her horrified expression made him laugh.

'Listen, Sukie, I don't expect you to get involved any more than you want to.'

'I'll do the constituency stuff, Pete, I've said that. But I don't think the rest is important. I mean, I won't be letting you down if I don't become an official parliamentary "spouse", will I?'

'Look,' said Peter, still opening letters. 'Here's one you might actually enjoy. I hope you won't say no to a reception at Number Ten Downing Street.'

Susanna examined the large stiff white card.

'Will there be other "spouses" there?' she said. She felt unable to say the word without inverted commas.

'I suppose so – do you mind?'

'It would mean I can't pretend I never come to London. I thought I might say that, to avoid joining their group.'

'Do come,' said Peter. 'It's in three weeks' time. Can I bribe you, with supper afterwards in the House?'

'Of course I'll come,' said Susanna.

* * *

Susanna wrote to Mark, still away at college. Letter writing to her children was a habit she tried to keep up, even after they had left boarding school. She wrote infrequently now, but whenever she had something worth saying.

> Believe it or not, *she wrote*, your mother has actually set foot behind the black door with the big ten on it. We didn't sweep up in a limousine, as they seem to on television, but struggled through wind and rain under Dad's rather inadequate umbrella, having left the car underground in the House of Commons car park. (That, by the way, is an unexpected convenience, because you get blown up on sight by the bomb squad if you park anywhere else around there.)
>
> When I say 'set foot' I actually mean a foot and a toe: in my inimitable fashion I managed to dislodge one of my newly bought high heels (why did I wear them? Oh, vanity) as I leaped nimbly onto the Whitehall pavement. So for the next few hours I had to remember not to put my weight on it.
>
> There were crowd barriers at the end of Downing Street, but no crowd, just a few onlookers who, having ascertained that we were nonentities, enjoyed watching Dad getting pinker as he tried all his pockets in turn for our invitation to show the policemen. Eventually he found it, and a policeman said, 'That's all right, sir,' and opened the gate. The spectators turned away in disappointment, having hoped for an Incident. A ministerial car sailed through after us, and we leapt out of its way.
>
> Downing Street is quite small, and narrow, and the only house numbers are ten, eleven and twelve. I said it wasn't very grand, and Dad said it was a typically modest British understatement.
>
> The famous door opened magically as we passed the policeman on the steps. I expect they have a peephole for viewing petition-presenters, meeja hounds, foreign dignitaries and the like. Two more policemen greeted us inside and took our invitation. Someone in black took our coats, and we were led past that mantelpiece, the one prime ministers on the telly stand in front of, smiling sideways and grasping distinguished visitors by the hand.
>
> We went down a passage, nice thick carpet, with portraits, no time to look at them, following another black back. A larger hall, our names checked again, and we were left to make our own way out of one corner and up a rather surprisingly narrow and unimpressive staircase. This was lined with etchings of past prime ministers, becoming photographs as they became

more modern. At the bottom there is a painting of Harold Macmillan apparently peering over the top of a wall.

A small landing at the top, just to catch your breath, and then we were suddenly in the Presence. I had got a smile ready and planned to make an intelligent remark in reply to whatever greeting was made, but I had hardly switched on my smile before my hand was in the firm prime-ministerial grasp and I was being drawn forcefully past the august front, as the well known voice said how good it was of me to come. My dicey heel gave way but I managed to disguise the lurch with a neat turn – I hope it didn't look like a curtsey – to see Dad not only shaken by the hand but recognised as well.

'Peter, isn't it – how nice to see you. Is this your first time in Number Ten? I hope you'll have a good look round. Was that your wife? You must get her a drink.'

And Dad too was propelled into the party.

So there we were, adrift in a throng of chattering, drinking MPs and their wives or husbands, known as spouses, all of our party, spread between two large rooms. We got drinks from trays that were circulating, and Dad said, 'Let's look at the pictures in case we never get another chance.'

This seemed a good idea, as everyone except us seemed to know everyone except us.

In front of a huge Turner we met another couple filling in time the same way. The man was from the last intake of new MPs and Dad knew him slightly. The wife asked me how I was enjoying 'the life', and I said so far not too bad, though I didn't know much about the London end of it. She told me about the 'support group' for MPs' spouses that holds meetings and goes on outings. I said it sounded like everything I had avoided since the Brownies, and she laughed and said what a relief – she had thought perhaps she was unnatural.

Then I was introduced to a government minister's wife who told me that when a minister moves to another department, or gets the sack, he is given a Red Box to keep. I didn't know what she meant, and she explained rather disdainfully that they all have red boxes, like that battered thing that gets waved about on Budget Day.

'It's rather a nice memento,' she said. 'My husband has collected two.'

I said, 'What on earth do you do with them?'

And she replied, 'Oh, my dear, they make wonderful jewel cases'!!!!! Note: I must remember to get myself a tiara . . .

We walked round the rooms, slightly bolder after a couple of drinks, celebrity spotting. The Foreign Secretary and the

Home Secretary were both mingling affably, and various other ministers I recognised but couldn't have named without Dad's help. Some cabinet ministers are quite juvenile-looking, and what they call junior ministers can be quite decrepit. We were talking to another new MP when he looked at his watch and said, 'It's five to seven – are you coming?'

Dad told me to wait for him till the vote was over (as if I could do anything else) and that he would only be about twenty minutes. Then suddenly, as if a plug had been pulled, the room drained of people till it was more than half empty, as MPs and ministers, including, to my surprise, the Prime Minister, dashed off to the House to vote, those with chauffeur-driven cars lingering till the last minute. Well, at least we could see the furniture then, which was, as you would expect, 'handsome'. Only spouses remained, mostly female but a few male, and talked rather desultorily until the members came back, when the party took off again. A strange performance, really. I asked one member what the vote was about, and he said, 'Some amendment to the Social Security Bill, I think.'

I said, 'Do you mean you don't know?'

He just shrugged, and smiled and turned away from me.

Later I had to rush to get the train home, and Dad had to go back to the House. The PM and spouse had long disappeared, so we didn't actually say thank you for the lovely party.

Do you notice how expressions like 'the House' and 'the PM' are beginning to trip off my tongue? I used to think they sounded pompous and silly, but you fall into the jargon. The whole thing is catching, but not, I think, really me. Perhaps I am just not spouse material. No reflection on Dad.

Your grandmother would send her love, but she is out with Ellie Fittall hunting fungi. They went together on a day's adult education course called Death or Dinner, and are now obsessed with living off the land. I expect any day to find them lying side by side, swollen and purple after a positive identification of some lethal variety.

Susanna, torn between loyalty to Peter and the demands of the stud, decided to limit the constituency to a reasonable percentage of her time.

'One event per fortnight,' she said to her mother. 'Just enough to let them know I support Pete, but not enough to make them think I am his permanent hand-baggage. Don't you think that's fair?'

'Very fair. Have you told your friend Peacock?'

'Peacock thinks I should come to everything, and a lot of things Peter can't get to as well. He says the last MP's wife did it all, and chaired committees for fundraising events, too.'

'Oh dear. A precedent,' said Rachel.

'She can't have had much else to do,' said Susanna. 'It's prehistoric, don't you think, to expect the spouse to give up everything for the party? I mean, she might not even support the same party, might she?'

'Do you?' Her mother looked at her with raised eyebrows.

'Me? I'm not political,' said Susanna.

'Would you like me to do you a schedule?' said Rachel.

'A *what*?' said Susanna,

'A schedule, or a spreadsheet, to help you keep your engagements in order. I can blow it up, so you could hang it on the kitchen door and read it at a distance, if you like.'

'Oh, Ma, you and your infernal machine. I tell you what you *can* do, if you like, which is a table of blood lines for me, with our ponies' breeding, and showing links to Royal Highland Show winners over the last thirty years. Then tell me what stallions we should be using and whether the one I have chosen is the best for us. That should keep you out of mischief for a while.'

'Oh, goody, goody,' said Rachel.

Susanna found, when she attended constituency events, that she was not as nervous as she had expected about raising her voice in public. Her teaching experience was useful here. She didn't feel that she was particularly good at it, but people seemed willing to laugh if she made a joke, and as long as she didn't have notes to lose she usually remembered what she was meant to say. She was firm about not making proper speeches, though on an occasion when a speaker had failed to turn up Susanna gave the mainly female audience an impromptu talk on the vicissitudes of pony breeding, which, to her surprise, they seemed to find entertaining and she herself quite enjoyed.

'You don't mean you told them about foaling, and things like that?' said Emma.

'Not in detail, but I told them how important it was to make sure all the bits of afterbirth had come out, and about when you were small, you remember, how I used to give you ten pence if you found the afterbirth before the foxes did, when a mare had foaled in the night. I painted a charming picture for them of my dear little children prancing round the field with a bucket.'

'Did you tell them about when the plumber found an afterbirth waiting for you to check it in the kitchen sink?'

'Of course,' said Susanna, 'but I didn't tell them what he said. There are limits.'

Peter held an 'advice surgery' for his constituents most Friday evenings, at different village halls round the constituency. Susanna took it in turns with Ellie Fittall and the treasurer, Reese, to act as his receptionist.

'He comes home very depressed sometimes, after his surgery,' Susanna said to Emma, on the telephone from Newcastle. 'People do have the most awful troubles, very often of their own making, but that doesn't make you feel less sorry for them. Dad worries about them too much, though. You would think being a solicitor would have hardened him to insoluble problems, wouldn't you? But it hasn't.'

'What does he do about them?' said Emma.

'He gets too involved. He spends days following up their stories, writing letters about them, trying to find ways of helping. Very often afterwards he finds they have solved the problem themselves in some way, but haven't bothered to let him know. Or else only half the story is true, and there's another very significant side to it, which of course they haven't told him. But it doesn't make him any less gullible next time.'

'They can't all be having him on,' said Emma.

'Oh, Lord, no,' said her mother. 'And the serious hard-luck stories really get to him. He has to learn to be more professional, like a doctor or a nurse. Have you noticed how he is losing weight?'

'Yes, I have. And he was never exactly paunchy. Do you think he's enjoying the House of Commons part of it, though?'

'I suppose so,' said Susanna, 'but he doesn't talk about it much. He's finding it quite tiring. For one thing, he hardly ever gets home before midnight.'

'You sound worried, Mum.'

'Yes,' said Susanna.

'Did you imagine it would be like this?'

Susanna considered.

'I tried not to,' she said.

'What I hate,' said Emma, 'is that I never see him. Or hardly. Do you know that the last three times I've been home he has been out, or in London? And the time before that he was working all weekend.'

'If you were one of his constituents you would be quite happy about that,' said her mother.

'Don't be so tiresomely reasonable,' said Emma. 'Stand up for my rights like a proper mother.'

Driving Peter home one evening after a particularly long surgery Susanna was aware that his silence came not from tiredness but from pent-up emotion.

'Something's worrying you,' she said.

'Leonora has gone too far,' he replied grimly. 'I had a suspicion that she was doing something subversive, but someone told me right out tonight that she has been going round the villages distributing pamphlets.'

'Pamphlets?'

'Green pamphlets.'

'But . . . what sort of pamphlets – what about?' Susanna was genuinely puzzled.

'Oh, hell, don't be stupid, Susanna,' Peter's voice was sharp and angry. 'Green! Green Party pamphlets! What do you think they're about? Attacking the government, pushing expensive notions – *my* daughter, in *my* constituency! What the hell does she think she's up to?'

'Oh,' said Susanna.

'God knows what's got into that girl. She's behaving like an absolute fool, just because she's piqued about her awful boyfriend.'

Suddenly Susanna felt angry too, but she spoke quietly.

'You might pause to consider whether you could be responsible yourself for some of this, Pete. I have tried to tell you that she was hurt, really quite hurt by your—'

'Oh, for Christ's sake,' said Peter roughly, 'you always take her side in this. I wasn't responsible for her rowing with her wretched boyfriend. Heavens, I only laid eyes on him once. And that was enough.'

'Can't you see, though? ' Susanna was trying to be reasonable, and knew she was failing to impress Peter. 'They quarrelled over you, your politics, and as Leo sees it, she chose you. And the point is you've never shown any sympathy or gratitude for her loyalty. She was genuinely unhappy and—'

'Gratitude? Are you both mad? Why should I be grateful to her for seeing sense?' Peter was beyond understanding.

'Well,' said Susanna, 'I guess what she is doing now is a sort of revenge. Anyway, she's grown-up, isn't she? She can choose her politics for herself. She doesn't have to follow yours.'

'Unlike you, I suppose?' said Peter, hearing through his anger the unpleasant note in his own voice.

Susanna did not reply, and they drove on in silence. Just before they reached Restings Peter said, 'I've taken a lease on a flat. I can't keep up these late nights. I am afraid that's what's making me so bad-tempered, Sukie. I'm sorry.'

'A flat? You never told me.' Already depressed, this news was another heavy blow to Susanna.

'Everybody does. Near the House. I hope you will come up and be there, a couple of nights a week, perhaps. We can have supper together, even if I have to go back and vote.'

'Thanks,' said Susanna. 'That sounds a load of fun.'

'Sukie, I didn't mean to tell you like this. Can we talk about it tomorrow? When we aren't, well, feeling low? It needn't be as bad as it sounds.'

Susanna nodded glumly, and they went in to the house.

It was June. Peter had been an MP for nearly a year, but to Susanna it seemed a great deal longer. She sat on the side of the bath in her mother's flat, watching her decorating. Rachel was dressed in jeans and a shirt that, judging by the variety of its colours, had done much of such work before.

'Quality time, that's what it's all about,' said Susanna miserably. 'Someone said to me, "How much do you see your husband?" "Lots," I said, loyally. Well, I see him, Ma, but that's about it. I see him in bed, when he's asleep. I see him at breakfast, at weekends, when he's reading his mail. We flog around together in the car without talking, because he is so deep into his files, or reading and signing mountains of letters that his secretary has thrown at him. Not much quality in that. On the way to meetings in the constituency he's always working on his notes for his speech, and on the way back he's usually asleep. It's not much fun, being a spouse.'

'Spouse. Mouse. House. Lots of rhyming potential there,' said Rachel.

'Ma, you're not listening. I don't blame you.'

'Louse,' said her mother. 'I am listening. But moaning is not the best accompaniment to artistic work. You have the weekends – well, Sundays, anyway.'

'Sundays are all right up to about four o'clock, and then I can tell that his mind is back in London. We were doing a bit of destructive gardening last Sunday, releasing some shrubs from being strangled by brambles. He was down on his knees cutting underneath, and suddenly I found myself pulling the whole bush out. He had gone right through the trunk. He was thinking about something else, he said. I told him it was my fault. It was a silly job to be doing in June, anyway, but somehow there was never time last winter.'

Rachel continued to paint as she listened to her daughter, drawing the brush in long, occasionally even strokes down the bathroom wall. Finishing at a corner, she stood back and looked at the effect.

'It's awful, isn't it? Not a success. I think I shall try sponging instead of dragging. Pass me that sponge.'

'Ma, you can't use that, can you? Your bath sponge? Don't they have proper paint sponges for this kind of thing?'

'I dislike that sponge,' says Rachel. 'It was sent me from Greece by a seriously boring friend, and it looks just like her. It will do admirably.'

'Is it not any better since you got the flat in London?' she asked.

'Nous – that's another one. And Strauss, of course. A reluctant political spouse, who developed a penchant for Strauss, bought a secondhand harp and played it, quite sharp, from a gallery seat in the House. Could be improved.'

'Silly Ma,' said Susanna. 'The flat helps a bit, I suppose. He is a little less tired since he stopped trying to get back here each night, but I think he finds the flat as depressing as I do.'

The one-bedroomed flat was in a huge characterless block, traditionally beloved of members of parliament, on the Thames embankment not far from Westminster.

'Of course it's just a sleeping place, but neither of us sleeps well there. Peter takes pills, something he has never done before. I've talked to some other wives – they come in late, late late, these MPs, part exhilarated, part exhausted, and need pills or a stiff whisky before they can wind down enough to go to sleep.'

Rachel stopped dabbing for a moment and looked at Susanna, who was sitting on the side of the bath, her hands hanging between her legs. She had seldom known her so depressed, nor so willing to talk about her problems.

'I am sure it must help him to have you there, even if it is only two nights a week,' she said sympathetically.

'I don't know that it does, Ma. He worries that he's keeping me awake too, and though I have tried not to show it, I think he guesses I hate the flat. I think it might be better all round if I gave up going there during the week, and concentrated on making the weekends better.'

'Are you quarrelling?' said Rachel. 'Oh dear, I should not have asked that. Sorry.'

'Not quarrelling, no,' Susanna sighed. 'Well, not much. But we argue about silly small things, which a psychologist would probably say are substitutes for bigger ones. We never used to do that.'

'What sort of things?'

'Household things, nothings; the colour of the front door; whether I should have helped Mark to buy a moped or not. You see, we always made decisions together, comfortably, and now Pete isn't there, or he's too busy, so I make them, and he resents it without realising he does. I suppose I make him feel unneeded.'

'Mmm,' said Rachel, working as she talked, not happy with what she was hearing. 'How are you planning to change your weekend life?'

'I thought I might have a word with the awful Peacock,' said Susanna, 'and see if he will persuade the branch committees not to hold events on Saturday evenings. It would give Peter one real evening off a week, and a time to see friends, and the children, if they are down. He always comes down during the week to anything that's on in the constituency, as long as the whipping allows it. It's too much. Then Friday evenings are always branch events or his advice surgeries, and there is usually something on Saturday morning.'

'Will Peacock play? Will he understand?'

'I can only try,' said Susanna. 'He is so obsessed with fundraising that he doesn't seem to see he's running Peter into the ground. We don't get on very well, I'm afraid, Mr Peacock and I.'

'What do you think of that?' said Rachel, her hands on her hips, her head on one side. 'Sponge on drag. Rather effective, don't you think?'

'You have dragged your nose, Ma,' said Susanna.

'How does it look?' said Rachel. 'Don't answer. The question was rhetorical. Susanna, isn't it time you told Peter what you're telling me? You need to discuss it together.'

'Absolutely no, Ma,' said her daughter firmly. 'If things are going wrong he must find it out for himself, not have me tell him. I will not have a part in disillusioning him. Anyway, we will probably get used to it. Other people do. Or perhaps he'll tire of it of his own accord. 1997 is the latest date for the next election – he should know before then if it's the sort of life he wants. But thanks anyway, for acting as my safety valve. I needed to let off steam.'

Peacock was pulsating with irritation. The accounts recently sent to him by the Young Conservatives showed a profit for the year of exactly twenty-seven pounds and six pence.

He had summoned the YC chairman to his office, to deal with him as severely as it is possible to deal with anyone who works in a voluntary capacity. Peacock would happily have paid Terry Lowther a salary out of his own pocket for the privilege of speaking his mind to him. As it was he had to restrain himself to sarcasm, which was falling on unnoticing ears. Pink, well fed ears too, he thought, looking at the young man filling Lelia's rejected chair to overflowing.

'Amazing number of YCs you have on your list, Terry,' he said.

'I do my best to haul them in,' said Terry Lowther smugly, 'and I think I run a happy ship. That's half the battle.'

'I am a little concerned about the other half,' said Peacock. 'How many of the crew of this happy ship are actually paid-up members of the Conservative Party?'

'Some and some,' said Lowther, unbuttoning his straining blazer for comfort. 'The main thing is to keep them on board, and if you keep asking for money there could be a problem.'

'Do you think once a year would be too much?' asked Peacock.

'Not in theory,' said Lowther airily, oblivious to the heavy sarcasm, 'but these are *young* Conservatives, remember, not all of them well heeled. I would look on it as a personal failure if we lost one of them through financial hardship.'

Terry Lowther worked in a firm of London moneybrokers. In his own terms, he was very well heeled. He saw his YC branch as the means to an end and the high membership figures as a feather in his political cap.

'The Conservative Party is, however, not a charity,' Peacock began.

'No, indeed, it is a crusade,' said Lowther. It had just dawned on him that he was under attack. He returned fire. 'As our agent, Leonard, surely you should persuade our MP's family that they should join my YC branch. I thought the elder daughter might take on the secretaryship.'

Terry Lowther had a secret agenda here. Although he had inexplicably failed so far to rouse Leonora's interest in him, he was persevering, partly because as a girlfriend she would help him in his dearest ambition, which was to become an MP.

'Bad luck,' said Peacock, 'she lives outside the constituency, and her last boyfriend was a paid-up member of the Socialist Workers' Party. Terry,' he continued wearily, 'the party needs money to fight the next election, and we can't take any freeloaders. The YCs have to pay their—'

Lowther's plump jowls quivered as he wagged his head.

'Never you worry, Leonard. If necessary I'll pay their subs myself. I need my YC troops behind me when the next election comes, out there on the hustings, battling on every doorstep . . .'

'I hope you will,' said Peacock bitterly, 'because if you don't at least get them out canvassing I don't see much future for you.'

Terry Lowther was surprised by this remark, but decided that it was not personal. The agent was speaking in national terms.

'You are right, Leonard,' he said. 'The future is in our hands. Don't you worry. Regard what I am doing now as a training programme.'

As he left Peacock sank his head into his hands. A left-wing MP, an alcoholic chairman, a Biggles-cum-Bunter freak running the YCs, a politically split executive committee – how much could a man bear? What was more, his MP's wife was coming to see him the following day. Peacock neither understood nor trusted Susanna. Why on earth did she want to see him? He sighed and looked at his watch. It was time to go home and kick his own wife. Even her meek support seemed to be wavering. She had actually criticised a government minister after a TV programme last week, silly cow. Nothing seemed certain any more. His future in the party seemed bleaker than ever and his dreams of preferment more and more unrealistic.

The small hatchback car was travelling fast. They had been late starting, because the London train had been delayed.

'I'm so sorry,' said Leonora. 'Children playing on the line, or something.'

'Poor little buggers – probably the only thing to do in Catford, or wherever. We can still just make it, because they hardly ever start on time. Get that belt on.'

The traffic lights were in their favour most of the way and by the time they hit the country roads they felt more relaxed.

'Just pray we don't meet a tractor,' said Andrew Manning.

'At this time of the evening? Surely not.'

'They often stay out late ploughing in the stubble at this time of year. Better than burning it.'

They did not meet a tractor, but coming round a bend they suddenly saw the pale shape of what looked at first like a huge wooden box lying full in their path. The car swerved violently to avoid it, and hit the object with one front wheel. It swerved again to recover. For a few heart-stopping seconds it was balanced on the two offside wheels, then, still travelling fast, it rocked back and as the nearside wheels hit the ground it crashed into the ditch. The bonnet was buried in the high bank beyond it and as the passenger door flew open the girl's body shot outwards onto the verge. The fall might have been soft, but there was a crack as her head hit a low post sunk into the ground.

Andrew, struggling against surging pain, reached a fumbling hand to the ignition key and was just aware of the engine fading as he slid into unconsciousness.

The silence was sudden, and pierced only by the clarinet voice of a lone blackbird perched high in an ash tree. In the fading light the lettering was still just legible on the green painted post by the girl's still form – WILDLIFE VERGE.

Chapter 9

'That girl Susanna Westerham does a damn good job, you know,' said Rupert Hascombe.

'He's lucky to have her, that's what I say,' said Ellie Fittall.

They were driving back from a branch wine-and-cheese party that the MP's wife had attended. Hascombe always gave the old lady a lift, not out of kindness, he told Florence, 'but because she is a breath of fresh air after all the waffle we get.'

'Mrs Westerham is the flavour of the month with the branches,' he said, 'because unlike our last unlamented MP's wife she has a sense of humour, looks pretty, and smiles.'

'And remembers people's names,' said Ellie. 'That last one called me Fouton, and if there's one thing I don't hold with it's an uncomfortable bed.' She chuckled.

'They all want her at their events, so Cyril Eversley tells me,' said Hascombe. 'It's a pity she hasn't more time to spare. She breeds hairy ponies, did you know that?'

'She came along to the Daffodil lunch at Pinthorpe, and there's a sour lot if ever there was, but she had 'em laughing just the way she drew the raffle. She's a pro.'

'Have you heard her making a speech at all?' said Hascombe.

'She'll introduce a speaker, and very nice too, or do a vote of thanks, but she won't speak herself. Dunno what her politics are.'

'Same at his, one assumes, Ellie.'

'Don't you go jumping to conclusions there, Rupert. Me and my Fred never agreed on politics. We was having a fight about Maggie Thatcher when he took his turn. She killed him, that's what I say. Surprising I'm still a Tory, really.'

They pulled up in front of Little Marden Hall.

'I'll just be a minute, Ellie, getting that list of donors for you, and then I'll run you home.'

He went into the house, leaving Ellie sitting in the car. He was back a few minutes later, looking serious.

'Sorry to be so long, Ellie. Florence was talking to me. She said she heard the local radio news. Evidently one of the Westerham girls has been in a car accident. I don't know how bad it is, but she's in hospital.'

'Ah, poor kiddie. I hope she's all right. Which one is it?'

'The elder one, I think. Isn't that Leonora?'

'Yes, lovely girl,' said Ellie. 'I suppose we'll hear.'

Susanna heard about the accident at about nine in the evening. She had not been unduly concerned on returning home to find a police car parked on the gravel. Routine visits by the police were normal since Peter had been in parliament, and she expected to find her mother giving an officer a cup of tea in the kitchen.

But Rachel met her on the doorstep, her face grave. Susanna felt her heart thud violently as she saw it.

'Oh dear God, what is it?' she said. 'Who is it? Is it Pete? Who is it?' she said.

Her mother put an arm round her shoulders.

'It's all right, love,' she said, 'but listen, and keep calm. Leo has had an accident. She's unconscious. She's in hospital.'

Susanna's skin prickled as the blood drained away from her face.

'Come in and sit down,' said Rachel. 'The police sergeant can tell you more.'

'There's not much I know, ma'am,' he said, as Susanna grasped his arm in the hall, refusing a chair. 'No other vehicles involved.'

'It was a crash?' Susanna gasped. 'Where is she? I must get to her.'

'I'm here to drive you, ma'am, and Mr Westerham, if he's here. They took her to the County – they have the intensive care unit there.'

'Oh, heavens, Peter. I must ring him. Does he know?' Susanna looked distractedly for the telephone.

'Here, drink this. Sit down just for a minute.' Rachel put a cup of tea in her hand. 'Then you go with the sergeant, and I promise you I will get hold of Peter.'

By the time they pulled up in front of the portico of the huge hospital Susanna was herself again, and determined to remain calm. The police officer had been able to tell her little, except that the accident had happened near Tunbridge Wells and that the car in which her daughter had been travelling was a write-off.

She was unprepared for the small group of pressmen who were waiting for her. Camera flashes popped in her face as she pushed her way past them and through the glass doors. Inside, an orderly in a white coat took her in charge and guided her at a fast walk down the wide hallway. She was aware of another smaller figure at her other side.

'Can you just confirm, Mrs Westerham, the name of the driver?

Is it true that the car in the accident is owned by Andrew Manning, one of your husband's opponents at the election?'

The reporter was walking crab-wise alongside her, his face eager, his pencil hovering over a notebook.

'I don't believe this,' said Susanna without slowing down. 'I am just going into the hospital where my daughter is injured, I don't yet know how badly, and you want to make some kind of political point?'

'No offence, Mrs Westerham, but it is interesting for our readers. Can I phone you later?'

'No, you can not,' said Susanna, and let the next swing doors swing in his face.

'I'm sorry, Mrs er . . . er . . .'

'Willoughby.'

'Mrs Willoughby. Mr Westerham is in the Chamber, and there is a debate in progress. It may not be possible to contact him for some time, because there'll be the division at ten, that's in a few minutes, and it may be followed by another.'

The House of Commons answering service was trying to be helpful, but failing.

'Listen, you must get a message to him,' said Rachel firmly. 'It is important. He must telephone me as soon as possible. Just tell him it is a urgent, but don't frighten him. He must ring quickly.'

'Well, we can put a note up in the lobby, Mrs Willoughby, and I'll ask the clerk to mark it urgent. He would see it as he comes through after the debate.'

'That's not good enough, I'm afraid. May I speak to whoever is in charge of your department?'

'Mum, is she all right? Is she bad? Oh Mum.'

'Emma, listen. I don't know much myself, yet. She's unconscious, and the doctors are examining her now. I'm in a sort of waiting room.' Susanna realised that the hand holding the telephone to her ear was shaking. And yet she felt so calm.

'I wish I was with you,' said Emma, sounding very young.

'I wish you were, darling.'

'What happened?'

'We don't know much yet. It seems there was a bale of straw in the road, and they must have hit it. I gather she was with a young man – what's he called – Andrew, you know, the candidate at the election.'

'Oh, him,' said Emma.

'You know about him, then? I didn't know she knew him.'

'Yes, she knows him. Is he all right?'

'Broken legs, I think. I don't know. They took him to a different hospital. His family have been told.'

'Is Dad there, Mum?' Emma was near tears.

'No, not yet. I hope he'll come.'

'Oh, Mum.'

The white-coated doctor faced Susanna with folded arms.

'It's hard to tell at the moment, Mrs Westerham. She has a very severe head injury, and cuts about her face. We do not at the moment think that the injuries are life-threatening, but there is always a danger of a clot. You asked me to be frank with you.'

'I am grateful to you, Dr Singh. I would rather know the truth, and my husband too.'

The doctor hesitated. He could see that the mother was keeping a firm control of herself. But she should not be alone. Her face was white with strain, and the news might become worse.

'Is Mr Westerham here yet?'

'Not yet. I am hoping he will be soon. It is difficult . . .'

'I will ask them to bring you a cup of tea, Mrs Westerham. Your daughter is in good hands, and you must trust us.'

'I do. When may I see her?'

'Now, if you like, but very briefly, if you don't mind. I will come with you. You realise she is not conscious.'

'I don't care how many more votes there are. Get Mr Westerham onto this telephone line or I will come and personally strangle the Prime Minister.'

'Hold on, please.'

Emma was staring through the windscreen of a car that Mark had borrowed from a student friend. Her eyes saw nothing of the road ahead, her mind being totally preoccupied with the ache of her thoughts.

'Mark, what if she dies?'

'Hey, bun-face, it's probably not bad at all.' Mark put an arm round his twin and pulled her close. 'Being unconscious is nothing – nature's way of solving a problem. She'll be fine.'

'I wish she didn't have this . . . this fight going on with Dad.'

She put her head on his shoulder, and the car swerved slightly.

'Watch it – one accident's enough. Em, I must just drive. Stop blubbing and guide me to this place. There'll be hospital signs when we get near, I imagine.'

Mark wished that he felt as confident as he was trying to sound.

'Whips' Office.'

'I want the Chief Whip.'

'Who is this? He's in the Chamber.'

'Then I want whoever is most responsible in your office.'

'Who is this?' asked the whip again. It was a woman's voice on the telephone; it sounded authoritative, but he did not recognise it.

'It doesn't matter. I am speaking for Peter Westerham's wife. One of his daughters has had a serious accident, and he is needed at the hospital now. AT ONCE. She is in a very serious condition. Who am I speaking to?'

'James Levalliant. I am Peter's whip, as it happens. I'm sorry to hear about the accident. I'll send in a note to the Chief Whip right away. Are you a relation?'

'Yes,' said Rachel impatiently. 'Why don't you send in a message to Peter?'

'Um. I think the other way will be more efficient. Can I ring you back?'

'Yes, but quickly, please.'

Rachel Willoughby sat staring at the telephone and tapping her fingers as she waited. She wished she still smoked. It rang again almost at once. It was Susanna. She spoke in a small voice.

'Ma? Did you manage to get Pete?'

'Not yet, Su, love, but I'm working on it. I should be speaking to him in a few minutes.'

'Oh. I hope he can come, They are going to operate in about twenty minutes. It seems there's a bit of bone may be pressing on her brain.'

'They are talking to you, then,' said Rachel.

'Oh, yes. There's a really nice doctor in charge. He promises to keep telling me everything, thank God. You've got the number here?'

'Of course. I had better get off the line, because I hope Pete is just about to ring.'

'All right. Thanks. Thanks, Ma.'

Rachel had heard the tremor in Susanna's voice, and she ached for action.

When the telephone rang again she forced herself to be calm.

'This is James Levalliant. Was I speaking to y—'

'Yes, it's me. What's happening?'

'Listen, I must apologise. I haven't spoken to Peter. The House is very crowded. The Chief Whip got my note, and he sent out a message.'

'For goodness' sake—' Rachel found it hard to contain herself.

'Please,' said the whip. 'I'm very sorry, and the Chief says to give you his—'

He heard Rachel's sharp intake of breath, and hurried on. 'The thing is, it's difficult to get Peter at the moment. The fact is, there are some absolutely crucial votes going through, three of them. They are all extremely tight. You can probably hear the division bell for the first now. And until they are over it is virtually impossible to get hold of Peter . . .'

Levalliant felt sickened by what he was saying. The call of duty had seldom been so hard to obey.

'Virtually impossible?' Rachel pounced. 'So you don't mean impossible, do you? What you mean is that you won't give Peter the message in case he misses a vote? That's it, isn't it?'

He gulped.

'It's not me, Mrs er – I am just repeating—'

'May you be forgiven,' said Rachel, her voice trembling with anger, in a tone that implied that his chances of forgiveness were slender. 'His daughter may be dying. If you don't have Peter Westerham on the line to me within two minutes I will ring the newspapers and tell them exactly what you have said.'

'I will do my best,' said the whip, running his fingers round inside his collar. There was not much to choose between the damage the Chief Whip could do to him and the damage this woman could do to the party. He decided to risk his neck.

Peter came into the whips' office at a run, and grabbed the telephone.

'My God, this had better be urgent, Rachel. They've just called a division.'

'It is urgent, Peter. It's about Leonora.'

'For heaven's sake, what has she done now?'

Rachel swallowed her anger.

'Pete, she's had an car accident. It's bad. You are needed. Susanna is waiting for you at the County Hospital.'

'An accident?' Now the alarm sounded in Peter's voice as the words gripped his gut. 'Why didn't you say so? Is she all right?'

'Pete, I don't know,' said Rachel. 'I only know it's serious, and Susanna needs you. It's taken me ages getting a message to you.'

'Oh my poor love – Leonora – I'm coming now. I'll borrow a car. Rachel – the County? I won't be long.'

'Take care,' said Rachel, to the dialling tone.

'I need a telephone. Can you . . . get me a telephone?'

'Later, dear,' said a nurse. 'When we've got you comfortable we'll see to that. They've telephoned your father, I know that, so you just lie quiet. The doctor is just coming.'

'I must find out . . . please would someone . . .'

But the nurse had left the small room, and Andrew Manning's eyes fell shut again. His legs were numb, or held down or something. All he knew was that he couldn't move, and that he desperately needed a telephone. But he couldn't quite remember why, as he drifted again into a doze.

'Pete! Oh love, thank goodness. Can you come?' said Susanna, standing in a corridor, her head and shoulders in a perspex canopy.

'I'm on my way. I borrowed someone's mobile. How is she?'

'It's not good, Pete. They're operating on her now – it will be at least three-quarters of an hour before we know anything, perhaps longer. The twins are on their way. I wish you were here.'

'Hang on, love. I'm coming. Be brave.'

'Take care. I can manage. Don't rush,' said Susanna.

'Bye.'

Peter pulled himself up in his seat and, gripping the steering wheel, drove faster than he should.

Susanna put the receiver down and walked along the corridor. Her feet made no sound on the shiny rubberised grey floor, as if she were a ghost. When she got to the swing doors at the end, she turned and walked back again, the words above the far door growing larger as she approached them. Cardiology. Radiography. Family Room. Exit. There was no U. All the other vowels, five Os, four As, four Is, one E, but no U. On the way back again towards the swing doors marked Operating Theatre A. Operating Theatre B. Physiotherapy. Lifts. Still no U. It's as if I don't exist, she thought. She made herself stop and look minutely at each of the oil paintings that hung at intervals along the walls. She tried to decide which she would buy, if she had to buy one. Uncertain, she turned at the end and started again.

Some time later silent footsteps overtook her. An orderly touched her gently on the elbow.

'Wouldn't you like to sit in the waiting room, Mrs Westerham? I can bring you a cup of tea there.'

'Thank you, I would rather move about, if you don't mind.'

'That's fine, dear, as long as you are all right. There was a gentleman asking for you. He may be in the waiting room.'

'Oh, why didn't you tell me?' Susanna cried out, then controlled her voice. 'I'm sorry. Thank you. Where is it?'

She half ran, back through the double doors, took a wrong turning down an identical corridor, and finally burst into the waiting room.

'Pete!'

But the figure turned and it was not Peter. Her heart plummeted and for the first time she felt near tears. It was a man whose face she vaguely recognised from the Kentish Weald executive. She remembered his name – Tom Wright. The Major with the big moustache. She stared at him. She looked round.

'Is Peter not here?'

'I haven't seen him. I'm sorry, Mrs Wes— Susanna. I came to see if I could help at all. Cyril Eversley was going to come, he felt he should, as chairman, but his wife was out, and you know he doesn't drive. He rang and asked me to come along instead. Sent you his, you know, good wishes and all that.'

'It's very good of you, Major Wright,' said Susanna, composing herself. 'I do appreciate it. But honestly, there isn't much anyone can do at the moment. I am just waiting to hear . . . I thought you might be Peter. He's on his way from London.'

'We were very, er, shocked, you know, to hear about the accident. We do hope it is not too serious. Cyril said . . .'

Susanna, whose initial feeling on seeing the stout, moustached, tweed-clad figure had been akin to despair, now saw that it was better to have someone to talk to, even if it was only Tom Wright. It would bring the moment of Peter's arrival closer, as well as the moment when the doctors reported on Leonora's operation.

'It's a good hospital, anyway,' Wright was saying consolingly. 'Damn good hospital. Know some of the doctors myself, from when I had a hernia done. Competent lot. Which has your daughter got, d'you know?'

'He's very good, I'm sure, the brain surgeon,' said Susanna. 'He fills me with confidence, anyway. And he explains things. Dr Singh, he's called.'

'Singh? Oh, my God,' said Wright, 'not one of those? Well, I shouldn't say that, I suppose, seeing your girl's under the knife, as it were, but I wish you had one of the home-grown ones. You could ask for a second opinion, of course.'

Susanna gaped at him, not sure if she was following his meaning.

'Don't you worry, dear,' Wright said, patting her on the shoulder. 'There'll be a team of them in there, supervising him. She'll be all right, don't listen to me.'

'I am not worried, at least not in the way you seem to think,' said Susanna at last.

'Atta girl,' said the Major heartily. 'That's the British spirit, keeping your chin up and all that. Peter would be proud of you. Here he is now, the man himself. Well, I'll leave you. You won't need me now.'

And he shuffled off, shaking Peter's hand as he passed him and muttering something.

Susanna laid her head against Peter's shoulder, and he held her very tight.

'I can't stand that man,' she said. 'Did he say I was a brave little woman?'

'Something like that. Come and sit down and tell me everything.'

They moved over to a cheerfully covered sofa and sat very close together. Small, brightly coloured fish wove back and forth, dragging long transparent tails and staring at them through the glass walls of a large tank. It all seemed rather unreal.

'Have you seen her?' said Peter.

Susanna nodded.

'Pete, she looked so frail. And, oh dear, mud, and blood still. I only saw her face. She hit her head on something.'

He took her hand and held it in both of his as they talked.

'What happened?' he said gently.

Now that he was here, Susanna felt that her coping ability seemed to have disappeared. She felt unable to talk sensibly.

'She was in a car, I don't know where they were going . . . with Andrew Manning . . . you remember?'

'*Andrew Manning?* That fellow? I don't believe it! Do you mean—' Peter's anger welled up as he clutched her shoulder.

'Pete, no,' said Susanna miserably. 'Don't be like that. It was an accident. They hit something, not a car – it was a bale of straw or something, I think they said. She was thrown out . . .'

'Drinking, I suppose, was he?'

'I don't think so. They haven't said . . .'

'Was she wearing a seatbelt?'

'I don't know Pete,' said Susanna, deeply upset. 'Yes, she was . . . it broke or came away or something.'

'How *could* she be with that fellow?'

'Pete, what is the matter with you? Leonora may be dying! Listen to me! Does it matter how it happened? Pete!'

Peter turned to her and she saw then the distress in his face.

'Oh, God, Sukie,' he said brokenly. 'Is it my fault? She wouldn't have been going around with him if – if I – oh, I don't know . . .'

Now his head was on her shoulder, and she was consoling him.

'No,' she said, stroking his hair, 'not your fault. Certainly not your fault.'

They were silent for some minutes.

'Someone's coming,' said Susanna, stronger now.

The door opened. Mark and Emma came in, their expressions anxious till their parents smiled at them. They hugged their mother.

'Hi, Dad,' said Mark. 'It's been a while . . .'

Emma slipped her arm through her father's. Her face was strained and pale, matching his.

'Is she going to be all right?' she asked.

'We're waiting for the doctor now,' said Peter. 'It shouldn't be long.'

A head came round the door.

'I'm sure you'd all like a cup of tea?' asked a smiling nurse.

Dr Singh, when he arrived, was grave.

'What we cannot tell at this stage is what permanent damage, if any, has been done. We have been able to lift the pressure, and the bone is in a position to knit. We will keep her under sedation for some time yet. We are a little concerned about possible displacement of the vertebrae in her neck, but I think what I can say is that everything has gone as well as possible at this stage, and that we are optimistic. I hope you will feel that is enough for me to tell you at the moment. I think you should all go home and sleep, and telephone me in the morning when I have seen her.'

'He gives me confidence,' said Susanna, in the car. 'What do you think?'

'Yes, I liked him too,' said Pete. 'He seems to know what he's doing – please God he does.'

Rachel greeted them at their front door. She scanned their faces anxiously and felt reassured.

'Just tell me quickly how she is,' she said, 'and then I'll go home. I've put the whisky out, and the kettle on. I guess what you all really need is a cup of tea.'

Chapter 10

It was nearly two weeks later that Peter and Susanna heard the news they had been waiting for so anxiously. Dr Singh, his normally solemn face warm with smiles, assured them that a second brain scan had revealed that Leonora had sustained no permanent damage; though her physical injuries meant that she must go through a fairly lengthy convalescence she would end up 'as good as new'.

It was Saturday, so Peter was able to spend much of the morning sitting with Susanna beside Leonora's bed. They found it hard to contain the joy that they felt. Leonora, who had not, since she resumed consciousness, been aware that either her life or her reason had been at risk, noticed the behavioural change in her parents.

'You are both rather noisy today,' she said.

She did not speak much, but her voice was now clear, if not strong.

'Oh, darling, are we talking too loudly? Sorry.' Susanna squeezed her hand.

'It's all right,' said Leonora wearily, turning her half-shaven head towards her mother. The scars on her forehead would soon be unnoticeable, but she still looked almost as pale as the pillow. 'It's nice of you to be here. I'm not complaining.'

A nurse came in.

'May I ask you to wait outside for a little while, please? One of the doctors wants to have a chat with Leonora. I think she will be able to sit up a little tomorrow.'

As Peter left the room, Leonora beckoned to her mother, who stepped back towards the bed.

'Mum, Andrew really is all right, isn't he? You're not just pretending?'

'He really is all right, I promise,' said her mother. 'Not very comfortable, I guess, with two smashed legs, but all right.'

'Will you get me his address,' said Leonora, 'and a card or something?'

'Of course, darling. I'll bring it tomorrow. You've got a lot of cards yourself – all sorts of people worrying about you.'

'Do you see that awful one from Terry Lowther, that fat YC? Thatched cottage and hollyhocks.'

'What, this?' said Susanna. 'Oh dear.'

'He's always ringing my flat.' Leonora giggled, and her mother thought with a pang that she had not heard that giggle for a very long time. 'If he rings you, Mum, say no visitors, won't you. For the next two years. Say I am hideously disfigured.'

Susanna kissed her and left.

In the waiting room Peter and Susanna stood hand in hand looking at the tropical fish. They were getting to know them quite well, and to Susanna they now seemed like small friends who had shared their pain.

'She's getting better, fish,' she said. 'She's much more like herself today, Pete.'

'So are you, Sukie,' said Peter. 'You've been looking like a ghost till now.'

'You look a bit grey yourself,' said Susanna. 'Any chance you can take a little time off? Of course, we'll be able to have a proper summer holiday this year, won't we?'

'Sukie, I have some news that I think is a bit exciting. I hope you will.'

'What's that?'

'Richard Blest,' said Peter, 'the minister of state at the Home Office, has asked me to be his PPS.'

'PPS? What's that?' she said blankly. 'Post post script is all I can think of.'

'Parliamentary private secretary, idiot,' said Peter. 'You don't get any extra salary, but it's the first rung of the ministerial ladder. You are, in effect, a very junior member of the government.'

'When did you hear this?' said Susanna, shaken.

'The day of Leo's accident. I was going to tell you that evening.'

'And you never told me!'

She could hardly believe it. She knew he had been longing for some kind of preferment.

'It didn't seem very important while all this was going on,' said Peter. 'I haven't given an answer. I asked for time to think about it, because they know about the accident. But I should give an answer now.'

'You mean you haven't accepted?'

'I wanted to speak to you first. Su – there is a catch to it. Though there's no pay as a PPS, you become, ironically, part of the so-called payroll. It would mean that I have to be a good boy. No rebellion, no controversial speeches.'

'So you couldn't talk on police matters,' said Susanna, 'or in immigration or asylum debates or anything like that? Or Europe?'

'You've got it.'

'Are they trying to shut you up, Pete, do you mean?'

'They could be,' he said, nodding, 'but I hope there's more to it than that.'

'I'm sorry,' said Susanna, wishing she hadn't said it, spoiling his triumphant moment. 'I don't know what made me say that.'

As she spoke Susanna was poignantly aware that this was a turning point. In general, though Peter was still overworking, since Leonora's accident he had seemed much less tense, more affectionate, more like his old self. Perhaps it was partly due to concern about Leonora, but they had been easier with each other, and his outbursts of irrational irritation had seemed less frequent. How could she guess whether this new, apparently exciting opportunity would be happy for him, or would bring back the pressure even more strongly? She knew that at this moment it was within her power to stop him taking this step: he was holding back the decision for her approval.

'It's more "of" the government than in the government, Sukie,' Peter went on. 'But it's getting there. It's an excellent stepping stone to being a real minister, if I do the job well. The fact is, Sukie, that if I turn it down, it is more or less saying that I am not interested in ever becoming a minister. And it's only by becoming a minister that you can manage to achieve anything. And I suppose I went into parliament to try to change things.'

'Cleft stick situation, in fact,' said Susanna.

They sat gazing at the endlessly circling and weaving fish, the highly coloured plastic weed and the bubbles rising unevenly from a plastic tube to the surface of the water.

'Do you know him well, this Richard Blest?' said Susanna, playing for time. 'Why did he choose you?'

'No, I don't know him well, but we have chatted together at times. I would be quite happy working for him, I think.'

Susanna paused.

'I suppose it means . . . even longer hours in the House?' she said.

'I'm afraid so,' said Peter. 'But interesting ones.'

'How do you feel about it, Pete?' His tone made her heart sink.

'No, I want to know how *you* feel about it.' He looked down into her face, smiling, his eyes unfocused. 'I suppose I feel awfully pleased to have been asked.'

Susanna would have been totally lacking in sensitivity not to feel the excitement in him. She made up her mind. Even if it was a mistake, she could not, would not dash it down.

She put her arm through his and kissed him on the cheek. She felt like an inverted Judas.

'I've never been to bed with a PPS,' she said.

Peter reached for her hand.

'Excuse me!' said a voice. A nurse was looking round the door.

'Leonora's free now,' she said, 'if you want to go back.'

'I'm glad they didn't ask you to become a whip,' said Rachel Willoughby when she was told.

'You don't like the whips' office, I gather,' said Peter.

'No,' said Rachel.

'Few people do,' said Peter. 'They rule by coercion rather than by consent.'

'They didn't manage to coerce me,' said Rachel.

'That reminds me,' said Peter. 'You never told us: how on earth did you manage to get me out of the Chamber in the middle of a series of votes? It's unheard of, when there's a three-line whip.'

'Oh, I just used a bit of coercion,' said Rachel airily. 'Some of their own medicine. The fellow recognised it at once.'

'What would you have done if they had refused, Ma?' asked Susanna.

'My other plan was to ring up with an Irish voice and say there was a bomb in the Chamber.'

'That would hardly have got me to the telephone,' said Peter.

'No, that's why I didn't do it,' said his mother-in-law.

'My God, Rachel, I'd rather have you on my side than against me,' he replied.

Leonora was allowed home after another couple of weeks, and for some months seemed happy simply to be there, slowly regaining her strength and confidence in the care of her mother and grandmother. The usual Scottish holiday had not happened, mainly because the twins had plans of their own with university friends, and August and September had passed by pleasantly at Restings. Only Peter seemed to be especially busy.

'This is the one time of year I can catch up with work in the practice,' he said.

Leonora was changed, and seemed gentler and quieter, if affected by a certain listlessness. The previous belligerence towards her father seemed happily to have drained away. It was not until midwinter that Susanna began to wonder whether the spark in Leonora was ever fully going to return. She decided to telephone Dr Singh.

'She has no medical reason not to make a full recovery,' he said. 'How is her love life?'

'I hadn't thought of that,' said Susanna, surprised. 'I'm not sure she has much at the moment.'

'Interesting,' said the doctor.

Susanna repeated this exchange to her mother, who said:

'Su, don't you know? Leonora's love life is learning to walk again at some rehabilitation centre near Portsmouth.'

'Andrew Manning? No, I didn't know. Is that serious, do you think?'

'The twins say so. Seriously serious, I gather, if only on our susceptible Leo's side at present. Haven't you noticed any change in your telephone bill?'

'I wonder what he's like,' said Susanna. 'I know he worked somewhere near Tonbridge. He's a land agent, it said in the paper at the time of the accident.'

'I rather guess that when he is back in Tonbridge Leonora will suddenly recover her spirits,' said Rachel.

It was three weekends later that Peter found out.

'Do you know who was on the telephone, wanting to speak to Leo?' he said explosively, coming in to the kitchen.

'Who?' said Susanna.

'That Green fellow, Manning!'

'What did you say?' said Susanna nervously.

'I told him she wasn't here.'

'Pete! You can't do that!' said Susanna, shocked. 'Tell her friends she isn't here?'

'Look, Susanna,' said Peter, his anger rising, 'I am not having that fellow hanging around Leonora. He nearly killed her once, as it is.'

'He nearly killed himself, too. And the accident wasn't his fault, you know that.'

'That may be so, but she should never have been in his car in the first place. She was only with him to annoy me, anyway.'

'Pete,' Susanna said, reasonably, 'that may not be so. She may be fond of him, and the accident is good reason why they should be in touch with each other. I mean, they were both badly damaged. Why shouldn't they keep in touch?'

'She'd bloody well better not get fond of him,' Peter was talking furiously, in a way that had become familiar. 'Listen, the fellow is my political opponent, apart from anything else. Can't she have the decency to see that, either? I won't have him in this house, and you can make that clear to her.'

There was a long pause, and then Susanna said quietly:

'I am not going to tell Leo who she can or cannot have as a friend. You are being unreasonable.'

Then she left the room.

She felt guilty in reporting this conversation to Rachel, but she was disturbed, and not a little concerned about Peter's lack of moderation.

'It's tiredness, I am sure, Ma, that's making him like this. It's not Pete, not the real Pete. Perhaps a bit of jealousy, too, about Leo. He loves her so much, and it's the second time she's had a boyfriend he disapproves of. Oh, what a mess. But I am quite sure that he wouldn't be taking this attitude if he were not under so much pressure.'

Susanna's meeting with Peacock, planned before the car accident, had been put off pending Leonora's recovery, and somehow never fixed again. Now she came to the conclusion that the potential problem between Leonora and Peter was a strong reason to ring Peacock again.

'I am going to tackle Peacock,' she said to Leonora one morning in May, as together they carried buckets of water to various plants round the garden. Leonora seemed physically completely recovered and, to Susanna's great pleasure, it appeared that during her convalescence they had grown closer in understanding and enjoyment of each other's company. She had watched Leonora's strength come back, as her hair, now cut into a close, shining cap, grew too. The sadness was that Peter was too concerned with his own life and away from home too much to enjoy this rebirth, or to get close to his new, milder daughter again. Leonora was seeing Andrew Manning, but he was not talked about at Restings, by common consent.

For the second summer running there had been a severe drought since mid-April, and now the hosepipe ban imposed by the local water authority was making garden duty a daily necessity. In early July, Rachel had rigged up a pipe from the bath to a tub below the window, and it was bath water that they were now using.

'Is this about Dad?' said Leonora. 'Are you sure this won't make your French beans taste of soap?'

'Not sure at all,' said Susanna. 'They may even taste of Wyberg's Pine Essence, in which your grandmother occasionally indulges. Yes. It is about Dad, and how Peacock plans his constituency days. How do you find Dad at the moment, Leo? Let's go in. I think you have done quite enough for one day.'

They walked up the flagged path towards the house, carrying the empty buckets.

'On the rare occasions I see him, you mean. Well, he's just plain tetchy,' said Leonora. 'You know as well as I do, Mum, Dad never used to be bad-tempered, ever. But now he loses his rag at the slightest thing, and sometimes for no reason at all.'

'I know,' said her mother. 'He's tired. He's perpetually short of sleep, so it's not his fault. But I agree with you. And it's become much worse since he became a PPS. I thought it would give him more sense of achievement, but you can tell he's not happy. But at least I can do something about the overwork. That's why I have geared myself up to talk to Peacock.'

Her visit to the constituency office the following day was not easy. The MP's wife and the agent had always been wary of each other, and had never arrived at using first names, as if by agreement. But the mild sense of discomfort between them had now become friction.

Peacock's body language – tapping fingers, the sideways glances at papers on his desk – achieved his intention of making plain that in his busy life he had little time to spare for Susanna.

'I thought perhaps we could arrange things better,' she said, after briefly describing Peter's signs of stress.

'I'm not sure what you are suggesting,' Peacock said shirtily. 'Is it that I do not know what is necessary for the MP to do in the constituency? Or that Peter is not up to it?'

He folded his arms and did not try to disguise his sneer.

'I am not suggesting either, Mr Peacock,' said Susanna patiently, 'but he must have a break at weekends. His work for the minister is really punishing, now, and he has been on duty in the constituency the last three Friday and Saturday nights. That's too much.'

'A lot of these people are commuters,' said the agent. 'They don't have time to attend events during the week. Friday and Saturday evenings have always been the best for raising money.'

'Only a proportion of them are commuters,' said Susanna. 'And if you gave them the chance, they might be quite pleased to have Saturday evenings to themselves. Then they could do these things on weekday evenings instead.'

'We can't get Peter on weekday evenings, because part of his job happens to be in the House of Commons,' said Peacock with unconcealed sarcasm.

'I had noticed, Mr Peacock,' said Susanna, controlling her urge to hit him. 'Look, I've got a deal for you. I know that having the MP's spouse is not the same as having the MP, but I will guarantee to come out to any function, on any day of the week, and any evening. In return, you make it clear that Peter is only available on Fridays and on Saturday mornings. The rest of the weekend is for his family.'

Peacock looked at her with his eyes slightly narrowed, doing gentle half-turns from right to left in his swivel chair.

'You must see,' Susanna went on, 'that it is in both our interests to keep him healthy. He is no good in parliament or in the constituency if he is exhausted.'

Peacock made up his mind.

'All right, Mrs Westerham. I accept what you say, and I will make sure all the branches are aware of it. But I expect a promise from you that you will stick to your side of the bargain.'

'I have no need to promise,' said Susanna coldly. 'Saying it is enough.'

'Did you have a fairly good day, dear?' said Mrs Peacock. Normally this question was Peacock's first irritation of the evening, but for once he gave it a friendly reply.

'Well, I did, as it happens. Quite a good day. Solved a couple of problems in one. The fact is, we were landed with a wet-behind-the-ears MP with radical views on just about everything, and not enough sense to keep quiet about them. His honeymoon period has already run out, and I was getting concerned about losing support among some of the older stalwarts.'

'Oh dear,' said Mrs Peacock. 'People like Mrs Fittall?'

'No,' said Peacock irritably, 'not people like Mrs Fittall. She's a one-off, a pinko maverick, surely even you must have noticed that? I can hardly trust her on the doorstep any more, so it's just as well she's got arthritis.'

'Yes, of course. Silly of me. I wasn't thinking,' said Mrs Peacock meekly, handing him a cup of tea.

'People like Tom Wright, I mean,' said Peacock, 'and quite a few others. The solid, right-of-centre, core of the constituency party, the people we can count on at election time. They are concerned about street violence and such like, but will our MP even consider the death penalty for aggravated murder? Not a chance. He won't even fudge a bit to keep them happy. Straight down the line, "No, Mrs Whoever, I do not believe in capital punishment," he says. Or "Britain's future is in Europe" – things like that. And they don't like it. Any idiot could tell that.'

He thought for a minute.

'Yes, dear,' said Mrs Peacock. She was wondering whether to mention to him that he was sitting on her knitting, but decided not to. He was in such a friendly mood. 'You were saying?'

'Yes, well, the other problem is the quota for Central Office. We've got to get more money in. And that wife of his, Susanna Westerham, is the answer. They like her, they'll pay to see her. Best of all, she never talks politics. Not a word out of place. Mind you, she probably doesn't know anything about politics anyway, and in this case ignorance is bliss.'

Peacock was not sure that he was right in classifying Susanna as ignorant, but he enjoyed doing it.

'I don't quite understand, dear,' said Mrs Peacock, 'how you are solving your problems.'

'No, you wouldn't, would you. But I am. A stroke of genius. A brainwave. I realised that she is worried about her hubby getting overtired, so I suggested a deal to her. I told her that I would make sure he had many fewer branch events to come to, if she would take them all on instead. And she agreed! So, in one fell swoop I can more or less muzzle him, and stop him putting people's backs up, and I make sure the events are well attended and the money keeps rolling in. And Central Office will notice that. Good fundraising is the sign of a good agent, they say.'

So they will raise your quota for next year, Mrs Peacock thought of saying. But the agent disliked any sign of shrewdness in his wife, so she didn't. She noticed later that the evening had passed without his raising his voice to her.

'Ma,' said Susanna to Rachel the following day in the stables. 'I have a bit of a problem.'

'I know that tone of voice,' grunted Rachel. 'Could we finish the job in hand before we discuss it?'

She was standing with her legs braced apart, her back to a pony whose head was resting on her shoulder. One hand was gripping a bar of the loose-box, the other holding the pony's muzzle in position, while Susanna tried to insinuate the neck of a bottle into the side of its mouth.

'Keep still, you idiot. We're only trying to help you,' she said, as the animal tried to jerk its head away.

When they had finished, Rachel wiped her shirt ineffectually with a handful of hay.

'Have you noticed, when you talk about "drenching" a pony with medicine, that not only the pony gets drenched?'

'Sorry, Ma. I'll do the holding next time if you like.'

'So what's the problem?' said her mother, as they walked side by side across a field towards the house, looking at the deep fissures in the parched soil. There had been little change in the weather since May. 'You want me to have a bath more often?'

'No,' Susanna laughed. 'Not that. I must say, it has been so good having Leonora here to help me with the bucket carrying. I wonder when they'll let us use the hosepipe again.'

'When it rains, I suppose – really rains, not this silly drizzle we've been getting.'

They walked slowly on.

'So?' said Rachel.

'It is about the ponies, actually,' said Susanna. 'I'm planning to run the stud down.'

'What?' said Rachel, incredulously. 'But you have been talking of expanding it all this time.'

'It doesn't make sense any more,' said Susanna, 'with the change in our life. I'm going to spend much more time in the constituency. It is something I have to do, because I don't see any other way of stopping Peter killing himself with work.'

'I think I begin to see the problem. Your stallion.'

'I've cancelled him, Ma. He's not coming.'

'Su!' Rachel stopped and looked at her daughter, who avoided her eyes.

'There is no way I could keep a stallion, have visiting mares, *and* look after the ponies we've already got if I'm going to be at coffee mornings and luncheon clubs and all that stuff.'

Rachel said nothing.

'I know what you're going to say,' said Susanna, 'but it was going to be a lot of work for two people, and you couldn't possibly manage alone.'

'No.'

'And I can't afford to hire anyone, and neither can you. Ma, don't try to make me change my mind.'

'I haven't said a word; not that I noticed, anyway,' said Rachel, mildly.

'No, but don't look at me like that.' A pinched look had appeared about Susanna's nostrils. 'The stud's not important, it's an indulgence. I don't need it. It's an irrelevance compared to what is at risk. You know I have always thought we were so safe, Pete and I, and the children, and you, of course. I am only realising now what a fragile thing family happiness is . . . It's a sort of balancing act.'

They were nearly at the garden. Susanna stopped and turned, and stood for a moment staring at the ponies grazing in the field behind her. Without letting her mother see her face, she went on.

'Anyhow, I have decided, Ma, and that's it. I can live without the stud, but I can't live without Pete. I'm losing him, Ma. Everything we have as a family seems to be slipping . . . ooohhh, *bloody, bloody, bloody politics! I hate it all.*'

Susanna threw the bucket she was carrying with all her might at the bars of the gate. It fell and rolled clattering back towards her as she stood with tears of despair rolling down her cheeks.

Rachel watched without comment. Things had gone further than she had realised. She looked away, leaning on the gate while Susanna recovered herself. Then she said:

'Can you talk to Peter about all this?'

'Pete?' Susanna laughed bitterly, rubbing her cheeks with the heels of her hands. 'I don't think he'll even notice when the ponies go. I have to do it, Ma. I will never forgive myself if we lose everything because I was selfish. I have to help Pete, you know, support him, until he has finished with this bloody business.'

'I hope you are right,' said Rachel.

'What do you mean, right?' There was still anger in Susanna's voice, and now she seemed to be directing it at her mother.

'I mean right to deal with it like this,' said Rachel slowly.

'I know Pete, don't I? I should by now, if anyone does.'

Rachel did not reply.

'You and Father,' Susanna began, with sudden intuition.

Rachel stopped her. 'That was different. This is not going to be like that.'

She spoke firmly, and Susanna knew better than to go on with the subject. She knew very little of the detail of the end of her mother's marriage, and she knew that Rachel found it hard to talk about. 'He wanted to live a different kind of life,' she had been told when she was younger, 'and we decided that you and I could not fit into it. But he loved us both, very much.' It was all Susanna had needed, as a child, that reassurance of love. The much later revelation that her father had become a monk had come not as a surprise but as a disappointment. It would have been easier for her, at school, if he had joined the Foreign Legion. She had been fifteen when he died, of double pneumonia exacerbated by lack of perceptive care. She had been sorry then that she never tried to see him, but that sorrow had passed. Suddenly, now, she felt it again.

She tucked her arm through her mother's.

'You'll tell me more, one day? So that we can share?'

'Yes, probably,' said Rachel. 'It wouldn't help now, though. At least, I don't think so. I'll think about it. Go on about the ponies.'

'I had better tell you what I have planned,' said Susanna, her voice steadier now. 'I'm selling the two three-year-olds to the man in Essex. It's a good home, and he will show them in Mountain and Moorland classes, under the Restings stud name. They will be a good advertisement for us, if we ever get going again. Then the two younger mares are going with their foals on loan to Janie Beck. She will breed from them and look after them. The old lady we'll keep, and the three youngsters, till they are ready to be sold. And the two geldings, for the time being. I'll have to give up schooling outsiders, too. And that's it.'

'And that's it,' echoed Rachel.

She had already decided that it would be foolish to try to argue her daughter out of the decision she had not only taken but begun to implement.

'That all sounds sensible, Su. I expect you are doing the right thing. So what was the particular problem you mentioned?'

'Telling you, actually, was the problem,' said Susanna. 'It hasn't been hard with outsiders. But you know how I feel. And I know you know. And you know I know. And so on.'

They paused on the back doorstep to take off their boots. They were both aware that there was a lot in their minds that neither was going to say.

'Well, they're damn lucky,' said Rachel, 'because they are going to get two MPs for the price of one, and I doubt if they deserve it. Oh dear. Just when I had got all the stud accounts onto the computer. Back to the drawing board. I suspect my future is in clip-art.'

Her flippancy was assumed. The clouds that had seemed so distant once seemed now to be massing overhead.

Chapter 11

It was a little later that week, while Rachel was standing at her kitchen sink, that she noticed a good-looking young man hovering uncertainly outside her window.

She opened it, and called, 'Can I help you? Sell you some insurance or double-glazing or anything?'

He laughed, and as he came to the window she recognised Andrew Manning.

'Come to the door,' she said.

He apologised as he came into her kitchen.

'Actually, I was passing by, and I thought I would look in and see if Leonora was about. But they seem to be out.'

'Yes,' said Rachel, returning to the sink, 'shopping. I'm her grandmother. I am just about to have some coffee, so if you would care to join me you can sit and wait here. I imagine they will be back in a few minutes. It's nearly one o'clock.'

Andrew was staring at the Pyrex bowl in front of her.

'What . . . what on earth are you doing?'

In the bowl was a glutinous pile of glistening grey and yellow matter, and with a small fork Rachel was probing inside a shell, which she threw, empty, on to a pile of others.

'Those are snails!' he said.

'Of course they are,' said Rachel, looking at him kindly.

'But, what are you doing with them?'

'My dear boy, cooking them, of course.'

'But, you can't just kill all those snails like that, can you?' said Andrew.

'Indeed you can. They were dropped into boiling water and – phhhut – dead.'

'But there must be fifty, a hundred, there!'

Andrew was torn between his innate sense of good manners and automatic horror at the ecological implication, which he hadn't yet quite thought out.

As Rachel poured two cups of coffee she answered obliquely.

'What do you think of slug pellets, Andrew?'

'Horrible. They should be banned. They kill the birds that eat the slugs.'

'I quite agree with you. They are banned in this garden, I can tell you that. But we have to control the snails, because we grow our own vegetables. What do you think of standing on snails as a mode of control?'

'Messy,' said Andrew, smiling. He was getting the gist of what this unusual woman was saying. He knew that Leonora was very fond of her, and he was beginning to see why.

'And wasteful. Much better to eat them,' said Rachel, 'which is what I do. I find any amount among the lettuces and on the walls, under the aubretia, in particular. I don't make a huge impact on them, but I have some delicious meals.'

'I've only tried snails once – rubber in garlic, I thought.'

'The wrong kind,' she said dismissively, 'the ones you get in restaurants. Ordinary garden snails are what the French call *petits gris*, and keep for themselves. Delicious. Much the best. You must come and try them with me sometime. That's the car, I think. They're back. Take your mug with you.'

Andrew turned in the doorway.

'I'd love to come and eat snails with you, I really would. Thanks for your hospitality. I believe you could have sold me some double-glazing too, if you had tried.'

A pleasant young man, Rachel said to herself. Willing to listen to reason.

It was Leonora's attachment to Andrew that caused the row between Peter and Mark.

'Mum,' said Leonora, appearing in her dressing gown for breakfast on a Friday morning in October, 'Andrew's coming to supper, is that all right?'

'Fine,' said Susanna. 'I shan't be in, I'm afraid, or not till about nine-thirty, but there are some lamb chops and lots of cheese and fruit.'

She was getting used to Andrew Manning dropping in. As soon as he was walking without crutches, some months ago, now, he had taken to calling at Restings fairly regularly, and Rachel's prediction had been right: Leonora was blossoming like a flower, and her laughter was again a part of the sound of the farmhouse, as it had been in the days before she had donned critical resentment with her student gear.

In unspoken acknowledgement, perhaps, of her father's disapproval, she and Andrew managed always to be out, at a football match, at a film, or just out, whenever Peter was at home. It saddened Susanna, who was sure that Peter could have come to like the young man as much as she did. She found Andrew as easy to talk with as he was pleasant to look at; his gentleness with Leonora pleased her, and so did his humour when his deeply held political beliefs were challenged, as they often were, especially by the twins – he submitted well to teasing. Most tellingly, he would notice, and pick up a teacloth without comment, if there were dishes to be dried. The atmosphere at Restings suffered no ripples when Andrew was there.

Susanna realised that Peter would be confronted that evening by the situation they had all been unobtrusively avoiding, because after his advice surgery he would be home for supper. Well, it had to happen some time, and perhaps this evening, when she would be out at a branch Quiz Night, was the ideal occasion. She felt that her absence might make Peter feel obliged to be hospitable. She could not be sure, for now she often felt that only half of him was with her, and that she had no means of contacting the other half. His mood swings alarmed her, as much when he became suddenly affectionate as when he lost his temper over minor things, as now happened frequently.

He came into the room now, and helped himself to coffee and toast. He had come home the night before, late. Susanna knew that he had not slept well, which always made her wary. As usual he opened his mail as he ate.

'Pete,' she said after a while, 'I have to go out this morning. Is there anything you need?'

'Where are you going?' said Peter.

'Only over to Burwood. They have a plant sale and I promised I'd drop in. I could shop afterwards.'

'I haven't been to the Burwood branch since last year,' he said. 'I might join you there later.'

'I'm sure they'd love that,' said Susanna equably, 'but why bother? They are only expecting me, and if you haven't got much work you could take the dogs for a walk instead. Give yourself a break – it's such a beautiful day, and you have a horribly early start for Brussels tomorrow.'

'You don't really want me to come, do you?' said Peter explosively. 'You can manage better on your own, I suppose.'

He gathered up his papers with sweeping gestures and got to his feet.

'Pete, love, for goodness sake—' said Susanna.

'Oh, forget it,' he said, as he left the room.

'You see what I mean?' said Leonora.

Peter, as he drove away into the constituency, tried to analyse his irritability with Susanna. Of course it helped to have her keeping the branches happy by attending their events. She did it well, and he was often told how lucky he was to have her. Well, of course he was lucky, he didn't need to be told that. Susanna seemed to have an ability to get on with everyone, which he knew he lacked, but then, they didn't talk politics to her. He wasn't jealous of her, oh no. Nothing like that. What he did mind, though, he had to admit, was that she had got rid of most of her ponies to be more available to help him. He couldn't believe such a dramatic gesture had been necessary. Not that she talked about it, in fact you would have thought she had lost interest in the stud. Perhaps she had, but it seemed to him that she must be feeling some resentment, though she was hiding it. She never seemed to want to talk about it, and it, well, made him feel uncomfortable, though he would have been hard put to it to say why.

Anyway, he had enough to worry about without her adding to it. His secretary was often forgetful, and he had missed an important committee that week; her excuse was the usual, that the correspondence was building up after two major lobbies, and she couldn't cope. Almost all his allowance for this year had gone on her salary increase and demands for updated equipment, and now she wanted more help. If he was sometimes tetchy, he thought, it was hardly surprising.

What Susanna did not know, was that Mark would turn up unexpectedly that evening and that by the time Peter got home the three young people would be deep into a game of Monopoly, spread all over the kitchen table. The MP had had a bad surgery, a stream of complaints from people he felt had no serious problems, and some deeply sad stories from people whose undeserved misfortune he knew from experience that he would be unable to alleviate. If he ever felt grateful for an unbroken family and a permanent roof over his head, it was tonight.

But he was tired, and he was hungry, and the sound of thumping music had reached him even before he had turned off the engine of his car. As he approached the kitchen door he was already feeling alienated; loud, unrecognised laughter made him feel even more annoyed and excluded. He opened the door to the kitchen and instead of seeing the table laid, as he had expected, for supper, it was covered with what his mind termed instantly 'puerile games'. Worst of all, facing him across the table was 'that fellow' sitting drinking Peter's whisky with his arm round the shoulders of Peter's elder daughter.

Before he even paused to think, he heard his voice snarling, 'What the hell do you think you are doing here?'

Andrew, shocked, got to his feet.

'Dad!' Unbelieving, accusing, Mark's voice.

Peter's head swung to his son, whose back had been towards him.

'And you too,' he shouted, 'have you nothing better to do? It's all I need, after a bad day, to find you've taken over the whole—'

He stopped. Mark stood up, clutching the back of his chair. His normally ironic, friendly smile was transformed into a pink mask of shock. Peter had not seen him for nearly three months, and suddenly, realising this, he saw himself through Mark's eyes, and shame and embarrassment swept through him.

'I'm sorry,' he said. 'It's just too loud. Do I have to put up with that bloody racket all evening? I have to work.'

He was fumbling, trying to slide his anger into something excusable, parent's reaction to pop music, anything.

All three stared at him. He turned and walked to the hall, hanging his coat, fiddling with his briefcase, doing anything except going back to face them. The silence continued. He was appalled at the thought of his outburst. He walked up to the bedroom and sat at Susanna's dressing table, staring at himself in the mirror. The music stopped abruptly. He heard the sound of quiet voices, and after a time the front door shutting, the starting of a car, then silence.

He undressed, dropping his clothes on the floor, and walked naked into the bathroom. He ran the bath and lay soaking in steaming water for a long time.

When he came down, soothed and contrite, he noticed at once that the kitchen table was spotless, with places laid for two.

'Mark,' he called softly.

There was no answer. He walked from room to room and found them all empty.

When Susanna got home an hour later the whisky bottle had rolled away out of sight, and she thought at first with a shock that Peter was seriously ill. She had never before seen him really drunk, and it was only when she smelled his breath as she leaned over him that she realised why he was sprawled over the table. Miserably, without asking questions, she helped him to bed.

The main result of the evening was that Leonora moved into Andrew's flat in Tonbridge. Peter, whose sense of guilt was as unreasonable as his behaviour had been, felt entirely to blame.

'Pete,' said Susanna consolingly, 'it was lovely having her at home all that time, but it was becoming almost unnatural. She's completely recovered, and she's twenty-four, for goodness' sake – no girl lives with her parents at that age.'

'But I drove her out . . .' said Peter, running his fingers through his hair.

'. . . And into his arms? Don't be melodramatic. You sound

Dickensian. I'm quite sure she will be perfectly willing to darken your doorstep again if you ask her nicely.'

So Peter wrote to Leonora and asked her to bring Andrew to Sunday lunch. Susanna prayed, and Leonora accepted.

'That's my girl,' said Rachel when she heard.

It was a strangely successful occasion, largely due to Leonora's tact and non-stop chatter, and Andrew's quiet good manners could not fail to have an effect on Peter. Afterwards he said to Susanna, 'I feel so impressed by them both. I hope Mark will be as forgiving.'

But he knew as he said it that it would be harder to restore the comfortable and trusting relationship with his son that had always meant so much to him. Mark's innate sense of fairness had been deeply bruised.

Over the following winter and spring, Susanna honoured her commitment to Peacock, and he had no complaint. The success of her efforts in the constituency was evident as the months went by, and the branches were buoyant and enthusiastic. She gave them ideas for fundraising that they had not thought of before.

'A sponsored bike ride?' said Ellie Fittall. 'Fine, if you can find me a tricycle.'

But she sat at a checkpoint all day drinking coffee laced with whisky, checking the bicyclists through. Susanna had more sponsor money on her front wheel than any other competitor.

At an auction of promises in December, her own promise to weed a garden for a day got the highest of all the bids. She regretted that one in June, but it made her even more popular.

Her idea of a sponsored dead wood collection in the Hascombe plantations raised hundreds of pounds, and the resulting sale of logs a few hundred more. It also earned her the Hascombes' undying gratitude.

Peacock was ecstatic.

'Things are looking up,' he said to Lelia in the office as they were doing the accounts one day, about nine months after his pact with Susanna. 'Getting her into action was the best idea I ever had. It doesn't matter if *he* ruffles a few feathers now and again; *she* makes up for it twice over.'

He almost found it in himself to feel some fondness for Susanna, but did not think that it was reciprocated. The charm so widely seen in the constituency never showed for him.

'How are you getting on with all these bazaars, or whatever it is you go to?' asked Rachel.

'Bazaars, mother, went out with cloche hats,' said Susanna. 'It is bring-and-buy coffee mornings and wine-and-cheese parties now. I'll probably die of a surfeit of cheddar and plonk. Actually, as I have to drive after anything like that, whether Pete's with me or not, the cause of my early death will be that disgusting non-alcoholic stuff, which no doubt saves Peacock's precious pennies, but doesn't make a rollicking party.'

'Apart from helping to keep Pete sane,' said Rachel, 'is there any fun in it?'

'Fun?' Susanna considered the question. 'There are some laughs, and I really like some of the people. Your friend Ellie Fittall, for example. She is so funny, and sharp, and kind, isn't she, and absolutely without illusions about anything or anyone. I asked her the other day why she was a Conservative, and she said, "I have to be something, don't I, to give me the right to complain." Actually, Ellie is just one of a lot of people whom I really do like. Conservatives are a very mixed bunch, I am beginning to find. Some really nice, some plain awful. Like the club, for instance. Membership of the Kentish Weald Conservative Club gives you a bar to sit at, a social position, a basis from which to moan about the government and everyone else, and an excuse for not canvassing or fundraising because you are doing your bit by being a member of the club. There you are! The club in a nutshell!'

'MP's spouse not totally enamoured, do I gather?'

'You gather,' said Susanna. 'Ma, I'm so glad I have you to talk to. I couldn't say all this to anyone else.'

'I won't repeat it to a soul who is not a member of the press,' said Rachel, 'and then only for cash.'

'There's something I want to ask you, Ma. What do you take Zantac for?'

'I don't.'

'No, what would it be for if you did?'

'Zantac?' said Rachel. 'Ulcers, I think. Why? Peter?'

'Yes,' said Susanna glumly. 'I thought that was it. Last year he said he had indigestion, but an ulcer makes sense. You get ulcers from tiredness and worry, right? And the whole point of my deal with Peacock was to take some of the stress off him. Sometimes I feel as if I got rid of the ponies for nothing. I just don't know what else I can do.'

Mark and Emma were seldom at home now. They both telephoned regularly, but Susanna was aware that the ties were inevitably loosening.

'They all right, the children, then?' Mrs Thomas would often say as she collected the newspaper.

'Hardly children now, Mrs Thomas. Growing up fast. That's why you don't see them much.'

It was usually hard to leave the shop in under five minutes, Mrs

Thomas's need for gossip being so pressing. It was her unusual silence one morning that first alerted Susanna to something having happened. She was about to escape with a polite 'Thanks. Bye,' when Mrs Thomas's bursting curiosity could no longer be contained.

'We was very sorry at the news, Susanna,' she said. 'I wouldn't pry, but I hope it will be all right, like.'

'What news?' said Susanna, frowning.

'Didn't you know? It's in the *Express*, front page.'

She thrust the paper at Susanna. The words MP's DAUGHTER ARRESTED leapt at her, and her heart thudded.

Mrs Thomas was all eyes as she read the article. This would make her shop the centre of attraction for days. To think of her mother not knowing about it, and her having to tell her!

'I don't believe it, love,' she said soothingly, 'not our Emma. Not in prison. I said to Harold, I said, there'll be some mistake, as like as not.'

'May I take this?' said Susanna weakly. She had to get away. 'I'll pay for it tomorrow, Mrs Thomas.'

'You take it, love. Anything I can do, mind. If you feel like a chat and a nice cup of tea . . .'

From home Susanna tried to ring Mark, but could not find him. Then she rang Peter. His secretary answered.

'Oh, it's you, Susanna. That's all right. I am afraid the press have been after him from first thing. He's trying to get on to the police in Newcastle now. He's going to ring you as soon as he knows anything.'

'Is it only in the *Express*?' said Susanna. 'It's not in the *Independent* – I haven't seen anything else.'

'I think it's only the *Express*, so far.'

'A pub brawl doesn't sound like Emma. Do you think it could be a mistake?'

Susanna realised as she spoke that she should no longer count on second guessing any of their children.

'Hold on a moment . . . Yes . . . Peter says he will ring you back in ten minutes, Susanna. All right?'

In the next office Peter was chewing his bottom lip as he waited, telephone to his ear. He had been passed between different numbers and was now waiting to speak to an officer who was said to know the details.

His mind swung between anger at Emma for the embarrassment and worry she was causing and, chillingly, fear of what he might be about to hear. A police raid on a pub could mean any of a number of things, but with students . . . So far, he had thought, he had felt in his gut, but he could not put his hand on his heart and swear, that his beloved children were free from drugs. Two years ago, he would have felt sure, but now? He no longer knew what Emma did in her daily life, nor Mark either, for that matter. Nor what they thought, any more. When had he last had a 'heart to heart' with either of them? What could he say to the police officer if the dread word was mentioned? 'Not *my* daughter, officer'?

He rubbed his hand across his aching eyes. Perhaps he should say, right away, 'Sorry, officer, I'm guilty, guilty of neglect of my own children, and of failure to—'

'Mr Westerham?' said a voice, and Peter grasped the receiver more firmly.

It was a painfully long ten minutes for Susanna, clutching her arms together and pacing up and down in the Restings kitchen. She leapt to answer when the telephone rang.

'Pete? What's happened? Is it true?'

'Oh, it's true,' said Peter, 'or true enough to make a story. But not what it sounds. I've spoken to the police, and to Emma.'

'Is she really in prison, Pete? I can't believe this.'

'No, of course she's not, nothing like that. There was a fight in a pub last night, like they said, and someone pulled a knife. The point is, the police rounded up a whole group of more or less drunken students, including Emma, and put them in the cells overnight. They kept two, and charged them, and let the rest go this morning. I don't think Emma was involved at all. She was just unlucky.'

'But – but –' Susanna's relief was tempered by her anger. 'If you read the paper you'd think—'

'I know. They spotted that she was my daughter, and the odd policeman isn't above making an easy buck, then some grubby little hack built it into a story. Don't worry, it'll be gone in a day. But I should leave the answering machine on, if I were you.'

'What did Emma say, darling? Is she very upset?'

'You can speak to her yourself. You've got her number. She's at her digs. We had a bit of a spat, I'm afraid. I have to go. I'm late for a committee.'

His manner was terse, and he sounded upset himself. Indeed Peter was upset, and once again full of guilt. His huge relief that Emma was clear of all trouble had manifested itself in angry words to her for getting herself into the situation. It was the same reaction as makes a mother smack a child for not being killed when it runs into the road. But that was not what was upsetting him now, as he strode down the committee corridor. He had convinced himself that Emma was playing with heroin, at the very least. How could he have doubted his sensible little daughter to that extent, and then been angry with her for having done nothing at all? How could he not have had more faith in her, his own daughter? What must she think of him? What did any of them think of him? He seemed to be losing his balance in relation to his entire family, and yet here he was walking into a select committee . . . Oh God, he had forgotten his briefcase.

When Susanna spoke to Emma she discovered what had happened with Peter. Her younger daughter was seething.

'He had the nerve to tell me I should be more careful! Me! I told him, Mum, I told him it was his own stupid fault. I am the only one whose name got into the paper, and he's only got himself to thank for that. Does he think I like being splashed all over the tabloids? Nobody asked *me* whether I wanted to be an MP's bloody daughter.'

'Love, calm down,' said her mother. 'You've had a horrid experience, but you mustn't—'

'Don't preach at me, Mum!' Emma's voice was still shrill. 'You're as bad as Dad. Everything has gone wrong since he—' Now she was near tears. 'Sorry, Mum, but he never thinks about the rest of us.'

'Oh dear, Emma. Don't be too hard on him.'

Susanna soothed her as well as she could. Her sympathies were with Emma, but she did not know how she could express them without being unacceptably disloyal to Peter. She did not feel she had been of much use to either of them.

Peter had been almost eighteen months as PPS to the Home Office minister when the crisis came.

He rang Susanna on a Monday night at about eleven o'clock. He often rang when he got back to the Westminster flat, so she was not at first surprised. But his voice told her that something was wrong.

'Pete? Are you all right.'

'I'm coming home, Sukie. I rang to say don't lock the door. I'll be an hour and a bit.'

'Where are you?'

'In the House. I'm just leaving.'

'Pete, what's happened?' said Susanna.

'I'll tell you when I get home. No, don't stay up. It can wait till morning. I can't talk now – I'm in the lobby.'

She stayed up, of course. She struggled and failed to imagine what could have caused the desolation in Peter's voice. She tried to watch television but her mind ignored the screen.

One of the dogs barked as his car pulled up outside, and Susanna got a bottle of whisky and two glasses out of the drinks cupboard.

Chapter 12

'No,' said Susanna firmly, 'you cannot speak to him. He came home very late last night, and he is not awake yet . . . No, I will not wake him . . . Yes, ring again if you like, but not before eight-thirty.'

She had switched off the telephone by their bed the night before, and crept out of their bedroom the first time she had heard it ringing downstairs. She had taken three calls by 7 a.m.

At eight she went up to the bedroom with coffee on a tray. Peter was still asleep. She woke him gently and he pulled himself up in bed, and sat staring blearily at her over his knees.

'You look like Mark in your pyjamas,' she said.

'You look like a younger version of your mother in your dressing-gown.'

'I think those can both be taken as compliments,' said Susanna.

'I heard the telephone,' said Peter.

'That's why I've come up. I can't fend the journos off any longer on my own. One was positively rude. It's all right, I was rude back.'

'I'm sorry,' said Peter.

'Why should you be sorry?' said Susanna. 'It's not a problem. Have some coffee. I think you had better tell me a bit more about last night, before I read it in the newspapers.'

Beyond telling her that he had resigned his position as PPS, and a little about the circumstances, Peter had not told her much and she had not pressed him. He had needed sleep more than anything.

'I'll tell you,' he said now, rubbing an eye with the palm of his hand. 'It's not much. It's a bit pathetic, I suppose. It was all to do with a new clause in the Housing Bill, which would remove the principle of priority for local families. I had told my minister that I couldn't support it, and he was sympathetic, even if he didn't agree.'

'So did you actually vote against the government?'

'No,' said Peter irritably, 'I didn't do that, I just abstained. And we won the clause, by twelve votes, on a three-line whip.'

'Then what is all the fuss about?' Susanna was mystified.

'Insubordination, that's what it's called. I was summoned to see the Deputy Chief Whip. He said at once that as I had failed to support the government they would have to ask for my resignation.

"Unless", he said, "you can assure me that your failure to vote was because you were unwell."

'"That wouldn't be true," I said. "I abstained because I was unable in all honour to vote for the clause."

'And you know what he said then, in his weaselly way? "Honour, my dear Peter, is a luxury that at this stage of your career you cannot afford. Not if you take your future in the party seriously. Come on," he said, "you've had your frolic. I'll tell the Chief that it was a mistake that won't happen again."

'I'm afraid I lost my temper then, Sukie. "No, you won't," I said. "You'll tell him that it was deliberate and you can have my resignation, as another matter of honour." And I rather fear I flounced out. And that was it.'

Susanna got up from where she had been sitting on the side of the bed, and walked to the window. She looked at distant trees, through a mist of her own making.

'Susanna,' said Peter, 'do you think I've been a fool? You know what it means, don't you?'

'I know what it means,' she said.

'It means I don't exactly have much future in politics. I have fallen at the first hurdle.'

'If you had jumped it I'd have been worried.'

She turned to look at him, and even though she was silhouetted against the light he saw the shine on her cheek.

'Sukie, you're crying. Please don't. Love, I'm so sorry. I've let you down.'

'You silly nit,' said Susanna, moving towards him. 'I'm not crying, but if I were it would be because I am so proud of you.'

'That's just simplistic. Most people would say I had been a total fool,' said Peter, sliding his legs over the side of the bed.

'If being honourable is being foolish,' said Susanna, 'then I am happy to be married to a fool. You have been compromising yourself for too long, and I know it doesn't work. I know you were unhappy after you had to support the government in those votes overturning the European court's rulings.'

She was half-kneeling on the bed, rubbing his shoulder muscles with the heels of her hands. He leant his head back in pleasure.

'That's not the only time I've had to deny my common sense,' he said, 'not to speak of my conscience, but I haven't always told you.'

'I know when it's been happening, though,' said Susanna. 'I can always tell.'

'I suppose you can,' he said. 'I'm sorry that I've been such a pain all this time.'

'Forget it. I'd rather have you around, being unpleasant, than not have you here.'

'There's another thing,' said Peter as they both started to dress, 'I'm afraid it will be in the papers.'

'I can tell that,' said Susanna, moving to the bedside. 'I'm going to take the receiver off for a bit. I hate those predatory hacks.'

Susanna replaced the receiver before she went down to get breakfast.

'Will you take it when it rings?' she said.

But it was the front door bell that rang first. There was a girl standing on the doorstep whose face was vaguely familiar.

'Good morning, Mrs Westerham,' she said. 'I am very sorry to bother you so early, but I wonder if I could have a word with your husband?'

Susanna hesitated.

'He is rather busy at the moment,' she said. 'May I ask who you are?'

'Kieran Mitchell,' said the girl. 'We met, do you remember, after the bye-election. I work for the *Wealden Echo*.'

The girl was holding out her hand, which Susanna touched reluctantly.

'You telephoned earlier,' she said.

'Yes, I am sorry it was so early.'

'It wasn't so early as the *Telegraph* and the *Express*,' said Susanna.

'Oh dear,' said Kieran. 'It's been like that, has it?'

'I will tell my husband you are here, and let you know what he says. Do you mind waiting in your car?'

Peter was firm.

'No interviews,' he said, 'until I see what the party press release says. I have got to see the morning papers first. We should have listened to the Today programme.'

'I did,' said Susanna. 'Just a brief item saying that you resigned last night, but not why. Pete, the implication, as I heard it, was that you had been sacked.'

She sounded indignant.

'Well, that's not unfair,' said Peter. 'I was sacked, in a way.'

'You resigned, because their ultimatum was unacceptable.'

'You are very loyal, Sukie, but it's all a matter of your point of view.'

'I am going to tell that journalist to come back later.'

She went to the door. Kieran Mitchell was still standing there.

'I'm afraid Pete – my husband wants to see the daily papers before speaking to you. So if you wouldn't mind . . .'

'I brought you the papers,' said Kieran cheerfully. 'I thought you would want to see them, and they told me in the village that you hadn't been down to get them yet.'

Susanna felt invaded and irritated, but accepted the bundle. In the kitchen she discovered that, as well as their usual *Independent* and *Times*, Kieran had brought the *Daily Mail*. On its second page she saw the headline ran SACKED MP RIDDLE. She looked up as Peter came in.

'They're making riddles about you now,' she said.

She spread the paper out on the table, and they read it together. The words 'known Europhile', 'sacked', 'rumoured incompetence', 'Westerham's inability to handle the job' leapt from the page.

'Peter, this is not tolerable,' said Susanna, deeply upset. 'They're lying! They must tell the truth, surely, about why you had to resign?'

'The truth? Who? The papers, or the whips?' said Peter bitterly. 'Don't be naïve, Sukie.'

The other papers ran the story, but with less prominence.

'So that's the end of you, is it?' said Susanna, her anger rising. 'Telling the newspapers you were sacked for incompetence – it's actionable! They can't ruin a man's reputation like that! Sue them, Pete.'

He laughed.

'Well, that would be a notable first. It's no good, Sukie. I just have to take it on the chin. Did you say that girl was from the local paper? I'll see her. At least I can make sure the constituency knows the truth.'

Kieran Mitchell, sitting outside in her car, was feeling dejected. She was not expecting to get an interview. She had heard the early morning news, and had come out to the Westerhams' house on her own initiative, hoping there was a story. Her editor disliked his reporters making their own plans, and she was fairly certain that she would be in trouble when she went back to the office; unless, that was, she had some good copy with her. The trouble was that interviewing a man she respected about his failure was not the sort of thing she enjoyed. Baiting the Tory Party was one thing, trampling on its better members was another. Perhaps she should head for the constituency agent instead of hanging around. Now there *was* a man she disliked: she could have a bit of fun with *him*.

Planning this, she did not see the front door opening. Peter tapped on the car window.

'Would you like to come in and have a cup of coffee?' he said.

In the Westerham kitchen, Kieran noted socks drying on the Aga rail, books piled on chairs, bright colours, elderly saucepans, comfortable chairs, crumbs on the tablecloth. It was somehow not quite what she had expected.

Peter Westerham was friendly; his wife, she thought, less so.

'I would like to do a piece on why you have returned to the back benches,' she said, as Peter passed the milk across the table. 'No, no sugar thanks.'

'That's very tactfully put,' he said, smiling. 'Will it get into this week's paper? I know you put it to bed a day or two beforehand.'

'Last night was the official deadline,' said Kieran, 'but a good story will always get in up to midday today. It's wonderful what they can do when they want to.'

'So time is short,' said Peter. 'Carry on, then.'

Kieran switched on her recorder as Susanna left the kitchen, shutting the door quietly.

'Well,' said Mrs Thomas, the next day, 'we are hitting the headlines, aren't we? It's a crying shame, I say, losing a man like Mr Westerham.'

'I don't know, Mrs Thomas,' said Susanna, paying for the papers. 'He may be able to do more now in parliament than he could as part of the government.'

'Oh, he'll still be an MP then, will he? I haven't read it proper. I just saw he resigned, and I thought that meant he was finished up there.'

No, unfortunately, said Susanna to herself, as she left the shop. Then she gasped as she saw the front page of the *Echo*. Kieran had certainly made sure the story was good enough to be included. Indeed, it had made the front page.

DISGRACED MP FIGHTS BACK

DIRTY TRICKS AT WESTMINSTER

Amid suggestions that he had been sacked for incompetence from his position as Parliamentary Private Secretary, Kentish Weald MP Peter Westerham yesterday accused the Tory Party of being economical with the truth over his ignominious return to the back benches.

'My abstention from voting was not a mistake,' he told our reporter. 'I was being asked to vote for a clause with which I strongly disagreed. My conscience and my duty to my constituents come first. I have no objection to being asked to resign in the circumstances. What gets me is that the rumour was deliberately spread that I was sacked for being no good at my job. This I resent.'

Asked whether there was any truth in other rumours that he had been sacked for his pro-European views, Westerham said he thought not, but that the party had been infiltrated at all levels by what he described as Eurosceptic wreckers.

'Good Lord,' said Peter, when she showed it to him. 'That last bit wasn't part of the interview. I only said that when we were chatting afterwards, as I took her to her car.'

'Oh Pete,' said Susanna, 'even I know that you don't say anything to the press that you don't want repeated.'

'It's true, though, that's the trouble,' said Peter.

'You are not economical with your truth, you are lavish with it. That's the way I like you. But it seems it's all right for solicitors, and not so all right for diplomats and politicians.'

'What you are saying,' he said, 'is that I shouldn't be a politician. Well, it's a bit late, Sukie. Perhaps you should have told me sooner.'

'It's not too late, Pete,' Susanna spoke urgently, 'you know it's not. It's not a life sentence – it doesn't have to be. You can get out – there will be dozens of people queuing up for your seat, you know that.'

Peter turned and looked curiously at her. This was Susanna acting out of character. His wife, against her nature, was not just advising him but urging him into a course of action, something she had never done before.

'What's this, Sukie? You, so vehement? This is not like you.'

'Pete,' she said, in the same tone as before, 'this is important. You know yourself what all this is doing to us, to you and me, to the whole family. We have been so separated these last three years – you've felt that too, haven't you? The children are losing you, and they need you. It's not just that you don't have time for them, it's that you don't even know what they think any more, and that's why things have been going wrong between you and them. They no longer talk to you the way they used to. If you were only happy, it might be worth it. But you're not.'

'Oh, hell, Sukie.' Peter stared despairingly at her. 'I know you're right. It has been a disaster.'

'You joined the wrong party, didn't you?' she said.

He sighed heavily.

'My problem,' he went on, 'is that I chose a party that no longer exists. It has been hijacked by people who would have had no place in it twenty years ago. Now it's becoming a party of right-wing reactionaries. The more isolationist and insular you are, the greater your chance of being listened to.'

The bitterness in Peter's voice was painful to hear.

'I feel full of guilt' he said, 'when I think of the pathetic, introverted sort of a country we are creating for our children.'

Susanna was shaken. She had never heard Peter speak so openly of his disillusionment, and it seemed deeper than she had ever guessed. She knew with even greater certainty now that he must get out, for his own sake, as much as for the sake of the family.

'Pete, there's a full year till the next election. That would give them more than enough time to find a new candidate and for him to work himself in to the seat. For our sake, for all our sakes, tell them that you won't go on. No one will blame you, or no one who matters. It would be the brave, the wise thing to do.'

'It would be such an admission of failure, Sukie,' he said. 'I should really stay and fight.'

'Surely you can fight for your beliefs outside parliament? And to leave would be honourable, Pete,' Susanna was leaning forward, emphasising her words with her clasped hands, 'because no one can work wholeheartedly for a party they no longer believe in. Pete, for the sake of the family, for my sake, please, please, say you will give up politics! Please.'

'Sukie, it's not as simple as that.' Peter was disturbed by her passionate pleading.

'Will you at least think about it?'

'Su, I always think about what you say, you know that. For one thing, you don't often say anything.'

They were interrupted by the telephone ringing.

'If it's the press, I'm not here,' said Peter.

It was not the press, it was Leonora.

'Is Dad all right? I heard,' she said.

'He's here,' said Susanna. 'Do you want to speak to him?'

She passed the receiver to Peter.

'Dad? I'm so sorry. I read that awful piece in the *Mail* at work.'

'It's only partly true, Leo,' said Peter. 'The main point is true, that I was sacked, in effect.'

'But Dad, Andrew rang me and read me the bit from the *Echo*. And I just want you to know that I have never been so proud of you. Really proud. Well done.'

'Leo, bless you.'

'I'll ring again later,' said his daughter. 'I have got to make sure the twins know about the real version.'

Peter put down the receiver.

'Thank God for families,' he said, stretching out his hand towards Susanna. But the telephone was already ringing again. Susanna took it.

'Yes, he's here. Hang on,' she said.

She made a face at Peter as she handed him the receiver. 'Peacock,' she mouthed.

He listened for a moment, and then said:

'I won't be able to leave till after the seven o'clock vote, so you could say eight o'clock. I shouldn't be much later. All right. Ring me at my office to confirm, will you . . . ? Yes. Goodbye.'

Susanna stared.

'He knows, presumably?' she said.

'He knows, all right,' said Peter. 'There is to be an extraordinary meeting tomorrow evening of the executive committee "to discuss your resignation" as he put it. And they want me there.'

'Would you like me to come too? I suppose there's nothing in the constitution against the MP's spouse turning up?'

'Who cares if there is?' said Peter. 'Are you sure you want to?'

'I'll come. Pete, was that all Peacock said? Not "bad luck", or "how are you feeling" or anything?'

'Not a word from my supportive agent.'

'Good God,' said Susanna.

The executive committee split neatly down the centre over the question of whether or not Peter Westerham should be censured over his refusal to accept party discipline.

In fact, Peacock was not convinced that to have his MP censured, much personal pleasure as it would give him, was a wise move politically. It would certainly be leaked by someone on the committee to the press, and Central Office would not approve. He never seemed to get anything right with them nowadays.

When Peter and Susanna arrived the committee was still arguing as to what they had to say to him, and had only decided that Eversley as chairman should say it, whatever it was, as they walked in. They were shown to seats at the end of the long table. Though there were some nods and smiles, other people seemed to avoid catching their eyes.

'We have, er, discussed the, er, events of the last . . . of Monday night, Peter,' said Eversley, after thanking him for coming, 'and we are unanimous, I think I may say, in regretting that you are no longer holding the position that you previously held, that is to say, at the Home Office, under the Home Office minister, of course, er . . . as . . . erm . . .'

'PPS,' said Peter helpfully.

'Exactly, of course,' said Eversley gratefully, 'and a very distinguished position too, and we are all very sorry that, er, you no longer hold it.'

'Bloody waste of a good man, I say,' said Ellie Fittall.

'Hear, hear,' said several voices.

Encouraged, Eversley went on.

'There are those among us, I think I am right in saying,' he said, 'who might have preferred a rather more robust support of the government on your part . . . Yes, Tom, you would like to say something here?'

Major Wright was heaving in his chair. He rose to his feet.

'Yes, I think you are putting a funny gloss on it,' he said. 'What we said was that we expect our MP to vote for the government on all occasions.'

He sat down again heavily, and muttered 'hear, hears' spread around him.

'May I say a word, Mr Chairman?' said Peter.

'Yes, yes, certainly. I hope you will.'

Peter stood up.

'If you have had an opportunity to read this week's *Wealden Echo*, Major Wright, it sets out in part why I abstained in a vote. I would like to enlarge on that. The issue was one of keeping local communities together, something that, as you know, I have always keenly promoted. In the past, you have agreed with me on this. Would you now have me vote against it?'

Ellie snorted, and dug her elbow into her neighbour.

'Now, look here,' said Major Wright, his moustache working frantically, 'it's all very well, but what about this Euro business? We don't agree with that. I fought in the war, you know—'

There were slightly embarrassed murmurs of support.

'Oh, sit down, Tom,' said Ellie, flapping a hand at him. 'You can stand for election as one of them Euro septics if you want to, but not now. We don't all agree with you, anyways. I bin to France too.'

Terry Lowther raised his hand, and the chairman nodded to him. He started ponderously.

'I would like to say, chairman, that I endorse the remarks made by Major Wright, in relation to Brussels, that is. But there is another matter that in my capacity as chairman of the Young Conservatives I feel should – well, it has been brought to my notice – well, it's a bit delicate, actually.'

As he spoke, he had looked at Peter and Susanna watching him from the end of the table, and suddenly wished he hadn't started. He swallowed.

'Carry on, Terry, we're all friends here,' said Eversley heartily, causing Rupert Hascombe to raise his eyebrows across the table at Ellie Fittall.

'Well,' said Lowther, his well padded cheeks reddening, 'it's just that somebody said that it was a bit unsuitable that Andrew Manning seems to be very friendly with, er, one of Mr Westerham's, er, children. It was just that someone said that, so I felt I ought to mention it. They said they thought Mr Westerham ought to know. I think they meant the political implications.'

'*Political* implications?' said Hascombe.

'Who's this Andrew Manning, then?' said Ellie. There was whispering across the table. Clearly not only she was mystified.

Peter cleared his throat.

'I can tell you that,' he said. 'Andrew Manning was one of my opponents at the bye-election. He represented the Green Party, and was a very good candidate. He is a fine young man and if he is a friend of one of my daughters, I consider it to be nobody else's business.'

Audible 'hear, hears'.

'Pretty girls,' said Hascombe under his breath,' are everybody's business.'

'Point of order, Mr Chairman.' A new voice, a woman whom Susanna recognised as having been on the panel that had two years earlier selected Peter for the seat.

'Yes, Mrs Williams?' said Eversley. Any diversion was welcome.

'As I understood it, this meeting was called to decide whether Peter Westerham should be disciplined – no – sorry, what's the word? Censured, thanks. Whether he should be censured for not voting with the government on a housing issue, not about Europe, or about his daughters' friends. And anyway, I think this censuring business is a lot of nonsense.'

Murmurs of approval. Most of them seemed to agree, thought Susanna, with whoever had spoken last.

'Thank you, Mrs Williams,' said the chairman. He had found his notes now. 'That's a very good point of order. And it brings me back to the point of the meeting. As I was saying, there are those who feel concerned that you abstained from the vote, and those who have indicated, er, their satisfaction that you have kept in mind the, er, needs of our local families, which seems to have guided your actions in this case . . .'

'Oh, go on, Cyril, say it,' said Ellie, 'you mean Peter did what he oughter. You can't say one thing and vote another, for anybody's sake.'

'Well,' Eversley went on, 'that, er, was more or less what I was intending to say, Ellie, thank you.'

'And thank you, Cyril,' said Peter, standing again, as if in answer to Susanna's unspoken prayer. 'I appreciate your support in what has been a difficult time for me. I assure you that my devotion to the welfare of my constituents will continue as long as I am your member of parliament.'

'Hear, hear,' said Hascombe loudly. 'Is that it, then? Any other business? I don't suppose so. I haven't had any supper yet, I don't know about the rest of you.'

'I declare, erm, the meeting closed,' said Eversley with relief. He had not enjoyed it, and he was gasping for a drink. 'Thank you, thank you all.'

As they collected their coats, several people came up to Peter and Susanna, friendly, slightly apologetic. Peter's most constant supporters stayed to the end.

'Are you all right, girl?' said Ellie to Susanna. 'He's a good lad, your hubby. Too good for this lark, maybe.'

'Thanks, Ellie,' said Susanna, unexpectedly comforted.

'And you give my love to that girl of yours. I'll never forget that poor little face when your mum took me to see her in the hospital. Like a little waif, she was, with all her lovely hair cut off. I'm glad she's all right now.'

'It was so nice of you to visit her. Yes, she's fine; blooming, in fact.'

'So I am hearing,' Ellie winked fiercely and nudged her. 'Mind I get an invitation to the wedding.'

'That may be premature, this day and age and all that,' said Susanna. 'But if my mother says so . . .'

'She's an old-fashioned girl. Well, you're an old-fashioned family, aren't you? Nothing wrong with that.'

Susanna watched the old lady as she went out. She thought about it. Strangely, there seemed to be nothing old-fashioned about Ellie.

Rupert Hascombe, leaving last, gripped Peter by the elbow.

'Peter, I'll vote for you at the next election, but there's a lot of people in your party who shouldn't be there. You may quote me, particularly to some of the more rabid members of the cabinet.'

And lifting his hat to Susanna, in what she enjoyed as being a delightfully old-fashioned way, he left too.

Peacock drove home deeply angry. He was angry with Eversley, but then he was permanently angry with Eversley. He was angry with Ellie Fittall, for voicing approval of Westerham to his face. He was angry with himself for not having engineered greater humiliation for Peter. And he was angry with Mrs Peacock simply for being there for him to look at when he got home. He punished her by telling her that his dried-up supper was inedible. He ate it, all the same, because it was actually quite good.

Sylvia Peacock decided not to ask him what had happened at the meeting.

A postcard from Mark was waiting for Peter when they got back to Restings. He read it, and passed it silently to Susanna.

'Dear Dad,' it ran, 'Whatever the papers say, forget it. You are ALL RIGHT and if we say so it must be true. Love, Mark.'

Peter took it back, and slipped it inside his coat.

'There were a few people there tonight that I would miss, if I were not MP any more,' he said. 'There are some real friends among the others.'

The memory of the warm handshakes cheered him, and he dismissed from his mind the averted looks of those who had avoided him at the end of the meeting.

Susanna only said, 'I must let the dogs out before we go to bed.'

She was happy about the postcard, and Peter's retention of it. She was warmed too by the memory of his words '. . . as long as I am your member of parliament.' They implied a certain impermanence.

She was sure his mind was working in the direction that she was longing for.

Chapter 13

By September of that year it was apparent that Leonora had undergone a transformation. She showered her family with leaflets about saving rainforests, sustainable energy, CS gases and global warming.

'I mean, these droughts!' she expostulated. 'We never used to flog around the garden with buckets of water every summer, did we?'

She expounded on ecologically motivated transport policies, and at meals during her visits all conversation was dominated by her statistic-riddled views.

'It isn't that she doesn't talk sense,' said Peter as he and Susanna went up to bed one Sunday evening, not long after Leonora and Andrew had swept off in her small car, 'it's that she just doesn't seem to think of anything else. I'm amazed she hasn't taken to riding a bike.'

'You mean,' said Susanna, 'that she is becoming a proper bore about it all.'

'Well, I wasn't going to put it quite so harshly, but frankly, yes. She's like a Catholic convert, all deadly devotion and meticulous adherence. The funny thing is that her young man isn't a bore at all. Like one born into the faith, he can laugh about it.'

'It's love, that's all,' said Susanna, yawning. 'She's taken an overdose of love's sweet nectar, and she's on a high. When they get engaged she'll calm down. She'll have more to think about.'

'*When* they get engaged? You sound very confident.'

'I am positive,' said Susanna. 'I think Andrew is just waiting to get a word in edgeways.'

When she had undressed, she sat in her dressing-gown on a small armchair in the bathroom as Peter lay soaking in the bath. He was on holiday and unusually relaxed.

'I shan't mind if you're right,' he said. 'She would be all right with him. He has a delightful way of winning an argument and then pretending he hasn't. Very diplomatic. I like him.'

'I get the impression,' said Susanna, 'that his political views are not unlike yours, whatever his green leanings.'

'His views on Europe certainly coincide with mine. He told me last time he was here that if he failed to get into Westminster he would try for the European parliament.'

'Do you ever wish you had done that, Pete?' Susanna said.

'Perhaps. I might have felt more at home in Brussels than in Westminster. I certainly think I would have felt freer there – I hate being so tied into the party system.'

Peter paused and sighed, rubbing his wet hands over his face.

'But I know now that I wasn't born for politics. Vanity, all is vanity. I was bored, and I suppose I fancied myself. I only got in to parliament because I was lucky. I should really get out and be the lawyer that I know in my heart of hearts I am.'

It was almost as if he were talking to himself. Susanna was mentally holding her breath. She did not interrupt him, for fear of changing his train of thought. On an evening like this, when he seemed so like his old self, her longing for his release was intense. His mood reminded her that their old, easy, teasing, joking relationship was still recoverable.

She felt an intense love for him as he lay there with a sponge on his chest.

'It's just a question of gearing myself up to it,' Peter went on. 'It will mean warning them that I don't want to fight another election. I must have a word with Rupert Hascombe sometime about timing. It's a pity Rupert isn't the chairman.'

When he fell silent, Susanna decided not to make any comment. Within eight months, the last possible date for a general election, what had begun to seem like a life sentence would end. She did not want Peter to realise how elated she was.

'I must go and shut the dogs up in the kitchen. What odds will you give me on Leo and Andrew being engaged by the spring?'

'None,' said Peter. 'You are far too perceptive.'

'Coward,' she said. 'Spineless, that's your problem. Too mean to risk a fiver.'

She closed the bathroom door just before the wet flannel hit it.

When Leonora broke the news, therefore, shortly before Christmas, it did not shake her family the way she had hoped. The twins expressed instant and deep sympathy for Andrew.

'We tried to warn him,' said Emma, 'but it was clear from the start that he was beyond redemption.'

'I don't suppose you'll need your car, now, as he's got one,' said Mark, hopefully.

'What do you mean, you knew? We've never so much as held hands in front of you,' said Leonora, and quickly put her fingers in her ears to suppress the jeers from her siblings.

'You can surprise Granny, at least,' said her mother, releasing her from a congratulatory hug.

'I want to tell her myself,' said Leonora, 'so don't you go and spoil it.'

She found her grandmother bending over an open drawer.

'Have you noticed,' Rachel said without looking round, 'that the thing that is lost is always the thing you happen to be looking for? It is one of nature's immutable laws. Oh, it's you, Leonora. Sit down.'

Leonora curled up in a deep sofa, and observed with interest that Rachel was wearing odd shoes.

'You know your shoes don't match, Granny?' she said, giggling.

'Indeed I do,' said her grandmother, turning round, triumphantly brandishing a screwdriver. 'I am not colour blind. I put on odd shoes to remind me that I want to watch the programme about whales and dolphins tonight, which I might otherwise forget. Now, your young man is probably interested in whales.'

'Actually, I wanted to talk to you about my "young man" as you call him,' said Leonora.

'Oh good,' said Rachel at once, 'I thoroughly approve. You show extremely good taste, and so does he, I have to say. So when is it to be?'

'Granny, you are horrible. I haven't even told you yet.'

'Not officially, no, but osmotically. I am not absolutely sure if that word exists. Pass me that dictionary on the table beside you, will you? What I mean is that the fact that you are in love has been oozing out of your every pore for some time, and I have long suspected that you are the marrying kind. Anyway, Andrew would be a fool not to marry you, considering how he feels about you, and he is not a fool, and so, *voilà*, my dear Watson. You will be glad to know,' she added, closing the dictionary and removing her glasses, 'that the word is in the dictionary, and means more or less what I suppose it to mean. What luck.'

'Granny, will you stop burbling and congratulate me? It may not be a surprise to you, but it is to us.'

'With all my heart, my dearest Leonora, and with all my love to you both. Bring him to see me soon, will you? I can give him a few tips about you.'

'Not on your life,' said her granddaughter. 'I'm going to keep you apart until he is safely in the family.'

Unusually, there was a fall of snow on Boxing Day. There was a frantic search in the stables for empty plastic feed bags, and the whole family slid painfully down the small hill behind the house. Susanna, watching Peter rolling in the snow, shouting furiously as the twins stuffed it down his neck, thought that it had been a long time since she had seen him so free of care. Her conviction that this was largely the result of his decision to leave parliament was reinforced by the slowly growing gloom that descended on him as the start of the new session approached after the New Year. He reminded her of Mark shortly before returning to prep school, growing detached and turning up late for meals.

She waited patiently for him to tell her that he had taken the first steps towards his release. She knew he had talked with Rupert Hascombe before Christmas, and that Rupert had been sympathetic. With the election due in the spring it was important that Peter should allow time for a successor to be chosen.

In late January, early one evening as she was unloading shopping from her car, she heard the telephone ringing. She ran into the kitchen.

It was Peter.

'Sukie,' he said, 'I thought you were out. I was just going to ring off.'

'I was,' she panted, 'but I'm not. Which train? What time do I meet you?'

'I'm sorry,' he said. 'I'm ringing to say that I won't be able to get down tonight after all.'

'Oh, what a shame, love. You were going to have an amazingly good dinner. I have actually done some creative cooking. What's happened? I thought you were paired.'

'I was,' said Peter wearily, 'but the whips have cancelled all pairing.'

'The buggers. Why?" said Susanna, failing to keep the droop out of her voice.

'Well, our whips' office has got wind of an opposition plot tonight.'

'What sort of plot?'

'You know the way,' said Peter. 'They pretend to go home, go around saying goodnight to people, and then hide in their offices. Then when the division bell goes, they suddenly all appear and get into the division lobbies, and hope it's too late for us to get the troops together.'

'What a nasty trick,' said Susanna,

'Oh, it's standard practice,' said Peter. 'We would be doing it to them, if they were in government with a tiny majority. I'm sorry to let you down, love. Perhaps your mother would be free to come and eat that delicious dinner I'm missing.'

'Don't worry about that,' said Susanna, hiding her deep disappointment. She had hoped this evening, their first quiet one together for a while, to find the right mood in which they would talk constructively about the future. Having taken the decision to give up his seat, Peter seemed to be lacking the impulse to implement it. With the last possible date for a general election now only three months ahead the matter was becoming urgent. And the meal was indeed special. She looked over to where she had laid the table, to the flowers in the centre, the newly made mayonnaise and the candles waiting to be lit.

'Don't worry,' she said again. But he wasn't worrying. His mind was firmly at Westminster.

'It is quite dangerous, actually,' he said, 'our Euro wreckers are involved, and the Ulster Unionists have been pretty volatile too, since the new deal with Sinn Fein, and no one knows quite which way they will jump. It must be hell being a whip on an evening like this.'

'Will you be home tomorrow, then?' said Susanna. 'Which train shall I meet?'

'I'll be late. After the ten o'clock vote there's a 1922 meeting. I'll ring when I'm leaving.'

Susanna sighed as she put down the receiver, and sat thinking for a minute. Although she was used to it now, it was still disappointing not to see Peter when she expected to. She supposed she was lucky that she knew his excuses to be genuine. If he had been a philandering husband, he would never have been able to hide it from her, because she knew him far too well. And she had no doubts about the strength of the love between them, though it frightened her when it seemed to disappear under the weight of Peter's other life, like a plant vanishing under encroaching weeds, strangled and starved of light and nourishment.

'Don't be fanciful,' she said aloud. Then she rang up her mother at the other end of the house, and invited her to dinner.

'Yes, dinner, definitely,' she said. 'White tie and tiaras.'

She was awoken much later by the telephone, and groped in the dark on Peter's side of the bed to find the receiver. At this time of night a call frequently meant a constituent in the glow of a good evening out who needed to put an urgent political point immediately to his MP. But, though they had had an answering machine installed, since Leonora's accident Susanna never put it on at night.

She tried her voice out, cleared her throat, and said, 'Hello?'

'Sukie? You there? We lost!'

For a moment she could not think what Peter was talking about, and then realised that he was still in the House of Commons.

'What? The vote? You lost the vote?'

'Yes. I'm sorry to ring you so late. You didn't hear the midnight news? It's shambles here. We lost massively, because they hadn't been able to contact a lot of our side. They're saying there's going to be a vote of confidence tomorrow, because the Irish lot all voted against us.'

'Sorry, I'm not sure what you are saying.' Susanna was still half asleep, and the implication eluded her.

'It was all the opposition parties,' said Peter, his voice quick and urgent, 'and if they vote against us again tomorrow the government could fall. We only need one or two mavericks, and you can never be sure, the way our party is now. Don't you see? That could mean a general election.'

'Heavens! Now I see what you are on about. No wonder you rang.' Susanna was more than just awake, she was sitting on the side of the bed. 'That's incredible.'

'I must go. There's a queue for this telephone. I'll ring you tomorrow.'

'Goodnight, darling,' she said. He had already rung off.

She lay back against her pillow. It was almost too good to be true.

The thought that a general election was now a real likelihood, not in a few months' time, but now, within weeks, kept coming back into her mind during the following day. She felt excited and disloyal. She felt she should not be hoping for the government to be defeated in this vote of confidence, but her longing to see Peter out of parliament dominated her feelings. This way, it would be quick and honourable, and in no time some other hopeful would be member for Kentish Weald.

She listened to The World at One, and heard speculation on the likely outcome of the vote of confidence in the evening. Elder statesmen and political pundits pontificated on the previous occasions that this had happened to governments with very small majorities. Too close to call, was the verdict.

Susanna went over that evening to her mother's end of the house to watch the ten o'clock news. They sat with drinks in their hands and listened to the commentator talking earnestly and excitedly about the implications of the vital vote that was taking place at that moment in the House of Commons. As the camera focused on the members trooping out of the chamber, Rachel and Susanna could feel something of the excited buzz that they radiated.

Other news intervened during the time that the division was in progress and was suddenly interrupted as the Chamber of the Commons reappeared on the screen.

'And now, back at Westminster, we are waiting for the tellers to announce the result of the vote of confidence that has just taken place, on the motion "That this House has no confidence in Her Majesty's Government". There is the Prime Minister, taking his seat now, chatting to the Foreign Secretary, showing little of the strain that he must be feeling. We have just seen someone – I think it was the Deputy Chief Whip – coming along the bench behind him and saying something in his ear, so he may possibly know the result of this crucial vote, but he gives no sign . . . Ah, now we can see the tellers for either side are moving into place, and it seems . . .'

The rising roar in the Chamber was drowning the commentator's voice. MPs on all sides were standing in their places and waving their order papers.

'. . . Guessing from the position of . . . and the Speaker is calling for . . .'

A hush fell and the voice of one of the tellers could be heard.

'The ayes to the right, 388, the noes to the left, 386.' The rest was lost in a howl of voices and the screen became a turmoil of waving, moving figures.

'For goodness sake, have we won, or lost?' said Rachel, leaning forward, her eyes fixed on the screen.

'It depends,' said Susanna, 'on what you call winning. And also on *who* is *we*?'

'The ayes have it, the ayes have it,' mouthed the Speaker.

The sounds from the chamber were faded to allow the commentator's voice to be heard.

'And as you may have gathered, the votes were 388 in favour, 386 against, which means that the government has lost this vote of confidence by just two votes, but that is enough. We will have an analysis as soon as we can of the voting figures, when our—'

'Turn it down. Where's the pad?' said Susanna.

The voice died away.

'Do you realise what that means, Ma?' she said, turning to her mother, her face alight with pleasure.

'Go on,' said Rachel.

'A general election! It means that Peter can get out! He decided not to fight another general election, and – Oh, Ma, I've been wanting this so much.'

'I know,' said Rachel. 'Hang on a minute, though. As far as I can gather, listening to all the boffins on the radio today, it is still up to the Prime Minister to decide whether or not to call an election. I mean, it's not automatic, is it?'

'Oh Lord. I forgot that. Well, surely he must, mustn't he?'

Rachel could hear the painful anxiety in Susanna's voice. She turned up the volume, and Michael Brunson was speaking earnestly at the camera.

'—stand that there will be a statement from Number Ten in exactly half an hour's time, so we will be bringing that to you at approximately ten-fifty, when there will be a short interruption of the next programme. And now we have two members of parliament waiting to be interviewed, one from the Labour—'

Rachel faded the volume again.

'Can you wait, do you think?'

She eyed her daughter with amusement.

'As long as you like,' said Susanna, smiling, 'as long as he says the right thing. Some more wine to steady our nerves?'

While they were waiting, the telephone rang. It was Peter.

'Sukie, you saw all that, I imagine,' he said.

'Of course. Ma and I were glued to the box. It was incredibly exciting.'

'Yes,' said Peter.

'Pete, I know I shouldn't say this, but I am so glad. There will be a general election, won't there?'

'I am sure there will,' he said. 'There has to be. There's going to be an announce—'

'I know,' said Susanna, 'we heard that. We're going to watch.'

'Sukie, I won't ring again tonight. I will be home tomorrow morning, and then we can talk.'

'Pete?' Suddenly Susanna felt anxious. His voice was strange.

'I must go. Good night.'

And he rang off.

Susanna, watching the Prime Minister speaking into a microphone in front of Number Ten Downing Street, thought he looked tired under the arc lights. Smiling nevertheless, he told the phalanx of journalists that the Queen had granted him an audience the following morning, and that a further announcement would be made after he had been to the palace.

'Prime Minister, what's the election date?' shouted a voice.

The Prime Minister smiled, waved and went back into Number Ten.

Susanna turned and hugged her mother.

'Good old Queen,' she said. 'She won't let us down.'

Peter was home in time for lunch. Susanna kissed him enthusiastically when he arrived, and suggested a drink, first, in the sitting room.

They sat on the window seat, the wintry sun warming them through the glass.

'So,' said Susanna, raising her gin and tonic towards him in a celebratory gesture. 'What do we do next?'

'Sukie,' said Peter, 'the first thing we do is talk.'

'Talk? Of course.' She smiled. 'Pete, I cannot tell you how—'

'Sukie, stop a minute.' His voice was strained as he interrupted her. 'Sukie, I know this is going to be a disappointment to you, but I have got to make this clear. I am standing in this election.'

Susanna lost her ability to speak. It was as if her throat was paralysed, and her mind anyway supplied no words. Her mouth opened soundlessly. She swallowed.

'Pete?' she said, certain that she must have heard him wrongly.

'Sukie, there is no way I can not stand for Kentish Weald in this election.'

He was looking down at his glass,

'You – you're going to stand again? Pete?'

'Yes. Sukie, this was not what I had planned, obviously. I meant to get out in time for them to find a new candidate before the election. I blame myself for delaying. But events have just moved too fast. I can't do anything else, you must see that.'

'Pete, no, you don't mean this.' She put her glass down, shaking her head.

He stretched a hand out to her, but she did not seem to notice it. Her eyes searched his face, imploring him to be joking. She found no reassurance there.

'Pete, you can't! It's a heaven-sent opportunity to get out, surely you see that!'

Her voice was low, but the passion in it was intense.

Peter felt anger rising in him.

'Oh, for goodness' sake, Sukie, don't be naïve. How can I possibly walk out on them all now? A month before a general election? I could never look myself in the face again.'

'What's naïve about the truth?' Susanna's voice was rising now, and she stretched her arms wide. 'For God's sake, Peter, the whole thing was a mistake from the beginning! It's made you miserable, you know that, we all know that. You said you wished you had never done it! You've said again and again that you wanted to get out. You – you told me so. How *can* you suddenly say you are going on? It could mean another five *years*, don't you see? How *can* you?'

She crossed her arms and looked at the ceiling, breathing deeply to steady herself.

Peter got up and walked to the other side of the room. He felt rattled and upset. He was not used to Susanna so passionate. He had expected her to argue that his decision was a mistake, but in her usual detached way, not with this strange desperation. He turned and looked at her. He must keep calm.

'Of course I know that, Sukie. I'm not stupid. But they chose me, Sukie, the local party, the Kentish Weald Conservatives; they chose me, and I can't let them down. There's always a fall in the vote with a new candidate, and with the government as unpopular as it is at the moment . . . Well, we just shouldn't be having an election now, midwinter, at the worst time for us.'

'That's not your concern,' said Susanna stubbornly. Her face was pale, and her lips held thinly together.

'Sukie, I can't just abandon them. I *have* to stand, don't you see? A new candidate just wouldn't have time to work himself in, and make himself known. The Lib Dem candidate, Horton, is both local *and* popular. He'd be in there with more than a fighting chance. Supposing we lost the seat to him? It would be like kicking them all in the teeth, all the people who have supported me these three years. I know some of them are pains in the neck, but there are friends, too, in the constituency, and they have given so much of their time to working for the party, and for me, too. You must see, Sukie? I just can't *do* that to them.'

He was pleading with her now. He knew that his own conscience would not let him drop out, but he needed her agreement as never before. And never before had Susanna shown him so clearly that she disagreed with him. The strength of her opposition shook him.

'Why should *they* come before your own family? Do they matter more than me and your children? We've had enough, Pete. More than enough.'

'Stop it,' said Peter sharply. 'Listen to me, Sukie, please! There is another risk if I walked out now: you know how right-wing our executive is now – they might choose an anti-Europe candidate. There is a minority of people on the committee who would vote for a Eurosceptic if he were blind, deaf and dumb. I would be handing the decent people of the constituency to the wolves! Now what do you say? Do you understand what I am telling you?'

Susanna had turned away and was looking at her watch.

'I have to go and fill the haynets,' she said, with a tremor in her voice. 'Lunch . . . after that. About twenty minutes. All right?'

Peter caught her by the arm as she moved towards the door.

'Sukie, please don't clam up on me. I need you to understand.'

'I understand, Pete,' she said, refusing to catch his eye, 'I just find it impossible to believe. Can we leave it now, please? I can't go on.'

She hummed wildly as she walked towards the stables, to keep the despair out of her mind. She needed breathing space.

Peter stared after her through the window. Why the hell, he wondered, had he not acted sooner? Still, he had been so sure that she would appreciate the jam he was in now, once he had explained it, and support him as she had always done. Of course the simple escape to normal life was tempting – God knew he had thought about it often enough – but Susanna had a perfectly good conscience too and she should have been able to see that he had no alternative but to go on. He knew, as certainly as he knew anything, that his decision to stand was the honourable one, however uncomfortable he found it. Why could Susanna not see it too?

He realised that never in their married life had she talked to him as she had today, or argued so passionately to persuade. In fact, she never normally tried to persuade or dissuade him at all, always displaying with him, or with the children, that conviction she had that sensible people knew what was right for themselves. She would discuss, but never overtly try to influence a decision.

And yet now, here she was, angry, obdurate in her refusal to accept that he knew, without question, exactly where his duty lay. He could not understand her attitude. He had expected her to be disappointed, but not this. He felt confused, and disoriented. The prospect of continuing with a life that now gave him no pleasure, and having to do it without Susanna's willing support, was unspeakably bleak to contemplate.

The telephone rang. He dropped into a chair beside it. After several rings he picked up the receiver. It was his constituency chairman.

Peter listened briefly, and then drew a deep breath, and let it out again.

'Yes, Cyril,' he said. 'As you say, here we go again . . . Yes, I can come to a meeting. I don't need to go back to London, so as early as you like in the morning . . . Indeed, there is a lot of planning to do . . . Yes, I'll tell her. And I'm sure she would send hers back. Goodbye.'

He leant back and shut his eyes. He felt as if he had swallowed a lump of lead.

Chapter 14

'Good morning. This is the election campaign office of the Green Party candidate for Kentish Weald.'

Leonora's voice on the telephone was bright with excitement.

'Hello, Leo! What's all this?'

'Mum, isn't this exciting? I'm going to be running Andrew's campaign office, and I thought I would ring Dad for a few tips.'

'He's not in at the moment,' said Susanna. 'He's – he's in Wraybury.'

'Mum? What's the matter? You sound funny.'

'Do I? Bad line. Leo, this may come as a surprise, but Dad is standing again.'

'What! But . . . but . . .' Leonora's voice tailed away.

'I know, I thought so too,' said her mother. 'But he is. It's all because of the election coming so suddenly. You had better talk to him about it, if you—'

Her daughter interrupted her.

'Mum, is this a good idea, honestly?'

'Leo, if he wants to do it, he'll do it. He's just gone to the first campaign meeting at the office.'

Leonora paused, disconcerted.

'The twins are going to be . . . well, surprised,' she said. 'They told me he was definitely going to be getting out. What made . . . ? Oh well. Mum, if he really is standing again, will he think I am being disloyal, helping Andrew? He won't mind, will he, do you think? After all, Andrew can't do him much harm – I have to admit that, if I'm being honest. But we are going to work on everyone's green consciences really fiercely and get Andrew a tremendous vote, you wait and see!'

'Well done,' said Susanna, with an attempt to echo Leonora's enthusiasm.

'Dad *will* understand, won't he?' her daughter burbled on. 'I don't really feel disloyal, because actually most of the time, about most things, Andrew talks just like Dad. It's just that he feels extra strongly about the environment and saving the world.'

'Don't worry, Leo,' said Susanna, trying to put warmth into her voice. 'I'm sure Dad understands. Of course he does. You *must* work for Andrew. It's what getting married is about. Good luck.'

'Thanks, Mum. I knew you'd be great. Bye for now.'

'Leo rang because she is worried it might upset Peter that she is working for Andrew's election campaign,' Susanna said to Rachel. 'I told her it's what getting married is about, and then I wondered.'

'Well, it is, isn't it?' said her mother. 'That and food. There's no greater bringer together or separater than, say, garlic. Imagine not agreeing on garlic. What's the matter?'

'Oh, Ma, I hardly know how to tell you. Pete's standing again.'

'What?'

'He's standing again in the election.'

Rachel put down her knife and the Y-shaped piece of hazel stick that she was whittling, and looked over her glasses at her daughter.

'I couldn't believe it either, when he told me,' said Susanna miserably.

'Did you talk?' said Rachel.

'We talked. Well, worse than that . . . I mean, we . . . argued. Not very happy, really. But there is no talking him out of it, and I don't suppose I should, even if I could. He is quite sure that it is Right with a capital R. It's all to do with not letting people down, and he's in one of those conviction moods, when you have to do something however much it hurts. You know?'

'Oh, I know, I certainly know,' said Rachel, her voice harsh with old sorrow. 'And I know how it is when you feel it is wrong to argue against that conviction.'

'It's like Father again, isn't it?'

Susanna would not have dared say this if her mother had not made an obvious reference to her own marriage.

'Not unlike,' said Rachel. 'Well, different, but it does produce a sense of *déja vu*. No, this is stupid. It is not like what happened to your father at all. He was giving a total commitment, a commitment for life, which is what Christianity means. Peter is only committing himself for five years, at the very most. It could be much less, Susanna.'

'But it won't be much less, you know,' said Susanna despondently. 'If he gets in, and of course he will, he'll say that he must stay and not cause a bye-election, because the Association would have no money left to fight it after all the expense of the general election. So he'll wait again until it gets near the next general election before he says he's not going to stand. He's stuck in there, don't you see? He is just too honourable, that's the trouble.'

Rachel said gently: 'Would you have him otherwise? In any case, I seem to remember you telling me that he hated the compromises of political life. You should be glad his honour is coming through undamaged.'

'Don't tease, Ma. I feel so depressed.'

She sat watching Rachel using her scissors to cut a long thin strip of rubber from an old bicycle tyre.

'Ma,' she said, 'tell me about my father.'

Rachel said nothing for some time.

'It's such a long time ago,' she began. 'Sometimes I wonder whether my memories are what it was really like, or what I think it was like. I think it had been in his mind for a long time, but he never talked to me about it.'

'Becoming a monk?' said Susanna.

'Not just an ordinary monk. Some monks live in the community, do things, run schools or whatever. I could almost have understood that. No, this was a closed order. Goodbye, shut the door, never see you again. Well, not quite. One visit, once a year.'

'Why, Ma? Why did he want to do that?'

'Oh, Su, can you imagine how often I asked myself that? Both then and since? I still don't know. He was totally – how can I express it? – gripped by his need for it. I wouldn't use the word possessed, because he was all goodness. I suppose the expression is "called". He felt he was "called".'

'Did it hurt terribly?'

There was another long pause, before Rachel spoke again. She was working on the hazel stick, cutting neat clefts in the wood.

'Yes, I suppose it did. It's hard to remember the feeling now. It made me feel very – redundant. I think the worst thing was feeling it was wrong for him, but not being able to be sure. You see, I couldn't disentangle my own need – my not unnatural need for him – from my gut feeling that he was making a mistake for himself. Do you remember him, Su?'

'Not at all,' said Susanna.

'No, you were too young. Perhaps just as well. My memory is that he was so happily certain at the start that it was the right thing to do. Then there are stages, points where you can draw back. It's a long process, and the joy seemed to go out of him as it went on, but his conviction never changed. I couldn't believe it wasn't all wrong for him, but I just couldn't bring myself to try and stop him. Probably I couldn't have stopped him, anyway.'

'*Was* it wrong for him?'

Susanna was shaken. She had always assumed that her father, at least, had been happy with his decision to become a monk, whatever it might have done to his small family.

'I am afraid so,' said Rachel, 'and the sad thing is that it took him only a relatively short time to find it out. I guessed things were not working when he asked me to stop visiting. He told me more, in a letter written only two years before he died. It was a tragic sort of apology, in a way. He didn't lose his faith, or anything like that, but he felt he had "misinterpreted the call", which was how he put it. I will show the letter to you one day.'

'Poor Ma. Poor, poor Father. Did you see him before he died?' Susanna was tentative about treading this ground that they had hardly ever met on before.

'No,' said Rachel, testing the strength of the rubber in her hand, 'he didn't want it. And I don't think I really did, either. Perhaps I should have gone, but like you, I still felt that people tend to know best what is good for them. He was only thirty-nine, you know, when he died.'

Susanna sat for a little, watching her mother's active hands.

Then she said: 'I suppose we are very alike, you and I.'

'Correction. You are like I was,' said Rachel. 'I have changed. I would never let such a thing happen now. But, as I said before, what Peter is doing is not for life.'

'It is, Ma, in a way. It is changing things between him and me and pushing us apart as nothing else has ever done. When we are easy together now, it's like an echo from the past. And his relationship with the children has changed. And the worst thing is that by the time he has finished they will all be grown-up, and gone, and that is something we can never get back. It is now that he should be available, and close to them. They need him, and so do I.'

She paused, and swallowed, then went on:

'Perhaps we could cope with it – I could cope with it – if only he were happy or fulfilled or something. But he isn't. He's disillusioned and miserable. And, oh dear, so am I.'

There were tears in her voice, and her mother heard them. 'You don't have to be,' said Rachel briskly, rolling the rubber round the hazel stick and putting it on the mantelpiece.

She patted the top of her computer.

'Give me a day,' she said. 'I have to do some thinking. I will feed it all into the system, and then – yes – I will write a programme. You wait.'

She was speaking metaphorically. What Rachel in fact did was get into her car and go and talk to Ellie Fittall. She had been going to go anyway. They had plans to deal with a tiresome cat that had taken a fancy to Ellie's window box. Rachel took with her the newly made catapult.

When Cyril Eversley arrived at the Association office, three rooms above an estate agent's in the High Street of Wraybury, it was humming, but the sound was not coming from the kind of activity that Leonard Peacock had planned. Lelia was pushing an elderly vacuum cleaner backwards and forwards over the contents of a packet of white granulated sugar that the agent had gesticulated off her desk as he argued with the man who had come to fix the office computer.

'It's not picking up,' she said. 'I told you dozens of times that it wasn't working right, so it's your own fault. Look at that, it's just not picking up.'

Peacock looked at the white grains, now fairly evenly distributed over a wide area of carpet.

'Can't you get a brush, or something?'

'Not if you want these agendas ready before they arrive,' said Lelia pertly. 'Anyway, the cleaners lock the cupboard when they go. And you'll all have to have your coffee without sugar. So.'

Peacock turned back to the computer fixer, who was standing with his hands in his pockets, grinning.

'How long?' said Peacock.

'Dunno. Few days. I'll have to take it back to the shop.'

'You can't have a few days. I haven't got a few days,' said Peacock irascibly. 'There's an election on, in case you haven't noticed. You'll have to get me another one while you're mending it.'

'I dunno about that,' said the youth. 'You'll have to speak to the boss.'

After he had left, staggering under the weight of the computer, Peacock thought how intolerable it was to have a spotty child making him feel a fool over his own office machinery. He wished he had accepted the Central Office computer course. He added these to his mental list of grievances, headed by being landed with a plain, stupid wife, a secretary with no sense of respect and an MP who should never have got the job.

'Stop that – noise, Lelia,' said Peacock, deleting his expletive just in time. Her attitude to him had never changed, however much he had varied his to her, and he had long since turned his attentions to the new girl behind the bar in the club. But to offend Lelia now could upset three weeks of campaigning. 'Just leave it, do it later. You're only spreading it.'

'Anything to oblige,' said Lelia, switching off. 'How many agendas do you want?'

Cyril Eversley crunched into the room, looked down in mild surprise, and said, 'What's all that?'

Peacock ignored him, except to say, 'The computer's crashed. I'm trying to get another one, while it's being mended.'

'Heavens,' said Eversley, 'what sort of crash?' He looked curiously at the white grains on the floor. 'I never knew . . . that stuff looks more like sugar than . . . Oh, I see. Crashed. Kaput. On the blink. I see. Well, it's not a very good time for that to happen, is it?'

Peacock showed his teeth to his chairman.

'Political timing is not something they program into computers, actually.'

Rupert Hascombe had entered and was hanging up his coat during this exchange.

'Morning, Leonard. Morning, Cyril,' he said. 'I suppose that means we won't have the canvassing lists for a day or two?'

'I'll have them, somehow, by Friday,' said Peacock. 'That's when all the branch chairmen will come here. I'll be distributing the posters and car stickers then, if the printers keep their promise. We've got some left from the bye-election, too.'

Other members of the executive committee arrived, followed by Peter Westerham. Peacock motioned them into chairs and the meeting seemed to get under way without any input from the chairman. Cyril felt irritated but helpless. Being Association chairman was not at all as he had imagined it would be. Peacock always managed to make him feel redundant.

'You know, I did wonder.'

Rachel and Ellie Fittall were in the kitchen of a ground-floor council flat in a close just off Wraybury High Street. A teapot swathed in alternate bands of purple and white knitted wool sat between them, and they were drinking out of mugs inscribed with rampant crabs. Rachel had just put Susanna's problem to Ellie.

'I did wonder,' Ellie repeated, 'before Christmas. He was looking so tired, and grey, like, and she never took her eyes off him while he was speaking. You could tell she was worried.'

'It's been going on for some time, actually,' said Rachel. 'And there's no doubt he was intending to get out before the election – he even told me that. It's just that the election has taken us all by surprise.'

'I don't see what's to be done,' said Ellie. 'He's a good lad, Peter, and he's right – I don't know how they would manage if he upped and off just before an election. You'd lose all his loyalty vote, if you got somebody new now, and the party's not exactly popular at the moment.'

'Ellie, they're having a meeting today, to plan it all. Why aren't you there? I thought you were always involved.'

'Not this time, dear. I told that Peacock I didn't want to be on no campaign committee. He was a pain in the arse last time, and I'm not working for him again. I don't like him, and I make no secret of that, and the way he treats his wife is something shocking. Treats her like dirt, poor Seelveea. But that's another story.'

Rachel returned to the subject in hand.

'Ellie, how are we going to deal with this? It's crazy for Peter to stay an MP when he really doesn't want to, and it's destroying his family. Couldn't we find someone to stand against him? Another Conservative?'

'No, dear,' said the old woman. 'You can't do that. All you'd do is split the vote.'

'And then?'

'Well,' said Ellie, 'if you did that, you'd have that Horton, the Lib Dem getting in. Bound to.'

'Would that be so terrible?' said Rachel.

Ellie cackled with laughter.

'I can see you're no political animal, Rachel Willoughby,' she said. 'Here, let's top up your tea. That's high treason, that is. My, I'd like to see that Peacock's face if that happened! It would finish him, that's for sure. And there's plenty people would like to see the back of him.'

'Ellie, I'm serious. Surely having a Lib Dem MP elected for a few years in Kentish Weald is a small price to pay to save Peter and Susanna's family life?'

But Ellie was still thinking about Peacock.

'I wouldn't mind having a go at him, I must say. They'd be sure to give him the boot if something like that happened. And then poor Seelveea could go too. She hates it here, with all the local girls laughing at her. There's not one of 'em he hasn't had a go at.'

'What's he like, this fellow Horton?' said Rachel. 'Is that the name of the Lib Dem candidate? I saw him at the bye-election, I suppose, but I never talked to him.'

'Pardon?' said Ellie. 'Oh, he's all right, as far as he goes, Lance Horton. He's chief executive of the water board and I'm still getting water out of me taps. No, I don't expect he'd do much harm, supposing he did get in. We'd get the seat back the next time round, anyway. No doubt about that. Kentish Weald has been Conservative since the Domesday Book, I reckon. My Fred used to say they could put up a monkey and it would get elected.'

'What do you think, Ellie? It's an idea, isn't it? You know everyone in the constituency. There must be someone who would stand, who is well enough known to take a good share of Peter's votes.'

'Well, there's quite a few as would get Conservative votes if they promised to hang the football hooligans on sight and to drop a bomb on Brussels. There's some real fancy voters, out there.'

'A real right-winger – yes!' said Rachel. 'Can you think of someone who'd be willing to do it?'

Ellie's not inconsiderable mind was now bent on the subject.

'I can think of one or two who'd like to do it; that Terry Lowther, you know, the Young middle-aged Conservative? But no one would vote for him – not enough, anyway. And I can think of one or two who would collect the votes, but they wouldn't want to upset the party. It's asking a good bit, you know, Rachel; and it's hard work, too, fighting a campaign.'

'That's what we need, then,' said Rachel, counting off on her fingers. 'Someone well known, popular, who's willing to work hard, who wants to help Peter, without saying so, who will preach pure right-wing propaganda . . .'

'. . . and who doesn't mind splitting the vote so that Horton gets the seat,' said Ellie. 'It's a tall order, whichever way up you look at it.'

They drank from their mugs and thought deeply. Suddenly Rachel raised her eyes, and met Ellie's. The same thought had occurred to them both.

After an hour, Ellie made another pot of tea.

'If it's not here by ten o'clock tomorrow morning, I will crucify you, I promise. If you let me down, you will never sell another thing in this town, I'm telling you.'

The Conservative Association had been regular customers for some years, though their demand for office equipment was not especially high. However, business was a bit slack, otherwise Don Smart, owner/manager of Smart Offices, would have told Leonard Peacock where to put his computer and slammed the receiver down. As it was, he drew in a deep breath and said:

'Mr Peacock, I will be there personally at ten o'clock, and I will personally transfer all the information onto the other disks so that this machine can read it. And I will personally show you and your secretary how to use it, which is no problem, because the keyboard and functions are almost identical.'

'They'd better be,' snarled Peacock, 'because otherwise you will personally be round here every day for the next three and a half weeks.'

Crashing the receiver down, he turned and glared aggressively at his wife, who was standing by his desk.

'What do you want?' he said.

'You asked me to come,' said Sylvia Peacock meekly.

'No, I didn't. Yes, I did. Tomorrow, though, not now. There's a bloody cock-up over the computer, and we have got to get a whole lot of paperwork done tomorrow morning. You're going to have to come in and use the typewriter, because Lelia needs help. I want you here at eight-thirty.'

'I was going over to the hospital to see Mother . . .' said his wife quietly.

'Well, you can't. Now get out. I'm busy.'

He got up and went to a filing cabinet and dragged open a drawer.

Sylvia Peacock stood looking at the back of his head for a few moments. She considered the greasy strands that were raked across a balding patch and wondered why he thought she put up with it. Perhaps the answer was that he never thought about it at all. But she had been thinking, for some time now, and wondering herself why she put up with it. And she had not come up with any good reason. But as long as her mother was alive, she would try to carry on. It wouldn't be long now.

Then she went home.

'Mother, have you finally gone totally mad?' said Susanna. She had been out for an hour on their one remaining riding pony.

'No, Susanna, it's a brilliant plan.'

Rachel talked eagerly, following her daughter as she walked towards the house, a saddle over her linked arms and a bridle swinging below it. 'And think what fun! Ellie, who really knows all there is to be known about Kentish Weald, is quite sure that you are the one person who could do it. You are well known all around the constituency, and she seems to think people like you.'

Susanna swung round to face her.

'But stand against my own husband! How could I do such a thing? And what's the point?'

'The point is that you are a good old-fashioned Conservative with far right-wing views and you are appalled at Peter's liberal, leftish, pro-European stance. And you think, in your feminine arrogance, that you could do a better job than him, now that you've watched him for a while.'

'But Ma, none of this is true! I don't, and I'm not and I most certainly couldn't, whatever—'

'Of course I know that, Su,' said Rachel impatiently. 'Don't pick nits. That is just the story. You have to have a story, for the press and for people who ask. The press are going to love it, by the way. Publicity certainly won't be a problem.'

'But I could never beat Peter. I wouldn't even want to.'

Susanna sat on the low stone wall surrounding the paved terrace and put the saddle down beside her.

'Let me explain, my dear child,' said Rachel, placing herself astride the wall and facing her bemused daughter. 'You don't need to beat him. All you have to do is syphon off enough votes from the loonier right-wing element in the constituency, and split the Conservative vote, so that the Liberal Democrat gets in. Then Peter is free! They may all wonder what sort of a dotty family you are, but what do you care about that?'

Susanna put her hand on her mother's arm.

'Ma, you had better stop,' she said firmly. 'I am not going to be rushed into anything like this. I really appreciate your taking the trouble to think all this up, you and Ellie, and I know you are both trying to help, but it is wild; I mean, what the twins would call really hairy. What I mean is that it is not, well, realistic.'

'Su,' said Rachel, 'unrealistic our plan may seem, but it is entirely practical. Promise me just to think about it.'

'I will, I promise, think about it.'

She hardly did, until during the night she realised that Peter, who had been tossing restlessly earlier, had left their bed and moved into the spare room next door. He had come in late, and they had talked very little before going to bed. Somehow, avoiding the main subject of both of their thoughts left them with very little to say to each other. They were polite, but distant.

Now Susanna lay with her hands behind her head gazing into the darkness, bleakly surveying the situation. In theory her mother's plan was very neat, and though she saw difficulties of implementation she could hardly fault it. There was just one problem. Suppose that it worked; suppose that in twenty-four days' time Peter was out and free, but suppose that he did *not* feel relieved and grateful? Suppose instead that he was angry and resentful, felt humiliated by this female conspiracy; suppose he never forgave her?

Her mind swung agonisingly between the possibilities. The feeling of their family happiness crumbling around them seemed at times worse than the possibility of a Peter weighed down by a personal loss of face. But minutes later the thought of his feeling permanently shamed by her action became unbearable, and she resolved to fight beside him, as she had always done. But then, how could she conspire to keep him in a life that made him so patently unhappy? Supposing his health started to suffer – it was suffering already, in fact. Surely he needed her help, now, to release him from an impossible situation? But would he see it that way? She felt weak with indecision, and incapable of sleep.

But she did sleep, and dreamed not of monks, nor of canvassers, but of tropical fish lying at the bottom of a glass tank, gasping weakly for air because they were not used to living under water. Somehow she must get them out, but her arms were not long enough.

When she woke in the morning she found that she had made up her mind. The reappearance in the bathroom cupboard of Peter's ulcer pills helped to sweep away any residual doubts.

'Ma, I will do it.'

'Good,' said Rachel. 'It's wonderful what a good night's sleep will do.'

She outlined some of the detail that she and Ellie had discussed.

'It's an amazing idea,' said Susanna, swept along by her mother's enthusiasm. 'But we'd have no helpers, or canvassers or anything.'

'Don't worry about that,' sad Rachel dismissively. 'Ellie will be your agent, and I shall run your office. That's going to be in Ellie's flat – very central, perfectly placed, and I'm taking my computer round tomorrow.'

'Good Lord,' said Susanna. 'You didn't even wait for me to agree.'

'No. I knew you would agree, when you saw what sense it made.'

'God knows what Peter will say when he hears.'

'Susanna!' Rachel glared at her. 'Not a *word* to Pete, until it's too late for him to stop you. Promise. Ellie has a plan for that too.'

'You and Ellie and your plans. What if I had said no?'

'I knew you better than that,' said Rachel, who had had severe doubts as to whether she would be able to persuade her daughter. 'But if you *had* said no, I had quite a fancy for standing myself. However Ellie thinks you have more street cred.'

It was a relief to Susanna that the twins were both working for their finals in the summer, and therefore not proposing to come home at all during the election campaign. This removed the immediate necessity to explain what she was doing, or to try to gain their approval. They would certainly hear, in time, but she would deal with that when it happened. Meanwhile she sent them each a postcard telling them that their father was standing again. She knew that Mark in particular would be saddened by the news.

Leonora was not a problem. She was totally wrapped up in her work for Andrew, and thought, ate, drank and lived for the campaign. Her parents expected to see little of her until the election was over. She turned up, however, on a flimsy excuse two evenings after her telephone call.

'Dad, you don't mind about Andrew and me, do you?'

'What an odd question,' said her father, looking up from his newspaper. 'You know we are all pleased about Andrew and you.'

'No, I mean that he is standing against you again in the election?'

'Ah,' said Peter, 'that's what you mean by mind. My dearest Leonora, anyone in the world can stand against me at the election without my taking the slightest offence and without losing a mite of my good esteem. He's still keen, then?'

'I think he really seriously wants to get into the House of Commons, and at the moment the Green Party is the only one that appeals to him.'

'Well,' said Peter, 'I wish him luck. He has a long haul ahead of him, in one of the minor parties.'

'It's sticking to your beliefs and doing what you feel is right that matters, and I quote my honoured father,' said Leonora.

'Yes,' said Peter, staring at her, looking through and beyond her. 'It sounds so simple, doesn't it?'

Susanna heard the hardening in his tone.

'We must remember to send Andrew a good luck message before the count,' said Peter after their daughter had left. 'I would hate him to think that there was any awkwardness between us. Because there isn't.'

'No,' said Susanna. 'She was a little worried.'

'Anyone has a perfect right to stand for parliament who can find ten sponsors to nominate them and five hundred pounds for the deposit. Whatever Andrew's political affiliations, I am proud of him, aren't you?'

'Oh, yes,' said Susanna. 'Of course. I agree with all you say. Anyone has a right to their political views. Um . . . and to stand for parliament.'

It seemed to Peter, to his intense relief, that Susanna had reverted to the interested observer of a wife that he was used to. He was desperately anxious for this to be true, and tried to persuade himself that the awkwardness that remained in the atmosphere was in his imagination. There was an air of distracted absorption about Susanna that he was not used to. They had still not talked again about Peter's decision to fight the election, or about their argument. This suited Susanna, as did Peter's apparent acceptance that she would not play any part in his campaign. So it was not mentioned. They both struggled slightly to keep conversation going at mealtimes, and each privately ached over the disagreement between them. Peter at least felt firm in his conviction that he was doing what had to be done; Susanna had no such feeling of certainty; she only knew that she was taking a bigger risk than ever before in her life. What they had in common, but could not admit, was their mutual longing for the new start they hoped they could somehow make once the election was over.

'Red for Labour, blue for Peter, yellow for Horton, green for the Greens. I haven't any more colours. Problem.'

Rachel was sitting at Ellie's kitchen table, which had now been pushed up against the sitting-room wall. On it sat the grey bulk of the computer, dominating and looking strangely alien in the small room. Ellie's parents stared from their frame on the mantelpiece, her mother sitting with her hands folded on her black-skirted lap and a bemused expression, her father standing behind her chair, one proprietorial hand on her shoulder, looking slightly apoplectic in his high white collar.

'What are you going to do with it, once you've finished?' said

Ellie, watching the monitor screen over Rachel's shoulder, her expression not unlike her mother's. 'Cook it?'

'Ellie, you can't run a political campaign without a pie chart,' said Rachel patiently. 'It gives us a visual image of how the parties stand, and, well, encourages us. That slice of the pie is Horton's share of the vote at the last election, that one is Peter's and so on. The trouble is only having four colours. Wait – I know what I can do. I'll make Susanna blue too, but dotted, and the fringe parties red dotted. That leaves two other dotty sections for imponderables.'

'What are we going to call our party?' said Ellie, giggling. 'Susanna's Party doesn't sound quite right. And I don't fancy the Dotty Party, not if I am going to work for it.'

'We'll discuss it when she comes,' said Rachel. 'She should be here soon. We may have a bit of trouble with her over the names on the nomination papers, so we can use the party name question to distract her. She's scared silly, you know, Ellie. We have to keep her courage up, or she'll change her mind.'

'I'll put the kettle on,' said Ellie. 'Then I'll pop down the road and get some more tea. We'll need a lot of that.'

'And I'll do a print-out of this. When we've got it right, and the spreadsheets, or rather, the bar-and-column charts, I'll get them blown up down at the copyshop. We want the walls covered with charts, for when we get the press in.'

'Blind them with science, eh?' said Ellie, putting her slippers in the grate and pulling on her outdoor shoes.

Mrs Peacock had been given Lelia's old chair, and after several hours of typing, her back, which had not done this sort of work for some years, was aching. She stretched. It was half past one. She supposed she would be allowed some time off for lunch. In the next room her husband and Lelia were still arguing over the computer keyboard. Mr Smart, having spent an hour working with them, had finally left.

Mrs Peacock walked quietly towards the door of the inner office. She saw Lelia's bent behind in her skimpy skirt and noticed that she wore stockings, not tights. She found it hard to understand how the girls now went for that. She remembered her own pleasure as a girl when the advent of tights had liberated her from the tyranny of roll-on and suspenders. She wondered if Lelia often showed her stocking tops in the office, and found to her relief that she no longer cared.

Peacock sensed her presence and swung round.

'Have you finished those lists?' he said curtly.

'Nearly,' said Sylvia Peacock. 'I could do with a break.'

Peacock looked at his watch.

'Yes. You go down to the corner and get us all some sandwiches,' he said. 'Cheese and pickle for me, and a bacon. What will you have, Lelia?'

As she took their orders Mrs Peacock thought it might be better to spend her own money, rather than ask for petty cash. He seemed in a reasonable mood.

'Take these,' her husband went on, 'and put them in the middle drawer of my desk. We'll need them when we get our own computer back.'

She took the computer disks from him, and did as he asked. Then, with relief, went down the stairs and out into the street. She stood for a moment and drew long draughts of air into her lungs, before crossing over and proceeding down the far pavement. She stopped by the estate agent's window, and read the cards below photographs of semi-detached houses for sale. Years ago she and Leonard had stood together, gazing in windows like this. Her brain was not taking in what she read, and soon she only saw her own reflection in the glass. It was of a drab, fiftyish face, not very fat, not very thin, not very anything, really. A face that stared miserably back at hers, and whose cheeks were running with the same tears.

'Are you all right, dear?' a voice said.

Sylvia Peacock gulped, and turned to see the kindly face of Ellie Fittall close to her shoulder.

'What you need, dear,' said Ellie, 'is a nice cup of tea. Come on. We'll go down to Pearson's and you can tell me all about it.'

Gratefully, Sylvia Peacock walked along beside her. She liked Ellie, and wondered only vaguely why they were not going to her flat, which was, after all, only just down the close that they were passing now.

'What on earth am I going to do about that?' said Susanna. 'The papers have to be in on Wednesday, that's the last day for nominations. I can't think of anyone I can ask.'

She had been helping her mother pin up huge sheets of paper on Ellie's sitting-room walls. She tapped her finger on a schedule giving vital dates up to election day. She had noticed an appointment in the office of the electoral returning officer.

'The nomination?' said Rachel. 'Your agent, Mrs Fittall, has it all in hand. She has already got you ten highly respectable names from the New Horizons Home. She helps there on Tuesday afternoons, and they love you, she says. You went to their Christmas party last year and you seem to have charmed them all. They are not entirely clear as to why you want to stand for parliament, and I suspect Ellie may have fudged the issue slightly. That, however, is not our business. The point is, if that is what you want, ten senior citizens, all on the Kentish Weald electoral roll, are quite happy to nominate you.'

Ellie had just come in, and was removing her coat.

'That's right,' she said. 'More than willing.'

'Ellie, you are even worse than my mother. You are ruthless,' said Susanna. 'Thank you.'

'I have promised you will come with me to get their signatures,' said Ellie, 'and mind you are nice to the matron, because she's a friend of mine, and she has turned a bit of a blind eye.'

'Evidently some of the residents have even offered to lick envelopes,' said Rachel.

'Envelope licking doesn't happen much nowadays, I gather,' said Susanna. 'All candidates get a free postal delivery of their election manifesto leaflet to every household in the constituency.'

'And that's not really what we need,' said Rachel thoughtfully, 'because we couldn't possibly afford to have sixty-five thousand leaflets printed. And even printing them on my machine, I could never do that number. In any case, we're not interested in the committed Labour and Lib Dem voters. All we want is a good number of the Conservative ones to vote for you.'

'That's it,' said Ellie, 'a selective drop. You can print them, Rachel, on your magic box there, just for the two or three thousand to the paid-up members.'

'We would need to get the names of all the known Conservatives,' said Susanna. 'But how would we do that? This is where Peacock and Peter have a real advantage over us, with all those files in the office. Ma, at the bye-election they had canvass sheets for every street in the constituency, with the likely voting habit of almost every person marked.'

'If we could only get our hands on those,' said Rachel longingly.

'Actually,' said Susanna, 'if we had the canvass lists, we could post to the paid-up Conservative members. We could afford it, with what we're saving on printing posters and campaign leaflets. And then in any spare time we could deliver as many as we can to other supposed Conservative voters. Not the country ones, that would be impossible, in three weeks. But we could have a good go at the towns and villages. After all, pushing slips through letterboxes is much quicker than canvassing. You are sure, are you both, that we really can do without posters?'

'What we are going to do is better than a million posters,' said Rachel. 'After all, the name Westerham is going to be all over the constituency anyway, on Peter's posters. No one's likely to forget it.'

'And just one meeting?' said Susanna.

'Yes, the church meeting. The old-fashioned single candidate meetings are out of date,' said Ellie dismissively. 'Too much telly now. Nobody comes. But they will come to this one, because they like to see all the candidates together.'

'I hope they ask me,' said Susanna.

'Oh, they'll ask you, all right, once your nomination as a candidate has been accepted. They ask them all. It will be in St John's. It holds hundreds of people, and being a church, it's neutral territory, see?'

'Ellie, you know so much about all this – is this just from being on the executive committee?'

'I'll tell you a secret,' said Ellie, laying a finger against her nose. 'My Fred was a trainee agent for a while, before he joined the railways. So if I have never been an agent, I have been an agent's wife, and you can't help picking it up.'

'Well, I think I'm incredibly lucky to have you working for me,' said Susanna. 'Even if we fail, I will never forget what you are both doing to try to help me.'

'Sound of distant violins,' said Rachel. 'The trouble is, it's all very well planning, but we can't do much of it without the canvass sheets. That's where we're stuck. Is there no way, no one who would have copies from the last election? No? I suppose not. Not the sort of thing you would keep to browse through in the long winter evenings. Ellie! Are you all right?'

The old lady was sitting rigidly upright, grasping the arms of her chair. Her eyes and mouth were wide open and she was staring at the computer. She turned slowly to look at them. She ran her tongue slowly over her top lip.

'Don't count on it,' she whispered, 'but it's just come to me mind that we may have a very valuable secret weapon.'

Chapter 15

Ed Forman, the deputy acting returning officer for the Kentish Weald constituency, looked at his watch. Nine forty-five. He had time for a cup of coffee before they all arrived. He opened the door of his office and stuck his head through.

'How about putting the kettle on, girls?'

But there were no girls there.

He was puzzled. He had heard them chatting only a few minutes earlier. Then he noticed that the door into the passage beyond was open, and he could hear their voices.

'Henny?' he called.

Henny's dark face surrounded by long, thin plaits appeared briefly in the doorway, with wide eyes and a huge grin.

'Oh, Mr Forman, come and look at this. You've never seen anything like it!'

'What is it? Could we have some coffee?'

'Just you come through here, Mr Forman. Or look out of your own window – out in the road. What's going on?'

Forman stood behind the two girls as they gazed down into the market square. There were vans, two large white vans parked on the other side, and in front of his own council office building stood a positive crowd of people, at least twenty, which in Wraybury on a Wednesday morning probably constituted a riot, or unlawful assembly. In Forman's normal position as director of finance to the council it was hardly his business, but as electoral returning officer it might be: the demonstration, or whatever it was, was after all taking place on his doorstep, or very near it.

'What's all this?' he said, reaching into his top pocket for his glasses. With them on his nose he could read the lettering on the vans. BBC. ITV. There were more cars parked about the square than usual, too. He could see now that some of the people in the crowd were carrying large black cameras, dangling from their hands or on their shoulders.

'Do you think it's a film they're making?' said Henny.

'A costume drama?' said the other secretary, Louise, excitedly. 'I wonder who's in it. Do you think they'll need extras? I did a crowd scene once, not costume, though, but I was there all day, and you know all they give me when it was over? Eight pounds, can you believe it?'

'Don't be dumb, Lou,' said Henny, 'it's the meeja, innit?'

There was an air of expectant inactivity about the gathering outside. The journalists were chatting to each other, always keeping an eye on the road round the square.

'Go down there, Henny,' said Forman, 'and see what it's all about. And ask them, politely mind, not to block the path up to the council offices.'

'Can I go too, Mr Forman?' said Louise.

'No. It's nearly time. And I wanted a cup of coffee. Oh, well.'

They watched as half a minute later Henny, her glistening dark plaits swinging around her, walked jauntily up to a man with a long boom and a huge padded microphone. He talked briefly to her, and was interrupted by a man with a notebook who appeared to be questioning her. Two others gathered close.

Forman tapped on the window. Henny didn't hear, but a few seconds later he could see her shaking her head, and then she glanced up at the window. He tapped again. Then Henny turned and ran back into the building. She reappeared in the office.

'You know what it is,' she said breathlessly. 'They're all from the newspapers and that, and it's because the MP's wife is going to stand against her husband! Our MP, wassisname!'

'Did *they* say that?' said Forman. 'You must have that wrong, Henny.'

'No, that's what they said,' said Henny, giggling. 'One of them asked me if I could get him into the building, when the candidates arrived.'

'Certainly not. What did you say?' said Forman.

'I said it was more than my job was worth. You know how much he was going to give me?' said Henny, her wide smile stretching to its limits.

'Henny! You are not to leave this office again.'

'Mr Forman,' said Henny, sulky, hurt.

'All right, Henny. I'm sorry. I apologise. Of course you wouldn't. I'm a bit rattled about this.'

'Ooh, look,' said Louise.

She had been watching two women walking round the square. They were both tall, slimly built and rather similar in appearance. The younger was listening attentively as they walked to what the older woman, with one hand on her arm, was saying into her ear. As they approached the council offices the older one drew ahead and spoke to a journalist. Within seconds the group had gathered round the pair like bluebottles to the scent of meat, cameras on shoulders, microphone booms swinging. The two women were almost invisible in the throng.

'Henny, Louise, get down as fast as you can to the doors, and don't let anyone in. Except the candidates – oh, and their agents. Got that? No one who hasn't got nomination papers. Fast!'

Noticing that some of the journalists were glancing up at his window, Forman decided it would be more dignified to return to his own office. He straightened his tie in the reflection of a print of the waterways of Venice.

Henny burst in through the door from the stairs.

'Mr Forman, I've got her in. They were all there, but I shut the door and locked it! But there's the other lady. Am I to let her in? She says it's her mum.'

'Yes, yes, of course – just no journalists. Can you manage?'

'Watch me!' said Henny, and disappeared again.

Back in the hall, the older woman could be seen through the glass doors, apparently making a speech to the crowd. Henny opened the door slightly, and tapped her shoulder.

'No statements till then,' the woman concluded, and slipped in.

'How do you do,' she said. 'I am Mrs Westerham's press officer.'

As they were led up the stairs, Rachel said to Susanna: 'I told them, in a quarter of an hour at the campaign centre. How's that?'

'Do you think they'll wait?' said Susanna.

'They'll wait all right,' said Rachel. 'I told them Peter doesn't know yet.'

'Oh, Ma.'

Forman greeted Susanna and Rachel in his office, then he excused himself for a moment, on the pretext of ordering three cups of coffee, and went next door.

'Louise,' he said urgently, 'get down fast to the car park. Catch Mr Westerham – you know what he looks like – and tell him to come in the back way. And anyone else who looks like a candidate. No, anyone else who *is* a candidate. Stand by the entrance gate and ask them as they come in. Make sure you see their nomination papers.'

In the absence of the chief executive of the council, who, if he had not been recovering from a hip-replacement operation, would have been the returning officer, Ed Forman was nervous. He knew that the depositing of nomination papers by election candidates was normally a quiet, if formal affair passing unnoticed by the general public, and that the scene out in the square was unprecedented. He also feared that it was unseemly, though possibly not unconstitutional. He was not certain if he had the right to demand that the reporters kept to the roadway, even on the grounds that they were damaging the municipal flowerbeds. But he could at least stop them harassing the candidates.

'May I take your nomination papers, Mrs Westerham?' he said. 'Thank you. Henny, will you check these against the register. And the deposit. Thank you so much. You will receive a receipt for this, of course. And just see if the coffee's ready, will you?'

He tried not to appear flustered, and knew he was failing.

'It is very kind of you,' said Susanna, 'but I don't think we have time for coffee, thank you.'

'No? Well, I won't keep you a moment. And – er – all the family well, I hope? I remember one of your daughters had an accident.'

'Oh, she's fine, now. You will probably be seeing her. She's working for the Green Party candidate. She's engaged to him.'

'*Really?*' said Forman. 'Most interesting. 'You are . . . really quite a political family, it seems.'

'You could say that,' said Susanna.

Henny came through the door from the other office and rushed up to Forman.

'Mr Westerham's here, and another one. I think it's the Labour. What am I to do? They'll have to come through here to get down to the waiting room.'

Forman felt the twitch starting below his right eye. His carefully formulated plans for an efficient and dignified registering of candidates was going hopelessly wrong.

'Mrs Westerham, I just have to give you the papers back, and a receipt for your banker's draft. It won't take a few minutes. But I'll just have to let the other candidates come through, if you don't mind.'

'Why should I mind?' said Susanna.

'Normally, of course, I would take you one by one,' said Forman. 'Yes, ask them to come through, Henny – Henrietta.'

'And how many cups of coffee, then?' said Henny, giggling.

'Oh, dear. Just boil the kettle. I don't suppose anyone will want coffee.'

Peter appeared first in the doorway, and stood for a moment open-mouthed.

'Susanna?' he said, and then smiled. He turned to the electoral returning officer. 'How are you, Mr Forman? I thought I was on time, but I see my wife is even more punctual.'

The two men shook hands, and Peter turned back to Susanna, smiling affectionately, his voice warm.

'Darling. How really sweet of you to come.'

For a moment Susanna's courage failed her. A jab in the back from her mother reminded her of her priorities.

'Pete, I'm here because I have just given Mr Forman my nomination papers as a candidate in the general election.'

There was a brief pause while Forman gulped. How on earth

was he expected to cope with this sort of drama in his office?

'You what?' said Peter, quietly.

'I am fighting this election, as an Independent Conservative,' said Susanna.

Peter stared at her, his smile dying.

Henny walked in again with sheets of white paper.

'Here are the lists, Mr Forman. Louise says they are all checked. And the receipt.'

'Thank you, Henny,' he said weakly, disproportionately grateful for the distraction. He turned to the Labour candidate who was standing near him, wearing a vast red rosette, a red rose pinned to his other lapel, and an incredulous and delighted expression on his face.

'Mr – er – I'm sorry. Good morning. I have to ask you . . . well, would you mind proceeding down the main stairs to the waiting room, this way, and one of the girls will bring you up shortly?'

With evident reluctance, the candidate walked past Peter and Susanna to the door, watching them over his shoulder.

'This is a joke, isn't it, Sukie?' Peter was saying.

'No, it's not,' said Susanna. 'It is quite serious.'

She was not finding this easy. She turned to Forman.

'If that is all I have to do, Mr Forman, I think I should be off.'

'Yes, that's everything, Mrs Westerham,' said Forman. 'Your receipt is in the envelope.'

Peter watched as they shook hands. Then for the first time he caught his mother-in-law's eye. Her face was expressionless. She smiled blandly at him.

'Rachel?' said Peter.

'I am her press officer,' said Rachel.

Peter shook his head wordlessly.

'If you don't mind, Mrs Westerham,' said Forman, 'Henny will show you down to the back entrance, which is into the car park.'

'No, thank you,' said Rachel. 'We'll go out the way we came in. We're not afraid of the press. In fact we have a press conference called for ten-fifteen at our campaign offices.'

She held open the door for Susanna.

'Good morning,' she said, smiling affably before following her down the stairs.

Dumbly, Peter handed Forman his nomination papers.

By the time Peter Westerham got back to the small car park, there were two reporters and a photographer there. They converged on him.

'Mr Westerham? Is it true, sir, that your wife is standing against you in the election?'

Peter stared at the young man. He was still feeling dazed, unsure of himself. The photographer was snapping away.

'Are you standing, Peter,' said the other journalist, 'or is she taking your place?'

'Are you both standing?' said the first. 'Have you both registered as candidates? What party is she standing for?'

Peter was walking towards his car as they followed him, questioning relentlessly. He unlocked the door, and spoke at last.

'I . . . I think you should ask her,' he said, as he got in and shut the door.

He drove out of the car park and down the main street towards the constituency office. It was the sight of the television vans at the entrance to Ravel Close that made him look down the short cul-de-sac. The house at the end, facing the main road, was decked in a huge sign that hung above the windows of the ground-floor flat. The corners were tied with cord stretching to a chimney at one end of the roof and the television aerial at the other, a feat that had been achieved with the help of Rachel's catapult and a great deal of string, and the lower corners were attached to pipes at ground level. The material looked suspiciously like a bed sheet, and the lettering was clearly done by hand. It read, very legibly, INDEPENDENT CONSERVATIVE CAMPAIGN CENTRE.

'Dear God,' said Peter.

His incredulity was warming into anger.

To say that Peacock was angry would be a blatant understatement. He was incandescent with fury, and he did not limit its evidence to Peter. He had thrown a journalist out of his office by the time Peter got there, and there had been time to stoke the flames of his wrath. His temper was already well out of control.

Banging his desk top with his fist he shouted at Peter.

'It has got to be bloody well stopped! I am not going to let some fucking woman do this to me! You get out there and strangle her, and if you don't, I will!'

'You are talking about my wife,' said Peter coldly.

'I know I am talking about your bloody wife. Can't you control her? You can't let her do this! Are you mad, or what? Why didn't you stop her?'

'I have known about this probably about ten minutes longer than you have,' said Peter, sitting down.

Peacock strode about the small room, kicking the furniture.

'She can't do it,' he said viciously.

'She has every right to do it if she wants to,' said Peter. 'Any citizen of the United Kingdom has the right to stand for parliament, representing any party at all or none.'

Peacock's rage was dissipating Peter's sense of bewilderment. He was still angry, he still felt that somehow his wife was trying to make a fool of him, but the agent's reaction, though even more hysterical than he had expected, suddenly began to make sense of Susanna's extraordinary behaviour.

'Oh, so we are going to be reasonable, are we?' snarled Peacock. 'We are going to let our little wife have her fun and not worry, are we? Well, let me tell you that she could lose us the seat with her little frolic. You should know—'

Peacock had worked himself into such a state that he now felt the need to sit down himself. He picked up the stool that he had just kicked over from in front of the computer and perched himself on it facing Peter and jabbing towards him with his finger.

'You should know that because they chose you for the bye-election we lost about eight thousand votes off our majority over the Lib Dems, right? On paper, we are only about four thousand votes ahead now, and this used to be a safe seat!'

He was positively spluttering with emotion, and a drip of saliva was sliding down his chin. The thought crossed Peter's mind that if Susanna's conduct annoyed Peacock as much as this it could not be all bad . . . but he put it aside as unworthy. He knew there was justice in what Peacock was saying. Peacock went on, his voice rising to a grating squeak:

'If she picks up two thousand of our votes – our votes! – and there are enough frigging idiots out there to vote for her just because she has the same name as you, if she does that then Kentish Weald becomes a muddy blarginal!'

Despite himself, Peter laughed, and the colour of Peacock's face deepened a shade.

'You'll laugh,' he hissed, 'when Lance Horton walks off with your seat. You'll laugh then, when you look the biggest c—, the biggest – jerk in England, because you couldn't control your wife.'

At that moment Peacock's own wife opened the door and looked timidly in.

'Leonard,' she said, 'you're wanted on the telephone. It's the *Daily*—'

'Get your fucking face out of here,' Peacock screamed at her.

Sylvia Peacock's face disappeared, and the door shut instantly.

'For goodness' sake, Leonard,' said Peter, horrified. He strode to the door and opened it. There was no one in the outer office.

Peter walked over to the open door opposite, and heard footsteps hurrying down the stairs. He went back into Peacock's office, and found the agent leaning against the desk, breathing heavily.

'If you can calm yourself down,' said Peter, 'we can talk about this rationally. That exhibition was quite unnecessary. Shouting at everyone is not going to solve anything. So listen, Leonard: we are going to have to ignore my wife, who will in any case not be able to run a serious campaign. She hasn't a chance. She will simply be another fringe candidate, with a minimum of helpers. I suggest we make no mention of what she is doing to the press or anyone else, and I think you will find that it will all die away. What we have to concentrate on is running a very effective campaign, and getting all our voters out.'

'Don't you teach me my job,' snarled Peacock.

Peter left him. He sat in his car, his arms folded across the steering wheel, leaning his forehead on his wrists. He felt now not so much angry as lost and confused. Somewhere a few hundred yards away Susanna was embarking upon a course that completely excluded him, setting herself up literally in opposition to him. He did not know how to take it, and his instinctive urge to defend her action to Peacock now seemed indefensibly wet. But how, he asked himself miserably, could he object to what she was doing? It was, after all, only a repetition of what he had done. But an Independent? She must have some political views, though he was blessed if he knew what they were, but standing as an Independent . . . what on earth did she expect to gain by that? She had been perfectly herself at breakfast, as far as he could remember. Had she gone mad during the day?

He sighed, and started the car. Who was fooling whom? He knew, really, that what Peacock had said was the clue. Peter himself was to blame for what Susanna was doing, with his prevarication and indecision. And she had not gone mad. She was just taking a very bizarre initiative. Anger would not get him anywhere, since she was now an officially registered candidate. There was nothing to be done, no way that he could think of out of this ludicrous situation. He simply had to make certain, which would surely not be very difficult, that she did not succeed. Apart from that, what could he do, but carry on?

He turned out of the car park, and found an old tune in his head.

'What can I do, but carry on? So I go on, clopin, clopant . . . whispering she's gone, she's gone, she's gone . . .' The words seemed strangely apposite.

Laughter was better than crying, in the circumstances. He felt like both.

The little office in Ravel Close was busy. After the journalists had left, the furniture had been pushed back into the room, and the computer monitor was glowing. Susanna was grateful to be rushed into planning. She did not want yet to consider the staggered dismay she had seen on Peter's face.

Rachel was sitting at the keyboard, and Susanna and Ellie sat on either side of her, all eyes gazing at the screen.

'I think "nationwide" is stronger than "nationally",' said Susanna.

'All right,' said Rachel, changing a word in the text.

'That should be just below the photograph,' said Ellie, pointing, 'because it makes the women's point. Just to remind them she's a woman.'

'I doubt if they'll forget that,' said Rachel, 'but it would fit in well there. Have you decided which photograph, by the way?'

'Well,' said Susanna, 'if my agent agrees, I think the one last summer on Beachy Head is the best. You can just see a fold of cliff behind me.'

'That's it,' said Ellie. 'That's the one. Standing firm on the bulwarks of Britain. They'll love it.'

'We need a bit more content, though,' said Rachel, 'a bit more inflammatory prose.'

'What about banning all violent films and videos?' said Susanna.

'Oh, I agree with that,' said Ellie.

'Scrap it, then,' said Rachel. 'It must be too reasonable.'

'Oh, I don't think so,' said Susanna. 'Censorship should go down pretty well.'

'All right,' said Rachel, 'shall we have a committee appointed by the Archbishop of Canterbury, Princess Diana and Mary Whitehouse to censor the film industry as a whole?'

Ellie cackled and Susanna fell back laughing in her chair.

'Oh, Ma,' she said, 'you've really found your niche. I think it's time we had a break for lunch.'

'Don't forget,' said Ellie, 'to leave space at the bottom for my name and address, as agent. Otherwise we'll be in all sorts of trouble.'

'I'll put it in now. What's the wording? Published by Ellie Fittall and—'

'Not Ellie, Ethelburga,' said Ellie, somewhat defiantly.

'What?' said Rachel, trying and failing to stifle her laughter.

'And what' s wrong with that?' said Ellie, raising two arthritic fists menacingly. 'I am Sussex born and bred, and it's a Saxon county, so we have good Saxon names, me and my sister. She's Gundreda. Me grandmother was called Gundreda too.'

'Ellie, you never cease to surprise,' said Rachel, tapping again on her keyboard. 'All right, Published by Ethelburga Fittall, 7 Ravel Close, Wraybury. You must get me your postcode. And printed by Rachel Willoughby, Restings Farmhouse, etcetera. Is that all we need? All legal requirements satisfied, Ethelburga?'

'That's the lot,' said Ellie. 'Now give me that telephone.'

'Lunch, first,' said Susanna. 'The sandwiches are in the kitchen.'

'And then,' said Rachel, 'I need to get printing.'

* * *

Mrs Peacock was at home, packing. She had always known that one day he would go too far, and now that it had happened she felt curiously calm. She would wait no longer. She would go first to the hospital, and if her mother was able to understand, she would explain to her what had occurred. Her mother, once, would have been delighted to hear that Sylvia was leaving her husband. Now, well, she might take it in, but probably not. She had been almost comatose for some weeks, and the nurse had said to Sylvia a few days earlier, 'Not long now, dear.'

The telephone rang. It would be her husband, angry that she had abandoned her post. Nervously, she lifted the receiver.

'Oh, it's you, Ellie,' she said, surprised.

When Peacock came home that evening and demanded something to eat, Sylvia Peacock was still there, and her suitcase was hidden under the bed.

He threw himself down in an armchair and told her to bring him a can of beer. Fumbling about in the crevice between the cushion and the arm he found the television pad, and pressed the button for BBC1. It was nearly nine o'clock.

Chapter 16

Peter, who got home only a little later than Peacock, found the answering machine in Restings flashing excitedly.

'Sukie?' he called, not hopefully, as he removed his coat.

He had already felt that the house was empty. The dogs were shut in the yard, and had greeted the sound of his car with frantic yelpings. He wondered if they had been fed.

There was no reply, and only one light on, which had probably been left on earlier in the day. He pressed some more switches and then went back to the telephone in the kitchen. The message tape was full, and he ran it back to the beginning, hoping for a message from Susanna.

'This is Don Masham, *Daily Mail*, for Susanna Westerham. I'd be grateful if you would call me on 0171—' Peter pressed the fast-forward button and stopped again. '. . . you, Mrs Westerham, and if you would do a telephone interview for Southern tel—' He switched off. Susanna could go through them herself when she came in.

Feeling particularly redundant, he let the leapingly grateful dogs into the house and fed them. Then he went to the refrigerator and found some cold sausages and salad. He put them on a tray, poured himself a glass of whisky and water, and carried it through to the sitting room. He needed distraction. He switched on the television, pulling a low table in front of the sofa for his tray. He should catch some of the nine o'clock news. Before he could sit down, the voice from the set took his attention. It was Susanna.

There she was, seated in a room he did not know, talking calmly into the camera in answer to a question.

'It is not unusual for a married couple both to stand for parliament.'

'But not for the same seat, surely, Mrs Westerham?'

'That is not so usual, of course,' said Susanna. 'But we all have to start somewhere.'

'Can you tell us your husband's feelings about this? He is, after all, the sitting MP.'

'At the moment,' said Susanna, 'my husband is a candidate for

Kentish Weald like the rest of us. And I cannot speak for him.'

The announcer's face appeared on the screen. He was smiling.

'We had hoped for a comment from Mr Peter Westerham,' he said, 'but according to his agent he was unavailable. And now to the sports news . . .'

'Oh, he was, was he?' said Peter wryly to the screen. 'Thanks, Peacock.'

Peter took a long draught from his glass. His eyes followed unseeing the movements of the rugby players across the screen. After a minute the telephone rang. He got up slowly and brought the cordless handset back to the sofa before he switched it on.

'Hello?' he said wearily.

'Peter? Rupert Hascombe. I've just been watching the news. What's all this about Susanna?'

'You tell me,' said Peter. 'I haven't had a chance to speak to her properly since it all broke.'

'Are you all right, you two?' Hascombe sounded anxious.

'As far as I know, Rupert. Actually, I think I am just about to find out. That's her car now, outside.'

'Well, you know,' said Hascombe, 'none of my business, and all that. But if I, if we, Florence and I, can help in any way, you know where we are.'

Susanna came in, carrying an armful of paper, which she dumped on a table.

'Don't say anything, Pete, till I've got a drink. I'm exhausted.'

'I'll get you one,' said Peter. 'What do you want. Whisky?'

'I think so. Lots of water. I'll be down in a minute.'

She came back without her coat, and sitting down in the armchair opposite the sofa, ran her fingers through her hair.

'What a day!' she said.

'Yes,' said Peter, handing her a glass.

She took it, and after a mouthful put it on the low table beside her. Peter was standing with his arm on the mantelpiece, looking into the fireless grate. Her behaviour, as if nothing unusual had happened, stirred his anger again. As if she sensed it, she said:

'Pete, I know you feel deserve an explanation.'

'Not unnaturally,' he replied coldly.

'Pete, I have just two things to say to you. The first, the most important, is that I love you. I love you totally and utterly, and forever. You must never, ever doubt that.'

Peter turned and looked at her, frowning.

'You have an unusual way of showing it.'

'The second,' Susanna went on, 'is a request. It won't be easy, but I beg you to agree to it. As long as this election campaign lasts, please will you not question me or ask what I am up to. I know what I'm doing, and I can only do it if you leave me to get on with it.'

'Do you actually expect me to accept all this without comment?' said Peter, incredulous.

'You can't stop me, anyway – Ellie made sure of that by getting me to go round to the council offices early in the day. She thought you might persuade me out of it.'

'Ellie! Ellie Fittall? Is she in this too?' said Peter, gaping.

'She's my agent,' said Susanna. 'And a very astute one.'

'I can believe it. Good God. And your mother. I thought she was my friend.'

Susanna looked up at him sharply.

'Oh, she is. Don't doubt that. But that is all I am saying. Listen, Pete. I remember how all rational life stops during an election campaign, and how long the three weeks can seem. But it is only three weeks, and because we must be rivals out there, please let us not bring it home with us. Let's keep our sanity and have no election talk in the evenings. Is it a pact?'

'Do I have any option?' said Peter, shaking his head. 'I see what you are up to, Susanna, and I find it quite weird. In fact, my first reaction was that you had gone stark raving mad. It was Peacock, in fact, who showed me what was likely to happen.'

Susanna said nothing.

'Is this determination not to discuss it starting now?'

'Yes, please,' said Susanna.

'Well, I just have to say that you can't expect me not to do my best to make sure you don't succeed.'

She was silent again.

'Bloody hell,' said Peter. He threw himself into the sofa opposite. 'Sukie, this is a crazy situation.'

She refused to be drawn.

'Pete, I'm going to make some supper,' she said. 'Those sausages look horrid. How about something hot and cheesy?'

For a moment Peter felt like refusing, but he realised that there was no point in making a martyr of himself. Ludicrous though the situation might be, but she had a point in wanting to keep the election out of their home.

As he sat later in the kitchen, mellowed by a drink, watching her back as she stirred something on the stove, a wave of despairing affection for her came over him. What was going to happen, he thought, was that she would make a total laughing stock of herself. It would serve her right, after this iniquitous behaviour. But he didn't really like the thought of her being hurt.

He got up and put an arm round her waist.

'That smells good,' he said. 'You know, I am extremely jealous of you, Sukie. I would give anything to have Ellie Fittall as my agent.'

The floor of the Fittall front room was strewn with newspapers.

'There's nothing at all in the *Guardian*,' said Rachel, in tones of accusatory disappointment.

Susanna folded back a page.

'Never mind. The others are brilliant, and there probably aren't that many *Guardian* readers around here. I like this: "My husband and I have never seen eye to eye politically, and I think it is time to take a stand." I never knew I sounded so royal.'

'What about this one?' said Ellie. '"Susanna Westerham, 44, looks much younger than her age, and despite her shy manner—'

'I didn't think I had a shy manner.'

'Listen, ". . . despite her shy manner, puts her arguments forcefully for an alternative Conservative policy on Europe. Her demands for a tougher line on immigration from the EU, curbs on French and Spanish fruit imports, and higher taxes for foreigners resident in the UK have a ring that will appeal to the extreme right in the Conservative party, and contrast strongly with the known views of her husband and present incumbent of Kentish Weald, Peter Westerham." That's what we are looking for, isn't it? And in one of the heavies, too.'

'Here's another good one – in the *Sun*,' said Rachel. 'I must say, though it would come better from you, your press officer did a fine job in getting them all here yesterday, didn't I? Headline: "MOVE OVER DARLING! Sharp elbows, down in Kent. Shapely blonde Susanna Westerham plans to oust hubby Peter in a takeover bid for his Kent seat at the election. 'It's time for a change,' she said yesterday. 'Let the girls have a go. We know what the voters are looking for, and it's not what's on offer . . .'"'

'I never did! Not a word of it, except "it's time for a change",' said Susanna indignantly.

'You don't have to say it, as long as they print it,' said Rachel. 'I probably said it, quoting you, of course. There's a bit about your all-female campaign team. Neither you nor I are described as shapely, Ethel.'

'You call me Ethel once again,' said Ellie, glaring through her glasses, 'and I'll describe you, Rachel Willoughby, to the next journalist who rings.'

'Will you be serious?' said Susanna. 'We've certainly got the coverage today. The question is, how do we keep it up till the election?'

'Leave that to the experts,' said Rachel, 'and get on with writing your speech for the church meeting.'

'And you'd better get back to your printing machine, Rachel,' said Ellie. 'I have to get those leaflets to the post office by Monday, or they just won't get delivered in time to make a real impact. We don't want to have to put on first class stamps.'

'I'm only printing on the one side at the moment,' said Rachel. 'I'll do the window-sticker side when we do the addresses. When are we going to get them, Ellie?'

'I'll have them by Thursday morning, I hope, if all goes well. Seelveea is quite nervous.'

'I don't blame her,' said Susanna. 'I would be, with that ghastly man.'

'I can't think what she thinks she is doing,' said Rupert Hascombe. 'All she will do is split the vote, She can't get in, and we'll have that Liberal fellow instead.'

'Perhaps that's what she wants,' said Florence, pulling their bedroom curtains closed.

'She's not a Liberal, is she?'

'Certainly not, she's a fascist, or so the papers say.'

'I never thought she was anything, actually,' said Rupert. 'She never talks politics, as far as I know.'

He watched his wife brushing her long hair. When she let it down at night it still seemed far more chestnut than grey. He trusted Florence's perception, and realised that she saw more in this strange business than he could fathom.

'Go on,' he said. 'What do you really think?'

'Well, it's a desperate measure, isn't it?' said Florence. 'She dislikes the whole political business, and she wants him out. And presumably she can't persuade him to stop, so she is doing it by force.'

'Good Lord!' Rupert Hascombe made the sound usually described as a guffaw. 'Do you think that's what she's up to? The little minx! I always thought there was more to that girl than meets the eye. Well. You can't help being impressed. It's naughty, but it shows quite a spirit.'

'Anyone can produce spirit when they are worried about their home or their family. But it's a dangerous game she is playing. I hope it doesn't backfire. I may be wrong, of course. Perhaps she just dislikes his politics and wants to try hers.'

'Well, she's certainly stirring it up. Quite fun.'

'Rupert, you are so nice,' said Florence. 'Lots of people in your position, I mean on the executive of the Association and all that, would be absolutely furious. After all, you're going to lose the seat. In fact, I bet Peacock is hopping mad.'

'Ho ho ho!' said Hascombe. 'I'd like to see his face. I think I had better drop in on him sometime and have a look.'

As they lay side by side in the large four-poster bed, Florence said: 'I suspect your old girlfriend has a hand in this too. Did you see her in the first shot, walking down the street with Susanna Westerham?'

'I did,' said her husband. 'I think they are two of a kind. Well, well. Should make the election more sparky than usual.'

'I want a ticket for the count,' said Florence, as she turned over to go to sleep.

The telephone rang, and Susanna took it.

'Mum, I've only just heard. I was out all day. What on earth are you doing?'

Leonora's call came early the next morning, and Susanna had to try out her voice before answering the telephone.

'Well, I'm doing what I suppose you've heard I'm doing,' she said, 'standing for parliament. Everybody's doing it.'

'Yes, but Mum, what about Dad? What about him?'

'He's doing it too,' said Susanna.

'No, Mum, you know what I mean,' said Leonora anxiously. 'Doesn't he mind?'

'You'd better ask him. He's shaving. Can you ring back?'

'You mean – he's there?'

'Of course he's here. What did you expect? He goes off canvassing early, but not that early.'

Leonora's voice sounded very unsure.

'It's just that I thought . . . we thought . . . perhaps . . .'

'We?'

'The twins and me, Mum. And Andrew. We were worried. We thought, reading the papers, perhaps you'd had a quarrel or . . . something.'

'Listen,' said Susanna, 'you'd better speak to Dad. Pete! Leo on the phone. Leonora, I mean. Can you come?'

Peter came in from the bathroom, wiping his chin with a towel.

'Mum, I'm so relieved . . . ' Susanna heard her daughter's voice tailing away as she handed him the receiver.

As she went into the bathroom she heard Peter say: 'Yes, she is. Anyone can. You can stand too, if you like.'

And she smiled. So far she had got away with it. Peter had not turned against her, but she could not throw off her deep anxiety about how he would feel if she succeeded. The stakes were so high.

The next call was from Emma. Peter had already gone out, and Susanna was about leave.

'Mum? Look, Mum, we think, me and Mark, that you shouldn't do this.'

'Do what?' said Susanna, mildly irritated, and deliberately misunderstanding.

'You know, stand against Dad. It isn't fair on him, and anyway, it's not the sort of thing you do.'

'Why not?'

'Well, Mum, you and Dad do things together, not against each other. You're just not like that.'

Emma knew that she was not expressing herself well, but the malaise she felt was coming over to her mother clear and strong. Since it echoed her own, Susanna found it particularly annoying. Surely someone, one of them, should feel she was doing the right thing.

'Emma,' she said, 'you're talking to me as if I were a child. Dad and I are both adults and capable of knowing what we are doing. You and Mark should consider that, before discussing us. Anyhow, you have made enough fuss yourself about Dad being an MP, so you've got a nerve to object to me trying to do something about it.'

'We're only trying to help,' said Emma, hurt.

'Look, I'm in a hurry,' said her mother. It was a bad conversation, and she wanted to stop it.

As she drove away in the car she wondered disconsolately whether she would end up turning the whole family against her. It was a relief to arrive in Ellie's house where the atmosphere was only positive.

Emma, upset, tried to ring her grandmother, but though she hung on for a long time there was no reply. So she rang Mark again.

The call from Conservative Central Office did not come until the second morning, by which time Leonard Peacock had got his act together.

'So what exactly is your explanation this time?' said Brinkman silkily. 'You always have an unusual one, Leonard. I'll say that for you.'

'Well,' said Leonard Peacock, keeping his voice lazy, 'it's a distraction, Ronnie, but not really a problem. Fifty, sixty votes, perhaps? She has absolutely no knowledge of politics, and as far as I know she has barely spoken in public in the last three years. Not to worry, Ronald. Nothing I can't handle. Now, I do have one or two things you can help me with. Your office says I am not going to get my posters till—'

He didn't get far. Brinkman cut in hard.

'Shut up, Leonard. You always talk too much. What I want to know is, why is she doing it?'

'Why? Your guess is as good as mine, Ronnie. A bit of mischief, I guess – women playing games. I think it's more of a practical joke than anything else. You know what her team is? Two old women! Her mother and that old troublemaker, Ellie Fittall. I told you about her before. She's based in Fittall's council flat, if you can imagine that. It's a farce; no canvassers, no office back-up. They haven't even been seen out canvassing. No, it's just a minor diversion. Frankly, we're too busy down here to bother with her.'

Peacock was managing to talk himself into believing this.

'Peacock, you fool,' Brinkman's disdain showed clearly in his voice. 'You don't need canvassers and office back-up when you have the national press eating out of your hand. She's the hottest news so far this election – a wife standing against her husband! The hacks are wallowing in it. If you don't watch out, she'll run away with the votes, and I'm warning you, if that seat is lost to the Lib Dems, don't call me for sympathy.'

'It won't happen,' said Peacock. The pencil that he was abusing snapped in two in his hand.

'You are going to make sure it doesn't. Get on to the returning officer and demand to see her papers. Somehow you have got to find some way that they are invalid. Check every name in the nominations. They're bound to have got something wrong.'

Peacock kicked himself mentally for not having thought of this first, so he could have told Brinkman that he had already done it. But then it would hardly have fitted the offhand attitude he was taking.

He started to speak again, but the line had gone dead. He put the receiver down, and almost immediately the telephone rang again.

He did not recognise the voice, and the caller refused to give a name.

'I have just put something through your letterbox,' the man said, 'in a brown envelope. I don't want to tell you who I am, because I'm a neighbour, and I wouldn't want him to know who it was. But I think you can use them. They've both got a date on. You'll see what I mean. All last June he was at it, early like, in the morning. I had to hide in a bush to get them. You'll see. Mind you use them well.'

Before Leonard Peacock could speak the man rang off. Some freak, of course, he thought, sending him some kind of rubbish. Sounded like photographs. A little bit of porn, perhaps. No time for that now. Still, he asked Lelia if she would be so good as to go downstairs and see if there was any mail. She went with a shrug and a toss of her head that implied eloquently that *she* didn't care if her work wasn't finished by the end of the day.

The brown envelope that she put into Peacock's hand was addressed to The Conservative Agent. Apart from that it was blank. When he opened it, and took out the contents, it took him some moments to realise what he was looking at; then, as he did, its potential dawned on him. His thin lips stretched into a tight smile. At last it looked as if the breaks were coming his way.

Brinkman's next call was to Ellie Fittall's number. It had not taken his office long to find it. A brisk female voice answered the telephone.

'Independent Conservative Campaign Office. How may I help you?'

'This is Ronald Brinkman speaking, from Smith Square,' he said, at his most unctuous, 'Conservative Party Central Office. I wonder if I could possibly have a word with Mrs Susanna Westerham?'

The receiver became muffled, and he could half hear, half imagine urgent consultation. The voice came back.

'I am so sorry to have to disappoint you. The pressure on Mrs Westerham's time is so great that she is only taking calls from the electorate and from the press. Do you by any chance vote locally?'

'Hardly,' said Brinkman, shortly, 'but—'

'Oh dear, what a shame,' said the voice. 'In that case, I am afraid I cannot help you. Goodbye.'

And Brinkman heard the line go blank.

'Bitch,' he said.

After another day of canvassing, all good candidates were tucked up in bed.

But there was unusual, if quiet, activity in a certain office in Wraybury.

'Over here,' said a whisper.

A second torch beam followed the first across the floor, and they both came to rest on the front of a drawer.

A slight rattling sound.

'It's locked.' The other voice was whispering too.

'Locked? It can't be. It's never locked.'

'Well, it is now.'

'There's no reason to lock it.'

'Are you sure this is the right one?'

One of the torch beams wavered around.

'Yes, quite sure.'

'Well, we'll just have to find the key. Have you looked in the bunch?'

'There are no small keys at all on his keyring.'

'Then with any luck it's here. Where would you hide a key?'

'In another drawer, usually.'

'Hush. What's that?'

The whispers stopped. A car had driven up and halted nearby. Tiptoe steps to the window.

'Who is it?' The question was anxious.
'Only a neighbour. Not the police!'
'Open all the drawers, but keep your light down.'

Eventually a small key was found in one of the filing cabinets. It fitted the desk drawer.

'There they are, at the back! Those are the ones, there. You take them.'

'I wonder why the drawer was locked. There's only pens and rubbish. And some photographs. Funny . . . some man in a garden, I can't see quite what he's doing. There's nothing worth locking up in here.'

'Better lock it again though. Give me the key. I'll put it back. Which drawer was it?'

The sounds of sussuration died away, and all was quiet again. Soon, further down the road, another car started up.

Later, as his bedroom door closed, Leonard Peacock twitched slightly, mumbled and turned over in his sleep.

Peacock had asked for a meeting with the Association chairman and the candidate. The fact that Sir Rupert Hascombe turned up as well did not actually suit him, because he had always found the ex-soldier a curiously disruptive element. But he could hardly ask him to leave, especially as he was a member of the executive committee and had come offering to do some canvassing.

'Canvassing party isn't leaving till ten, actually,' said the agent. 'They're not here yet. It's only nine-thirty.'

'Well, I had to drop my wife off to catch the London train, so I thought I would just come along,' said Hascombe cheerfully. He could tell that Peacock didn't want him, and he was interested in finding out why.

Peter Westerham and Cyril Eversley arrived together.

'Well, what's going on, Leonard?' said the chairman. 'You said you had some good news.'

'More than good news,' said Peacock. 'I have something here that will totally eclipse the little matter of the difficult wife. What I have here is a piece of dynamite, which, if we handle it correctly, will blow the Lib Dem candidate right out of the sky.'

'Sounds interesting,' said Cyril Eversley.

Peacock drew two photographs from the drawer of his desk, and handed them to him.

'Nice garden,' said Eversley. 'Whose is it?'

'That's the point,' said Peacock impatiently, taking them from him and passing them to Peter Westerham. 'Don't you see who it is? It's Lance Horton.'

'The Liberal candidate?' Eversley still looked blank.

'Of course,' said Peacock. 'The Lib Dem, in his garden. And look what he's doing!'

'Seems to me to be holding something . . .'

Cyril Eversley, as always when he was with Peacock, knew he was somehow being made to feel stupid. Peter had passed the photographs to Rupert Hascombe, who was frowning.

'Well done,' said Peacock. 'And the dates printed on the bottom?'

'I didn't look,' said Eversley. 'But I realise what he's doing now. I thought at first he was having a pee.'

'June 2nd and June 9th last year,' said Peacock, addressing them all.

'We-e-ell,' said Hascombe, 'I get your point, but a lot of people, you know, when no one's about . . . It's in his own garden, presumably, after all.'

'You're missing the point,' said Peacock shrilly. 'Think who he is! Think of his public position! He's a county councillor! He's the chief executive of Wealden Water! They imposed a hosepipe ban all last summer, and there he is watering his own garden regularly in the early morning!'

There was silence for some seconds.

Then Eversley said, 'I see the point now.'

And Hascombe said, 'Where did you get these?'

'Anonymous,' said Peacock. 'Someone pushed them through my letterbox. And a call, saying what Horton was up to in his garden, right through June, in the early morning, before anyone was up. That's clear evidence you've got in your hand. He's finished!'

'A neighbour, I suppose, watching from his own garden.' Hascombe smiled wryly. 'Vindictive sort of thing to do now, nearly a year later.'

Peacock was hardly listening.

'It's just a matter of timing now,' he said excitedly, 'and whether we go national or local. One of the local papers, I think. Either the *Echo* or the *Tun Wells Gazette*. The *Gazette* comes out on Thursday, the *Echo* on Wednesday. If we get it in next week, a week before polling day, there'd even be time for a follow-up. What do you think?'

Hascombe tossed the photographs back onto the desk, and Peter spoke for the first time.

'Look, I'm sorry, Leonard, but we can't make use of this.'

A pause.

'What?' Peacock spat the word out.

'I can't be a party to using this sort of material,' said Peter. 'I don't want to win the seat through this man's private behaviour. I just won't do it. It isn't – it isn't –'

'It isn't cricket,' said Hascombe, enormously relieved. He had been feeling distinctly uncomfortable.

'Thank you,' said Peter. 'You express it admirably, Rupert. Sorry, Leonard. Can't do it. It isn't cricket.'

Peacock was for a moment speechless. He looked from one to the other in undisguised horror.

'Yes,' said Eversley, 'it would seem a bit . . . well, perhaps not quite . . .'

Peacock ignored the chairman.

'Are you telling me,' he said at Peter with venom, 'that after all you've done, after letting your wife play these silly games, you're going to refuse this? It's a gift! It's a lifeline – it's our only hope! Don't you see? We play this right, make sure everyone in the constituency knows, and it'll cut Horton's vote to the bone. They won't stand for it, not after last summer and—'

'It's all right, Leonard,' interrupted Peter. 'I understand exactly what you're saying, but I won't do it. And that's that. It's not the way I play. You had better tear those photographs up and forget about them, and we'll beat Horton in a fair fight, just as we did before.'

Peacock was breathing heavily and his face was puce, but before he could say any more his office door opened and a face looked round it.

'Morning, everyone. Reporting for canvassing duty,' it said cheerfully. 'Is this the briefing room?'

Peacock was forced to turn his attention to the canvassers in the next office. Hascombe said quietly to Peter: 'I'm glad you scotched that one. I never like playing dirty, though the other lot would do it.'

Peter shrugged.

'Thanks for your support. But we don't exactly have a happy agent.'

He turned to the chairman.

'Can I come in your car, Cyril? I believe we're heading for the industrial estates this morning.'

A short way down the High Street, in Ravel Close, Ellie Fittall and Sylvia Peacock were anxiously awaiting the arrival of Susanna and Rachel. Sylvia had arrived via a back alley to avoid passing the Conservative Office.

'What if they don't work? They're not floppy, are they?' she said, her normally anxious expression more apprehensive than ever. 'They seem quite hard and stiff, and Rachel said they would be floppy. To think we'll have been through all that for nothing. I thought I would faint when that car arrived. I was sure it was the police. If you hadn't come with me I think I would have died.'

'Was Leonard still asleep when you got home?' said Ellie.

'Oh, yes, thank goodness. I don't know what I would have said. It was as bad as when I was taking his keys. I kept thinking, what'll I say if he wakes up?'

'We should have given you a story,' said Ellie. 'Never mind. It wasn't needed. You were a brave lass, Sylvia, I'll say that for you.'

'I don't think I could have done it if I wasn't leaving anyway,' said Mrs Peacock, still twittering. 'I wouldn't have had the nerve. Ellie, I rang my sister yesterday, like you said. It's all settled.'

'You're not off yet?' said Ellie anxiously. 'Not till after the election? We need you, girl. You're the spy in the camp.'

Sylvia Peacock fluttered nervously.

'I s-suppose, as long as he doesn't suspect, I could stay just till it's over. But I don't want anything more like last night. It would finish me.'

'No, no more burglary,' said Ellie comfortingly, 'not if these things fit, that is. Here they come now. She says they have to be compatible, whatever that means. I don't understand this computer stuff.'

Susanna and Rachel came into the small room, and they all held their breath as Rachel examined the three flat, grey computer disks.

'Yes!' she said. 'Same as mine. We're in luck. They'll do.'

'A little prayer. Say thank you nicely,' said Ellie, giving Sylvia's arm a squeeze.

'I'd better put them in the machine, all the same,' said Rachel, 'just to make sure.'

They all watched the screen as she slid a disk into a slot in the side of the computer and pressed a few buttons. A lot of titles came up on the screen and she selected one. There was a pause, and a hum, and up came a screenful of names and addresses, headed 'MEMBERS, subs paid.'

'Bingo!' shouted Rachel.'Got it first time!'

'Fantastic,' said Susanna.

'What's more,' said Rachel, 'they're all in label format. We just have to print them out.'

She inserted another disk, and tapped the keyboard.

'That's it. The canvass sheets!'

She waved a fist above her head.

'Yip – yip – yip!' squeaked Ellie, grabbing Susanna's hands with her own arthritic ones. 'Here we go, here we go, here we go!' she sang shrilly as they spun round. Rachel grabbed the sides of the computer table and hung on.

Chapter 17

The second week of an election campaign is always the hardest on all parties: the initial exhilaration of going into battle has worn off; the second wind has not yet blown through the lungs of the canvassers and exhaustion has set in; the public is getting hardened to the knock on the door, and has started tuning out the politicians on the TV screens. The days seem endless, and the goal of election day is too far away.

Apathy had not, however, hit Kentish Weald. If not exactly in the grip of election fever, the voters were certainly showing an unusual interest. 'What about this man and his wife, then?' was a common question on the doorstep.

The traditional meeting organised by the Council of Churches, in which all the contestants met face to face, attracted unprecedented numbers. In the outsize Anglican church of St John, built, like the town hall, in the days of Wraybury's affluence, every seat had been taken well before the advertised starting time. The excitement of pushing past the journalists and television cameras waiting outside had infected the crowd, who were talking animatedly like a congregation at a wedding awaiting the arrival of the bride.

The vicar of St John's, the minister of the United Reform Church, and the local Catholic priest were in discussion in the porch about whether or not the media should be allowed into the church.

'Why not?' said Father O'Connor. 'Let's have a bit of fun. You'll like people to see your church full for once, Christopher.'

Before the vicar could reply, the minister spoke with distaste.

'I think it is totally unsuitable to make a media circus of it. The idea was to give people a chance to compare the candidates, and to ask them the same questions in a sober atmosphere. It was not to make it a subject for television viewers.'

'Voyeurs, I would call them,' said Father O'Connor, giggling. 'You'll have to make up your mind, though, Christopher. It's time for the off!'

'It is awkward,' said the vicar, vacillating. 'After all, those unable to come have the right to know what is being said by their candidates, and the parish newsletter will come out far too late.'

'It's your church,' said the minister coldly.

'That's true,' interjected the priest, nodding.

'. . . but I would not allow mine to be so defiled.'

The vicar was torn. He did not like the minister but his disapproval worried him. In the end he compromised, which pleased no one: he allowed the journalists in, while keeping the cameras out. The anger among the television crews was enough for him gratefully to claim sanctuary within his own portals.

As chairman, the vicar stated the rules. Five minutes each, to state their policies, was all the candidates would be allowed. Then several pre-planned questions would be asked, which each in turn was required to answer. Then, if there was time, a few questions would be accepted from the audience.

The Monster Raving Loony candidate, who was dressed in a gorilla suit, and removed his head in order to speak, was the first to perform. He was a wag, and reduced his audience to helpless laughter. None of the next three candidates in their short speeches said anything out of the usual or much different from their election manifestos. Since they were called in alphabetical order, the Westerhams came last, and after some slightly convoluted explanation by the vicar, on the lines of Peter's Christian name having the earlier initial, but in any case he would call a lady first, Susanna was invited to speak. She rose, looking composed, and no one could have guessed how her pulse was racing. The three deep breaths she took to steady herself were disguised as a slow look round the audience. This produced a low murmuring from the crowd, and a 'Silence, if you please' from the vicar.

Susanna hardly looked at her notes, and spoke in a clear, carrying voice.

'I do not intend,' she said, 'to refer to any other party contesting this election, but simply to tell you the particular policies on which I am standing.'

They were few, but draconian, and each drew excited whispers from the audience. She was in favour of longer sentences for offenders and removing such comforts as television sets from prisoners' cells; of restricting immigration numbers to a level that did no more than maintain the current total population of the British Isles, with a strong bias towards those of Caucasian and preferably Celtic origin; of giving financial inducements to those who wished to return to their country of origin; of banning homosexuals from the armed forces and of immediate withdrawal from the European Union.

Peter sat watching her with a blank expression. She seemed so confident and clear-cut in her views. He could hardly believe what he was hearing, and it was not in any way the sort of thing he had expected. He felt unnerved, and tried to concentrate on what he was going to say.

Then he rose to take her place at the lectern, and the chairman had once again to quell the murmuring. At no moment did Peter feel that he had the full attention of the audience. His leftish and rather liberal views were well known, and after Susanna's opinions his thoughtful moderation was as stimulating as a garden bonfire after an *auto-da-fé*.

The questions began; first the prepared ones, on homelessness, on overseas aid, on nuclear disarmament. The candidates answered, one after the other, and then further questions came from the floor. In both sessions, each answer Susanna gave elicited gasps of amazement and sometimes prolonged applause.

'I would refer you,' she said, 'to the programme followed in Atlanta, in the United States, in preparation for the Olympics. All dossers and drop-outs were cleared from the streets which gave an entirely new image. It was very successful. Afterwards, I believe they were housed in the Olympic village. In our case, I suggest unused Ministry of Defence property.'

In response to a question on capital punishment, she was emphatic.

'I have no doubt that hanging should be reintroduced,' she said. 'What is the point of filling our prisons with unrepentant monsters, all at the expense of the taxpayer, when we need the space, anyway, for rapists and child abusers, quite apart from burglars and false claimants of unemployment benefit?'

Peter, pale and grim, stared straight ahead. In reply to the same question, he said, 'I have never made any secret of my aversion to the idea of capital punishment, and I would never vote for it.'

A low hissing grew stronger in the audience, countered by some clapping.

A man stood up near the front.

'Can I ask Mrs Westerham whether, if capital punishment were reintroduced, she would be prepared to pull the trigger, as it were?'

Susanna rose again, cool and firm.

'I should not wish to be the one to do it,' she said, 'but in those very unlikely circumstances, as an Englishwoman I hope I would never fail in my duty.'

As the clapping and expostulations died away:

'My God,' said the questioner, 'you're a hard one.'

'Please,' said the vicar, one finger in his dog-collar, 'the candidates must be questioned equally. Mr Fawcett for the Loonies is next in the firing line. Oh dear, I mean—'

But his gaffe went unnoticed in the rising burble of talk. No one was interested in the gorilla's views on hanging. After a glance at his watch and in response to a furious look from the United Reform Church minister, the vicar brought the meeting to a close, and the audience left, some of them arguing heatedly.

The waiting TV men pounced on individuals, and found many delighted to be questioned, expressing their views with enthusiasm.

'What I say is, it's nice to hear an honest politician,' said one woman, her two companions nodding agreement as they moved in behind her to get themselves into the camera shot. 'I may not agree with it all, but she's not afraid to say what she thinks, that one, not just a lot of waffle, and she's going to get my vote.'

Soon the candidates emerged from the church, and Susanna was surrounded by a crowd of admirers. Major Wright and his moustache were among them.

'Is this "for real", as our American cousins say?'

Peter turned to find Rupert Hascombe at his elbow.

'I feel slightly winded, Peter,' he went on, 'as if someone had kicked me in the stomach. I don't know about you?'

'I know I have got to talk with her,' said Peter grimly. 'She doesn't normally give me the chance these days.'

He pushed past a man with a microphone who was trying to speak to him, and elbowed his way to Susanna. And so, unplanned, he gave her just the scene she needed, and provided the cameras and the microphones of the waiting media men with the shot and soundbite that appeared on the television screens of the country that evening.

Seizing his wife by the arm, the Conservative candidate said forcefully: 'Susanna, what is this? What on earth are you doing?'

And Susanna, looking him straight in the eye, said: 'All I am doing is giving the people of Kentish Weald a choice, and a chance to vote the way that they think.'

As the cameras clattered and whirred Peter turned away, his face warm with anger and embarrassment. This was no longer a joke. He was shattered by what he had heard Susanna say. How could she make a speech like that? It was true that she never expressed political thoughts, but he had always simply assumed that her views were roughly in line with his own. She avoided political discussion. 'I am apolitical,' she would say; and 'One in the family is quite enough.' But now she was demonstrating such totally unexpected oratory skills, such extraordinary adeptness in handling an audience that, despite himself, he found he was wondering whether there could possibly be other things about her that he had never discovered. He felt slightly sick.

'Do you think I went too far? I may have put some of them off,' said Susanna later in Ellie's flat.

'You got it just right,' said her mother. 'You frightened me out of my wits. But for some of them you probably didn't go far enough. You never even touched on castration.'

'I did wonder whether my DIY execution bit was rather over the top,' said Susanna, giggling. The adrenalin was still flowing, and she was riding high.

Ellie, armed as usual with a teapot, put it down on the table and looked speculatively at Susanna.

'We were just as well to leave hanging and such out of your paperwork, I think,' she said. 'They're going to find your manifesto strong enough meat as it is, when it comes through their letterboxes, and we've got to keep it so's they can believe it. We've got to please more than just the Nazis among them.'

Rachel was stacking piles of envelopes and putting rubber bands on them.

'Thank goodness we don't have to stamp them. They frank them all at the post office. I think we are ready to go.'

Carrying plastic bags full of envelopes they all walked together down the High Street.

In the Conservative office, a few doors down, Peacock and Lelia were arguing about the replacement computer.

'I'm not changing again in the middle of all this,' said Lelia. 'We'll just keep this machine until after the election and put our own one down the passage.'

'They'll charge us rental for that one, though,' said Peacock irritably, 'now that they've brought ours back. I can get the man to come and set up our own machine, and he can take this one away. It won't take half an hour.'

'No,' said Lelia firmly. 'I'm not changing again. I've just got used to this one, and I'm not changing again now, not with all this work to do, and that's flat.'

Peacock gave in, and Mrs Peacock, quietly folding leaflets in the next room, silently blessed the secretary. Her heart had almost stopped when she realised the office computer was back, repaired. At any moment they might have discovered that the disks that fitted it were missing. Rachel had copied them for her own use, but Sylvia so far had not dared risk being spotted returning the originals to the desk drawer, with the office permanently manned. And another night visit was not on.

Passing the window, Peacock glanced into the street and saw Susanna and her companions carrying their bags towards the post office.

'What are they doing now?' he said, staring at them as Macbeth might have eyed the three witches. His loathing, especially of Ellie Fittall, had greatly increased since discovering that no flaw could be found in any detail of her registration of Susanna as a candidate.

Lelia, attracted by the malevolent tone in Peacock's voice, joined him.

'Well, they're not shopping,' she said.

As they watched, a single envelope slid from the top of one of the bags in Ellie Fittall's hand, and fell unnoticed to the pavement as she walked on. Peacock and Lelia looked at each other.

'Get it,' said Peacock, and for once his secretary did not demur.

'This is a disaster,' said the agent a few minutes later, having read the leaflet. On the front was a notably attractive photograph of Susanna, her hair blowing back from her face as she stood above a chalk cliff. Even the poor photocopied reproduction did not disguise her good looks. Profiled against the sea she was the image of the young Britannia.

'They'll vote for her on that alone,' said Peacock miserably. 'And the rest of it is what half of them want anyway. Listen to this: "Homeless and unemployed people must be encouraged to move from the South East to less populated parts of the country, by making their benefits payable only in those localities. There they will find moderate rents, more vacancies and lower unemployment." It's sheer rubbish, but they'll love it! And look at this drawing – war graves in France. "They fought to keep Britain British. And we will keep faith with them!" They'll fall for it. They'll vote for her. She'll get half our votes. Bloody, bloody, bloody—'

'One more word like that and I'm off,' said Lelia, reaching for her handbag.

'Oh, sh— I'm sorry,' said Peacock, 'but I've had enough. Get me Cyril Eversley on the telephone.'

'Get him yourself,' said Lelia automatically.

In the next room Sylvia Peacock smiled.

The only message on the answering machine that interested Susanna when she got home was from Mark. Something was wrong, she could tell by his voice, and with her heart beating faster she rang him back. But it was not the sort of thing she expected. His tone was harsh, and he launched in at once.

'They had you on the PM programme, with all the things you said, Mum, at that meeting. What the hell has got into you? It was unbelievable! I know we've got at Dad for doing this political thing, but at least he's – well, he has decent views at least . . . I mean, you couldn't be ashamed of what he does, but—'

'Mark—' Susanna tried to interrupt.

'Then you go and stand for his seat, as if Dad didn't have enough problems, and now . . . Someone sent me your leaflet – it's vicious – it's shameful—'

'Mark, listen! Will you let me—'

She had never heard Mark like this. He shouted back:

'No! It's indefensible. I won't listen to your excuses. You could have persuaded him to give up without going to those lengths, if you had only tried—'

'Mark,' she said desperately, 'that's just the point—'

'No! Between the two of you, you're tearing our family apart, and I'm not going along with it. Goodbye.'

Susanna stood staring at the dead receiver in her hand, tears welling to her eyes. A sound behind her made her look round. It was Peter, standing in the doorway, his face hard and unfriendly.

'What?' he said, jerking his chin.

'Mark,' she said.

'Mm,' said Peter, turning away and leaving the room.

Susanna rang Mark's number again, but there was no reply.

Peacock was deliberately late in keeping his appointment with his chairman at the Conservative Club that evening. He knew it would cost him less to get Eversley into a receptive state if he had already spent half an hour or so alone at the bar.

'Sorry, Cyril,' he said, patting the tweed-clad shoulder. 'Pressure of work. Thanks for coming. I thought I could do with a break for a drink and a chat.'

Eversley looked at him warily. Friendly overtures from Peacock were unusual, and therefore suspect. What was more, the agent offered to buy him another drink, which was unheard of.

They moved to a table and talked for a little about the football match playing silently on the television screen above them.

'Well, how'sa the campaign going, d'you think?' said Eversley, remembering his position as chairman.

'The campaign?' Peacock sighed heavily. 'I don't know, Cyril. I've never known anything like this. Everything that woman does is winning her votes. She never puts a foot wrong. It's that bloody old Fittall who's helping her. She knows the ropes. Unless we can pull something out of the bag they're going to make us lose this seat to the Lib Dems. And you know where that will leave you and me.'

Eversley frowned. He was well aware that Peacock's promotion chances would not be good, and he was sorry about that. He would have liked to see him move on, as far away as possible. But he did not see how he himself, as chairman of the Association, would be affected.

'You *and* me?' he said.

'Well, you know how it is,' said Peacock, shaking his head and gazing mournfully into the middle distance. 'They keep an eye on things, up there in London. I heard a whisper that you were in line for . . . Well, you know, the birthday honours list will be out in two or three months. You haven't heard anything, have you?'

'Heard anything? No. D'you think . . . ?' Eversley was beginning to get the gist of what he was being told.

'No, well. They usually write to you a few weeks before. It could be in the New Year ones, I suppose. But if this all goes wrong, and it is going wrong, Cyril, believe you me, we'll have to say goodbye to all that. That's life, I suppose. All ups and downs.'

Peacock gazed deeply into his glass, the picture of gloomy resignation. For once he seemed to have his defences lowered, and Cyril felt for him. They were both in the same boat. He considered, and took a long drink.

'S'jus my wife, really,' he said, 'who was hoping for something. Y'know what the ladies are like. She'd've liked to see me get, well, y'know, something.'

Peacock did know, and he knew that it had been a long-held wish of Cyril's too, that MBE.

'Let's have another round, shall we,' he said, 'and drown our sorrows. A double, Cyril?' he said, nodding to the bartender.

Over their fresh glasses, after they had drunk for a little while in silence, Peacock started the next stage.

'It's just a pity,' he said, 'that Peter wouldn't let us use those photographs. If we'd got them in the paper, with a nice little story, it would have made all the difference. There's no way that Lance Horton could win then.'

'Y' think so?' said Eversley.

'I know so,' said Peacock. 'Not a shadow of doubt. We could lose a few thousand to that woman, no problem, because the Lib Dem vote would fall right away. We might even pick up some of them ourselves.'

'Thass what we need.'

'So are we being stupid? After all, the man was breaking all the rules, wasn't he? He was asking for it. If those photographs got in the paper, no one would know where they came from, would they? And then all our problems are solved!'

'Couldn't do it, though,' said Eversley blurrily. 'Not cricket. Defn'tly not cricket. 'Sa pity. 'Sa real pity.'

'Of course,' said Peacock, going in for the kill, 'you could give me permission to do it. You're the chairman after all. It's your life they're messing around with.'

''Sright. My life. And my wife.' Eversley's head hung over his folded arms.

'Why not, Cyril?' Peacock nudged his elbow. 'I'll do it, if you just say yes. It's our duty, isn't it, to get Peter re-elected? No one will know, only you and me. I can just send on the photos anonymously.

I mean, he might have sent them straight to the paper anyway, mightn't he?'

'Yeh, 'sright,' said Eversley. 'But he din't. He sent 'em to us. But we can't do it. Defn'tly not cricket.'

His head was nearly on his arms.

Peacock's patience went.

'For Christ's sake, Cyril,' he said. He got up and walked towards the sign saying Gents. By the time he got back, Mrs Eversley had arrived and was coaxing the chairman to his feet.

'You should be ashamed of yourself,' she said coldly to Peacock, 'letting him get like this. Come on, Cyril.'

Eversley stumbled away, holding his wife's arm and still muttering, 'Defn'tly not cricket . . .'

Peacock was left staring after them, cursing under his breath. But he had already made up his mind. With or without authority he would act to save the election. But he would not give the stuff to that cow Kieran Mitchell on the *Echo*. In any case, her editor was Lib Dem.

The Editor of the *Tunbridge Wells Gazette* was contemplating retirement. Not just in general terms but specifically, this Monday morning. He had had a good run, all things considered, and he could fairly say that, now that his term as chairman of the golf club committee was due to begin, he had more or less reached the summit of his ambitions. Years ago, his aims had been higher. The *Daily Telegraph* had been in his sights; if not the editorship then a leader writer perhaps. But somehow his stars had not led him that way, his great moment had never quite come and only a lingering nostalgia for what might have been clouded his sunny horizon.

He looked at the letters in the unopened pile on his desk. Pile was perhaps an exaggeration. There were two. One was a plastic-covered leaflet which, he could see through the transparent cover, would enable him to reclaim money from his debtors more easily if more expensively. The other was a brown envelope, marked with his name and the words Private and Confidential. Slitting it open he pulled out two photographs and an unsigned typewritten note.

He recognised the Liberal Democratic candidate at once. He had been rather proud of the series of political interviews he had carried at the time of the last local bye-election. Though he was a lifelong member of the Conservative Party, he felt he could say with his hand on his heart that he had allowed virtually no bias to creep in.

He also noticed the dates: in the middle of the previous hot summer. It took him longer to make out that what the man held in front of him was the nozzle of the hosepipe that curled out of the grass behind him, and that he was directing its jet into a small fishpond, in one photograph, and into a border full of bedding plants in the other.

It took him longer still to put all three observations together and to realise that what he was looking at was not only politically explosive, but gave him the opportunity to use the line he had only ever expressed in daydreams.

He opened the door of the next room and said, to the two surprised youths sitting there, 'Hold the front page!'

One of them said, 'Wha-a-at?' vacantly.

The other, more astute, picked up the previous week's paper and looked at it.

The editor sighed.

'Ring the printers,' he said, 'and tell them I want a word. Urgently.'

And he turned back to his word processor.

Three days later Susanna was pushing a leaflet through a letterbox when the owner of the house walked up the garden path behind her.

'What's this, more junk mail?' she said.

'No,' said Susanna. 'It's my election manifesto. I am the Independent Conservative Candidate, Susanna Westerham. How do you do?'

'Oh yes, I saw you on the telly.' The woman smiled, interested. She looked Susanna up and down. 'You only come around at election time, you lot, don't you?'

Susanna had heard this comment before, and her usual resentment rose to the surface.

'You could hardly expect an MP to go round thirty thousand doorsteps between elections. My husband has weekly advice surgeries when you can come to him with any kind of problem. Had, I mean.'

'Why are you standing against him, then?' the woman said over her shoulder, as she had opened the door.

Susanna flushed.

'You'll have to read my leaflet, and find out,' she said.

'Well, I might. I don't normally vote,' said the woman, picking up a newspaper from the windowsill inside. 'Do you wonder we get fed up with all you politicians?'

She waved the paper in Susanna's face, and the words, ELECTION CANDIDATE'S GUILTY SECRET flashed in front of her.

'You're all the same,' said the woman triumphantly, and shut the door.

In Ellie's office, when they had all read the paper, there was amusement.

'It won't do him much good, when it gets round,' said Ellie. 'I wonder where it came from? One of his neighbours, seemingly, and I don't blame him, when everyone else was carrying water in buckets and basins all summer. I never once used a hosepipe on me windowbox – stuck to me milk bottle, I did.'

There was also some concern.

'It certainly doesn't look good, for the chief executive of the company that imposed the ban,' said Rachel. 'I have a feeling that this could give a lot of his votes to Peter, and cancel out what we're doing. Just when we thought we were getting there.'

'Oh God, the thought that we might be going through all this for nothing,' said Susanna.

In Peacock's office, where Cyril Eversley had burst in and thrown the *Tunbridge Wells Gazette* on his desk, there was anger.

'Yes, of course I did it,' said Peacock. 'For goodness' sake, Cyril, you agreed that I should, on Tuesday evening last week at the club, don't you remember? You'd had one or two.'

'You – you bastard, Leonard. I never agreed! I remember every word, and you wanted to do it, and I said we couldn't. I never agreed! Ask my wife. You can't pin that on me, so don't you try.'

In the Liberal Democrat office there was despair.

'The bloody fool,' said the agent miserably. 'Just when we had it all tied up. He's lost us the best chance we ever had to win this seat.'

In the office of the *Wealden Echo* there was unrestrained fury. The editor had Kieran Mitchell pinned to a chair, unable to evade his anger as he towered over her.

'Not only do you let this – this rag, this toilet paper, get the story, but you let a good friend of mine drown in it. Lance Horton would make a better MP than all the others put together.'

'Not if he does that kind of thing,' said Kieran bravely, extending a hand to tap the rival newspaper on the desk.

'Bloody fool, letting himself get photographed like that,' said the editor, adding self-righteously, 'not that I approve of what he did, mind you.'

'The story was sent to the *Gazette*, it says,' said the girl, 'so it's hardly my fault we didn't get it. You think you'd have used it, then, do you?'

'Well,' said the editor, abashed, 'there are ways and ways of using things. I might have kept it till it was too late to matter. But the point is, we have to be first with the news, Kieran, always, understand? You should have been out there, getting this story.'

He thought it better not to give her a chance to reply.

'We have one more issue,' he went on, 'the day before the election. I want our front page on fire, Kieran, blazing, that day. I want selling headlines. A good story, and preferably an anti-Tory one. It's only fair, to keep the balance, you see?'

'I see,' said Kieran.

Saturday evening, with less than a week to go. Susanna, home and tired, flicked through the letters lying on the table. Her heart sank as she saw her own handwriting on an envelope. It was the letter she had written to Mark after that unhappy telephone call. She had been confident that she had put everything right with him, but here it was, returned unopened, and marked RETURN TO SENDER. He hadn't even read it. One glance at her handwriting had been enough.

'Ma,' she said tearfully to Rachel a few minutes later, after explaining her distress, 'I can't go through with it.'

'Infirm of purpose,' said Rachel in, she hoped, a fair imitation of Sarah Bernhardt's most withering tones. 'Give me the daggers ... Susanna, we are nearly there – you can't give up now. If your children really think you are a reactionary fanatic they are stupider than I thought.'

'Do you think they all believe it?' said Susanna. 'They must have had such a low opinion of me all these years.'

'Su, of course they don't. They're just embarrassed at what you're doing. Perhaps you had better talk to Peter, despite your rather sensible agreement.'

'I think I will,' Susanna nodded, downcast. 'I can't take much more of this.'

On the Sunday before polling day there was no canvassing for the Conservatives. This traditional Sunday break was observed by the Independent Conservative party as well, Ellie said authoritatively, as long as she was a member, and firmly closed the front door of her flat.

So Peter and Susanna found themselves at home together for a day, the first time since the previous weekend.

'Pete,' said Susanna, 'if I put the lamb in the slow oven, will you come for a walk with me before lunch?'

He hesitated, then agreed.

They followed signed footpaths that led into relatively unspoiled countryside behind their farmhouse, the two dogs running ahead, barking excitedly, having been long deprived. They walked for a long time in virtual silence, by mutual unspoken consent. The day was bright, and the earlier frost had mostly vanished, leaving only a white encrustation in the shade of the hedges.

They paused in a gateway, to lean on the cracked grey oak rail and look at the view over gently heaving fields.

'Mark isn't speaking to me,' said Susanna.

'No?' said Peter, non-committally.

'Pete,' she said, '*you* don't believe that I'm for hanging and flogging and all that stuff, do you?'

'Am I hearing you right?' he said.

'All that stuff in my pamphlet. You don't believe that's what I really think?'

Peter turned to her with a look of exaggerated surprise.

'Aren't we in danger of talking about the election? About campaigning? I thought that wasn't allowed.'

Susanna swallowed.

'Could we have a truce about that? Just for this morning?'

'It's you that makes the rules,' he said, shrugging.

'Pete, the children don't understand what I'm trying to do.'

'Does anyone, Susanna? Do you yourself?' Now there was an acid edge to his voice. He seemed fascinated by the swooping wires of the distant pylons.

'Pete, how can you ask that?' she flared up. 'You know what our plan is – you told me yourself that Peacock made it clear to you. I'm doing it for *you*, Pete, for goodness' sake! In the end it is all for you, you know that! You becoming an MP was a mistake I helped you make, and now I'm helping get you out of it. I'd much rather take the flak myself than have you go on.'

'Take the flak' was not an expression he had heard from her before, and he was to remember it later.

'Calm down,' he said, shrugging again. 'I haven't tried to stop you, have I?'

He looked at her, and the tension and pallor he saw in her face softened his approach. He turned and leant his back against the gate.

'Oh, look, Sukie, your dreadful speech at the inter-church meeting certainly shook me up. It was so bloody realistic. But obviously as soon as I really thought about it I realised that it had all been cooked up to give you a platform. You may think you don't ever talk politics, but even you couldn't have hidden opinions as extreme as that from me for all these years. It was ridiculous – you are the most moderate, un-racist person I know, and as European as – as Ted Heath.'

He looked at her again, without smiling.

'There is, of course,' he went on, 'a question of the morality of asking for votes on a false prospectus. Thought of that, have we?'

'That's my problem. I'll deal with that in my own conscience,' said Susanna. 'But Pete, would you do something for me? Would you talk to the children, say what you've just said to me? I would like to do it for myself, but they . . . they won't answer my calls.'

'You've got a nerve, Susanna, asking me that,' said Peter. 'But I suppose I will. Let's go on. I'm cold.'

'Thank you,' she said. 'Yes, I suppose I have a nerve, as you put it.'

The path was narrow, and she walked in front of him.

'It would be nice,' she said, 'if we could stop now.'

He understood.

'Not go through this final week? Yes. You get swept along towards polling day on Thursday. It's like white-water canoeing. No stopping now.'

'Or like going into labour, when you're having a baby,' said Susanna, 'particularly the first time. You feel like saying, "Oi, I'm not ready. I think I want to change my mind about this," and you can't, however scared you feel.'

Peter came up beside her as the path widened.

'I wonder how the *Tun Wells Gazette* got that nasty little story,' said Susanna.

'Peacock said Cyril Eversley told him to do it,' said Peter, 'or approved it, anyway. I simply don't believe him. Cyril felt as strongly as we did about it. I have refused to comment to the *Echo*, and I just hope it'll all die away. But I'm afraid they may refer to it too, because their paper comes out the day before polling day. I hate this sort of thing.'

'I know you do.'

They walked on, side by side on the wider path, the sun on their backs.

'I am glad we had this morning, Pete,' said Susanna. 'We needed it. A bit of dramatic calm. I'm sure there's a name for it. You know what I mean? Like the long duet in the last act of grand opera, when the hero and heroine don't know what's going to happen, but they sort out a few misunderstandings and have a nice nostalgic time, and so does the audience, before the emotional stress of the conclusion. And you all feel the better for it.

'No, no, don't say anything,' as Peter looked like protesting. 'I'm not being flippant about what you said. I'm just moving on, in an intellectual and imaginative way that you may not appreciate.'

'Oh, I appreciate it. I just don't feel like singing.'

It was a relief to be able to joke again, and they both felt it, although the strain between them could not be banished. Peter found himself torn between disapproval of what Susanna was doing, and a feeling he could hardly admit to himself that in the unlikely event of her plan succeeding a lot of problems would be solved.

Susanna, reflecting later on her operatic analogy, remembered that such interludes could foreshadow disaster as often as deliverance. She knew intuitively that Peter's calm came from conviction that she could not succeed in making him lose his seat. What she could not know, was how he would react if she did, and that was the thought that kept her awake at night.

Chapter 18

It was seven o'clock on the morning of election day. The frost was again bristling white on the grass round the house, and the sun was rising through a pinkish haze into a clear, cloudless sky, loftily oblivious of how this might affect the voting patterns of Great Britain. Peter and Susanna were breakfasting together at Restings. Peter was to be picked up by the chairman of the Young Conservatives, who would drive him on the customary whistle-stop tour of polling booths and party committee rooms around the constituency.

Both the Westerhams felt a sense of unreality about their situation, and each was determined to behave very normally.

'I can't say I'm really looking forward to a day spent entirely in the company of Terry Lowther,' said Peter. 'For one thing, I can hardly forget his childish attack on Leo and Andrew, and for another, he keeps asking me if I will endorse his application to go on the candidates' list. I wish I was unkind enough to tell him to give up now, or at the very least to grow up first. Though, actually, I can think of some people on the candidates' list selection panel who would see our Terry as a gift from heaven. What's your programme for today?'

'A long walk with the dogs, first,' said Susanna, helping herself to marmalade. 'Then a bit of pruning. I'm going to hit the climbing roses really hard, this year. And I think I may have lunch with Ma.'

'Am I going mad, or are you?' said Peter, incredulous. 'On election day? Do you mean you are not even going around in the constituency? It is, after all, normal behaviour for a candidate.'

'Not much point, really,' said Susanna, munching toast. 'We don't do things like that in my party. You can't tour the committee rooms when you don't have any committees, and we don't have a vehicle suitable for standing and waving from. We thought we would all have the day off, actually.'

Peter privately found her offhand attitude infuriating, although what she said was obviously the plain truth.

'Well,' he said, determined not to rise, 'I have to hand it to you for coolth. My day is going to be hell. It's always exhausting, and with opinion polls the way they are, everyone will be in deep gloom.

I hope to get back for a quick shower at about eight-thirty, and then off again to Wraybury town hall. As you have so little to do, I suppose you won't mind getting me some supper.'

'A strong drink is what you'll really need,' said Susanna. 'You'll have been eating tidbits all day, remembering last time. I'll have something ready, though, delicious but gobble-able, in case you get late. I'm hoping you'll give me a lift to the count. It seems silly to take two cars, and Ma is picking Ellie up.'

'Oh, you are planning to come to the count, then?'

Nothing would surprise him now. But his sarcasm was wasted.

'I thought I would,' she said.

'I would be sorry if you didn't have the courage to face up to what you're doing,' he said coldly.

'You'll give me a lift, then?'

'I suppose so. This is all quite dotty,' said Peter, shaking his head. 'It must be unique for opposing candidates to arrive together.'

'You can drop me around the corner if you like,' said Susanna, 'so that your supporters don't see.'

She had not meant to annoy him, and was sorry that it had happened. It would make the bridge-building afterwards all the harder.

Peter, as he was driven away, reflected that she would not be so casual if she had any real confidence in her plan working. She was preparing for the humiliation of defeat by pretending she didn't care. He felt comforted by this thought, and resolved in that event to be generous and forgiving. If she succeeded, and the Liberal Democrat got his seat, he would have to try and remember that she had done it, however perversely, for their family's sake. He thought he could manage that.

Lowther interrupted his thoughts.

'What?' said Peter. 'Yes, that's right, Terry. Bratscombe village hall first.'

In the office of the Independent Conservative Party there was an atmosphere of almost excessive calm. The computer sat blind and silent in a corner, the piles of papers that had littered every surface and most of the floor had all been disposed of. Apart from the wall charts, all a little tatty now, the room looked almost like a sitting room again. Ellie Fittall was shuffling about in her bedroom slippers at eight-thirty in the morning, wondering what to do.

At ten she telephoned Rachel Willoughby.

'I can't stand it no more,' she said. 'I have never been so bored in me life. I can't remember an election day when I wasn't out there fighting for votes, and driving people to the polls, too, when I was younger. And the last few times, I've always been a teller somewhere.'

'Well,' said Rachel, 'why shouldn't you be a teller now? You can be a sort of straw pollster.'

It was all the encouragement Ellie needed. Within minutes she was trotting down the road to Wraybury's biggest polling station, a primary school in peacetime, with a folding stool under her arm. The plastic bag in her other hand held a notebook, Rachel's mobile telephone, two Thermos flasks of hot tea and other comforts.

Telling is an essential part of election day, for each party needs to know who has voted, in order to chase up any of their supporters who have not. It can also be a tedious and chilly job, and as an old hand Ellie knew most of the tricks. She also knew this polling station, and her eyes narrowed as she saw that the Labour, Liberal Democrat and Conservative tellers were occupying all the space in the only sheltered spot beside the entrance. After placing her stool beside them, but in the wind that whistled round the corner of the building, she said to the company in general:

'I wonder whose car that is; the green one just by the gate.'

For a minute she thought her shot had misfired.

Then the Labour teller, a pale girl in a huge sheepskin coat said, 'Why?'

'Oh, is it yours?' said Ellie. 'It's terrible, this vandalism, isn't it? Day and night. Can't leave anything, nowadays. Now, when I was young . . .'

While the girl was out of sight Ellie moved her stool into the shelter of the wall, and pushed the vacant chair out. By the time the owner of the car returned, mystified at finding her vehicle just as she had left it, the old lady had poured tea all round, and was deep in conversation with the other tellers.

A woman came out of the polling station. She headed straight for the teller with the huge blue rosette.

'Mrs Amy Welsh, 19 Craghill Way, and I don't mind saying you did not get my vote this time. Nor you either. Neither of you.'

She glared at the orange and black rosette decorating the lapel of the Liberal Democrat teller.

'My roses were dying in all that hot weather last summer, but I never once done them with the hose, like what your man did. It was disgusting. But as for that Tory lot, going and telling all the papers, just to get more votes, that was just as bad. Diabolical, I call it. You're all the same, and you can tell them I said so. I love my garden.'

She threw a copy of the *Wealden Echo* on to the lap of the woman with the blue rosette and marched off down the path towards the road. She paused to throw a parting shot over her shoulder:

'And I can tell you, some of my friends are so fed up after all these shenanigans that they're not voting at all!'

'That's what they're all saying,' said the girl with the red Labour rosette happily. 'Hypocrites, though, aren't they, the whole lot of them? They'd all have watered their gardens if they'd thought they could get away with it. And the same goes for telling on their neighbours. Hypocrites, that's what I think, bourgeois hypocrites.'

Ellie took the paper. She had already seen the article, but she read it again. Kieran Mitchell had done a magnificent job for her editor. She had had a stroke of luck: the aggrieved informant had missed seeing his story in the Tunbridge Wells paper, which was not one he subscribed to; intent on publicity, he had telephoned the Wealden Echo, and it had not taken Kieran long to discover where he had originally sent his photographs. As a result, the main headline in Wednesday's *Echo* was a seller.

NO BLOW TOO LOW FOR TORIES

Conservative hosepipe leaks

Kieran had been pleased with that line. Her sensationally worded revelation that it was the Conservative agent who had passed the photographs of the Lib Dem candidate to the press read well. Peacock's unconvincing denials read even better. And the quoted outrage of voters she had interviewed about his 'below the belt' tactics were everything she had hoped for. Apparently there were limits in Kentish Weald to what was considered fair in politics. Kieran and her editor were not alone in their satisfaction about the piece.

'Nasty piece of work, that Peacock,' said Ellie Fittall, smiling and rummaging in the depths of her bag. 'Now, would you all like something a little stronger in your tea?'

Unlike the bye-election count four years earlier, the Kentish Weald general election count in Wraybury town hall was a cliffhanger. Again and again the scene inside the old council chamber came up on the television screens nationwide. The thing that made this particular election result of special interest was, of course, the fact that a husband and wife had been standing against each other. Now, to add spice to the situation, there had already been two recounts, and a third was taking place.

The first recount had been ordered by the returning officer because of the closeness of the votes for the leading contenders. All it had achieved was to bring the votes of the two leaders slightly closer together. The second recount had been at the demand of the runner up, and had reduced the already narrow gap by two more votes. For this reason, the electoral returning officer had permitted a third recount.

When it was over, the counting clerks sat back, folding their arms and chatting among themselves, and the result was once again passed to the candidates. The figures were unchanged this time. It would have surprised the political analysts in the television studios, as well as those viewers who stayed up late into the night to watch the election results coming through, to know that at this point the leading candidate urgently, even passionately, requested a fourth recount.

'I have two identical results,' said Ed Forman firmly. 'There will be no more recounts.'

He invited all the candidates to follow him onto the platform for the announcement of the result.

'I just don't believe it,' said Susanna, standing beside her mother, staring at the long rows of white slips stretched out along the tables. 'This is some sort of nightmare.'

'Pinch me, would you?' said Rachel.

'Five votes, just five votes,' muttered Susanna, as Ellie propelled her up the steps. 'I thought it couldn't possibly go wrong . . . Ellie, what am I to do?'

'You're to get up there with your chin up and a smile on your face and not let us down,' hissed Ellie. 'Have a bit of pride, woman. You're on television.'

The swingometer faded from the screen and the commentator said into the camera:

'And finally we have a result from Wraybury, where there was an unusually low poll for this general election. In any case, after three recounts it appears that they have agreed on a winner. The candidates are gathering on the platform for the announcement of the result. From the look on the Independent Conservative candidate's face, the challenging spouse of the sitting MP, I would say the result is not to her satisfaction, though it is hard to tell just who *is* looking at all pleased up there . . .'

The voice of the returning officer was faded in.

'. . . to represent the Kentish Weald constituency, do hereby declare that the number of votes cast at the said election are as follows . . .'

When he got to 'Manning, Andrew John, eleven thousand, six hundred and ninety-seven' a roar of surprise burst from the listeners on the floor, and the commentator said hurriedly, 'You can hear the amazement here, over an astonishingly high vote for a Green candidate, beating the Lib Dem, whose vote has fallen very considerably. This is really a—'

Once again the returning officer's voice was heard.

'May I ask for silence, please? Myers, Reginald Arthur . . .'

'(Labour),' said the commentator.

'. . . five thousand and thirty-four.'

'Lower than last time,' murmured the commentator, 'but then it was a low poll.'

'Westerham, Peter James . . .'

'(Official Conservative).'

'. . . eleven thousand, nine hundred and seventy-four.'

Another burst of excitement, and another plea for silence; a quick 'Again, a huge drop for the sitting MP,' from the commentator.

The returning officer raised his voice a little, as if anticipating a reaction.

'Westerham, Susanna . . .'

'(Independent).'

'. . . eleven thousand, nine hundred and seventy-nine. I therefore declare the said Susanna Westerham duly elected Member of Parliament for the Kentish Weald constituency.'

For a moment there was a stunned silence, and then a rising babble of voices all round the council chamber.

'Well,' said the commentator, facing the camera again, 'there we have it. An astonishing result in Kentish Weald. The Green Party have picked up a huge number of votes, beating the Lib Dems, whose vote has fallen considerably, into fourth place, and the Conservatives have lost the seat which they have held since – how long, James? – since before the last war, and it has been won by an Independent, Independent Conservative, I should say, the wife of the last MP, in a nailbiting finish. And now we have another result from Scotland coming in . . .'

And the programme moved on.

'Good God, Mum has won,' said Mark.

Emma felt almost unable to reply.

'I don't believe this. You – you realise she hasn't just got Dad out, she's got herself *in*. *She's* the MP now!'

'Oh, well done, Emma,' said Mark.

They were standing watching from the gallery of the council chamber. They could see Leonora busy embracing Andrew Manning just off the platform.

'No one cheered her,' said Mark.

'She hasn't any supporters, that's why,' said Emma.

'Are you surprised she hasn't got any supporters,' said Mark, 'with all that stuff she had in her election address? All that racist, right-wing little England stuff?'

'*We* know it wasn't for real, but people voted for her,' said Emma. 'A lot of people. Where are they now?'

'You'll always find fascists out there,' said Mark gloomily. 'I suppose there's no one cheering because she didn't have a committee and all that.'

'Mark, think,' said Emma, 'it must be awful to win like that and have *no one* pleased. No one cheering.'

'Well,' said her brother, 'that's what she deserves, isn't it? Standing against Dad and spreading all that Nazi stuff around.'

'Mark, we have got to support her,' said Emma. 'I promised Dad we would. She's our mother, for goodness' sake. She wouldn't let *us* down at a big moment like this. And if we're going to do it, let's do it properly. Come on, we're going down.'

She took him by the elbow and pulled him towards the stairs.

On their way through the crowd in the hall, as they neared the platform, they met Rupert and Florence Hascombe. They were talking together, looking serious, but greeted the twins with smiles.

'That's a turn-up for the books,' said Rupert.

'We're going to give Mum a cheer,' said Mark.

'Quite right too. Someone must,' said Florence. 'We'll come with you. Come *on*, Rupert. Susanna is a friend.'

From below the platform, Mark called out at the top of his voice, 'Three cheers for the new Member of Parliament for Kentish Weald, hip, hip—'

To his surprise, by the time he got to the third hip, several voices had halfheartedly joined their small, cheering group. Ellie's reedy tones rose above the others. The flat, abruptly ended little cheers came to Susanna's ears, as she struggled to think how to deal with the microphone that had been placed in front of her. Something was expected of her, so something would have to be said.

Eventually, grim-faced, she spoke.

'I . . . I have to say that I am as surprised as you must all be to find myself in this position. I have my agent and my press officer to thank for putting me in it. And my family. I would like to thank my family for, well, being my family. And as for all those people in Kentish Weald who decided to vote for me, I hardly know what to say.'

It was the view of those who heard her that as an acceptance speech it was rather inadequate, but then the poor woman was obviously in an emotional state. The other candidates remembered to thank the returning officer, his staff and the police, in the correct fashion, so the honours were done.

Rachel Willoughby, having listened to Susanna's careful phrasing, thought it wiser, on the whole, to offer Ellie a lift home right away and not to intrude on the new MP's time until the dust had settled. Ellie seemed to be equally eager to leave. What they really needed, they agreed as they set off, was a good night's sleep. It might even help to clarify the situation, which had left them both in a state of considerable mental disarray.

Slowly the event wound down: the voting slips were poured back into the ballot boxes, and the boxes were resealed; the counting clerks cleared the tables and collected their coats; the supporters of the different parties dispersed, one or two congratulating Susanna politely as they passed, most of them intent on getting home.

Andrew Manning came out of the chamber with his arm round Leonora and surrounded by a crowd of Green supporters. They were grinning and exuberant, and an observer would have assumed that this was the camp of the winning candidate.

Leonard Peacock strode out through the entrance hall, a leather wallet of papers under his arm, his features rigid. He ignored Susanna completely, but walked up to Peter and glared into his face.

'Happy, now?' he grated.

Peter stared back, and then turned away.

Cyril Eversley, some unsteady paces in Peacock's wake, paused by Susanna and coughed.

'What a thing, then,' he said, patting her on the arm. 'You winning it, what a thing. Never 'spected that. What a thing . . .'

He leant heavily against her, not entirely on purpose and causing her to put out a hand for support on the table behind her, and muttered into her ear.

'Y're a r'markable woman, thass what I say. A r'markable woman.'

'Goodnight, Cyril,' she said. 'Thank you.'

He shambled past Peter, too overcome to do more than lay a heavy pat on his shoulder.

When they had all gone Susanna moved towards Peter. He had not been near her since the announcement of the result. She looked past him as she spoke.

'I can't believe this has happened. I never meant this to happen,' she said.

'No?' said Peter, looking down at her. The expression on his face was not inviting.

'You must believe me,' said Susanna. 'This is the very last thing that was meant to happen. We never even contemplated this happening.'

'You are asking me to believe the impossible,' said Peter.

'Pete, I mean it!'

'You may not have expected this result,' he said coldly, 'but don't tell me you didn't secretly hope for it.'

He turned away to the pile of coats on the table behind him.

'I not only didn't expect it,' she said urgently, following him, 'I most certainly did not want it. Peter, listen to me – what I am saying is the truth!'

She looked up sharply into his face. He did not meet her eyes. Pulling on his coat, he said: 'Leonora used to have some caustic little aphorisms about truth and politicians.'

'I am not a politician, Pete!' she said angrily.

'You are now,' he replied. 'And I wish you joy of it.'

He tossed her coat to her, and walked ahead down the steps and to the car.

Peter drove home, and they did not speak. He was unwilling, and she was far too upset. As they pulled up outside Restings, he said: 'I think it best if I slept in the spare room. We may both have trouble sleeping.'

The following morning for Susanna was like waking into a nightmare. The unthinkable having happened, she was now forced to think about it. But the 'cold grey light' was far more conducive to rational thought than the heat of the night before. She was certain, at least, that Peter, in the room at the end of the passage, would be realising, now that he had calmed down, that her intentions had been no worse than he had supposed; it was just that her plan, with her mother and Ellie, had misfired most horribly. To deprive him of the Kentish Weald seat had certainly been their object. But to supplant him, no. That was a scenario no one had for a second contemplated. She would surely not have to work convince him of that.

For the rest, Peter would help her over what to do next. She badly needed him to advise her on who to get in touch with during the two-week post-election parliamentary break.

She was mildly surprised to see the spare room door already standing open; then she heard voices in the kitchen. They were all down already, reading the newspapers spread over the table. The Labour landslide and the defeat of the Conservatives filled the headlines, but it was the local result that held their minds.

When she walked in, they fell silent, then all started speaking at once.

'Good morning. You slept, I hope?' from Peter.

'Hi, Mum,' from Emma, 'where do you want to sit?'

'Get down,' said Mark to one of the dogs. 'Get off that chair.'

'Good morning,' said Susanna.

'Want some coffee?' said Mark.

'There are a couple of messages on the answering machine,' said Peter, 'Ellie Fittall and some news man.'

'Mum, come and sit here.' Emma looked anxiously at her. It was as if none of them dared allow a silence. They were saved by Leonora.

She slammed the front door and burst into the room, her face glowing as she smiled round the table.

'Didn't Andrew do brilliantly? They're saying it's the biggest vote ever won by a Green candidate. Do you realise he beat the Lib Dem by nearly two thousand votes? And jolly nearly beat you two! He's coming round a bit later. He's got the press ringing him!'

She looked over at the telephone on the side table and saw that the receiver was lying off it.

'Aren't you going to congratulate your mother? She was the winner, actually,' said Mark, his usually warm expression noticeably absent.

'Yes, of course I am. Mum, you're amazing. Dad, are you all right?'

She kissed Susanna's cheek, and then put her arms tentatively round her father's neck She looked solicitously at him.

Peter was sitting at the table in his shirtsleeves. He looked tired, but the smile he directed at his daughter was genuine.

'Of course I'm all right,' he said. 'And Andrew really is to be congratulated. Not just for putting the case of his party well – I read his article in the *Echo*, and I thought his leaflet was extremely sensible and professional. I couldn't disagree with any of it. Not just for that, though, but for an efficient campaign, and for recruiting an excellent agent. You should both be congratulated. It was a tremendous vote he got.'

'Dad, you're great.' His daughter hugged him again. 'I wasn't really his agent, but I did run the office. But it was all him, he just was so convincing. You should have heard him on the doorsteps! And he's going to do an interview tonight, and I wondered if I could possibly borrow the video. I'll bring it . . . Mum, I don't know what to say. You're an MP. It's all a bit of a shock. Everything changes so fast, doesn't it – one minute Andrew doesn't have a hope, then suddenly he's getting all these votes. And you two – oh dear, am I being . . . ?'

Susanna, who had said very little that morning, smiled at Leonora and dipped her head to her coffee mug. The twins had slid out of the room as their sister was running on.

Leonora noticed. 'Oh, I must catch them,' she said, heading for the door. 'We want them to come to the flat tonight and . . .'

The door shut, and Peter and Susanna were left together. He got up and moved to the stove.

'You are going to have some breakfast, I hope?'

'Pete? Will you talk to me?'

She could not believe that he was still so distant. She had been so sure that the passing of the night would have brought them to think alike.

'I am talking to you, am I not?' he said, his eyebrows raised. 'I am offering you some excellent sausages, cooked by Emma.'

'No, Pete, you know what I mean.'

'Do you mean talk to you about last night?'

Turning, a serving spoon in his hand, he was smiling at her now, a polite smile that did not involve his eyes.

'I don't think that is necessary, Sukie,' he said. 'We were all there, so there's nothing much to be gained. Two sausages or three? I'll put some more toast in.'

She sat staring at her plate. The nightmare seemed still to be happening.

'Pete—'

He looked at his watch.

'If you want to discuss anything about the household, I should be back about seven. After three weeks away from the office I have a lot of catching up to do. If anyone rings, they can get me there. I'll be off now. Have a good day.'

Peter had been thinking too. The cold light of dawn had cleared his mind as well. The more he looked at it, the more plainly he saw that to win the Kentish Weald seat had always been Susanna's intention. The way she and her companions had run their campaign was proof enough, if it were needed. They had done far more than was required to let Horton in, and it was perfectly possible that the remarkable Mrs Fittall was in some way behind the débâcle over the hosepipe that had affected both Horton and himself so badly.

There was also the evidence of Susanna's devoted work in the constituency, her apparent enjoyment of it, her soaring popularity which Peacock had commented on so frequently and so pointedly to him. It should have been obvious to any fool that she was nursing the seat for herself, while trying to persuade him to give it up. She had regularly played on his tiredness and told him he was damaging his health. That phrase she had used, it came back to him now: 'I would much rather take the flak myself than have you go on.' If that had not been a statement of intention, what was it? He should know what it was to want to be an MP. He remembered being jealous of others in the job, so why should not Susanna, so resentful of being a spouse, 'an MP's handbag' as she had called herself, feel the same? There was no doubt she believed the family would benefit from his getting out of parliament – he had become convinced of it himself. But her intention, he knew now, had been far more devious. He had been the victim of a carefully laid plot, and this he found impossible to forgive.

Susanna sat long at the table, till eventually the twins reappeared. They seemed busy, fully occupied. She would have liked to have talked to them, to have explained her feelings, but they avoided her. She felt too stunned to pursue them. It was Peter she was most worried about.

Later in the morning Rachel tapped at the window.

'Sorry to bring you a problem,' she said. 'I need a hand in the stables. I think we have a frozen pipe. Could you bring a kettle? Or a hairdryer?'

'I'll go,' said Mark, passing through.
'No,' said Susanna. 'I will.'
Anything for distraction.

As they walked down the path together Rachel said to Susanna: 'You don't have to say anything. I've been awake most of the night thinking all the things you have been thinking.'

'I was convinced by your plan,' said Susanna. 'A few thousand votes and let the Lib Dem in. How *could* it go so wrong?'

'I reckon it was that wretched hosepipe business,' said Rachel. 'It took votes away from them both, and they divided between you and Andrew.'

'That is obvious,' said Susanna. 'But oh dear, Ma, it's far, far worse than you realise: Peter believes that we went out deliberately to win the seat.'

Rachel stopped in her tracks and stared, as Susanna walked on and into the stables. When her mother joined her she was already wrapping strips of material round the pipe. They talked only of the problem of preventing a leak but later as Susanna swept a pool of water into a gutter Rachel spoke again, indignantly.

'How can Peter think that that was what you wanted? It's beyond imagining, Su.'

'Well, he does.'

Turning away from her mother, keeping her hands busy, Susanna tried to hide her face. She was finding it intolerably hard to maintain the pretence that she was calm. Then it was too much; the broom fell to the ground and she stood with her head drooping as the tears started to flow.

Rachel touched her hand. She turned and dropped her face onto her mother's shoulder.

'Oh God,' she said, her voice shaking, 'I have been such a bloody fool.'

'We both have,' said Rachel, 'arrogant, bloody fools, and I am the bloodiest.'

'I thought I had family troubles,' Susanna snuffled, 'and look what they're like now. The children all think I've been disloyal to Pete, I know they do, and I have, but not the way they think. And Pete – Pete is behaving like a stranger, Ma. It was dreadful, last night, and again this morning. He won't talk to me, he won't even discuss what happened. He is all polite and distant. I don't think he is ever going to believe me, or forgive me.'

'Oh come,' said Rachel briskly. 'He'll get over it. Give it a few days. Let the dust settle. Let a little time pass, and he will see it all differently. Just behave normally and ride it out.'

'I hope you're right, Ma,' said Susanna.

But she was not. At no point over the next week did Peter waver in his behaviour. He was polite, helpful, considerate and as far away as a distant star. He asked Susanna no questions about what she was going to do, and he gave her no inkling of what he might be going to do. He did not, in fact, seem to be thinking of her at all, but appeared simply to have settled back into his legal life as if he had never interrupted it.

More than once Susanna tried to approach him.

'Pete, surely you will at least talk to me about everything that has happened?'

'Why? We both know what has happened, and quite honestly I have other things to think about now. If you don't mind, I have to make a couple of telephone calls before I go out . . .'

It was the same every time.

One of his partners telephoned to speak to him one evening, and got Susanna instead. He seemed slightly embarrassed, and after some stumbling congratulations said warmly what a difference it made to have Peter in the office again every day.

'We seemed to have gone into neutral over this period that he has been so busy, Susanna. Having his ideas and his drive back with us is a great thing. Has he told you what he's planning?'

'No,' said Susanna.

More embarrassment.

'Ah, well. I expect you've been very busy. I am sure he will want to, well . . . discuss it all with you. You are an unusual couple, you Westerhams, very . . . er . . . unique, and all that.'

'I think you really want to speak to Peter,' said Susanna, helpfully. 'Hold on while I tell him.'

The twins were away again, and Susanna's desperate efforts to speak to them were continually frustrated by answering machines. They did not return her calls. Leonora seemed busy, too, and when Susanna did get through to her, she was always 'in a rush' when her mother tried to engage her in explanatory talk. It was as if no one wanted to hear Susanna's side of the story. She felt intensely lonely. Rachel was the only person to talk to, but she wasn't much help.

'I am sure you must just be patient,' she said. 'Have you tried to talk to him?'

'Ma, of course I've tried,' said Susanna impatiently. 'I told him only this morning that we couldn't go on like this, that we would both feel happier if we could sit down and have a proper discussion, and you know what he said? He said he was perfectly happy, and I should be too, so there was really nothing to discuss. It's inhuman.'

'That's what it's not, I'm afraid,' said Rachel. 'It's all too human. He's hurt, that's all. He'll come round.'

'I think you are wrong,' said her daughter. She was beginning to find Rachel's apparently unflagging confidence in her own judgement intensely irritating.

As the days went by, a sense of injustice grew in Susanna. She had apparently to carry all the blame for their situation, and this isolation was her punishment. She did not feel she deserved it, and it was unfair. Where she would have been ready with sympathy and understanding for any of the other members of the family, she was met with blank indifference.

Out of her resentment at this treatment grew a determination not to be crushed by it. She would not crumble, and humble herself. She would fight back, and surprise them all. She would, she thought, warming with some pleasure to the idea, show Peter that she had indeed the courage of which he was accusing her.

It was as if a permanent frost had set in to the Restings farmhouse, and only Peter was getting on with his life. Susanna, too, became strangely uncommunicative, and it seemed to Rachel that the stand-off was to be unending.

Nine days after the election she went to see Ellie. Despite the act she was putting on, she was suffering like her daughter from loneliness and self-doubt, and needed the cups of tea and common sense she knew she would find in the little council flat.

But Ellie for once had no advice to offer.

'They're going to have to sort it out between themselves, love. There's not much we can do now, except keep our heads down, as I see it. We've meddled enough, that's what.'

'It was such a brilliant plan, Ellie, that's the sad bit.'

'It was neat, wasn't it?' said Ellie. 'It's not everyone can win an election with a committee of three.'

'Four – we couldn't have done it without Sylvia,' said Rachel.

'Ye-e-eh,' said Ellie, 'Seelveea, poor Seelveea – but she was all right, wasn't she? It'll be the making of her, you mark my words. That was a great night. I quite fancy a little burglary on the side.'

They were like two old troopers, proudly reliving their past battles, the triumphs tinged with regret.

'Ye-e-eh,' said Ellie again, 'it was a good plan, and we had a good team. We done it well. It just got out of control. Ain't you got nothing in that computer to help?' she added, trying and failing to make her friend laugh. But Rachel was feeling too downcast to be cheered.

She did not manage to talk to Susanna till Monday, two days later. Seeing that her car was in its place, she slipped rather sheepishly into her daughter's kitchen. She heard sounds in the larder behind. There she found Susanna by the big chest freezer.

'Su,' said Rachel, 'I just wanted to tell you, I went to see Ellie, and she agrees with me that—'

Susanna interrupted her. She looked different today. She was different. She was brisk and confident, like someone who has come to a decision. She spoke firmly.

'It is very good of you and Ellie to concern yourself with my problems, but I really don't need any more of your joint advice.'

'No, I understand that, darling,' said Rachel humbly. 'I wouldn't take my advice now either, but I just—'

'Ma, I am quite busy, actually. These are for Pete, for when I am not here.'

Susanna turned back to the freezer, which she was filling from a cardboard box with large numbers of packets of ready-made meals.

'Frankly,' she said as she worked, 'I know you both meant well, but I would not be in the position I am if you weren't both so well-meaning. From now on I'm going to think for myself.'

'Su, don't rub it in,' said Rachel wretchedly. 'You couldn't make me feel more guilty than I do already. What are you going to do?'

'Do?' said her daughter. 'What do people normally do, after they've been elected? You don't think I'm going to chicken out now, do you? Allow me a little pride.'

'Susanna?' said Rachel, unbelieving. 'You're not going to . . . ?'

'Of course I am, Ma. I'm going to take my seat in parliament. What else can I do?'

Stupefied, Rachel watched her dumping Ocean Pies on top of the rest. If she had an opinion she was not in a position to express it.

'I suppose,' she said, after a pause, 'there is nothing else you can do.'

'No,' said Susanna, shutting the lid with a bang. 'I've got just a week, till parliament starts again. Actually, I'm quite curious to see what it will be like. I may even enjoy it. And meanwhile, I hope you will give me a bit of peace and quiet. I do not want to be constantly questioned about it all. I need a break.'

Rachel nodded meekly.

'I do understand,' she said, though she did not.

Chapter 19

One week later, Susanna went to London, going by herself despite an offer from her mother to keep her company. Peter made no such offer, and there was no change in his usual courteous but remote manner as he drove her to Wraybury station. She ached, longing for him to say something, anything, encouraging.

'I hope you will find it interesting,' he said, as his farewell words.

The doorman at the block of flats greeted her as usual, and then, remembering, looked at her again.

'It's you that's the MP now, I saw,' he said.

She nodded, and felt his eyes on her as she went towards the lifts.

She walked along the Embankment to the House of Commons in the afternoon. To get in, she showed her old pass with the large S stamped across it. She went to the office where parliamentary passes are issued. After being photographed – 'Let's have a cheerful smile, then' – she was told that her new MP's pass would be available the following day.

'Your husband will know where to come, Mrs Westerham, when he wants his spouse's pass,' said the clerk with a smile.

'Yes, he would know,' she replied flatly.

Then she went, asking her way, to the office of the Sergeant-at-Arms and confirmed that she was ready to take the oath of allegiance that afternoon. His clerks were friendly, though she felt again that she was being eyed with some curiosity.

'Anything we can do to help,' said one of them, 'just let us know. It takes a few days to find your way around, and learn the ropes. Though, of course, you have been . . .'

'Please treat me as a beginner,' she said.

'Don't worry, we're here to help you. Anything we can do . . .'

This kindly attitude left her unprepared for the reaction of a small group of Conservative members, some of whom she recognised, walking along one of the corridors. As she approached there was nudging and whispering, and no smiles.

'Isn't that the Independent? Westerham's wife?' she heard.

She was meant to hear, which made her say 'Good afternoon'

firmly as she passed them. One or two nodded in acknowledgement and murmured in embarrassed response as they walked on.

Susanna, her face flushed, kept her chin up and soon heard footsteps hurrying behind her along the tiled floor. One of the MPs had turned to follow her. As he came up beside her she stopped and faced him. Peter and she had shared a table with him in the café more than once.

'I thought I should say something, Susanna,' he said. 'I'm sorry if we all seemed a bit, well, unfriendly, just now.'

'That's quite all right,' said Susanna.

'You're not going to be greeted with open arms, you realise?'

'I had no reason to expect it,' she said.

'We haven't got a glut of members in the party at the moment,' he said, 'as you know, and deposing a sitting MP is not exactly popular. Especially standing as an Independent.'

He was uncomfortable, apologetic even.

'Don't worry,' she said. 'I know what I've done.'

'Nothing personal, of course.'

'That's nice to know. Would you mind telling me the way to the Upper Corridor?'

Relieved, he gave her directions, and hurried to rejoin his friends.

Susanna smiled wryly. She remembered how Peter had been helped through his first few days by another member of his party. She, as the sole representative of hers, would have to rely on the officials of the House, her basic knowledge of its layout and her native wit.

She had been allocated a small office in the main building of the Palace of Westminster. There was just space for two desks, an armchair and some filing cabinets. The window looked onto an inner courtyard whose dark walls reflected little light. An overhead fluorescent bar in the ceiling burned night and day. The clerk who gave her the key told her that, until new office space had been provided in other buildings in recent years, a room like this would have held three members.

'You're lucky,' she said. 'You have room for a decent-sized desk now. And seeing you are not a member of any party, you and your secretary will have the room to yourselves. You're a rare bird.'

After she had gone, Susanna sat at the desk, trying to imagine how it had felt for Peter. Had he felt low in those first days, as she did now? Probably not. It had been some months before she had seen the growing detachment in him, the early signs of disillusion setting in. If she had not seen at first hand what had happened to Peter, now, as a new MP, she would very likely be fizzing with energy and fervour, longing to get going on the job of reforming the world.

She sighed. She had no plans for reform, but she did have a point or two to make.

Susanna went down to the Chamber just before the swearing-in ceremony. No one spoke to her, except a new Lib Dem member standing beside her as they took the oath in front of the Speaker.

'Never actually thought I'd ever find myself doing this,' he whispered.

'Nor did I,' said Susanna.

It was three days before she had any real contact with another member. She had spent the afternoon working in her office on a pile of constituency mail, mainly about future engagements, all of which she refused. She went down to the members' tearoom at about six, and was followed to her table by a Conservative member.

'Mind if I join you?' he said, sitting down.

'Not at all,' she said.

'Susanna, isn't it? Peter was a good friend of mine.'

She noted the past tense, and replied, 'He's very well, thank you.'

'Good, good.' He sounded a little uncertain. He was thin, narrow-faced, with glasses, and geniality did not sit easily on him. He introduced himself as Martin Fryer, and she was sure she had never met him before.

'Well,' he said, 'if you've finished that, why not come along and have a drink. Have you been in the Pugin Room yet?'

'No,' said Susanna, 'not recently, but yes, please.'

They went together to an elegant, high-ceilinged room off a crossing of corridors where the green carpets of the House of Commons met the red carpets of the House of Lords. The windows looked onto the terrace and the river.

Fryer suggested she grab a vacant corner table while he got the drinks.

When he returned and sat down he said at once: 'I'll come clean with you, Susanna. We are all very interested – why did you stand for parliament as an Independent? As far as we can gather, you are as Conservative as I am, and you were elected basically on the same political principles as my own.'

'Tell me about your principles,' said Susanna, helping herself to a potato crisp. She had been hoping for an approach like this.

'Well, you know,' said Fryer, quietly, leaning his folded arms on the table, 'I'm firmly on the right of the party – I believe we have drifted too far to the left.'

'I'm very interested in what you say,' said Susanna, cocking her head sideways and smiling at him. 'Do go on. And on the European Union?'

The member still spoke in a low voice but with more confidence, feeling he had a sympathetic ear. This was what he had been told he might expect.

'Well, the sooner we are clear of that the better, of course. If we had never gone in, we would be the greatest power in Europe by now. And that's what it's all about, Susanna. Power. When did Britannia ever take her orders from foreigners?'

He was intentionally keeping it simple. He didn't think there was any great brain here, but she was a good-looking girl, which made a change.

'You know, you could be quoting from my election address,' said Susanna. 'I did a rather good leaflet.'

'Good, good,' he said, rubbing his hands together. 'I'm sure we'll get on. Well, now. We've got a little lunch tomorrow, myself and some colleagues. We call ourselves the Britannia Group, actually. Like thinkers, you know, and with quite a lot of influence with our front bench. I hope you'll come along. The Kolossi restaurant, off Millbank, at about one o'clock. You'll enjoy it. I'll introduce you to everyone.'

Susanna agreed, and Fryer was satisfied. Mission accomplished. They would have this independence nonsense knocked out of her in no time at all.

She telephoned Restings. As always when she had not spoken to him for some hours, she had a flicker of hope that the stony front would be cracking, that some word, some inflection would indicate a softening of his attitude.

'Pete, it's me,' she said.

'Oh, yes,' he said flatly, and her hopes wilted again.

'Pete, I'm going to stay at the flat again tonight, and not come home till late tomorrow. There's a sort of lunch at some restaurant that I've been invited to. Is that all right with you?'

'Why should it not be?' Despite his determination not to show any interest, Peter could not resist asking: 'Who's giving the party?'

'A bunch called the Britannia Group. They seem very friendly.'

'They would be,' said Peter. His voice was even more glacial than usual.

'So I'll ring you to say which train,' said Susanna. 'Listen, I'm going to do my maiden speech on Tuesday of next week. I got in early, so I'm in luck. Will you come?'

Peter paused, disconcerted.

'I . . . er . . . I have a rather busy week,' he said.

'I came to yours, Peter.'

'Yes.'

'I'd like you to be there, Pete,' she said softly. 'And in spite of what you all think of me, I hope the rest of the family will come too.'

'Well,' he said, non-committally, 'I don't know what they'll be doing.'

When Susanna entered the Kolossi she mentioned the name of her host, and was led at once to a back room where about twelve people were standing around with glasses in their hands. They had clearly been there for some time, and briefcases and scattered papers indicated that a meeting had taken place. Two waiters were laying the table for lunch. She was seized by the elbow and led round the group.

'Have you met Susanna Westerham, the new member for Kentish Weald?'

To her surprise her hand was shaken with enthusiasm, even kissed by one male member, and the welcome was warm.

'We're going to put you next to someone you know,' said Fryer, showing her to the table.

'We've met before, I think,' said the man who sat down on her left, smiling.

His ingratiating expression was familiar, but she could not place it.

'Geoffrey Lyne,' he said. 'I was on the shortlist for your constituency before the bye-election four years ago. But they chose your husband.'

'Of course,' said Susanna, 'I remember you. You got a seat, then?'

'Well, of course, dear girl,' he said, offended. 'I am one of the Home Office team.'

'Oh, yes,' said Susanna. 'So you are. Do tell me your views on immigration.'

Lyne obliged willingly, and Susanna listened. She listened all through lunch, never allowing herself to be drawn into discussion. Occasionally she asked a question, and her companions were eager to explain any detail she might not have understood.

Later, after she and most of the rest of the party had gone home, Lyne blew a long stream of smoke from his cigar and said to Martin Fryer, 'I think you're right. A good listener, doesn't say much, I guess because there isn't too much up top.'

'But it seems her heart's in the right place,' said Fryer. 'And she's a good looker, which makes a change from, well, you-know-who.'

'A definite addition, I should say,' agreed Lyne with a wink. 'Yes, a definite addition to our side. A little tuition, and she'll vote straight down the line. I think you should go and see the Chief Whip, tell him what we've achieved and get the credit. After this he will owe us one, which is the way we like it.'

* * *

'What's it like?' said Rachel to Susanna at the weekend. 'Are you enjoying it at all?'

She had run into her while shopping in the village, and they were walking home together.

Rachel's sense of guilt at the turn events had taken had left her with a serious deficit in confidence in her own instincts, but concern for Susanna nagged at her. She felt that she should give her the chance to talk if she needed to. Also, she would have been the first to admit, she was consumed by curiosity.

'Enjoying it.' Susanna considered for a moment. 'I am learning a great deal, if that's what you mean. And I am beginning to understand why MPs feel important. You are encouraged to feel important by everything that happens there. From the moment the policemen salute you as you walk through the entrance, you feel different. And all those signs on doors saying Members Only . . . I haven't felt so elevated since I stopped being a school prefect.'

'Do you like feeling important?' asked her mother.

'Elevated. I didn't say I felt important,' said Susanna. 'When I walk through that wonderful old Westminster Hall, with the plaques on the floor inscribed with names from our history – "Warren Hastings was impeached on this spot"; "Charles I stood trial here" – and I look up at those beautiful rafters that have survived fire and war . . . Or when I see the mace carried into the Chamber, before proceedings can start, I feel about as important as an ant on Everest. It is the *fact* of parliament that is important, not the people in it.'

'I suppose,' said her mother, 'that what the people do there is important, what they achieve.'

'Oh yes, of course,' said Susanna. 'I have to achieve.'

'Leave your mark?'

'That's right, I plan to leave my mark, one way or another. Otherwise, what's the point of being there?'

Rachel did not feel she had found out very much, apart from her daughter's apparent preoccupation with this new life. If Susanna, in being so uncommunicative, was intent on making her mother suffer, she was succeeding, thought Rachel ruefully, but she was hardly in a position to complain. It was not surprising if Susanna felt she was responsible for what had happened.

In the afternoon she decided to speak to Peter. She did not expect it to be easy, since he had been as distant with her as with her daughter since before the election.

While Susanna was busy indoors, she found him on a ladder removing wooden clapboard from the side of a log shed that was linked to the back of the house. It was a windless corner and the sun helped to take the chill off a cold day. He was working in jeans and a sweater, with his sleeves rolled back, which made him seem younger than in his usual dark suit. Rachel sat down on a large chunk of wood and wondered how to begin. She was not even sure what she wanted to say.

After a little Peter said: 'Are you here simply as a spectator? I don't mind constructive criticism. I'm not sure whether these batons are good enough to hold the new felt.'

Grateful that he sounded so normal, Rachel started picking up debris and putting it into the wheelbarrow.

'Peter, it sounds a bit wet, but I need someone to talk to.'

'Would I do?' he said, looking down at her. 'I guessed you hadn't just come over to admire my prowess as a handyman.'

'Thanks,' said Rachel. 'Honestly, Pete, I'm floundering. I have helped to get you all into a mess, and I certainly don't want to interfere any more, but I need someone to tell me what's happening.'

'Rachel, come off it,' said Peter, sliding down the ladder. 'I don't feel at all convinced by the new you, all meek and indecisive.'

'I don't suppose it will last,' said Rachel. 'I'm afraid I have developed a pro-active nature. Anyhow, I have good reason to be meek, seeing the damage I did by being aggressive.'

Peter sat on the log.

'Can we talk about me? First, anyway?' he said.

Rachel spread her hands in agreement.

'I am not so stupid,' he said, 'that I can't see that, between you all, you have got me *out* of a mess of my own making, and as each day goes by I feel more grateful for it. I am not a politician, I am a solicitor with strong political beliefs, but that's it. Won't you sit down?'

'Really?' said Rachel, weak with disbelief, perching on the side of the wheelbarrow. 'Do you mean that? No regrets?'

'I have regrets, of course,' he said, picking up a stick from the ground and tapping it on his palm. 'Failure is regrettable. I wish I could have achieved something worthwhile while I was there. But at least I'm out of it before it's too late for me to do something else with my life.'

Rachel was pleased beyond measure that her son-in-law was talking to her so easily.

'You don't find it hard, then,' she said, 'to go back to what you were doing before?'

'I'm not,' he said. 'I'm going to go back to school, and so is our junior partner. I'm going to specialise in European law, which is the big growth area of the future. We have some great plans to expand the firm. Fancy an investment, madam?'

'That's . . . that's exciting,' said Rachel. Then, hesitantly, 'And Susanna?'

'Well, that's another matter altogether,' said Peter, his voice hardening. He started hitting the stick against his boot. 'Rachel, Susanna and I are not exactly communicating, as you probably know.'

'Join the gang,' said Rachel.

'I'd like to get it right again, but . . . Hell, perhaps we shouldn't talk behind her back like this, but have you any idea what she is up to now?' He looked at Rachel aggressively. 'I mean, if she really did this crazy thing just to help *me* back to reality, what on earth is she doing up in London now? How do you explain that?'

'Look,' said Rachel helplessly, 'I don't understand any more than you do, Pete.'

His face was grim as he attacked the stick with both hands and snapped it in two.

'Well, I'll tell you what I think. What may have started as a sort of game is serious now. She likes the idea of being an MP.' He shrugged. 'Fine, fine. She's welcome. I hope she does better than I did.' His voice had grown bitter. 'But where does that leave me? Doesn't she care that I'm left here, looking after everything and feeling a bloody fool? Rachel, honestly, wasn't she planning this all along?'

'I know just what her plan was, Peter, and—'

But he wasn't listening. He was standing up, with his hands jammed in his pockets, kicking the log he had been sitting on.

'All this stuff about family – what is *she* doing for her beloved family now?'

'Peter—'

'She was jealous of me, that's what I think, and she was bloody well going to get into the action herself. Jealousy, that's all it was. She started by doing things in the constituency, and then that wasn't enough for her—'

Rachel instinctively came to Susanna's defence.

'That's not fair, Peter! She was trying to help you in the constituency. And she was good at it. If there was any jealousy, it wasn't in Susanna—'

'Oh, ha bloody ha,' his voice was loud and angry. 'All that stuff about taking the load of me! She was taking the constituency off me, Rachel, and you were helping her do it!'

'Peter!' said Rachel indignantly.

'Oh, for God's sake, Rachel, let's stop. I shouldn't have said that. Leave it alone.'

Rachel reacted furiously.

'Leave it alone? When you are accusing me of conspiring with Susanna to get her your seat? Are you going off your head, Peter? She said you were getting bad-tempered and unreasonable, but this takes the cake. You can't seriously think that?'

'I don't know what I think,' said Peter, quieter, but his voice was still shaking. He picked up the pieces of stick and threw them far into the bushes. 'I just think between us all we've destroyed everything we ever had.'

Rachel could not trust herself to speak again. She turned away, walking blindly back along the path round the house. She was appalled by her own lack of control and, as she calmed down, deeply saddened by what she had seen of Peter's pain.

At a first-floor window, Susanna stepped back. She had heard most of what had been said, and could still see Peter sitting on the log with his head in his hands.

'Dear God, what a mess,' she said aloud. 'I don't deserve it, but please, please help me try to put it right.'

She turned back to the table, where her papers lay beside an open bound copy of *Hansard*. She stared at them for a minute, before sitting slowly down again.

Peter, upset at having lost his cool and broken his determination to keep aloof from his relations, got into his car some minutes later and drove to Wraybury. He had no particular plan, except to get away from the house and recover himself. He parked near his office, from habit. He could, he thought miserably, go in and do some work. He walked along the street, his hands in his pockets, hunching himself in his sweater. It was a cold day, and he had not stopped to put on a coat. Suddenly he felt fearful of the quiet and chill of his empty office, and on impulse he turned into the teashop next to it. It was not something he would ever normally do, but what was normal at the moment?

Being a Saturday the place was full. He looked round for a seat, and asked a woman alone at a table if she minded . . . ?

'No,' she said, smiling shyly at him. 'You're welcome.'

She appeared to recognise him. His heart sank. As a little-known backbencher he had seldom been recognised, and especially not when dressed like this. The last thing he felt like was a chat with an ex-constituent.

But the woman did not chat. She sat quietly, taking tiny nibbles at a biscuit and sipping her tea while he waited for his.

Her soft little round face seemed familiar. Peter tried to place it. It wasn't important, but it nagged him.

The waitress put a pot of tea in front of him, and he felt for his wallet. Of courses it was in his coat pocket at home.

He shut his eyes briefly, and ran his fingers through his hair.

'I'm sorry—' he began.

'Will you let me pay? It's no trouble.' The woman opposite was looking anxiously at him.

'Well . . .'

The waitress was hovering.

'Really. I'd be glad to. We do know each other,' said the woman.

'You are very kind,' Peter replied, smiling at the implied warning of the dangers of accepting tea from a stranger. 'Forgive me – you must tell me your name.'

Having paid the waitress and put her purse away, she looked up at him again, apologetically.

'It's Sylvia Peacock,' she said.

'Oh yes,' said Peter. Of course, he thought, he should have recognised that down-trodden expression. 'How stupid of me.'

'No,' she said, 'not stupid. You wouldn't recognise me without him.'

She said it factually, not inviting protest. She seemed very undemanding, and it did not appear that she was going to say any more. Perhaps she was not well.

'Are you all right?' Peter said impulsively.

'Yes,' she said. 'Yes, I think so. I'm all right. Are you? I have been wondering about you and Susanna.'

Somehow her question was not offensive. Peter paused, as thoughtfully as she had.

'No. I don't think we are,' he said. 'Not really.'

'No,' said Mrs Peacock, 'I thought you might not be. I'm sorry . . .'

Her voice dwindled away. Once again, it did not seem as if she would go on.

It was Peter who spoke again.

'He doesn't like me much, your husband,'

'It doesn't matter,' she said at once. 'He deserved it all, you know.'

Peter thought about this too.

'I suppose we all deserved it all,' he said. 'Except you, Mrs Peacock.'

'I wouldn't know,' she said, a little wistfully. 'I have to go now, I'm afraid. Though I expect you . . .'

Her voice faded. She seemed preoccupied as she pulled on her gloves and buttoned her coat.

'Goodbye.' She held out her hand.

He stood up and took it.

'I am glad we met,' he said. He felt sorry that she was going. It had been restful to share his sense of defeat with someone who understood.

She nodded and walked away, weaving between the tables. Peter sat and wondered about Mrs Peacock and her life. Suddenly he was aware that she was standing beside him again.

'If you don't mind,' she said, hesitantly, 'please take care, you and Susanna. If it all goes wrong, it . . . it lasts such a long time. It isn't too late. Maybe if you talked to Mrs . . . to Rachel . . . She helped me, you know, her and Ellie.'

'I have talked to Rachel,' said Peter forlornly, 'and it didn't help at all.'

'Oh.' The small anxious face looked disappointed. 'Oh well.'

And she left him again.

On Sunday evening, Peter drove Susanna to the London train, just as she had so often driven him.

'Will you come on Tuesday?' she said, as she got out of the car.

'Susanna, I don't know.'

He spoke emphatically, inviting no further exchange.

She got on the train with little hope, and spent the journey gazing out through the dark window.

By the time he got home, Peter had made up his mind to follow Mrs Peacock's advice.

'Rachel, I've come to grovel, to apologise. I didn't mean to shout at you like that.'

Peter was standing in her doorway, filling the frame with his dark silhouette.

'Perhaps you just needed a good shout. I don't blame you,' she said at once, from where she stood at the stove.

'I don't even believe half of what I said,' he said without moving. He wasn't sure whether he was staying or going.

'But it made you feel better to say it, I bet. Come in, and leave that wind outside.'

He shut the door and, crossing the room, stood beside her staring down at the sauce she was stirring in a pan.

'What are we going to do?' he said at last.

'I am the last person you should ask,' said Rachel. 'Sit down, anyway, and let's have an inordinately large drink.'

Chapter 20

Monday was a day of telephoning. Peter spoke to Leonora.

'I have to, Leo,' he said to her. 'She gave me her support when I was doing my maiden speech, and it meant a lot to me to see her in the gallery. She seems to want me, so one way and another, however I feel about it, I have to be there. But for you and Andrew, it's your decision. I just thought I would let you know. Will you tell the twins?'

Leonora spoke to Mark.

'Wouldn't it hurt Dad,' he said, 'if we went? It would look as if we approve of all this.'

'He's going himself,' said Leonora.

'*Is* he?' said Mark. 'Well, that's generous of him, in the circumstances. But in that case, she doesn't need us as well.'

'Why are you so sour?' said Leonora. 'It's not doing *you* any harm, her being in parliament.'

'I don't know how you can forgive her so easily for what she did to Dad.'

'Listen, Mark, speak to Emma, will you?'

'Em, you decide.'

'Of course we must, Mark. Look, the great thing is that Dad is going. If he can accept her being an MP, surely we can. We can't freeze her out for ever. All that matters to us, Mark, is them getting together again, right?'

'Right, I suppose. Yes.'

'Well,' said Emma, 'if Dad is being generous enough to go and listen to her speech, the least we can do is support him. We can't let him go alone.'

'I don't suppose he'd be alone. Granny would go, I bet.'

'Well, ring her and ask her.'

'Of course,' said Rachel. 'Not least because I am intrigued to know what sort of speech she will make.'

'That's a point,' said Mark. 'I only hope it's not all that fascist stuff again.'

'Hardly,' said his grandmother. 'But I still don't know what she really thinks, do you?'

'Not really. But I have to admit, Em and I are quite impressed by her going ahead with it.'

On Tuesday morning the House of Commons answering service took a message. After the telephonist had failed to find Susanna in her office, it was inscribed on a slip of paper and put in her pigeonhole in the Members' Lobby. It read, 'We will be there. Peter.' Susanna never saw it, partly because she spent time nervously going over her coming speech in St James's Park, partly because she had not yet got into the habit of checking the message board.

She went early into the Chamber. She wanted to be able to choose her seat, and calm herself. She was nervous; not so much about the occasion, the momentous sensation of addressing the British parliament for the first time, nor even about what she was going to say; far more alarming was the possibility that her idea was wrong, and that instead of producing the solution to her unhappy predicament it would only make the damage irreversible. But it was the only idea she had, and if it failed . . . The thought did not bear looking at. She had no reliance now on her judgement. It had proved faulty before, and there was no reason to suppose it had improved. Yesterday, while she had still had a measure of confidence in her plan, she had desperately hoped for a call from Peter, saying that he was coming to London and would be in the House. Now, when her confidence was at its lowest ebb, she felt relieved that she had not heard from him. Without him there listening, it would be less nerve-wracking for her, and in any case he would hear soon enough.

Members going by to take their seats looked at her curiously. Martin Fryer, passing along the row in front of her, nodded.

'Maiden today? Good luck,' he said.

There was a statement on Northern Ireland by the Secretary of State at three-thirty, so when Susanna got to her feet at ten past four it was a still full and mildly interested House that faced her. Maiden speeches are always listened to, partly from traditional politeness to a new MP and partly because who knows what supernova may be born at that moment? And on this occasion they were looking at something out of the ordinary.

Susanna's reputation had gone before her. The Labour benches were intrigued by a woman who had stood against her husband and deposed him. Independent candidates are never normally elected, and the fact that Peter Westerham had been on the left of the Conservative Party and that Susanna's politics were said to be those of the extreme reactionary right made things all the more tasty. It looked as if the senior frontbenchers of the Conservative Party would be much discomfited by her speech, which would emphasise party divisions, while the pleasure of the Tory extreme right faction, which they would find hard to conceal, would give the other parties yet more political ammunition. It was, all in all, worth hanging around in the Chamber for a further ten minutes.

Knowing she would be called soon, Susanna concentrated on calming herself by looking round the upper galleries of the chamber; the *Hansard* clerks, the press, the empty benches of the peers' gallery, and the steeply raked tiers of the Strangers' Gallery. Her heart thudded violently as she caught sight of Emma in the third row, and then of the rest of her family beside her. Susanna's dread of failure flooded back, engulfing her in momentary panic. But she breathed deeply and managed to control her beating heart. At each pause in the debate, she rose with other members trying to catch the Deputy Speaker's eye. Without warning, he called her name. She remained standing, her papers clutched in her hand. Luckily most of her speech was to be read, word for word, so she knew she had only to concentrate on keeping her voice clear and steady.

Peter, sitting in the gallery with the twins on one side of him, Leonora, Andrew and Rachel on the other, was doing his best to feel relaxed. The place, as always, was too hot. He knew that down below in the chamber the opposite benches seem much closer than from above. You could almost smell the hostile breath of your opponents across the way, and it was an audience as critical and unforgiving as you could get. Susanna down there below him looked unexpectedly vulnerable, and his concern about what she might be going to say disappeared in his sudden and unexpected wish that she should do well. He looked at the Labour benches. They were all listening as she started speaking, some frowning, one or two whispering to each other. On the Tory benches there was the same attention and concentration.

He too should pay attention to what she was saying.

'Dad! Dad!' hissed Mark, leaning forward from his seat beyond Emma.

'Hush. I want to listen,' said Peter.

'Yes,' said Mark. 'Listen! Don't you recognise this, Dad?'

Susanna's voice was low-pitched but clearly audible through the tiny loudspeakers in the backs of the gallery benches.

She was pacing it well, thought Peter, not rushing it. Then suddenly the words registered with him. He listened for a few more sentences, and then turned open-mouthed to Mark. 'Get it, Dad?' said Mark. 'It's your speech!'

It was indeed Peter's speech. Omitting only the sentences relating to constituency issues at the time, Susanna was repeating, precisely, the words of Peter's own maiden speech as a new member, with its pleas for moderation and balance, and with its statements of the principles and beliefs belonging to the left wing of the Conservative Party. And not only Peter and his family were recognising it. There were mutterings on the benches below as members leaned towards each other.

As the noise rose, so did Susanna's voice, to make finally a ringing declaration of the endorsement of the European Union that Peter had given nearly four years earlier.

'Mr Deputy Speaker,' she concluded, turning to the Chair, and laying down her notes, 'the Honourable Members on both sides of the House have clearly recognised the plagiarism in my speech. I hoped they would. I am not ashamed of it. I believe in everything I have said, and I could think of no way of improving on the words of the previous member for Kentish Weald. I commend his speech to you. It is as true and as relevant now as it was then, when it was spoken by the most honourable member ever to take his seat in this House. I thank the House for its courtesy in listening to me.'

Susanna sat down, and the Chamber burst into a confusion of noise. Conservative pro-Europeans were waving their order papers and cheering, Labour members on the Government benches opposite were laughing, members of the Britannia Group were arguing angrily in the aisle, frontbenchers on both sides were sliding away, a Liberal Democrat MP was trying to speak and the Deputy Speaker was almost inaudible as he called for order.

Peter sat back.

'Well, Dad?' said Mark, his face spread with a huge smile. 'What do you think?'

'Good old Mum,' said his twin. 'Why didn't we have more faith in her?'

Rachel looked along the bench at Peter. He was still staring down at Susanna, and she was unable to read the expression on his face. Andrew and Leonora were talking in excited whispers. Susanna did not look up to the gallery.

The House was settling down, and one of the 'chains' signalled to the family to be quiet.

'Shall we go?' said Peter.

Susanna was still in her seat as they left, listening politely to the next speaker. Some minutes later, a note was passed hand-to-hand along the bench to her. It was from the Whips' office. She looked at it and then at the green card with it. She saw Peter's writing: 'Can you meet us on the terrace?'

She looked up and saw that her family had gone from their seats.

A boatful of sightseers was passing down the river, mostly Japanese, well-wrapped in anoraks and scarves. Camera lenses glinted as they photographed the Palace of Westminster lying long and languid in the March sunlight by the water's edge. Emma and Leonora waved enthusiastically back at them from the terrace wall.

'That's right. Make their day. "MPs waving from Westminster, 1997,"' said Rachel.

'No one would ever mistake you two for MPs,' said Mark. 'But *you* could be getting in some practice, Andrew.'

His prospective brother-in-law grinned. 'Hearing your mother today in that place was pretty inspiring, you have to admit. The trouble with my party is that I doubt if I'll ever be able to practise what I've been preaching.'

He looked speculatively towards Peter, who was a little further along the wall, gazing at the river. He took a step towards him, but then saw that Susanna had just come up the steps onto the terrace and was walking towards her husband. Andrew did not think they would want company at this moment.

Susanna stood beside Peter and they both looked down at the ebbing tide of the Thames.

She was full of hope, but as yet no certainty. She wished he would say something. When he turned to face her, she realised that they had not looked each other in the eye for a long time.

'I don't know how to put this,' said Peter. 'It sounds trite, but I owe you an apology.'

'An apology?' she said. 'For goodness' sake, what have *you* done to apologise for?'

'It's not what I've done, it's what I have been thinking about you. And it seems I was wrong. That's what I feel guilty about. Your mother has told me a great deal that I didn't know.'

She drew a deep breath.

'You do believe me now, then, Pete? That I never planned to be an MP?'

Her face was openly pleading. He smiled.

'To put it in other words,' he said, 'I believe you really did go through that charade for my sake.'

'And for mine, Pete,' she said. 'Our sakes are intertwined.'

'Your maiden speech, Sukie. It was the most generous thing I have ever known anyone do. That was the moment for your own speech, your big moment, Sukie, and you gave them mine, with all the credits. I had no idea . . .'

'It was for you, Pete,' she said. 'My present to you. My way of telling you how much I love you, and how much I admire you. And I wanted to say it in public.'

'You certainly said it in public,' said Peter. 'It was quite the most astonishing thing. Su, you are a constant amazement to me. You always have been.'

'Well, I'll try to keep it up,' she said. 'I just want to say, too, that I deserved everything I have had from you, and from the children.'

Further down the terrace Rachel was trying to restrain the twins and Leonora, who saw no reason why they should not speak to their mother.

'For goodness' sake,' she said, 'have you no dramatic instinct, any of you? You should stay in the wings till the principals have finished their big scene.'

'The Reconciliation?' said Mark. 'The tearful coming together? Thank God it's happening, anyway.'

'We've all got a part in this scene, though,' said Emma. 'We all thought she had gone round the twist.'

'Come on,' said Leonora, 'they've had quite enough time to make it up. Let's bring on the commercials. I'm gasping.'

'You spoke so well,' Peter was saying. 'No, I'm not joking. I mean your delivery, the way you held the House. They don't always listen like that. You'll make a good MP, because we know the constituents love you, and they'll go on doing that, even if you have changed your colours somewhat.'

'Yes, somewhat,' Susanna said, grinning. 'But they may not like what I'm going to do next.'

'Sukie!' Peter caught her hand as she turned away. 'I love you, too,' he said.

'Tell me later. Here come the gang.'

'Hi, Mum,' said Mark slightly sheepishly as they approached.

Susanna kissed each in turn.

'Thank you,' she said, 'thank you all for coming. It meant a lot.'

'Can you come home with us,' said Peter, 'or is there a heavy whip?'

'For me, yes,' said Susanna. 'A three-liner. But I will be home this evening, on the six-twenty. Will you have some supper ready, and some champagne?'

'You're on,' said Peter. 'See you then.'

After seeing her family leave, having walked them through the vast and moving magnificence of Westminster Hall, Susanna kept her appointment with the Conservative Chief Whip. She was on a high, and she knew it. A huge weight had been lifted from her soul, and she had never felt so confident.

She headed for the rooms at the heart of the House of Commons whose shabby old-fashionedness belied their importance in management of the party or, when it was in power, the government of the day. In the outer office she was greeted by James Levalliant, who had been Peter's whip, and was still the whip in charge of the Tory members for the South East of England.

'Susanna,' he said in greeting, 'the Chief will be just a couple of minutes. Take a seat.'

She sat at one of the whips' desks. The room was like a small classroom, she thought, with too many desks for comfort. 'How is Peter?' said Levalliant, sitting back at his own desk and fiddling with the top of his pen.

'Peter's fine, thank you,' said Susanna.

'I, er, I don't think the Chief will be long. Would you like some coffee? Or tea?'

'No, thank you.'

She noted his discomfort and felt that it was not surprising that he was at a loss as to what to say to her. He could hardly congratulate her on someone else's speech. She did not feel dIsposed to help him, and he shuffled some papers on his desk.

The Chief Whip appeared, towering in the doorway to the inner office. He shook hands with Susanna and invited her in. It was a much smaller room of no greater distinction. A large desk, a small green leather-covered sofa and two armchairs.

'I apologise for keeping you waiting,' he said. 'I am most grateful to you for coming to see me.'

'Not at all,' said Susanna, 'but I am sorry it is here that we are meeting. I would have liked to have had the chance to see inside Number Twelve. I believe it is not a very common experience.'

'Your husband has had that privilege,' he said. 'We cannot see into the future, but there is no reason, in theory, why you should not one day have it too.'

He patted the back of an armchair near his desk.

'I doubt it,' said Susanna, seating herself in it.

'Come, come,' he said genially, sitting down behind a pile of papers. 'Your future is bright. You spoke extremely well, if unusually, in the Chamber today. And that is what I wanted to have a word about: talent needs to be channelled where it can be used effectively, as I know you have the wit to see. Otherwise it is wasted on the desert air, if I may put it like that.'

'Oh, you may,' said Susanna.

'And this seems to me where we may be able to come to terms,' he went on, not appearing to notice her interjection. 'Not to beat about the bush, Susanna, as we are both busy people: you will never get anywhere as an Independent. I have been given to understand that you might be prepared to accept the Conservative whip.'

'Oh, really?' said Susanna. 'And who gave you to understand that?'

She took pleasure from the thought of Martin Fryer misinforming the Whips' office.

He frowned.

'That,' he said, 'is immaterial. Let us just say that in the circumstances I am prepared to consider offering you the whip. What you would have to accept, of course, is the importance of our party discipline, something your husband failed significantly to understand.'

'Go on,' said Susanna steadily.

'It seems that there is a certain ambivalence as to your position in the political spectrum. We had been led to expect you to lean on the whole to the right, but I was somewhat reassured by your final words in your speech today—'

Susanna interrupted him.

'I don't think it is necessary for you to know where I would stand in relation to your party, if you will forgive my saying so, since I do not intend to attach myself to it.'

'I beg your pardon? Am I hearing you correctly?'

The smile disappeared from the big face.

'Perfectly correctly,' said Susanna. 'I came to see you because I wanted to tell you to your face why I am here; indeed, why I stood for parliament at all. My husband joined your party and was bitterly let down. He was allowed no scope for his own thinking, which is wise and moderate. He has wasted four years of his life, and I resent it, though he doesn't. He was too loyal and too honourable to let you down, so I had to get him out in the only way I could, by standing against him. And I only beat him through some lucky breaks, and because I appealed to the lowest and most foolish instincts of a gullible portion of the electorate, instincts which I blame the extreme right wing of your party for fostering.'

The big man seemed about to interrupt. Susanna raised her hand.

'Please – I have nearly finished. In losing Peter, you have lost just the sort of MP you should be recruiting, and I suggest, for your party's sake, that you think about that very carefully. That's about it. You will not be bothered by me any more. Thank you for listening to me.'

She felt she had ended lamely, but the expression on the Chief Whip's face had become rather intimidating.

After a long pause, during which he never took his eyes off her, he said: 'And may I ask to which party you are planning to affiliate yourself?'

'Oh,' said Susanna, attempting to look apologetic, 'to no party. I should have explained more clearly. By this evening I will no longer be a member of parliament.' She stood up. 'I wonder,' she said, 'if you would be so good as to direct me to the office of whoever it is who awards the Chiltern Hundreds?'

'What's that?' said Mark, hours later.

The kitchen table at Restings was aglow with candlelight and surrounded by the whole family, with Andrew in his usual place beside Leonora.

'I would just love to have been a fly on the wall,' said Peter, when he had finished laughing. 'It's the quick way out, Mark. A device. Historical, and mad, but still used. By law, a member may not resign a parliamentary seat, once elected. But he cannot be an MP if he holds an office of profit under the Crown. And that is what stewardship of the Chiltern Hundreds is. It's an area in the Chiltern hills that once needed a steward to protect everyone from the local bandits. An ideal job for your mother, I would have thought, even if only a nominal one. But if I'm right, she can only do it until someone else applies for the job.'

'I would love to have seen that Chief Whip's face,' said Rachel, stretching luxuriously.

'It was interesting,' said Susanna, smiling. She had enjoyed telling her story. 'I didn't stay long, after that. He seemed extraordinarily cross at the idea of fighting another bye-election. I didn't feel that was any of my business, so I said goodbye and left. There are some nice prints in the passage outside. I had a good look, as it was the last time.'

'A bye-election might be Andrew's business though,' said Leonora enthusiastically. 'Do you think he'd have a chance, Dad?'

'In Kentish Weald? I wonder. It was a huge vote you got for your Greens,' said Peter.

Andrew leaned forward, his elbows on the table, his face eager. 'What would you think, Peter, if I stood for the Tories? *Your* sort of Toryism, and Susanna's, is fine by me. And if I got in I could go Green again, and actually achieve something.'

'Andrew,' gasped Emma, 'the hypocrisy! Leo, is this what you are thinking of marrying?'

'Andrew,' said Peter, laughing incredulously, 'building on what you've done already, you really might make it. You are right to think of the Tories, because despite everything, it is the most likely party to win round here.'

'People have changed parties before now,' said Mark, 'including Churchill. Didn't do him any harm.'

'Frankly everyone locally is going to be so fed up with the local Tories, and the Lib Dems, that you personally would have a real chance,' said Rachel. 'You could easily keep your own Green vote, and gather quite a few of the moderate Conservatives. It's worth a try, if it's really what you want. What both of you want. You *and* Leonora.'

'Here we go again,' said Emma, in horror.

'It's all right – we've talked about it, Granny,' said Leonora smiling.

'We'd be going in with our eyes open.'

'What about Peacock?' said Susanna. 'I bet he'd never allow anyone to be considered who has the faintest relationship to our family.'

'Well, I don't intend to sever my connection with your family, for Peacock or anyone else,' said Andrew, squeezing Leonora's hand.

'I've got news for you,' said Rachel. 'I spoke to Ellie earlier. I had to tell her about Susanna's speech. She sent her love, by the way, to both of you. But listen – she's celebrating because the executive has voted to get rid of Peacock. They seem to have decided that leaking that letter to the papers lost them the election. So with Peacock gone Ellie will be back in the Conservative fold, and if you can get *her* on your side, Andrew . . .'

'. . . you can hardly fail,' said Susanna, clapping her hands. 'She is a formidable lady, Ellie, and a serious strategist.'

'Sukie, come over here.' Peter had got up and was standing near the window.

'Hi,' she said, joining him. The rest of the party went on chattering noisily.

'I have got a serious question to ask you, Sukie,' he said. 'Will you answer it seriously? And honestly?'

'Of course,' said Susanna.

'I'm trusting you to be honest,' he said, 'because it matters a lot, I want to be sure. This Chiltern Hundreds lark; are you doing it for me?'

'No,' she said happily, placing both her hands against his chest, 'this time it's not for you. It's entirely for me. I have had my fifteen minutes, and that was quite long enough; I don't want to be an MP; I never wanted to be an MP; I want to be a pony breeder, and I want to see my spouse in the evenings, like other pony breeders.'

'That's all right then,' he said.

He covered her hands with his. Then, very lightly, he stroked her cheek with the tips of his fingers.

'Thank you,' he said.

Holding hands, they went back to the table. Peter picked up his glass.

'This is a toast,' he said. 'To Mrs Peacock.'

He drank.

'*What?*' said Mark.

'I didn't know there was a Mrs Peacock,' said Emma.

'Oh, there's a Mrs Peacock all right,' said Rachel, 'but why your father should be—'

'Never mind,' said Peter. 'I'll give you another. Let's drink to Ellie Fittall's long life and health.'

'To Ellie,' said Rachel, raising her champagne glass. 'And to you

– to two ex-MPs, and perhaps one future one.'

Leonard Peacock had telephoned Central Office four times during the morning. Brinkman was never available. Finally, when Peacock was near despair, the area agent had come on the line.

'Ronald Brinkman. Who's that?' he said curtly.

'It – it's Leonard Peacock, Ronnie.'

'Oh yes, Peacock. What can I do for you?'

'You've got to help me, Ronnie.'

In his own ears his voice sounded uncomfortably like a bleat. He cleared his throat.

'They're trying to get rid of me. My executive. It's ridiculous, of course. They are trying to blame me for that stupid woman, when it was entirely the fault of the chairman—'

'Oh yes,' said Brinkman, his voice distant and cold. 'I heard there were going to be some changes down there. It's hardly my business.'

'But it is, Ronnie,' said Peacock, sweating profusely. 'Look, Ronnie, I need your help. If we are going to win a bye-election it would be madness for them to get a new agent here now, anyone can see that. All they need is a word from you. If you would just come down—'

'My dear Peacock.' Brinkman's voice had assumed that silky tone that the agent had heard before. 'My dear Peacock, you are their employee, not mine. In any case, you know very well that Central Office *never* interferes in the internal affairs of local Associations. They are, as I have said before, entirely autonomous. Oh, no. It wouldn't do at all. I'm sorry. And now, you must excuse me, I have a call on another line.'

Peacock was left with the receiver purring gently into his ear.

He picked up the whole telephone with both hands and threw it across the room where it hit the face of the computer, causing a starburst of cracks across the glass. Looking malignantly after it he noticed a figure standing hesitantly in the doorway. It was his wife.

He stared murderously at her.

'Get out,' he said.

She looked back at him quietly for a moment.

'Well,' she said then, 'that's just what I'm doing, dear. I came to say goodbye.'

Peacock saw that she was dressed in what she referred to as her 'good' coat, with her best handbag over her arm.

'Where are you going? To see your mother?' he said, without thinking, uninterested to the point of exhaustion.

Sylvia Peacock gave a slight shake of her head.

'Mother passed away last week, dear. I did mention it, but you were, well, very busy. No. I am going to London.'

'What for?' said Peacock more aggressively. 'What time will you be back? There's a rail strike on, as you won't have noticed.'

'You misunderstand me, dear. I am travelling by air. I am going to London, Ontario. To Jack and Emmie, you know, in Canada. And I won't be back. I have left their address in the kitchen, but I don't think you will want it. I have taken everything I need. I just dropped by to return these. We had to, er . . . borrow them, for our campaign.'

Stepping forward she placed three grey computer disks on his desk.

'Goodbye, Leonard,' she said, and left the room as he stared at them.

As she walked down the stairs, Sylvia Peacock reflected that in all the years that she had known him she had never, till this moment, seen her husband reduced to silence.

She stepped into the waiting taxi and drove away without looking back.

Miss, say goodbye to your daughter

To Kathleen, Nathan, Matthew and Carrie.
I love you all very much.

Miss, say goodbye to your daughter

EMMET O'REILLY

A true story of self-actualisation against all odds

First published in 2022 by
Emmet O'Reilly
Dublin
Ireland
emmetbooks.com

All rights © 2022 Emmet O'Reilly

Paperback	ISBN: 978 1 78846 230 3
eBook	ISBN: 978 1 78846 231 0
Amazon paperback edition	ISBN: 978 1 78846 232 7

All rights reserved. No part of this book may be reproduced or utilised in any form or by any means electronic or mechanical, including photocopying, filming, recording, video recording, photography, or by any information storage and retrieval system, nor shall by way of trade or otherwise be lent, resold or otherwise circulated in any form of binding or cover other than that in which it is published without prior permission in writing from the publisher.

The right of the author of his work has been asserted by him in accordance with the Copyright, Designs and Patents Act 1988.

Permissions:
'No More Tears' reproduced with kind permission of
Jewel Kilcher and Tommee Profitt

Produced by Kazoo Independent Publishing Services
222 Beech Park, Lucan, Co. Dublin
kazoopublishing.com

Kazoo Independent Publishing Services is not the publisher of this work. All rights and responsibilities pertaining to this work remain with Emmet O'Reilly.

Kazoo offers independent authors a full range of publishing services.
For further details visit kazoopublishing.com

Cover design by Design for Writers

Printed in the EU

Contents

Chapter One	*Connection*	9
Chapter Two	*Home*	15
Chapter Three	*KNOCK ... knock*	22
Chapter Four	*Romance*	27
Chapter Five	*Progression*	41
Chapter Six	*News*	49
Chapter Seven	*Decisions*	57
Chapter Eight	*Wedding*	66
Chapter Nine	*Pivot*	79
Chapter Ten	*Which Direction?*	86
Chapter Eleven	*Newborn*	93
Chapter Twelve	*Intervention*	100
Chapter Thirteen	*Newtownforbes*	108
Chapter Fourteen	*Growing Up*	112
Chapter Fifteen	*Rosie*	120
Chapter Sixteen	*Second Chance*	124
Chapter Seventeen	*Father Figure*	133

Chapter Eighteen	*Sisters*	144
Chapter Nineteen	*School of Life*	154
Chapter Twenty	*Johnny B. Goode*	162
Chapter Twenty-one	*Giorgio*	173
Chapter Twenty-two	*April 29th*	184
Chapter Twenty-three	*Family*	192
Chapter Twenty-four	*Das Kapital*	204
Chapter Twenty-five	*Education*	214
Chapter Twenty-six	*1990s*	224
Chapter Twenty-seven	*2002*	229
Chapter Twenty-eight	*Granny*	239
Chapter Twenty-nine	*Illness*	246
Chapter Thirty	*Acceptance*	255
Epilogue		263
Acknowledgements		267

You see love is a mystery
And I still see its shining face
There are no more sad songs, just blue skies
And no more tears to cry

No More Tears, Jewel, 2019

Chapter One

Connection

Ellen O'Connell was twenty-nine, single, petite in stature and mild mannered, but well able to speak up for herself should the situation require it. Ever since finishing school at the tender age of fourteen, she had worked on refining her skills as a seamstress in a local dressmaker. Local for Ellen was the square mile in south inner city Dublin known as the Liberties. The area had its name since the arrival of the Anglo-Normans in the twelfth century and was so called as it was the only part of Dublin to be free of the laws of the city by existing outside its old medieval walls.

It was July 1944. The allied troops had just landed in Normandy and there was a palpable sense of optimism amongst those nations that the end of World War II was in sight. On the fringes of the fractured European continent, Ireland was just over twenty years distanced from the political separation of north and south. Whilst the British had departed seventy-five per cent of the country, the void left was filled by an overbearing Roman Catholic Church interlinked with a political class that was still burdened by a vicious civil war. To a significant extent, the Irish identity was inextricably linked to being Catholic and the Church played on that linkage to control its flock following the establishment of the fledgling Irish State.

At that moment, Ellen's focus was on an upcoming dance in the local church hall. At twenty-nine, most of Ellen's peers were married – the average age of brides was twenty-six – and, although secure in the knowledge that she hadn't yet met the man for her, time was marching on and some of the neighbours were questioning whether spinster life was in store for her. This was typical of a close community like the Liberties, that espoused to do anything for each other in a time of difficulty, but would chatter behind twitching net curtains about the latest scandal. The most recent gossip related to a local woman, mother of four children under six, who was admitted to a mental asylum with her nerves – the husband, who was fond of a Guinness or two of an evening and liberal with his fists, was in no better shape and the neighbours farmed out the four children to three houses whilst the woman recuperated. Great community to rally around, but couldn't help themselves but spread the news in an innocent, naïve but, ultimately, indelicate manner. Ellen felt empathy towards that family and dropped in a bob or two in the local collection for those unfortunate children.

The dance was organised for Friday 21 July. The local parish hall was a basic building used by the church and local community for gatherings, dances, bring and buy sales and youth clubs. The dance was ostensibly run by a group of young folk that were trying to bring brightness to the seemingly unending austere times that existed in wartime Dublin, but the local church was in the background, taking rent for use of the hall and overseeing the sound level of

Connection

music from the local band. Ellen, who was always up for some fun, had bought her ticket to the dance when they were sold two weeks earlier and now, three days before the big day, was focused on what she was going to wear. Being a seamstress, she had access to a variety of dresses, but given the mild weather that July week, she sought something a little summery. She opted for a knee-length, short-sleeved, green dress, with buttons going diagonally from the neck to below her hip, complemented by a gold belt. She also wore a small pearl necklace given to her by her mum. Ellen was blessed with an hourglass shape and the dress accentuated the curves on her diminutive frame.

On the evening of the dance and with her best friend Mabel Quinn getting dolled-up with her, Ellen got dressed for the night. Armed with some light make-up and deep red lipstick, she took one final look in the mirror and said to Mabel, 'Ah sure, I'm a bit over-dressed, but let's go.' As Ellen and Mabel walked into the dance hall, they were both struck by how it had been turned into something from the Roaring Twenties. The high windows in the hall were covered with dark paper to prevent the evening summer sunlight invading the room. Bright, almost gaudy, gold tinsel hung on the walls on each side of the dance floor, with uplighters and tall plants designed to give the space a decadent and luxurious feel, far from the standard Liberties look. Given the Church's involvement in the dance, no alcohol was permitted, but the innocent revellers were in such good spirits, there was no need to add anything else into the mix. Soon into the night, Ellen spotted a group of men arriving. There were three of them, but the one at the front intrigued her – he seemed to be the chatty one of the group, dressed in a dark brown three-piece suit, short well-groomed jet black hair, clean shaven, cheeky smile and relatively small in height. When he saw Ellen glancing over at him, he quickly looked away and retreated behind one of his taller friends. This only intrigued Ellen more and she instantly decided this was a man she wouldn't mind knowing a bit about.

A tradition at Irish dances at the time was that certain sets were Men's Choice and others were Ladies' Choice. It was 10.45 p.m. Ellen had had great fun, especially listening to the live band playing a mixture of traditional Irish songs and a few international numbers, including one from Bing Crosby, but the night was drawing to a close. She danced a couple of times with men that asked her onto the dancefloor, but neither fella piqued her interest – she wondered whether she was simply too choosy or maybe she needed to broaden her horizons beyond the Liberties. Then, the Master of Ceremonies for the night declared Ladies' Choice. In those days, women generally sat on one side of the hall, men on the other and, at times such as this, it was only the more forward women that had the courage to walk out from their side of the hall, cross 'no man's land' with everyone watching their every move as if happening in slow motion, and ask a man to dance. It was convention that no man or woman refused a request to dance, but the very act of stepping out of line, especially as a woman, open to being seen as desperate to have to ask a man to dance, was nerve wracking. Most of those thoughts ran through Ellen's head as she sat beside Mabel. Her friend was more of an old-fashioned kind of woman – she looked thirty, which she was, acted like she was

Connection

forty, dressed like a fifty-something and the blend tended to confuse those simple men who were just looking for a dance. Ellen was different – her dress sense displayed confidence, her inner feeling slightly less so, but there was something in her that night that drove her on.

She took one look across the floor, one final glance at Mabel, stood straight up and headed over to the sea of men on the other side of the hall. She saw the well-dressed young man that she had spotted at the start of the night. He was partially obscured by his two tall friends, so she peeked around and said, 'Would you like to dance?'

He looked a bit surprised, but grinned back and, of course, said, 'Yes!' They immediately held hands, as was normal, and he led her onto the floor – it was a waltz and, as the music started, Ellen immediately felt comfortable in his company despite not knowing his name yet. Given the box step nature of waltzes, it was more likely than not that he would tread on Ellen's toes, but their collective timing just clicked. As the song ended, the norm was that each would walk back to their respective sides of the hall. For some reason, they both walked down the middle of the hall together, hand in hand. As they reached the door end of the hall, they stopped and he said, 'Hi, I'm Joe. What's your name?' He was captivated by Ellen's stunning dress and welcoming face.

Ellen instantly replied, 'I'm Ellen. You're a lovely dancer,' and they giggled like teenagers. It was clear to both that there was a connection. Right then, the Master of Ceremonies encouraged everyone to disperse and Ellen and Joe said a quick goodbye, but not before he got a glimpse of her sparkling blue eyes, as they reflected in the overhead lights.

Miss, Say Goodbye to Your Daughter

It was possible that they would never see each other again – however, they knew that the six degrees of separation that connects everyone on the planet was more like two degrees in Dublin. It was a small tight community, where everyone knew each other, so they were comfortable that having each other's first names would suffice for starters.

Chapter Two

Home

Ellen's normal working day started at 6 a.m., when she got up, washed and readied herself for the treadmill of life. Ellen was the youngest of four children of the O'Connell family of Ebenezer Road – the irony of the street name was not lost on its residents, given that money was not plentiful in that part of Dublin. However, these salt of the earth people were generally happy and content with what was a subsistence life. Luxuries were having decent fruit and veg in the house, with a few spuds and meat on the plate, and some fresh fish on a Friday.

Given the fact that her sisters, Annie and Mary, passed away aged three months and fifteen years respectively, and her brother, Peadar, had long since left the family home, Ellen's role in the house involved an element of caring for and financially supporting her parents. In what was a challenging time for the whole family, her father, Mick, passed away three years earlier. Mick had a tough exterior, was from the school of raising his children with a sense of responsibility for their place in the house and was very reluctant to accept any excuse for chores not being completed well and on time. However, under that strict exterior lay a man that would defend his offspring, and wider family, with his life and he had a soft spot for Ellie, as he called her in the house. The two of them would often go on walks into town, crossing those medieval walls, and they both particularly enjoyed going to Moore Street in the north inner city to chat to the pure bred Dubliners running the stalls and stock up on fruit and veg for Ellen's mother, Dee.

Ellen never forgot the day she came home from work in January 1941. With the only sound being a mantelpiece clock ticking inexorably, Mick was in the parlour, a room at the front of this standard working class house that was reserved for special guests only. Given its northerly aspect, it was a cold room and, although it had a working fireplace, it was rarely lit and the dark patterned carpet and brown wallpaper made it a dour enough place. Mick was sitting on the sofa and had his head down. When he looked up at his youngest child, tears streamed down his face and Ellen just hugged him with all her strength. Over recent years, Mick's lungs had been causing him significant issues and Ellen knew that he was due to visit the hospital that morning. To the shock of everyone in the family, that visit confirmed Mick's worst fears – his lung capacity had deteriorated and the doctor informed him that he should get his affairs in order, as something as simple as a common cold would likely lead to a rapid decline in his health and ultimately result in death.

'What's wrong, Da?' asked Ellen, knowing something was amiss.

Mick replied, 'It's fine, Ellie, I'll need you to look after your ma. Don't cry, child, I'm going to a better place and I'm ready.' Stoic in the face of such a prognosis, Mick wiped

Home

away his tears, took Ellen by the hand and said, 'Let's make a nice cuppa for your ma,' as he brought her through the living room, past a sorrowful Dee, and into the scullery.

Two months later, following a brief fight against bronchitis, Mick O'Connell passed away in his sleep at Saint Vincent's Hospital, then located on Saint Stephen's Green. Ellen couldn't get to grips with the suddenness of it, but mustered enough strength to go through the standard Irish funeral ceremonies. The mass in Saint Teresa's Church, Donore Avenue, was a big affair with many of his Arthur Guinness & Sons' colleagues attending, followed by a traditional burial in Mount Jerome Cemetery, Harold's Cross in the same plot as his daughter Mary, who had passed away some fourteen years earlier. When she got back to Ebenezer Road after the funeral, Ellen readied herself for the next stage of life, helping provide for her mother and her maternal uncle, Peter, who, as a bachelor, lived with Dee and her family.

Although dealing with the loss of her father, the next three years went by quickly, with Ellen combining her home duties with an ever more enjoyable job working for the local dressmaker. She sacrificed a lot during that period, but although there were times that she would have liked more space and time to focus on herself, Ellen always knew that her father passed away safe in the knowledge that she would help look after the house and family. It was her duty, but she really enjoyed the 'craic' in the house of an evening when dinner was finished, maybe some of her cousins would call around and they'd have a couple of drinks in the small living room with her ma and uncle.

It was 10 a.m. on that Saturday morning after the dance.

Miss, Say Goodbye to Your Daughter

When Ellen awoke, she had a cloudy feeling of excitement – why she felt that way became clear when her eyes adjusted to the bright sunlight peeking in between the drapes and she caught sight of her dress from the previous night. She remembered that dance, the giggles when she introduced herself to Joe and the laughs she shared with Mabel as they ran home afterwards. Her mission that day was to find out more about Joe. But firstly, she went downstairs to share the spoils of the previous night with Dee.

Dee, who was in her early seventies by then, was born in Wexford but moved to the Liberties area with her family in the 1880s. Like Ellen, she was on the small side, with thinning grey shoulder length hair, and her silhouette was unmistakeable as she'd walk back from the shops pulling her 'old lady trolley'. Her parents were pure working class, with her father a labourer with Guinness and her mother a housewife until she passed away in 1894, two years after Dee's youngest sibling was born. Dee was born in 1873 and had witnessed utter deprivation in a post-famine Ireland, with poverty in Wexford forcing her family to move to Dublin in search of work. Back then, the British ensured that the inhabitants of this island were wholly and exclusively focused on putting food on the table for their next meal in priority to dreaming of a time when Ireland's children could be free.

Although only minimally educated, having left school at twelve, Dee had a strong work ethic, having been a laundress before bearing children, and sought to pass that onto her offspring. Having lost her eldest, Annie, aged three months, she also missed the opportunity to see what her third child

Home

could achieve, when Mary died of tuberculosis in 1927. Her only boy, Peadar, picked up some of the work ethic of his mother, but raising his five children took its toll. He lived in Dolphin's Barn and, despite its proximity to Ebenezer Road, the strange behaviour of Peadar and his wife meant that family visits were few and far between. However, one of their children, Bridget, aged eight in 1944, took it upon herself to call by the house on the odd weekend and Ellen would ensure that her niece received a warm welcome and some food during each visit.

Although never said, there was no doubt that Dee's 'favourite' child was Ellen. When raising her children, Dee maintained the exterior of a serious mother that wouldn't tolerate any antics, but she melted inside every time she received a squeeze hug from a young Ellen. She never called her Ellie, with that nickname reserved solely for use by Mick, but she always enjoyed Ellen's feisty spirit and hard-working attitude, and acknowledged that her daughter was her rock of stability after Mick passed away.

That morning, Ellen bounded down the stairs to find her ma sitting in the scullery at the back of the house having a cuppa. This was Dee's favourite room, where she'd come up with interesting meals for her family from the barest of ingredients. The room was effectively an annex off the living room and had a galley kitchen, with a gas cooker and some units on the left hand side and a sink on the right hand side under a window overlooking the backyard. On the floor was off-yellow patterned lino that led to storage at the rear of the kitchen, with an external toilet located in the backyard. This was the most basic room in the house, but Dee was quite content sitting at the small table with a cuppa, a biscuit and enjoying any bit of heat generated from the sun streaming through the side window.

'How did you get on last night? Did Mabel make it through to the end?' Mabel was known for getting sleepy on nights out.

'Yes, she did,' replied Ellen, with Dee giving her a surprised look in response. 'Ma, it was a great evening. You should have seen what they did with the hall. I thought I was in America!'

Dee loved to see her daughter's blue eyes glint when she imparted exciting news. Those eyes witnessed their fair share of sadness over the years, but Dee detected that Ellen was in a happy place that morning.

'What was the music like?' inquired Dee.

'You know yourself, Ma,' replied Ellen, ''twas a mixed bag' of all sorts.'

She was only dying to tell her that she was asked to dance twice, had the craic with the girls and plucked up enough courage to ask a lad for a dance. Dee felt Ellen wanted to talk more about the evening, so rather than keep her on tenterhooks, she threw out a question.

'Did you have any dances?'

'I did. I was asked to dance by a fella from Newmarket. He's two left feet, God help him.'

'Anyone else?' inquired Dee, pretty certain that it wasn't only one dance.

'Some lad from Inchicore, but sure he must be double me size. Fr McHugh made sure the lights were put on immediately after the last dance and I came home after that.'

Home

Dee sat back, put her cup on the saucer, into which some of the tea spilled, and a little smile crept across her wrinkled face. 'I thought you'd have more news than that.'

'I wouldn't tell you everything, Ma,' said Ellen.

Both mother and daughter knew the importance of seemingly simple conversations and, although it was never said, they valued their open relationship and the ability to talk about almost all things.

Chapter Three

KNOCK ... knock

Later that day, Ellen left the house and called up to Mabel to gossip about the goings-on from the previous evening. But Ellen had purpose in this visit to her best friend's house.

'You were brave to step out and ask that fella Joe to dance,' said Mabel, who preferred to blend into the background in most circumstances.

'Sure, I'd nothin' to lose. He was hardly going to say no, was he?'

'S'pose not,' replied Mabel, 'but did you like the look of him before asking him?'

'I did, to be sure,' Ellen said, letting out a girly laugh. 'I spotted him at the start of the night. Now, you need to help me find him.'

In the fifteen years she had known Ellen, Mabel had never seen her be so forward and direct in seeking out a man. In the 1940s, a woman's place was to do as she was told, wait to be asked out and never risk being accused of being forward on matters of the heart.

Mabel said, 'Right so, what's his surname?'

'I haven't a clue,' replied Ellen, followed by a look

KNOCK ... knock

of bemusement when Mabel, who generally knew who everybody was, gave her back a blank stare. After ten minutes of trying to map out various ways in which they'd seek to find out who Joe was, they decided to head out for a short walk in the summer sunshine. They were going to Oscar Square, a small park five minutes' walk from Ebenezer Road, and, on the way there, they bumped into Jenny Connolly, a former classmate of theirs from school. Jenny couldn't help herself.

'Ellen, I hear you asked Joe Comerford for a dance at the end of the night?'

Ellen didn't know where to look. She didn't mind people having a giggle at her expense given her willingness to ask a man for a dance, but didn't like that Jennifer, and presumably others in the neighbourhood, knew more about Joe than she did. 'Sure, I did,' responded Ellen, trying not to miss a beat. 'I didn't see you there yourself, Jenny.'

'Sure I'm past those dances. This little one has put paid to me energy levels,' as she pointed towards her bump. 'I hope I've more energy when the baby arrives.'

Ellen and Mabel said goodbye to Jenny and, when she was out of sight, they both laughed heartily. 'You have his name, so no stopping you now, Ellen,' said Mabel.

Ellen, happy that this part of the investigation was complete, replied, 'Too right, Mabel. Now, let's find out some more.'

Over the next few days, in between work and household chores, Ellen and Mabel found out that Joe Comerford lived off Thomas Street, was the age of Christ and worked in a butchers in Rialto. This was great to know, but Ellen had no idea what to do to try and 'bump' into him. She also couldn't be sure if he felt the same connection she had that night.

Joe himself woke the morning after the dance and, whilst washing, looked in the mirror and couldn't help but smile. Although they had only shared four or five minutes and barely ten words together, he thought Ellen was gorgeous, with her beautiful eyes and engaging smile, and decided that morning that he'd try to find out more about her and whether this was a relationship worth pursuing. He worked six days a week in the butchers, so didn't have too much time for private investigation. However, one of the tall men that Ellen peeked around to ask Joe to dance was tasked with finding out as much information as he could that week. His name was Jimmy Joyce and, by the following Friday night, when Joe met him for a couple of pints in the Robert Emmet pub at the corner of Thomas Street and Thomas Court, he had plenty of information.

'What ya find out for me?' queried an excited but impatient Joe, before either fella had time to take a first sup of their pints.

'Slow down there, Joey,' replied Jimmy, trying, in his own way, to build suspense. 'Her name is Ellen O'Connell. She lives on Ebenezer Road, or somethin' like that. She works with a dressmaker and she's a few years younger than you, I think.'

'Not a bad start,' said Joe to himself. When out with his friends on a Friday or Saturday evening, he was good company and always had a witty one-liner to keep the chatter going, but was daunted by the idea of plucking up enough courage to ask this woman out. He was a simple man in a lot of ways, but knew the importance of having someone to share his life with and, 'Ellen might be the one,' he thought to himself.

It was Friday 4 August, exactly two weeks after the dance. Joe finished work early and went home to wash away the 'scent' of the butchers – a standard part of Joe's hygiene ritual, but, on that day, he was keen to look and smell his best. He confirmed Ellen's address as No. 12 Ebenezer Road, or Benzer as it was referred to locally, and decided to call by to see if she was there. He'd been to and fro in his mind on whether to do this, but decided today was the day. He put on the same three-piece suit he had worn to the dance and made sure every hair was in place.

As he came downstairs, his mother, Josie, piped up. 'Where ya goin' all dressed to the nines?' Josie was always interested in what Joe was doing, given he was her only child.

'Just out to see a friend,' replied Joe, keen to end this conversation quickly.

'Well, I'm not saying you're meeting up with a girl, but, if you are, here's a few pennies to get an ice cream or somethin',' Josie said, as if she was talking to a young child.

'Ah, Ma, will you leave it out. I'm grand.'

Josie told him to enjoy himself and not be back late, given his early start the following morning. Joe almost tripped over the mat at the front door in his haste to leave the house and then paced purposefully in the direction of Ellen's house, right hand in his trouser pocket and left hand swinging in carefree fashion with every stride, belying his inner sense of dread at calling to Ellen's house.

As he rounded the corner from Cow Parlour onto Benzer, Joe wondered whether this was a trip to the dentist such were the knots in his stomach. He'd been talking silently to himself since he left his house, trying to distract his mind from what was ahead. But he was now outside a 1920s house in this charming little road that led to Donore Avenue. No. 12 was a well maintained house, with a small front garden surrounded by a waist-high hedgerow and part-rusted metal fencing – as with most houses in this neighbourhood, the outside walls were splashed with greying pebbledash, although some of the neighbours tried to spruce up the dash by adding some colour, but to mixed effect. All of this was analysed by Joe's eyes in the five seconds it took him from spotting Ellen's house to walking to the front door – but he said to himself that he just needed to get on with it. He was at the door and noticed the knocker was quite high – Joe was about five feet six inches tall, always had fun poked at him for his less than average height and maybe this was a sign that he shouldn't be there. 'Enough of this nonsense,' he said to himself. He took his right hand out of his pocket, reached high for the door knocker and rapped it twice, first one too firm and the second one a little lighter. 'KNOCK ... knock.'

Chapter Four

Romance

Ellen was upstairs in her room organising some clothes and the rap on the door startled her. She ran down the stairs, opened the door and was even more surprised when she saw Joe outside smiling sheepishly at her. His hair was even darker than she remembered and, with her one step up from him, he seemed smaller. Trying to act calm, she said hello and Joe, also trying to act like everything was normal, said, 'Hello, Ellen. Do you remember me?'

Ellen knew fine well who he was, giggled and replied, 'Are you the fella I danced with a couple of weeks ago?'

'I am,' replied Joe, struggling to remember the opening chit chat he had rehearsed to himself over the preceding days. 'Would ya like to go for a walk?' asked Joe, more in hope than expectation and, to his surprise, Ellen quickly and emphatically said yes.

'I just have to tell me ma,' she said, after which she turned and dashed inside.

She quickly told Dee that she was going out for a walk, to which Dee replied, 'Wrap up love, the wind is expected to pick up this evening.' Ellen then got her coat on the way back to the front door.

Miss, Say Goodbye to Your Daughter

As Ellen and Joe started walking up Benzer, and despite the conversation still being a bit of a struggle, they both felt comfortable in each other's company. Though, through their respective research since the dance, they knew more about each other than they were letting on. 'What time do you start in the shop each day?' asked Ellen.

'How'd ya know I work in a shop?' replied Joe.

Ellen quickly thought of a way to cover her tracks. 'Sure I thought I recognised you from the butchers in Rialto.'

'What has you around those parts?' inquired Joe.

'Me ma sometimes shops there and me da always said your pork chops were the best in Dublin.'

These were innocent first conversations, with each party trying to sound sophisticated, interested, but not too keen. For a man of the 1940s, Joe was reasonably intuitive and he decided to ask a question.

'You said your da said we had the best chops. Does your ma get them somewhere else now?'

Ellen mentally came to a halt, but tried not to break physical stride. Apart from the odd time to Dee and Mabel, she never really talked about the sadness she felt without her father – it brought back acutely painful memories, but, for some reason, she felt comfortable talking about it to Joe, an almost stranger to her. The connection she felt at the dance made her feel open and nicely vulnerable.

'He passed away three years ago,' replied Ellen.

'Ah jaysus, Ellen, I never knew – if I did, I wouldn't have asked.'

'No problem,' said Ellen, ''twas very difficult for all of us, but time does help.'

Romance

'What was wrong with him?' inquired Joe, himself feeling awkward about probing such a delicate subject, but he sensed Ellen wanted to be heard.

'His breathing was bad and an infection got the better of him, but he passed away quickly and in no pain, thank God.'

Joe touched his hand against Ellen's and she instantly gripped tight. This wasn't the conversation Joe had mapped out in his head, but he felt the connection from the dance get stronger – Ellen was of a similar mind, a feeling she never had before.

After walking for a few minutes, they reached the Grand Canal at Sally's Bridge. That breeze Dee had mentioned was starting to pick up and Ellen was glad she had brought her coat. Despite it being early August, an Irish summer day can consist of four seasons in an hour, sun splitting the stones one minute, then clouds come in, breeze picks up and the rain hits – that day was no different and, as they walked up the canal towards Dolphin's Barn, the wind was firmly rustling the browning leaves on trees that would soon be shedding their autumn harvest. Just before they reached Dolphin's Barn Bridge, there was a bench beside the canal – Joe asked would she like to take a seat and Ellen was happy to stop.

'Were you close to your da?' asked Joe.

'I was. I still think he's with me, if you know what I mean. We had some great times together.'

'I'm close to me parents as well,' said Joe. 'Me ma still treats me like a chisler, but it keeps her busy.' Trying not to overthink what he was saying, Joe said, 'I'd like you to meet them someday.'

Ellen replied, 'That'd be nice, but let's get to know each other first.'

'I'd like that,' said Joe.

Without ever saying it, it was implicitly assumed that, in the fifteen minutes from Ebenezer Road to Dolphin's Barn, Ellen and Joe were 'courting'.

After another thirty or so minutes chatting with ease, Ellen said she had to get back home and Joe walked her back to Benzer. As they approached No. 12, Joe, being inexperienced with women, didn't know whether he should give Ellen a goodbye kiss. She also wasn't sure what he would do. In the end, Joe gave her a gentle peck on her right cheek and said, 'I'll call around at seven o'clock tomorrow.' She thought the peck was the most romantic thing ever and, as she stepped into the house and Joe walked away from the front gate, they both took a glance over their shoulders and let out more giggles.

Bang on 7 p.m. the next day, Joe rapped more confidently on the door at No. 12. Ellen answered quickly. She was literally waiting on the other side, as she wanted to make sure Dee didn't answer the door. Holding hands as they walked towards 'town', they were almost skipping down the road, with both anxious to learn more about each other.

'Where'll we go?' asked Ellen inquisitively.

'How about Moran's?' Joe had no idea if Ellen took a drink, but thought he'd suggest the pub at the corner of Kevin Street and New Street.

'Sounds good,' declared Ellen – she was keen to have one drink to relax as, despite feeling comfortable with Joe, she was still nervous as to whether they really had that connection or would they be able to keep the conversation going. Moran's was a typical Dublin pub of the times – a bar area exclusively

Romance

for men, with only stools to sit at and some standing room for those hardy enough to stay upright after a few pints of the 'black stuff'. The 'lounge' area had marginally more comfortable seats and women were welcome in that part of the pub. The final part was a snug, separated from the bar and lounge area, and exclusively for use by women.

The 'black stuff' is Guinness, a stout made in the Saint James's Gate Brewery since 1759. Moran's was located less than a mile from the brewery and, to a seasoned Guinness drinker, it's known that when a pint travels a shorter distance from the brewery to the bar it makes it exponentially better than one that had to travel further. So, this bar was one of Joe's favourites and he loved the silkiness of a pint of Guinness from its taps.

He opened the door to the lounge area and ushered Ellen in first. There was a quiet area in the corner free, with a round mahogany table and two soft-seated low stools. Joe asked her what she'd like to drink and she instantly replied, 'I'll have a glass of Guinness, with a dash of blackcurrant.' He liked her taste in drink, albeit the blackcurrant was sacrilege to many customers of that establishment. Ellen loved a glass of cool Guinness, especially during summer, and the blackcurrant gave a sweet contrast to the hops taste of the real drink.

After a few minutes, Joe arrived back with the drinks and the next two hours flew by. There were plenty of years to catch up on and it seemed that every time one person would finish a story, the other had another tale competing for air space.

'Where did you learn to sew?' inquired Joe about Ellen's work with a local dressmaker.

'Me ma taught me a little bit when I was a chisler. I also did some sewing in school and ma talked to Mrs Fogarty about taking me on when I finished,' replied Ellen, with a relaxed smile, as she loved to talk about her dressmaking.

'How do you decide what to do with the dresses?' asked Joe.

'Mrs Fogarty listens to what the customers want and she turns it into ideas. I then get on the machine and that's it really,' said Ellen, playing down her expertise at producing a finished product from basic ideas and raw materials.

Joe was impressed at how easy Ellen made it all seem and was in awe of anyone who could use their hands to such great effect. He had left school at twelve, and whilst he knew mincemeat from a sirloin cut, he had no particular 'skills' that he could call his own. However, he had a full-time job in a thriving local business and had no complaints.

For Ellen, there wasn't a moment that evening where she felt this wasn't right. They just seemed to be on each other's wavelength. As they left the bar, there was no stopping this young couple from soaking up the late summer heat. They made their way back to Benzer and, this time, Joe gave Ellen a kiss on the lips that lingered that little bit longer than the peck on the cheek the previous evening.

A couple of weeks after their first date, Joe organised for Ellen to meet his friend Jimmy, the fella that found out key information on who Ellen was. 'What's Jimmy like?' inquired Ellen with a certain sense of trepidation at what lay ahead of her that evening.

'He's a great fella. I've known him since I was about fifteen and he's got me out of a few scrapes over the years,'

Romance

replied Joe, who hoped that Jimmy would keep the detail of some of those incidents to himself.

They were meeting in the Robert Emmet pub, where Joe and Jimmy had met to discuss Ellen a few weeks earlier. Pubs, or public houses, have always had a special place in the heart of the Irish nation, where friends and family mix in a casual, relaxed setting, and publicans ensure that drink flows with freedom no matter what struggles are going on in the outside world. This pub was typical of those of its day. The floor was rustic, with almost every tile cracked and broken, the bar was a deep mahogany colour and customers could feel the history and sense the stories exchanged at the bar by just touching that old stained wood. Both parts of the pub, but particularly the 'men only' bar area, were shrouded in a smoky haze, as most customers would light up a cigarette as they supped their drink. As the sunlight coming through the partly stained windows hit the cigarette smoke, it made for a surreal environment, with a rainbow of colours projected onto heavily embossed wallpapered walls. This pub was named after one of Ireland's renowned freedom fighters, Robert Emmet, who led an unsuccessful rebellion against British rule in Ireland in 1803, was captured, tried for high treason and executed in public on Thomas Street.

Far from thoughts on Ireland's struggle for freedom, Ellen was solely focused on making the right impression with Joe's best friend. Joe showed her into the lounge area and Jimmy was already there nursing a pint of Guinness. 'Jimmy, this is Ellen, Ellen, this is Jimmy,' blurted out Joe, keen to move the evening on from this awkward start.

'Delira' to meet ya,' said Jimmy in a flat Dublin accent.

'Likewise,' replied Ellen, trying to keep eye contact with Jimmy, despite the distraction of the back of his hair sticking out like a rooster.

'Right so, that's the hard bit out of da way,' exclaimed Jimmy. 'What can I get you love birds to drink?'

'A pint for me,' said Joe, inadvertently jumping in front of Ellen.

'I'll have a glass of Guinness, thanks,' said Ellen – although she felt comfortable to add a dash of blackcurrant to the order on her first date with Joe, she decided not to stand out to Jimmy and kept it to a glass of plain.

The night went well from there – Jimmy didn't disclose any embarrassing Joe stories; Joe kept the conversation going whenever a gap presented itself, which was rare given Jimmy's ability to fill any void; and Ellen came across to Jimmy as a genuinely nice person that was clearly falling for his best pal. As they left the pub, Jimmy headed west towards Kilmainham, as Ellen and Joe headed back towards Benzer to drop her home.

'What'ya think of yer man?' inquired Joe.

'He's a gas ticket and seems like a real friend.'

That final comment struck a chord with Joe. He valued the small group of friends he had around him and was loyal to those that placed their trust in him. He inferred from Ellen's statement that she also strongly valued friendship and this was another trait he admired in her.

Of the many firsts that Ellen and Joe shared in those early weeks, the most nervous was when they met each other's families. For both, it seemed right that Joe be introduced to Dee before Ellen was brought down Thomas Street direction

Romance

for tea with Josie and her husband Davey.

It was September and only six weeks since they had met at the dance. Ellen came downstairs and Dee was listening to the wireless for the weather report. The forecast was invariably wrong, but Dee religiously listened to it on Radio Éireann every evening at 6.30 p.m., so she felt she knew what to wear the following day and also to give her something to talk to the neighbours about when she'd stroll around chatting to anyone that had the time of day.

'Ma, can I have a word?' Ellen asked sheepishly.

'After the forecast, love,' replied Dee.

Ellen sat nervously on the second-hand faded brown cloth sofa that Mick had acquired about ten years earlier. All she remembered from that wait was hearing about 1010 millibars falling slowly – her heart was falling not so slowly for Joe and she did wonder whether it was all happening too fast. However, as she thought to herself before coming down the stairs, this must be what love was all about, so she was determined to go with her heart.

'No problem, love, what'ya want to talk about?' inquired Dee, as she surfaced from having her ear next to the wireless, her head still taking in the forecast and what it meant for the following day's attire.

'I'd like to bring someone over for tea tomorrow, if that's all right with you?'

'That's fine love, is it Mabel? I always enjoy her chitter chatter.'

'No, it's a lad that I met at the dance a few weeks ago,' replied Ellen.

Dee understood that this was a difficult conversation for

Ellen, so used whatever sensitivity she could muster and made it as easy as possible for her. 'Of course, Ellen, I'd like to meet him, but I've one important question for ya.' Ellen looked up, dreading what the question might be. 'What's his name?' added Dee with a big grin on her heavily creased face.

Ellen breathed a deep sigh of relief. 'His name is Joe Comerford. He works in that butchers in Rialto and lives near Thomas Street.'

'I look forward to meeting him,' replied Dee putting her daughter at ease, 'and tell him to bring some of those chops your da used to love.'

'Leave it out! Thanks, Ma. How about tomorrow evening around six?'

'That's no problem, Ellen, and relax, I won't eat him.'

Ellen ran upstairs, incredibly relieved that her ma had made that conversation easy. She just hoped that the following day would be as 'relaxed'.

It was Saturday. Ellen finished work at lunchtime and went to the shops to get some cakes for the tea with Joe. She bought some coffee cake, a favourite of the O'Connell family, and a fresh sliced pan of white bread to make up some corned beef sandwiches. She knew she was over-preparing, but she wanted this meeting to go as smoothly as possible. Joe finished up a little early from the butchers and got dressed up in 'that' suit again to try and make the best impression possible. He told Josie what he was doing – she decided to say very little, as she felt that Joe was in his own world preparing for conversations with his girlfriend's mother. 'Make sure to shake her hand, call her Mrs O'Connell and mind your language.' Joe was known at home for his colourful use of

Romance

English and Josie was keen that he didn't show up her family by letting out unnecessary expletives.

'Thanks, Ma,' responded Joe, 'see ya later.'

As Joe left the house, Josie looked out the front window. Joe was known for having a quick and purposeful walk, but that day he was meandering slowly, deliberately, and Josie felt for him, but she was confident that his good rearing would stand to him as he met the 'opposition'.

About fifteen minutes later, Joe arrived at No. 12 and, once again, rapped the knocker. He was bang on time and Ellen knew it was now or never. She opened the door, took Joe by the hand, led him past the parlour and into the living room. This was the main socialising room in the house, with a three-seater sofa against the window that overlooked the back garden, a matching single seater and Mick's old armchair immediately on the left near the hearth. The carpet matched that of the parlour, but the wallpaper was a lighter shade of brown with an embossed pattern. There was a teak sideboard at one end of the room, which housed an inordinate amount of knick-knacks that had been accumulated over the years. Dee was sitting in her usual sofa chair and, thankfully, Uncle Peter was out for a couple of jars with a friend.

Ellen introduced Joe to her ma and, with a reasonable level of confidence, he reached out to shake Dee's hand. 'I'm very pleased to meet ya, Mrs O'Connell. You've a lovely house.'

'You too, Joe. Now call me Dee. Mrs O'Connell makes me sound like an aul dear.' This immediately defused the tension in the room.

'All right, Dee it is,' said Joe, and Ellen then went into the scullery to get the tea ready. The next hour went well, with Dee adopting a friendly stance towards her daughter's consort.

'Do you come from a big family, Joe?' inquired Dee.

'There's just me and me parents, Josie and Davey – no brothers or sisters, so it was a quiet enough house growing up,' replied Joe. Complications during Joe's birth meant that his mother couldn't have any more children and this made her especially protective of her only child.

Joe chatted about his job and even managed to mention something about the weather autumn was throwing at Dublin – Ellen had tipped him off about her ma's love for the weather. 'I reckon we're in for a cold winter, if that breeze out there is anything to go by,' said Joe, opening up the conversation to Dee's favourite topic.

'You're not wrong, Joe, but hopefully it's a mild one. Otherwise, I'll need a new coat,' replied Dee.

The coffee cake went down well and, with that, Joe stood up, shook Dee's hand firmly and expressed his genuine thanks for a lovely evening. Ellen brought him to the front door, whispered a quiet, 'Well done,' to him, he gave her a goodbye kiss on the cheek and they agreed to meet up the following day after mass. Ellen went back into the living room and Dee immediately put her daughter at ease.

'He's a nice young fella. You've picked well, love.'

'Thanks, Ma,' said Ellen, as she went about cleaning up the place. This felt like an important test to pass and attention then turned to the reciprocal meeting with Joe's parents.

Ellen and Joe met up at lunchtime after mass the following day and planned when might be appropriate for her to meet Josie and Davey. They agreed that the following Friday

Romance

evening would be best, and in the run up to that day, Josie was in a flap – this was the first woman that Joe had brought home and she wanted to ensure the evening went smoothly. Joe called over to No. 12 to pick Ellen up and bring her to Bonham Street to his version of the two-up, two-down house that was typical of inner city Dublin in those days. The house was standard red-brick on the outside, but, when she stepped inside, it was clear to Ellen that the Comerfords took pride in their humble abode. She could feel the relatively plush carpet underneath her low-heeled shoes and remarked to herself that the living room wallpaper was in immaculate condition. There was also a tall glass cabinet in the corner of the room that housed various trinkets and, after politely greeting Joe's parents, Ellen made sure to compliment the house. 'Your house is beautiful, Mr and Mrs Comerford. I love your cabinet,' said Ellen, as Josie beckoned her over to have a look.

'Thanks, Ellen,' replied Josie, as she took out a butter dish and knife set that was handed down to her by her own parents and showed it to Ellen.

'That's lovely. Me ma has a similar dish, but not as nice as this one,' said Ellen.

This was a relaxed start to the evening, but Josie had inordinately high standards for any woman that was to be with her beloved son. After sitting down, Ellen politely ate a couple of sandwiches and a little slice of homemade fruit cake and sought to make small talk, with Joe jumping in when required. Josie was particularly interested in Ellen's seamstress work. 'I hear you're mighty at the sewing machine, Ellen,' said Josie, inviting the conversation to explore the types of dresses she made and the range of customers that she encountered.

'I wouldn't say that,' replied Ellen, trying not to sound boastful, 'but I do love to put me own twist on the standard dress.'

Given this clear passion for her work, Josie was surprised that she didn't wear something more elaborate. Being a dyed in the wool inner-city Dubliner, Josie was also intrigued by Ellen's calm and confident manner, which, to her, appeared above her station, as if she picked up a level of self-assurance from her well-to-do customers.

After saying their goodbyes, Joe walked Ellen home and then made his way back to Bonham Street to see could he get any feedback from his parents.

Joe walked into the living room and immediately said, 'Well, what do you think of Ellen?'

Davey just looked down at the ground – he had been given orders by Josie to stay quiet, as she was to take the lead and assess Ellen's earlier 'performance'.

Josie jumped straight in. 'She's a lovely looking girl, but is she trying to be something she ain't?' Despite being the controlling partner in her own marriage, Josie would prefer that her only child be the assertive one in his relationship and felt that Ellen might be driving the agenda with her son.

Joe was taken aback at the directness from his mother, but rather than defend Ellen, he decided to respond passively, 'Ah Ma, you're not funny.'

She wasn't trying to be funny, but put a marker down in his head that Ellen hadn't fully passed the Comerford test.

Chapter Five

---*---

Progression

It was Wednesday 20 September. Normally, Joe would spend his Wednesday evening at home with his family, have dinner and get an early night in advance of another busy day in the shop on the Thursday. However, that Wednesday was a big day for the special lady in his life – it was Ellen's thirtieth birthday. Given Joe's status in Dublin life, he was not a man of great means, but he was keen to get this first birthday right.

As with all matters, he first consulted with Josie. 'Ma, what should I buy her? What would she enjoy?'

Josie, who hadn't particularly thawed in her views on Ellen, didn't give much help, but did say, 'It has to come from you – you know her better than I do – what will make her smile?' Joe went to bed that night and felt he had the kernel of an idea.

Since Mick had passed away, there weren't many smiles in No. 12, but the morning of Ellen's thirtieth birthday was a good one. Although Ellen missed her father with all her heart, Dee and Uncle Peter made a fuss of her from the moment she got up. She took the day off work and Dee made her favourite breakfast of burnt bacon and white pudding, with white bread, lashings of butter and a hot cup of tea. On the present front, money was tight, so Dee didn't splash out too much. But she did open her jewellery box the previous weekend and picked out her favourite bracelet, a rose gold chain with a run of three tiny diamonds, and a prized possession that was passed down to Dee before her own mother passed away.

'Ellen, happy birthday, there's something inside,' she said as she handed her an envelope with a birthday card in it.

As it rattled in her hands, Ellen felt the weight and thought there might be a few shillings in it. To her joy, she opened it and instantly knew that this was a treasured family heirloom, one that Dee only wore on special occasions.

'Are you sure, Ma? This is your favourite.'

'Absolutely, Ellen, you deserve to have it now.'

Ellen immediately put it on and felt very special, as she walked around the living room showing it off. She was ecstatic and it was the ideal start to her birthday. She was looking forward to seeing Joe later and did wonder what he might give her – she was always thinking of others and her heart was wondering whether Joe felt too much pressure to get a 'good' present.

She was right. He felt a lot of pressure, not from Ellen expecting a wonderful gift, but from himself to not mess this one up. Now, Joe was in front of her, with a little brown bag by his side. He went into the house and Ellen decided to take him into the front parlour to avoid the prying eyes of Dee and Peter.

Bursting to give her the gift, Joe gave her a quick kiss on the lips, then pulled away and said, 'Happy birthday Ellen. Here's a little present.' He was so anxious that he'd got the

Progression

wrong gift, that she'd hate it, and then his eyes were attracted to her right wrist. 'That's a lovely bracelet. Where'd ya get it?' His voice was trembling.

Ellen's face lit up. 'Me ma gave it to me. It's her favourite bracelet that was passed down by her ma. I just love it!'

Joe's heart sank. Ellen ripped open his brown bag, read the card and thanked Joe with a kiss on the cheek. She then opened the gift wrapping to find a little black rectangular box. With excitement, she opened it and instantly saw a yellow gold chain – a plain bracelet made up of tiny links.

'I love it!' said Ellen.

'But sure ya already have a bracelet,' replied Joe. 'I can bring it back to the shop at the weekend.' His voice was low, as he had put a lot of thought into what the right present might be and Ellen's mother had beaten him to it just hours before.

'No way,' said Ellen, 'this one's from you and it's perfect.'

Joe's face beamed with joy and he felt a rush of emotion, the likes of which he had never experienced before. A man that sometimes couldn't find the words to match those emotions, he just uttered, 'I'm delira' you like it.'

Then, Ellen took off her mum's bracelet, placed Joe's gift on her wrist and immediately ran in to Dee to show her.

Dee saw the happiness all over Ellen's face and said, 'It's beautiful and looks lovely on your little wrist.'

Three weeks later and, this time, it was Joe's birthday – thirty-four years of age. Not a fella to look back on what might have been, he had a mindset of looking forward and there was a lot to be positive about. He was beginning to think he had found his one true love and the signs were that Ellen felt similarly.

Miss, Say Goodbye to Your Daughter

Ellen told Joe to keep the evening of Saturday 14 October free and, to her surprise, as she awoke that morning, it was a bright, sunny and calm day. She decided to wear a different dress this time – an ankle length, pale pink chiffon dress, with a v-neck and short sleeves. Once again, she wore her mum's pearl necklace and the bracelet Joe bought for her thirtieth birthday. She took one final look in the mirror before heading for the door – sometimes, she could be self-conscious of her appearance, but, that day, she felt comfortable in her own skin. In a break from the norm, she decided that she would call by Bonham Street to pick Joe up, which meant another opportunity to meet Joe's parents.

She arrived at Joe's house promptly at 5 p.m. and gently knocked on the door. Joe quickly answered and, immediately, a broad smile shot across his freshly shaven face. 'Ya look fantastic, Ellen.' He had no real idea of female dress sense, but knew what he liked and he thought Ellen looked picture perfect that night – he was also thrilled that she was wearing the bracelet he'd bought for her.

'Thanks Joe and happy birthday,' replied Ellen, as she walked into the living room to greet his parents. 'How are you, Mr and Mrs Comerford?'

'Ah sure we're survivin', Ellen. You look lovely,' replied Josie, with Davey looking at the ground again.

Ellen could tell that Josie wore the trousers in the relationship and understood that she could try to get to know Davey as much as she wanted, but his view on Ellen would be determined by Josie and no one else.

'It's hard to believe you're thirty-four Joe. I remember changing yer bum over me knee like it was yesterday.'

Progression

At that point, Joe knew the best thing to do was aim for the door, but Ellen decided to open up the conversation. 'Mrs Comerford, what was he like as a chisler?' queried Ellen – she had a gift of asking open-ended questions that gave the other person ample opportunity to go down various avenues.

In any event, Josie loved talking about her only child and duly took the bait. 'Well, as a baby, he cried a lot. If he stayed in school, he could have done anything,' Josie declared, with the pride that parents have for all their children. She continued, 'He could be quite a mischief when he was younger and there was one time we ended up in Dr Kenny's surgery to retrieve a button from his little button nose.'

'Ah Ma, will you stop this nonsense. Ellen doesn't want to know about that.'

Everyone chuckled a bit and the young ones took that opportunity to head for the door. As they were about to open the front door, Ellen decided to give her present to Joe. For starters, a card she made herself. She had procrastinated for hours one evening during the week about what to say inside – she went with 'Have a lovely birthday. With Love. Ellen xx'. She thought about saying the three magic words, but didn't want to scare Joe off in case it was too early for that – that's the way she felt, but she had no idea if it would be reciprocated. As for the present, she went with the tried and tested 'shirt and tie' set from Frawley's Store on Thomas Street – she knew it would probably be a little underwhelming for Joe, so she whispered in his ear that she had another little gift for him later.

Ellen and Joe then dashed out the door. Her plan was that they'd go for a 'one and one' in Leo Burdock's near Christ

Miss, Say Goodbye to Your Daughter

Church Cathedral, Ireland's oldest chipper having opened some thirty years earlier, and then a few drinks afterwards. They gleefully walked down Thomas Street onto High Street and past the Cathedral, hand in hand, chatting, laughing and without a care in the world. They crossed Christchurch Place onto Werburgh Street and went to the back of the line. This wasn't a restaurant, just a take-away, so Ellen planned, weather permitting, to pick up the fish suppers and then head for the gardens of Saint Patrick's Cathedral. The cathedral was built in the twelfth century in honour of Ireland's patron saint and, despite several times of utter poverty in Dublin, its keepers, who by then were the Church of Ireland, maintained the gardens to an exceptional standard to provide inner city Dubs with a green resource to get away from the harsh concrete life of a city resident. The weather played along with Ellen's plans and, with sunset due around 6.30 p.m., there was just enough light to allow Ellen and Joe have a romantic open-air meal in those heavenly gardens.

The food went down well and they worked it off by walking around the gardens a few times before the gates closed.

'What a beautiful fountain,' said Ellen, as they walked past the water feature in the middle of the gardens – it was an oasis of calm in a busy city and gave these lovers the chance to just chat to each other. Next up on Ellen's agenda was a trip back to Moran's for some drinks. It was 7 p.m. before they arrived and the pub was already bustling with a mix of local lads sharing what had happened to them during the preceding week and a few couples, both young and starting off in life, and old and 'stuck' with each other. One elderly couple intrigued Ellen – they sat in the corner and appeared to share only a few words for the hour that she observed them – however, there was something about the way he helped her out of the chair and carried her handbag for her when they were leaving that put Ellen in no doubt that he cared deeply for his wife. 'Maybe old relationships don't need many words to keep the spark,' said Ellen to herself and she thought this might be her and Joe in thirty years. But, on that evening, conversation wasn't a difficulty for either of them – they squeezed in a third drink before deciding to call it a night just before last orders and both were feeling a little lightheaded as they hit the fresh air.

As they walked down Ardee Street hand in hand, Ellen remembered that she hadn't given Joe the final part of his birthday present. As they crossed the street known as The Coombe, she pulled him in the direction of a small alleyway. She had an urge to show him how she felt, maybe what wasn't said on the card. They walked to the end of the lane, out of sight of passers-by, and she grabbed both sides of his face and gave him the extra present, a French kiss – words didn't seem enough and she thought it was time to physically show the deep feelings she had for him. He reciprocated, as he similarly felt the desire to physically express his love for Ellen.

In 1940s Dublin, any displays of affection in public were shunned – pre-marital sex was considered a 'sin', but neither Ellen nor Joe were thinking about rules at that moment. They were both caught up in the emotion of the night – a perfect night for an innocent couple finding their way in life, which ended with love-making intercourse.

Afterwards, as they continued down Ardee Street, they knew they'd crossed the Rubicon in their relationship — without saying it, both felt they may have gone too far, but there was no regret, just a sense that they should keep the physical side more subdued in the future.

As they got to the door of No. 12, Joe held Ellen's hands and gave her a warm embrace. Quite the birthday for Joe and he certainly had a pep in his step as he made his way back to Bonham Street.

Josie was still up when he got back home and couldn't resist putting the boot in again. 'Ellen's a bit forward, isn't she?'

Once again, Joe didn't rise to it. 'Ma, she's lovely and that's that.'

Josie tried to keep the 'debate' going, but Joe just said he was tired and went to bed. As he lay his head down, his thoughts turned to Ellen — in No. 12, as she lay down, her thoughts went to him. The late evening adventure wasn't far from their thoughts and they were both on quite a high.

Chapter Six

News

Ellen and Joe hadn't talked about the events of the Saturday night in October and there'd been no repeat of that love-making embrace. They spent each Saturday evening together and, generally, a mid-week evening, where, weather dependent, they took a stroll around the Liberties and sometimes beyond. Ellen was particularly busy with work, as those more endowed than her were having dresses made and altered for the pre-Christmas party season. With being so busy, it wasn't until the third week of November that she started to wonder why her time of the month hadn't arrived. Never a consistent twenty-eight day cycle, but rarely more than thirty-five days, she recalled that her previous cycle started around the end of September.

'Maybe it was later than I remember. I thought we were careful. What if I'm pregnant? What will ma say? Is Joe the one?' All those thoughts and questions were spinning around her head, but Ellen didn't dare voice concerns to anyone about her late cycle.

It was 1 December, almost a full nine weeks since her period. She again thought back to that night in the alleyway – naïve but not stupid was what she thought about that encounter.

However, by the following week, Ellen was panicking. No sign of blood. 'Could this be happening?' she thought to herself. 'How can I go to the doctor in this state?' She contemplated having to visit the local surgery to seek confirmation, or otherwise, of her predicament. Ellen's head was in turmoil, but she didn't feel she could turn to anyone for help.

Her doctor was an elderly man called Dr Smith – he was the O'Connell family doctor for several years and tended to Mick during his illness. Since Mick's passing, he called in to see Dee at least once every six months – a social call, but he felt that Dee valued the connection they each had with Mick in his final weeks of life.

Ellen rarely went to see him and worried that he would inform Dee if the news was not what she would like, but, by then, there was no choice. She made an excuse with the dressmaker and headed to South Circular Road to the doctor's clinic, registered with the receptionist and sat down beside a doting mother and her young child.

Worry was etched into Ellen's normally relaxed and smiling face, but she knew she had to find out one way or the other. In the fifteen minutes before seeing the doctor, Ellen took in every square inch of the walls in the waiting area, read every notice and listened to every word between the mother and child beside her. Her mind was so alert, despite the anxiety at what lay ahead.

Dr Smith then came out and asked Ellen into his office. He asked her what was wrong and she just blurted it out. 'I think I'm pregnant.'

To her surprise, Dr Smith displayed great compassion for her situation, given that he knew she was unmarried, and

News

said, 'Things are never as bad as they seem. Let's examine you and we'll take it from there.'

Dr Smith had known Ellen since she was a teenager and understood first-hand what she had gone through when Mick passed away – he didn't want to pile more pressure on her, just when she needed a friendly ear and a caring and calming presence. He carried out the exam and, as expected, he said to Ellen, 'It's probably not the news you want, but you'll get through this.' He didn't need to say the words, 'You're pregnant,' but the message still hit Ellen hard. She shed a few tears, to which Dr Smith responded by opening the window to let some fresh air in and gave her a couple of soft tissues to wipe her eyes. 'Can I ask when your last cycle started?' inquired the doctor.

'Around the twenty-eighth of September,' replied Ellen. He informed her that, by his calculations, she was due her child in the first week of July.

'Ellen, you'll have to tell your mother, but I'm here for you any time if you need to talk about anything.' This was a comfort to Ellen, but that conversation with Dee terrified her. She found it odd that Dr Smith didn't ask about the baby's father, but, in these circumstances, the father wasn't top of mind.

Ellen didn't know whether she should tell Joe first or her mother – either way, it would be a challenging conversation, but Ellen was never one to shy away from what needed to be said. It was difficult to find the words, but gauging the range of reactions was terrifying her. She didn't fear becoming a mother, but dreaded what people might think of her. 'Will this be what I'm judged on?' she thought to herself, having never strayed too far from the well-trodden path over the years.

After a few days tossing it around in her increasingly muddled head, Ellen made the decision to talk to Dee first – she knew they had a strong relationship, solidified after Mick's passing, and sensed that her ma would know how to manage such a calamitous affair with the steady hand of experience that a woman of her age possessed.

It was Sunday. Uncle Peter had just left the house for his usual evening visit to the 'local' for two medicinal pints to set him up for the week to come. Ellen made some fruit scones that afternoon, which herself and Dee enjoyed with a cuppa – although 'enjoyed' is not how Ellen would have described that snack on that evening. Her heart was beating fast, her mind equally racing, but she knew this was the right time to impart the news.

She'd just put away the dishes in the scullery and Dee was sitting in her usual place at the table. As Ellen looked out the window towards the backyard, she said, 'Ma, can I tell you some news?' She was hardly able to get the words out, such was the dryness in her mouth. Tears were not far from her eyes, but, with all her strength, she tried to keep it together.

'Of course, Ellen, what's troubling you?' Dee knew her daughter's tone of voice and had an immediate feeling that this news wasn't 'good'. Ellen then turned around and sat down opposite her.

'You know I've been seeing Joe for a few months now.'

Dee responded, 'Go ahead Ellen, what's wrong?' sensing that Ellen was struggling to find the words.

News

Despite trying with all her might to hold back the tears, Ellen started crying. Instinctively, Dee got up from her chair, sat beside Ellen and grabbed her hands. 'It'll be fine, Ellen, what's wrong with my little girl?'

With this natural maternal thing to do, Dee gave Ellen that final bit of strength to utter the words that would change things forever – although the die was cast, it seemed to Ellen that voicing her next sentence made everything that bit more real, that bit more permanent, that bit more serious. 'Ma ... I'm pregnant.'

Dee had a strong Catholic faith, which was passed down to her by her own parents. When Mick passed away, she briefly questioned why God would let such truly sad things happen to good people. However, it was her faith that got her through the dark days. She was comforted to believe that Mick had gone to a happier place and that they would be reunited for eternity when she herself left this Earth. In her eyes, if the Church declared that something was a sin, it was so, and one of those 'sins' was engaging in pre-marital sexual intercourse. The Church was unequivocal on the matter and she never once questioned that point in her own mind. Now, she was having to deal with the fact that her daughter not only committed that sin, but was expecting a child from that activity. She harboured thoughts of one day welcoming Ellen's children into the house as an adoring grandmother – she didn't see much of her grandchildren from Peadar and was hoping for a second chance in that role if Ellen was blessed with a child or two. Now, she was having to digest the thought that she would be the grandmother of an 'illegitimate' child.

Miss, Say Goodbye to Your Daughter

Moments before, Dee and Ellen had had an intangible bond they both treasured, but now she couldn't make eye contact with her daughter. She wanted to hug her, tell her everything would work out, tell her she would look after things, but her overriding feeling was one of shame. For now, all Dee could say was, 'Jaysus Ellen, get out of me sight. I can't look at you right now.'

Ellen, left the room, ran upstairs and lay on her bed hugging her pillow and a little fluffy teddy bear she had had since she was eight. It was not how she had hoped this would play out, but, for now, Dee needed time and space to digest the news.

A mother with limitless love for her daughter sitting in a cold kitchen. A daughter on her own, in her bedroom, not knowing if she had anyone to rely on for support at such an incredibly difficult time. 'How has it come to this?' Ellen thought to herself. If only they could talk it out, find some solutions that worked. That just wasn't the way, but Ellen thought, before telling Dee, that she would support her unconditionally. Now, she wasn't sure, and that just added to the turmoil in her head. It was about two in the morning before she managed to fall asleep. It was something similar for Dee, with both running multiple scenarios around their heads, but neither of them able yet to share those thoughts.

The next morning, they both got up early, ate breakfast at the same table, but, other than functional words, not a syllable passed between them. Ellen knew she had to tell Joe and tell him soon.

The following Wednesday, they'd arranged to meet on Cork Street to go for a walk. Ellen was thankful that Joe wasn't calling to the house, as she didn't know how Dee might react to seeing him at that moment – Dee wasn't prone to angry outbursts, but

News

nothing was off the agenda in Ellen's mind at that stage. So, that Wednesday, and ironically in Ellen's mind, she stood outside Paddy Whelan's pram and bike shop, which was where she had arranged to meet Joe. He was running a few minutes late, as there was a late rush of customers to the butchers, and this just made the knots in Ellen's stomach even tighter. He arrived about fifteen minutes after the agreed time, full of apologies and gave her his usual peck on the cheek.

As they walked down towards Dolphin's Barn Bridge, she grabbed Joe's hand. 'I've some news, Joe.'

Joe was immediately alerted by Ellen's serious demeanour. In the five months since they had first met, he had never experienced that and had no idea what to expect.

'Are you all right?' he asked.

Again, Ellen uttered those few short words that would change everything. 'I'm pregnant.'

'Are you sure?' asked Joe, as he sought to process what Ellen had just said, hoping that it was possible that this wasn't happening. 'How could this have happened?' he said to himself. His mind went back to that night in the alleyway, but he, like Ellen, thought they had been careful.

'Yeah. I was at the doctor and he confirmed it.'

Joe's heart sank even further on hearing this news.

'What are you going to do?' uttered Joe.

Of that sentence, all Ellen heard was 'you'. 'How has this become just my problem?' she thought to herself. This felt like a betrayal. More thoughts ran through her increasingly scrambled mind, 'Joe was there in the alleyway that night. Joe was the one who danced with me back in July. Joe was the one who held my hand every time we met up. Joe was the one who bought me that dainty gold bracelet. Joe was the one whose actions were always of love, or so I thought.'

But now, at her time of greatest need, it felt like not only her mother, but also the de facto love of her life, were abandoning her. She couldn't find the words at that moment to respond to that part of his sentence, but replied, 'I've talked to me ma and we'll try and figure it out.'

Joe was put out that her mother had heard the news before he did, but part of him was hoping someone else would come up with a solution. They continued their walk in silence, which was difficult for a couple used to chatting freely and easily.

After a few minutes, Joe put his foot in it again. 'Whatever you decide to do is fine with me. It's your decision.'

This time, Ellen stood up for herself. 'This is our baby and we'll decide together and with our families.' She felt better for getting it out and Joe understood where she was coming from, but the shock of the news imparted only minutes earlier had not yet diminished.

He chose to just nod and say, 'I know.' There wasn't a lot of conversation after that and they went their separate ways – for once, before parting, Joe didn't give Ellen his customary kiss on the cheek. As she walked up the path to the house, Ellen felt entirely on her own – it was probably the shock affecting Joe's abilities to think straight, but it surprised her that he didn't seek to reassure her, either physically or verbally. She felt hurt and alone and walked into No. 12 unsure whether her mother would be willing to talk it through and find solutions.

Chapter Seven

Decisions

She opened the front door, hung up her coat on the usual third hook along and went into the living room. Dee was listening to the wireless, having just got her daily weather fix – at least some things were still normal, thought Ellen. Peter was up in his room, so Ellen decided to try and open up the conversation. 'Ma, can we talk about things? I really need your help. I just met up with Joe and I've no idea what to do.'

'Don't mention that man's name in this house. If I see him, I'll string him up for what he's done.'

This upset Ellen even more – Joe and Dee got on well to that point and, if there was to be any future for the relationship, she needed her ma on speaking terms with Joe. 'It's not all his fault.'

'Don't say that Ellen. Joe's responsible for his own actions.' Ellen decided to leave that aspect of the discussion for another day.

'Help me out of this mess, Ma.'

'It's a mess for sure. At least we agree on something,' as Dee lightened the mood fractionally. As Ellen did herself, Dee spent the past three days thinking of possible solutions and they were both open to a conversation around those options that evening. Dee took the 'conch' initially, 'As I see it Ellen, you have two options: One is to marry that man,' unable to even utter his name, 'and the second option is to give the baby up to the orphanage.'

Ellen had a third option of having the baby out of wedlock and raising it herself in her family home and she decided to proffer that alternative in response. 'Would you consider letting me have the baby and stay here and raise it?' In her version of events, this would still mean that Joe could be part of her and her baby's life, but that idea was immediately quashed by her mother.

'That can't happen! That won't happen! That child has come from a sin and we can't have it in this house.' The 'B' word wasn't mentioned, but it was clear that it was close to Dee's lips and Ellen was shocked.

'Don't be like that, Ma. This baby will be a human being like us all and I'm not having you thinking of him or her in any other way.' Ellen put all her passion and emotion into the second part of that sentence – she was not having her baby being likened to a mortal sin. Dee half back-tracked and then went again.

'I'm sorry Ellen. But, if the cap fits.'

'Ma!' exclaimed Ellen. 'Please give me and this baby some respect,' again expressed in forthright fashion, as she pointed to her tummy.

'Ellen, I just don't see that option working in this community. It's marriage or the orphanage.'

Ellen couldn't bear to think of the second option. Giving up on her baby like that just wasn't in her nature. The first

Decisions

option of marriage required Joe to be on board and, after her earlier conversation with him, she'd no idea where his head was at. 'Ma, I think I love Joe, but this is all so sudden. Can you have another think about my option?'

Dee once again stamped out that possibility, 'Absolutely not. Marriage or the orphanage, that's it!' It sounded so simple, but so far from it, thought Ellen. She decided retreat on that evening was the best course of action.

'We'll have another talk tomorrow,' said Ellen.

'I'm not changin' me mind, Ellen,' replied Dee.

Ellen headed for bed for what would be another restless night. Joe was due to call for Ellen a few days later for their usual Saturday night meet up. Despite the cool December weather, they agreed a walk was needed to talk things through. Ellen put on her coat, gloves and scarf, waited at the bottom of the road to prevent him from having to face Dee and they headed up for a walk along the canal. As they left Donore Avenue and crossed South Circular Road, Ellen started the discussion. 'Joe, you really hurt me the other night. This is our problem, not just mine and I want us to agree what we're doing together.'

A pretty firm opening statement to which Joe replied, 'You're right. I'm sorry. I haven't a clue what to say.' He was like a rabbit in the headlights and, even though the man is expected to be the strong one, it was clear that Ellen was going to have to think for both of them.

'I talked to me ma and it's the altar or the orphanage. She won't let me have the baby on me own.' When put in such stark terms, it scared the bejaysus out of Joe. He'd obviously been thinking about options for the past three days, but hadn't manage to distil it down to two simple words: 'altar' or 'orphanage'. He knew what they both felt for each other, but the idea of a shotgun wedding wasn't how he'd mapped out his life.

'What'ya think yourself Ellen?' Again, another sign that maybe Joe wasn't as mature as she thought.

'Surely, he has his own opinion?' thought Ellen to herself. 'I can't give up on this baby. So, what about the other option?'

In a rather embarrassing and low key reply, Joe said, 'I'll have to talk to me parents.'

'Do you have your own brain Joe?' retorted Ellen sternly to make sure he got the message that it was time for him to stand up and be counted on this issue.

'I do, but jaysus, we only know each other five months.'

'You weren't saying that in the alleyway,' as the temperature rose another level in the discussion.

'Let's not fight. I think marriage is the only option then,' in what must have been the most subdued marriage proposal the Grand Canal had ever seen. 'But I need to talk to me parents tonight. They don't know yet.' Ellen's normally polite and calm disposition dropped completely.

'For God's sake Joe. You've had three days to tell them. You need to grow up.' Suddenly, this fairy tale love story was unravelling at pace and, again, Joe played for time.

'I'll tell them when I get home and we can meet up tomorrow after mass. Is that all right?'

'Yes, that's fine,' replied Ellen, as they both agreed to call short their stroll. They walked back to Benzer, said their terse goodbyes and Joe made his way over to Bonham Street. As he crossed Thomas Street, the irony of passing by the site

Decisions

of Robert Emmet's hanging wasn't lost on him – this felt like a trip to the gallows, as he prepared to face his parents, well, particularly Josie, whose temper was renowned. To his disappointment, his parents were in and he knew he just had to come out with it.

Joe went into the scullery, got himself a glass of water, headed back into the living room and sat down beside the fire. His hands were cold from the chilly December breeze and thought he'd spend a few minutes warming up before facing the music. However, Ellen's words earlier telling him to grow up hit home – he just had to grasp the nettle, knowing that the sting could last for quite a while.

His opener to get it started was direct, if a little clumsy, 'Ma and Da, I'm in a mess … eh … we are … Ellen's with child.' The reactions of his parents couldn't have been much different. Davey did his usual and started counting the scuffs on his worn shoes, but Josie hit the roof.

'Ya fuckin' eejit Joseph. Did you let that floozy trick you into this?'

'Don't call her that Ma. I need help here.' Once again, his choice of the first person in that sentence said a lot about where he felt the problem resided – he appeared to be looking for help to get himself, not themselves, out of the situation, notwithstanding that he agreed to get married less than sixty minutes before. Josie made a couple of suggestions, again more aimed towards solving her son's issues and to hell with Ellen.

'She can give it up or leave Dublin and have it somewhere else.' It was like as if exporting the problem to another community meant that there was no longer a problem.

Joe then piped up, 'We could get wed?' Josie knew this was an option, but her reticence to suggest it echoed her general reservations about whether Ellen, or any woman for that matter, was good enough for her Joe.

'It's a possibility. Is that what ya really want?'

'Me head is all over the place. I do love her, but it's all so sudden,' said Joe.

'Love is no part of this. This is about the right thing for you, not that woman.' In echoes of Dee's thoughts on Joe, all blame from this mother was being firmly laid at Ellen's door. The discussion on options went on for another thirty minutes, with Davey adding very little and Josie trying to control the direction it was taking. By the end of it, she reluctantly agreed that a quick wedding might be the best option, but there was no final sign off just yet.

The following day, Joe left the house around 10.45 a.m. and headed for Donore Avenue Church for 11 a.m. mass, where he agreed to meet up with Ellen after the service. He walked towards the back entrance of this magnificent building. Originally built in 1924 and later extended to cater for the increasing population in the local area, Saint Teresa's was typical of churches of its time, granite-faced, imposing from the outside, vast space inside with solid oak pews lined up like soldiers in formation facing a two level sanctuary that hosted a natural stone altar. In the middle of every Sunday mass, the parish priest would give a sermon to his flock, sometimes a sermon from the Archbishop of Dublin, John Charles McQuaid at the time, or even from the Pope himself.

On this day, Fr McHugh, a man that came to Dublin from his native Donegal to attend seminary in Holy Cross

Decisions

College, had 'free' reign for his sermon. He decided to focus on the upcoming Christmas celebrations and chastise his parishioners, in advance, for letting their morals slip during any pre-Christmas gatherings. The Catholic Church, at that time, had immense power over the Irish people – those people of little means clung onto the belief that weekly, and sometimes daily, attendance at mass and doing everything the Church asked of them would somehow guarantee an everlasting life after death. That grip over its people only strengthened under Archbishop McQuaid, who 'governed' his flock with an iron fist and was known to have excessive influence over successive Irish governments, such was the interlinkage between State and Church at that time. His friendship with Eamon de Valera, one of the 1916 insurgents and Taoiseach at that time, from their links with Blackrock College had significantly influenced the framing of the Irish Constitution of 1937.

Joe wasn't particularly listening to the sermon that day given he was in the grip of a crisis that his naïve and simple mind was struggling to comprehend. A small part of him was genuinely excited by an upcoming wedding to Ellen, but this was far outweighed by the feeling that everything was out of control. He didn't yet have the connection that Ellen felt for this unborn baby. As he walked from the top of the church after taking communion, he caught a glimpse of Ellen on the right hand side. They exchanged the briefest of smiles, but this belied their collective sense of concern at how things were playing out. As the parishioners rose for the final prayer, Joe snuck out the back of the church for a quick cigarette before meeting up with Ellen. He wasn't a regular smoker, but his nerves kicked in and felt a cigarette would calm him enough to be able to have a sensible conversation with her, as he waited at the side entrance where they agreed to meet. As Ellen approached Joe, she could smell cigarette smoke and, to herself, said he won't think he can continue to smoke when this baby arrives.

After exchanging pleasantries, Ellen jumped in, 'How did your parents take the news, Joe?'

'Me ma was hopping mad, but I think she agrees that we should be wed.' Ellen felt that Josie appeared to be calling the shots and that Joe was childlike in his inability to make his own decisions.

'But what do you want, Joe?' as Ellen was concerned that she was the only one in the partnership focussed on their future.

'I'm happy if you're happy,' responded Joe, in another example of him not wanting to stand up and be counted. Trying to make the best of the situation was a trait that Ellen had in abundance following her father's passing, so she decided that pushing Joe, at that point, to be someone he wasn't would be futile.

'Right, we're agreed we'll get married as soon as we can?'

'Yeah,' was the reluctant response from Joe in what didn't sound like a man who was about to marry the woman of his dreams.

'I've arranged a meeting with Fr McHugh tomorrow evening at 5pm. Can you be there?' Ellen asked, having briefly talked to the parish priest before mass that morning.

Again, 'Yeah,' was the only response he could utter – he was just about aboard this 'train' and was nowhere near the

Decisions

driving cab – he just hoped the destination would be a Garden of Eden for himself, Ellen and their unborn child and, in that thought, at least he was thinking of more than just himself. As they parted, Joe's mind turned to the awkward conversation they'd be having with Fr McHugh to agree arrangements – those sermons from various priests over the years 'preaching' about what the Church deemed to be 'immoral' acts were ringing in his ears.

Chapter Eight

Wedding

It was the following day. Joe and Ellen had their usual work days in the butchers and dressmaker, but they'd no doubt the real work lay ahead of them and that 5 p.m. meeting with Fr McHugh.

McHugh's role models growing up were his father, who toiled day in day out on the family farm, and his mother, a typical housewife who ran the home with supreme efficiency, if lacking a little empathy towards her seven children. He had arrived in Donore Avenue Parish in 1940, four years earlier, and the local community were in no doubt that it was McHugh's way or the highway.

Dee, Josie, Ellen and Joe were all outside the vestry of the church. This was the first time the mothers had met and it was clear from their respective frosty attempts at greetings that both blamed the other's child for this predicament. As they trooped into the vestry, Ellen recalled being in that room on the night before her father's funeral and it brought back difficult memories. The room was basic, with a tall cabinet to one side, which housed various parish files, but everyone's attention was grabbed by the strange scent being emitted from a small gas heater in the corner. There were three chairs in the room, one large one for the priest and two others facing that chair – Ellen and Joe chose to sit, with the mothers standing behind their respective children in a physical show of support.

Fr McHugh walked in, sat down, and, in a gruff tone, opened up proceedings. 'What do you need? I've another meeting to get to in half an hour.'

The four of them didn't know who should start. Josie jumped in, 'These two want to get wed as soon as possible, Father,' which was code for a shotgun wedding.

'Did you two cavort with each other?' was the direct response from McHugh. He asked it in a way that seemed to take pleasure in probing the sexual act that had led to this meeting.

'We love each other, don't we, Joe?' replied Ellen, trying to move the discussion on.

Once again, Joe let himself down, with his usual insipid reply of 'Yeah.'

Fr McHugh then got on his high horse about what marriage meant. 'Do you both realise that marriage is for life and you must bring up your children in the faith of God? This is not a decision to take lightly or in response to making up for an immoral act in the past.' It was a clear nod to the brazen ignorance of Church teachings that Joe and Ellen had practised some time previous.

'Yes, we do,' was the simple and straight answer from Ellen.

Fr McHugh then spent some time asking Josie and Dee about their own families, the strength of their respective Catholic faith and outlining that this wedding ceremony would not be a 'celebration' in the conventional sense. He continued, 'I will give you a wedding service in this church, but only direct family are allowed attend. The bride must wear an ivory dress and there are to be no celebrations.' This was a needs must event and Fr McHugh made it clear that God would not look down on it with any sense of pride for these immoral young people. Ellen had a strong faith, but, even in such a moment of crisis, she could clearly see that this part of the conversation was an attempt by Fr McHugh to exercise Godlike judgement and make her and Joe feel dirty, shameful and that they'd disrespected themselves, their families and, more importantly, the Church.

'When could we get married, Father?' inquired Ellen, as she tried to put some flesh on the bones of this ceremony.

'Miss, you'll get married when it suits me,' retorted McHugh in one final act to ensure everyone in the room knew who had the power. 'Let me look at the book.' He hummed and hawed whilst flicking through the church diary. 'I can do nine o'clock on Tuesday ninth of January.'

Fr McHugh knew he needed three Sundays to provide the necessary clearance for the wedding, so this was the earliest date he could do and there would be no questioning of him. He was omnipotent in that room and took pleasure in exercising that power against his weakened 'opponents'. In those times, people played by Church rules or had to be prepared for the severest of consequences. Dee, Josie, Ellen and Joe then left the vestry.

Outside, Ellen took Joe aside and asked him only one thing. 'Are you totally sure about this, Joe?'

She was giving him the chance to speak up, speak for

Wedding

himself, speak the truth, and all he could say was a softly spoken 'Yes.' Marginally better than 'Yeah', but it was obvious that he still needed time for all of this to sink in – three weeks left for that and Ellen crossed her fingers that it would all work out.

In the 1940s, weddings were pretty much organised by the bride and, notwithstanding the non-standard nature of this nuptial celebration, it was up to Ellen and her family to get things ready. With just over three weeks to go to the 'Big Day', there was plenty to do and, despite Fr McHugh's declaration of 'family only' in the church, there was no way Ellen was doing this without her best friend, Mabel. When she got back to Ebenezer Road that evening, she headed straight to Mabel's house and broke the news on all fronts.

'Mabel, will you be me maid of honour?'

'Jaysus, you're getting married? When'd ya get engaged? When's it all happenin'?' exclaimed Mabel, with a childlike feverish excitement expressed in her naturally high-pitched voice.

'Where do I start, Mabel?' Ellen brought the mood back to earth. 'I'm with child.'

'Jaysus, Ellen, how did that happen?' inquired Mabel, after which they both chuckled at the innocence of the question.

'Don't ask, Mabel. We're getting married on the ninth of January. So, will you be me maid of honour?'

'Of course I will,' replied Mabel, as she gave her friend a consoling embrace rather than the excited hug that would normally follow such wedding news.

'Thanks, Mabel. I'll need a lot of help over the next few weeks to get everything ready.'

'I'll do anything for ya, Ellen,' said Mabel, which was exactly what Ellen wanted to hear. Unconditional friendship and support when she most needed it – there was no judgement, no condemnation, no tut-tutting from Mabel.

They spent the next couple of hours doing lists up, with Mabel's mum, Betty, bringing in regular supplies of tea. Betty was brought into the know and gave Ellen that look of pity. She was trying not to judge, but a sin was a sin in her eyes – however, she had the decency to let her daughter help her best friend in a time of need. Those little gestures meant a lot to Ellen.

The list involved the following:

- Invitations – Mabel had artistic flair and agreed to draw up handmade invitations

- Wedding Dress – given Ellen's role working for the local dressmaker, she said she would talk to her the following morning and see what could be done

- Bridesmaid Dress – Mabel went straight up to her room and pulled down her favourite 'night-out' dress – although her style was not to Ellen's taste, this was not a time to be choosy and Ellen ticked the box

- Flowers – Betty was roped into this one – her sister had a flower stall on nearby Camden Street and she would organise bouquets for Ellen and Mabel and single flowers for the men

- Church Readings – again, Betty sorted out this one – she pulled out the bible from the top drawer of her

Wedding

dining cabinet and picked out two short readings – nobody questioned the style of readings, just another box ticked

- Mother of the Bride's Dress – Ellen knew that Dee had her favourite dress that could be tailored, if required, at the dressmakers
- Groom's Suit – she left this for Joe and presumed that he'd be able to get his suit pressed for the occasion
- Rings – Ellen was fully aware that she hadn't yet received an engagement ring – this didn't bother her, but she knew that she needed to organise wedding bands. The two ladies left this box unticked, but Ellen said she would talk to her mother later.

There was no talk of a honeymoon – Ellen and Joe's honeymoon period was the preceding five months. Now it was serious and there was no time or money for even a short break down the country. There was also no reception to plan for – this was a wedding day in name only, but Ellen decided to organise sandwich platters to be served to guests back in No. 12 after the church ceremony. This was far from the day she had envisioned when, as a young girl, she dreamt about walking up the aisle to her betrothed. 'Whatever it takes,' she would say to herself whenever she thought about the rushed arrangements.

It was 10 p.m. before she left Mabel's house and, she felt that at least the main items for the wedding were in hand. She stepped into her house, walked into the living room and immediately picked up on an atmosphere between her ma and Uncle Peter. 'What's wrong, Ma?'

Miss, Say Goodbye to Your Daughter

'Uncle Peter thinks it's all happenin' too fast.'

Ellen initially stayed quiet, but her uncle looked sullen.

'What would your da be sayin', Ellen?' said Peter, once again condemning Ellen for her situation, but bringing up her da was a step too far.

'Don't bring Da's name into it. Above all, he'd want me to be happy. If getting married to Joe fixes this, then he'd be fully behind me,' responded Ellen in a grown-up forthright manner that made Dee quite proud.

'Peter, this is happenin' and let's just support Ellen,' said Dee. She herself had serious doubts about how everything was playing out but, without her late husband, she was trying to step up and provide Ellen with the backing she would normally be getting from Mick. Peter just muttered to himself, decided retreat was the best form of defence and headed upstairs.

'Thanks, Ma,' said Ellen, as she went over and patted her mother on the arm. 'Can I ask your help with one thing for the wedding?'

'No problem, Ellen, what'ya need?'

'I need two wedding bands. Could you talk to Pat and see if he has any cheap ones in the shop that we could buy?' asked Ellen, referring to the local pawnbrokers.

'Wait there,' said Dee as she too went upstairs. After a couple of minutes, she came back down and held something in her right hand. 'Close your eyes, Ellen,' she said as she brought her daughter back to her childhood days when, on a Friday evening, her da would ask her to close her eyes, put out her hands and then place a Friday surprise in those small fingers. It might be a piece of fruit, a small chocolate bar or

Wedding

some jellies – it never mattered, the joy was in the expectation on a Friday afternoon, as Ellen must have looked at the clock on the mantelpiece every five minutes, as she listened for the latch on the front door, and then closed her eyes before Mick even came into the living room. She was now thirty years old, eyes closed, hands out and not knowing what to expect from her mother this time. 'Open Sesame,' said Dee, which was the magic phrase her husband had used every Friday evening.

Ellen opened her eyes and a little black box was in her hands. She looked at the box, at her ma and back to the box again.

'Open it!' exclaimed Dee.

Ellen opened the box and inside were two plain gold rings, nothing fancy, but just what she needed for the wedding.

Ellen immediately recognised the small rings and said, 'Is that da's ring and your ring?'

Although Mick never wore his wedding band, like most men of that time, Dee always wore hers and only took it off when washing up in the scullery or when rubbing moisturiser on her hands each evening.

'Yes, Ellen, they're the rings we exchanged all those years ago and you should have them for your wedding.'

'Are you sure, Ma?'

'Of course, Ellen. Your da would have wanted it.'

This moment lifted Ellen's spirits after a wearing day – it was a vitally important start if herself and Joe had her ma's support.

Apart from wedding preparations, Ellen was busy with work and herself and Joe only met once per week in the run up to the wedding, for a mid-week walk around the

Liberties. Notwithstanding that this was their first Christmas as a couple, they agreed not to buy presents for each other, as money was best saved towards their future life together. They exchanged cards on Christmas Eve and then met up for the final time before the wedding on Wednesday 3 January.

'Happy New Year, Joe,' said Ellen, as Joe pecked her on the cheek outside No. 12. Ellen had her coat on already and they headed for a walk along the canal.

'Thanks, Ellen. You too,' replied Joe, but he didn't seem as present as he normally was on those walks. After less than forty-five minutes, he said he had to head home, as Davey had asked him to move some furniture in their living room. Before reaching the Cork Street end of Donore Avenue, they said their final goodbye before the wedding.

'Next time we'll see each other will be at the top of the church,' said Ellen, attempting to gauge how ready he was for the following Tuesday.

'Yeah, hard to believe,' replied Joe, which gave a sense that he was still struggling with the enormity of what was coming. After kissing Ellen goodbye, he said, 'Take care of yourself over the next few days.'

'You too, Joe. See you on Tuesday,' said Ellen.

Joe then headed for Bonham Street, with Ellen walking home on her own. Ellen felt Joe's distracted nature, and rather emotionless goodbye, were down to pre-wedding nerves and, after getting home, she shared a pot of tea with Dee whilst warming herself beside the fire.

Mabel and Ellen went up to the dressmaker on the Saturday before the wedding for a final fitting. The dressmaker pulled out all the stops and produced a beautifully classic wedding

Wedding

dress for Ellen – she opted for a full length ivory dress, with a sweetheart neckline, and a fitted bodice, with fitted sleeves gathered at the shoulder. As Ellen came out from the dressing room, Mabel, being a sensitive soul, couldn't keep the tears in and went up and hugged her friend. 'Ya look amazing. Joe's a lucky man.'

'Thanks, Mabel,' was all Ellen could come out with, as she was struggling with her own emotions, memories of her own father flooding back. She was thinking how lovely it would have been for him to walk her up the aisle, even in the circumstances. 'It's a lot of effort for one day, but I love it,' said Ellen, after she composed herself.

Despite the unusual and rapid run-up to this wedding, Ellen was coming to terms with her new life and felt optimistic for what the future would hold for them and their unborn baby.

That night, Ellen asked Mabel and two other friends over to her house for a couple of drinks and sandwiches – nothing flash, but it was nice for Ellen and Mabel to have some downtime given the frantic weeks they'd just had, running hither and thither to get things done. The four young ladies and Dee laughed, cried and joked – normal banter was exactly what Ellen needed as she prepared herself for the rest of her life.

It was 6 p.m. on Monday 8 January, the day before the wedding. Ellen was in the scullery making ham, chicken and corned beef sandwiches as if she was feeding the masses. Dee had cleaned the windows earlier that day and even Peter was in on the act and washed down the front step. No matter what anyone thought, the following day was an important one for the O'Connell family and everyone was pulling together in the same way they did when Mick passed away.

Then there was a knock on the door. This wasn't uncommon that week, as the local community, having got word of the impending nuptials, were dropping off cards and presents for Ellen and Joe. Peter went to the door and, a few seconds later, Joe's friend Jimmy was in the living room.

Ellen came into the room and was taken aback to see him. Maybe he had one final message from Joe before the wedding. 'Hi, Jimmy. What'ya doing here?' she asked slightly nervously.

Jimmy was fidgety and, for a lad that was not normally stuck for a word, he didn't seem to know where to start his sentence.

'Eh ... Joe ... yeah ... eh ... '

'Spit it out, Jimmy, ya eejit,' said Ellen, as she sought to relax the mood.

'Jaysus Ellen, Joe's gone.'

'Gone? Gone where? Is everything all right for tomorrow?' It was dawning rapidly on Ellen that there was something seriously wrong.

'I'm sorry, Ellen. He's gone away. He can't go ahead with the wedding,' said Jimmy, finding his voice and making sure that the message he was sent to deliver was getting through. He took no joy in this act and he himself was trying to come to terms with what had happened in the preceding days.

'Where's he gone?' asked Ellen, hardly believing what was happening. 'Is he coming back?'

'I don't think so, Ellen. I think he's left Dublin forever.'

Wedding

'What do you mean forever, Jimmy?' Ellen realised that this might be it in terms of the relationship she'd been fostering with Joe since the previous July.

Jimmy had no more answers for her and he left sheepishly a few seconds later. Dee went over to a devastated Ellen and hugged her tight.

'It's all right, Ellen. Maybe it's for the best.'

'What do you mean the best? This baby has no father. I have no husband. What's going to happen now?' asked Ellen as she started the groundwork on defending her position against her mother's orphanage plan, which was something she dreaded.

'That's for another day, Ellen. You're in shock.'

Ellen went back into the scullery, tried to wipe away the tears and restarted making sandwiches. She was completely stunned. Notwithstanding her obvious fears, she did love Joe and, before Jimmy's outburst, could see a future for them together. Now, he'd left Dublin to Lord knows where. 'Will I ever see Joe again? Have I lost my one chance at love? Will my child ever see its father? Will I be able to keep my child? What will my friends think? Will I be isolated in my community? Will I lose my job?' were all questions in Ellen's mind. This mix of emotional and practical questions were running around her head and all her body could do was stand in the scullery making sandwiches for the wedding that would never happen. Dee was in the living room trying to figure out if this was good news or bad news, what was Plan B, was there a Plan C, what would Mick have done? All questions, but no answers.

For now, all Dee could do was walk back into the scullery,

give Ellen one more hug and say, 'Ellen, I love you very much. We'll figure this out.'

Ellen just stood there, tears streaming down her soft cheeks and onto the table.

Mabel called to the house later. More hugs and tears ensued and she stayed over that night, the only tangible support she could offer her best friend after receiving such devastating news. But, as Ellen's head hit the pillow, she tried to process what had just happened. In the three hours before she fell asleep, her only clear thought was that she wanted to keep this baby – but she had no idea if that would be possible, would she get the support from her family and could she even manage on her own? Her eyes closed. Tomorrow would be another day.

Chapter Nine

Pivot

Going back three weeks from that visit by Jimmy to Ebenezer Road. From the moment Josie and Joe left Saint Teresa's Church, she started at him. 'How could you be so stupid to get her pregnant? How did you pick a woman with notions? Sure, didn't she make the first move with that dance in July? Didn't she make all the running in the relationship since then? Didn't she trick you into that sexual encounter? Didn't she fill your head with ideas of everlasting love?'

This was psychological warfare from Josie and one that Joe was incapable of defending. His mother had subjected him to this coercive behaviour for as long as Joe could remember and he was no match for her. Not only had she had sixty years practice of it, but she was also able to play out various scenarios in her head and devise strategies to address each scenario. Joe was in the lion's den and maybe his fate was preordained.

'Joe, let's sit down and chat some more about the wedding,' said Josie, as they arrived back to Bonham Street.

'Ma, I know you don't like Ellen, but it's all set for next month,' responded Joe. Unfortunately, as with most times like this, his words were right, but the tone with which he delivered them lacked intensity and left far too much room for Josie to exploit.

'Joe, I know you love Ellen, but you have your whole life ahead of you and tying yourself down to a woman you've only known for five months is not what you want.'

'I know it's scary, Ma, but we can make it work.'

'I've no doubt you mean well, Joe, but can you really say that you know this woman?' replied Josie, as she used Iago-like skills to play on Joe's insecurities. 'You're a good boy,' she added as she worked on making him feel like a helpless child, 'but this is not the solution.'

Like a fly landing in a spider's web, Joe's next move was exactly how Josie would have played it out. 'What's the solution, Ma?'

Josie needed to be careful not to jump to an extreme solution in case it pushed Joe back in the direction of the wedding to Ellen.

'There are other options, Joe. You could encourage Ellen to give the baby up to the orphanage. Maybe Ellen could move away from the area.' Then she decided to land a third option that was firmly in Joe's hands. 'Or you could start afresh somewhere else.'

Joe didn't have the intellectual capacity to consider multiple scenarios and relied on those around him to guide him, but, as he listened to what Josie was mapping out, he wondered how leaving the scene of the crime could be the right solution. He would lose connection with his lover, never see his baby, not that he felt that bond yet, lose his job and give up day-to-day contact with his family and friends in the Liberties community.

Pivot

Although Josie was, by that stage of her life, a bitter woman in a loveless marriage, she still protected her family and, ordinarily, would have wanted Joe to be close by so she could keep an eye on him, live vicariously through his actions and achievements in life and, maybe, someday, enjoy having his 'legitimate' children, her grandchildren, over to Bonham Street for regular visits. But, in her mind, Ellen and Joe's actions would lead to a permanent impact on the perception of the Comerford family in this tight community. Most of the families in this particular locality were linked by being 'on the bread line', so any family's status was fragile and once one family member stepped out of line, and particularly if that misstep was linked to one of the Church's core principles, that family could subtly be pushed to the fringes. Such was the situation facing Josie – Joe had sinned, even if, in her eyes, he was cajoled into it by Ellen, the community would know it and the only way to get rid of the problem was for Joe to move away and condemn the problem to one for the O'Connell family only.

Joe's next move proved pivotal. He opened the door to her options and Josie ran in. 'What do you think, Ma? I'm confused.' She knew she had poor helpless Joe exactly where she wanted him.

'You could go to London and start a new life. Your da has a friend that went over there years ago and I'm sure he could put ya up before you find your feet.'

'London?' thought Joe – he'd hardly ever been out of Dublin and had never been in another country – he had this image of London as a massive city, with people and buildings everywhere. 'How would I settle there? How would I get to know people? What would I work at?' he thought to himself.

Josie had thought out the escape, even if she was a little sketchy on some of the answers to those questions about what life would hold for Joe after he got there.

'You could get the train to Belfast, ferry to Scotland and get a train from there to London.' Josie made it sound like he was going on a little holiday. 'We have a suitcase you could take. You don't have to pack too much.'

After some more strong arm tactics by Josie, Joe was beginning to think about the practicalities of packing his life's belongings into one suitcase, but it all sounded far too surreal to happen.

'Jaysus, Ma, I don't know. London is very far away.'

'It'll be exciting, Joe.'

Exciting was going to a Gaelic football match in Croke Park and then back to the pub for a few jars to discuss whether the Jackeens were good enough to regain the Sam Maguire Cup following their win two years earlier. For Joe, exciting was most definitely not running away from the situation with Ellen, but Josie painted this picture of opportunity and wonder in moving to a big city like London. Three or four years earlier at the height of the German Blitzkrieg bombing of the city, she wouldn't have recommended that destination, but the D-Day landings pushed the war eastwards and London was now considered 'safe'. 'I hear there's wealth over there like you wouldn't believe and the people love to see the Irish coming over.' She had no basis for that second statement, having never actually had a conversation with an English person in her life, but Joe was no match for her hyperbole.

This more forth than back conversation went on over

Pivot

the following two weeks. Through her skilful manipulation, Josie would progress Joe's thinking a few steps towards a new life in London each evening, with Joe then maybe taking a single step back towards his Dublin life as he fell asleep each night, but that steady persistence from Josie brought them to Amiens Street Station on Saturday 6 January 1945.

Three days from when he was due to be wed to Ellen, he was standing beside the Belfast train, holding a small suitcase with some clothes in it. Josie paid for his journey and gave him five English pounds to start his new life in London. In his pocket was a scrap of paper with an address in Ealing, a suburb in north-west London where Davey's friend lived. Josie and Davey were with him at the station. Although Joe had no idea at the time, this was the last time he would see his parents. Since the famine days one hundred years earlier, emigration was a way of life for Ireland's young. Most left the Emerald Isle in search of a job, food and a better life for themselves and their families. Joe's situation was different. He had a steady job in Dublin, something which one-third of his peers didn't have, he had someone who was willing to be his wife and he had the prospect of becoming a father for the first time six months hence. But each time he thought about what he was leaving, Josie would sense his wobble and assure him with some encouraging words of the new life he was headed for. He never felt the shame that Josie had and, if Davey had found his tongue, the entire situation could have been avoided.

As the three of them stood on the platform, Josie opened their last collective conversation. 'Joe, this will change your life for the better and, in time, maybe we can visit you in

London,' she said as she sought to encourage Joe onto the train.

'I'll miss you, Ma and Da. I'm sorry for all the problems I've caused, but I didn't mean for it to happen.' Joe was close to tears, as he began to realise the enormity of his decision to leave Dublin.

'Joe, we love you and we know that you'll have a great life in London,' said Josie, trying to focus on the positive.

After a few more minutes, Joe walked slowly up the four steps to the train, carrying his little suitcase. As he stepped inside the train, he took a glance over his shoulder and gently waved at his parents. They waved back, smiled and, as the train departed the platform, Josie breathed a sigh of relief that she and her family, what was left of it anyway, could continue with their normal life and status in the Liberties community. For her, losing her only child was an appropriate cost for regaining this status amongst her people and she never re-thought the handling of that crisis. She did what she had to do – she would be judged in the afterlife and surely the Church would reward her for ridding society of this 'problem'. However, the problem still existed in No. 12 Ebenezer Road.

In the forks of life, Joe made the stark choice of departing for a new life in London rather than going in the opposite direction and marrying Ellen. As he turned back after his wave goodbye to his parents, he took a seat on an uncomfortable bench in the crowded carriage. All manner of people were on the train – families clutching onto their life's belongings, as they sought a better life in England, a few honeymoon couples who married that morning and ran to the train to have some special early days of marriage and single travellers, both men and women, that mostly looked on the verge of tears. For them, maybe they weren't running away from problems of the magnitude of Joe's predicament, but they were similarly leaving families, friends and lives, with no idea what lay ahead of them. Joe sat hunched over, with both hands holding onto the handle of his suitcase. His thoughts ranged from what Ellen would think when she heard of his departure, would he ever be back in Dublin, would he ever see his parents again, would he ever see his child? As much shock as Ellen felt when Jimmy visited No. 12 the following Monday, Joe was also in shock at what the last few weeks had brought him.

About six hours later, the ferry arrived in Stranraer. Joe got up from his seat, walked down the gangway, made his way to the railway station and boarded another train he had no control over. He had chosen one fork in life and the impact of that choice on Ellen and her unborn baby would last forever.

Chapter Ten

Which Direction?

Unbeknown to Ellen, on the night Jimmy imparted the news of Joe's flight from Dublin, Dee paid a visit to Bonham Street to try to figure out what had happened. Josie answered the door.

'Where has that son of yours gone?' queried Dee angrily.

'That's none of your business and that baby is no longer our concern,' responded Josie.

Dee couldn't believe that Josie was so forthright, willing to give up on her own flesh and blood. She chose to walk away from the house after her other questions went unanswered.

Ellen got up on what was meant to be her wedding day. As she came to, after a far too brief and restless sleep, at first she didn't remember the shocking news of Joe's departure from the previous evening. She opened her eyes and saw Mabel asleep beside her. It then hit her like a tidal wave – there was no wedding, no groom and no certainty as to what would happen with her baby. She felt an incredible weight on her shoulders, that cloud over her life, as she started playing out various scenarios. She was also dealing with the loss of Joe – although their dalliance had been brief, she felt it was a deep relationship and, because she knew he was gone,

the connection was more intens[...]
broken in two.

Although effectively grievin[...]
her primary focus, as she lay i[...]
think of any way in which she c[...]
she'd have to start with Dee and try and use their close
relationship to her advantage. Growing up, she often used
her female charm to improve an outcome in the house, not
in a bad way, but just to eke out a slightly better situation for
herself, and mostly relating to the trivia of life. This situation
was far from trivial and it was going to take all her strength
and determination to drive the outcome she desired most.
She got up, washed, ate a quick breakfast with Mabel and the
rest of the day went by in a blur – nothing was said between
Ellen and Dee about Plan B that day.

It was the evening of Wednesday 10 January and the
weather had taken an unseasonable and early turn towards
spring. Although the living room fire was gently smouldering
away in No. 12, both Dee and Ellen were readying to discuss
Plan B and the temperature between mother and daughter
was decidedly wintry. Before the wedding was agreed as the
best plan, Dee was adamant that Plan B was the orphanage.
Her logic was that this was the only way that Ellen could
reasonably stay in the community – she sinned, fell pregnant
and they must be cleansed of this illegitimate child if everyone
in the O'Connell family was to return to normality. Ellen had
the opposite view and wanted to stay living in Dublin and
keep her child. Mothers and their adult children often have
close relationships, and Dee and Ellen were a prime example
of that, but the bond that exists between a mother and a small

Say Goodbye to Your Daughter

once a mother finds out she's expecting – the child dependent on the mother for that first nine months to a similar extent, the mother symbiotically feeds off that dependency to define herself as a 'mother'. To consider a break of that bond is anathema to a mother-to-be. Ellen thought to herself that Dee would be able to empathise with that feeling, but the shame caused by Ellen's actions had each 'side' going to battle to find a palatable solution.

After tea that night, Ellen decided to broach the topic. 'Ma, we need to talk about this. It's not going away.'

Dee knew that, but she felt Ellen might need a week or so space between the 'wedding day' and discussing options.

'You know my thoughts on this, Ellen. You're going to have to give the baby up to the orphanage.'

Ellen had this conversation with Dee before the wedding option was agreed and had her arguments ready for her mother's opening gambit.

'Ma, you don't understand how I feel. No matter how this baby came about, it's my baby and I can't give it up. Can we come up with a solution that means I can keep the baby?'

'How do you think that's goin' to work, Ellen? It's not acceptable to have an unmarried mother keep her baby. That's that!' Dee tried to double underline her position.

But Ellen, knowing that society would find it difficult to accept her bringing up her baby close to home, wondered whether there was anyone in her own family that could bring up the baby as their own for as long as Ellen remained unmarried. In that way, maybe Ellen could stay physically, and to some degree emotionally, close to her baby, with the possibility of reclaiming her child at some point in the

Which Direction?

future. Rumours abounded in the Liberties about families whose daughters disappeared with their mothers for a few months, only for the mothers to re-appear cradling a newborn alongside their daughters. Without being certain, the community knew that these were illegitimate children, but a blind eye was turned to a pragmatic solution. But Dee's age and widowhood ruled out this possibility for Ellen.

'Ma, is there anyone in the family that could bring up the baby as their own?'

'What about your brother? This has to be kept close, so that's your only option.'

Ellen immediately baulked – she knew that was the only likely option but she had hoped that Dee might be able to consider other 'families'. She had seen first-hand the issues her brother was having rearing his own children and this was not a future she could consider for her baby.

'So, Ellen, we're back to orphaning the child as the only option. I know it's not what you want but, if the baby is adopted, its new parents will be able to give it a life that you can't. It will be cared for without the shame that this area will condemn you and your baby to.'

Due in part to the stigma of illegitimacy, adoption had been a feature in Irish society for many decades and thousands of babies had found loving homes with caring adoptive parents. Many of those children were handed over or taken into care, as their families, mainly single mothers, couldn't cope with the children and orphanages arguably provided a safe haven and the hope of a second chance for those children. However, Ellen didn't want her baby to be someone else's child – it was hers and that indelible bond she felt was only getting stronger with each day and with each discussion she had with her mother about the future.

Ellen regrouped and said, 'What if I went away to have the baby and came back home after a while?' This didn't make sense to Dee, as the illegitimate child and its mother would still be ostracised by the community, but she pursued this further with Ellen, as she had knowledge of a situation that was managed initially in a way like this.

'What about if you were to go down the country and have the baby in a home? I've heard there are ones that are run by the nuns.'

Ellen initially bristled at this idea, at the nuns being involved – although she still had her faith, she wasn't sure how the Brides of Christ would help and she still didn't understand how this would make it any easier for her to keep the baby long-term.

Dee continued, 'You could have the baby there and they would mind you and the baby after that. The baby would always be yours and you could bring it back here once you're married.'

Marriage was at the heart of everything. A baby born out of marriage was viewed by the Church and State as a second-class citizen and Ellen would have to be wed for her to bring up the child without the stain of illegitimacy being branded on the child.

Joe wasn't strong enough to stand up to his mother and had been hunted out of Dublin, so Ellen didn't see how she could ever find a man that would not only take her on knowing that she'd been with another man, but also take on the 'burden' of her illegitimate child. However, this was the only solution being proposed that gave Ellen the chance to keep control of her baby's future.

'Ma, do you know where such a place is? It might work, but only if I have control over my baby and its future.'

'Let me look into it,' replied Dee.

Dee had gone up to Fr McHugh on the Monday evening to cancel the wedding and they had already had a brief conversation about a 'mother and baby' home in Tuam, Co. Galway, run by the Bon Secours Sisters. Despite his obvious disdain for women such as Ellen, Fr McHugh was still a Christian and had visited that home some twelve months earlier. He said to Dee that the head nun ran a tight ship and had several well-trained nuns to help with delivering the baby and looking after mother and child from then.

The following day, knowing that Ellen had had twenty-four hours to let the seed of the 'mother and baby home' idea permeate her mind, Dee restarted the conversation with her daughter. 'Ellen, I was talking to Fr McHugh about that idea we talked about yesterday.'

'Go on, Ma, what did he have to say?'

'He was quite helpful and understands you're in a difficult situation. He said there's a place in Galway that's run well and you'll be able to stay there for at least the first year of the baby's life.'

'Sounds interesting. When would I go down?' asked Ellen.

'I don't know the details, but Fr McHugh said he'd call the Reverend Mother over the next few days.'

This gave Ellen hope that she would have some control over the next stage of her and her baby's lives and that gave her grounds to build back some of the optimism dashed by

Joe earlier that week. By the end of the conversation, Dee and Ellen agreed that Galway was the option to go for and, for the next three months, Ellen sought to return to relative normality by continuing her seamstress work. Each week, she grew larger, as her baby stretched into the space, and she began to wear slightly baggier clothes. Given Ellen's frame, those with an eye for detail would have gathered what was happening. Some talk was going on behind her back, but Ellen chose to keep her head up and think positively.

During that three-month period, Dee imparted details to Ellen of her encounter with Josie on the day the wedding was cancelled and they both agreed that, much like the Comerfords were walking away from the problem, the O'Connells would bury any memories of that family and seek to move on as best as possible. But the aborted wedding, coupled with the Comerford family denial of the issue, had a significant impact on Ellen's ability to trust people, given how much she felt let down by the actions of Joe. Thoughts of the relationship, the possible future they could have had together and the devastation she felt on the day Jimmy visited No. 12 were buried, as Ellen believed that this was the best coping mechanism for the stress she was experiencing.

Chapter Eleven

Newborn

It was April 1945. Ellen had given up sweet treats for Lent, so she enjoyed a couple of slices of cake with Dee and Uncle Peter on Easter Sunday evening. 'I'm eating for two,' had become a bit of a joke around the house, albeit the 'problem' was still a raw subject with Dee.

It was agreed with the home in Galway that Ellen would get the train down on the Friday after Easter to live for the last three months of her pregnancy. It was an express condition of the home that no family members could travel down with her, as it was felt that, once a mother-to-be boarded the train, she was to stand on her own two feet. This felt harsh to Ellen, but she couldn't impose any conditions.

The train was leaving from Kingsbridge Station, near Kilmainham, at 1 p.m. – so, after Ellen said goodbye to Uncle Peter and received a surprisingly warm embrace, she and Dee took the thirty-minute walk to the station.

As they approached the train, Ellen had a strong feeling that this was not the right thing to do – leaving her family, friends and community in her time of need. She stopped on the platform and said to Dee, 'I can't do this, Ma. I want to stay in Dublin to have this baby.' She didn't know how her mother would take a last minute U-turn.

'What do you mean, Ellen?' exclaimed Dee. 'This is what we agreed.'

'But Ma, I can't have this baby away from here. I'm frightened.' She strongly appealed to her mother's emotions. With fifteen minutes to go before the train departed for Galway, there was little time for debate, but this to and fro went on for at least ten of those minutes. Ellen gesticulating, Dee with her head down, it was a scene that no doubt played out in various scenarios on that platform over the years.

With a few minutes to go before the train departed, they both slowly trudged their way back to the main part of the station. As they sat down outside the tea shop, the long high-pitched sound of the platform guard's whistle gave Ellen an indescribable sense of relief as that Galway train departed. She didn't know if Dee would insist on her coming back the following day, but, like a death row prisoner receiving another day's reprieve, she felt relieved to be heading back to No. 12 for another night's sleep in her own bed.

The next few days were challenging for Ellen and Dee's relationship, but, ultimately, Dee reluctantly agreed to Ellen's request to have the baby in Dublin and the next three months, with Ellen getting ever bigger and tongues increasingly wagging in the Liberties, were spent preparing her room for the arrival of a newborn. It was almost thirty-one years since Dee had made similar preparations for Ellen's arrival, not to that house, but to a tenement building off Usher Street. Ellen sourced a crib and some neutral baby clothes from friends and family and, by early July, it was feeling very real.

On Friday 6 July, three days before the baby was due to

Newborn

arrive, Ellen sat down with her ma. Whilst Dee had agreed that Ellen could have the baby in Dublin, it was unclear for how long she would tolerate having an illegitimate child in the house. In what was a repeat of many conversations the two had had previously, Ellen said, 'Ma, can we see how the first few months go and then decide?'

'Ellen, you know that you can't be allowed to keep the baby for any longer than a few months,' said Dee, in what was, at least, some concession on her part that Ellen might be allowed a short time to bond with her new baby.

Ellen closed that conversation by saying, 'Ma, I know this is difficult for you, but thanks for everything so far.' Ellen really appreciated how Dee was allowing her previously articulated red lines to be somewhat moved.

Three days later, Ellen was in the Coombe Hospital, an institution dating back to the early 1800s – her waters breaking earlier that day confirmed the baby was on the way. She was brought into a dimly lit, cold, clinical room by an elderly nurse, who was dressed in shabby bluey-green scrubs. The nurse's name was Sister Francis. She had pledged to be a Sister of Charity in 1901 when the careers of choice for Ireland's daughters were simple – nurse, teacher or nun. Her face was heavily wrinkled, with eyes deep set and a hook nose that made her look more like a witch than a nun, but she was highly experienced when it came to delivery rooms. However, it was clear that she looked down on this first-time mother-to-be.

'Get up on the bed,' ordered Sister Francis gruffly.

Ellen sidled up to the edge of the bed and, despite her size and the awkwardness of late stage pregnancy, managed to get her backside onto the firm mattress and swing her feet up, with a little help from Sister Francis. The delivering obstetrician was all business. He never once made eye contact with Ellen and used Sister Francis as his intermediary to communicate to his patient. It was like Ellen had wronged him and he felt no compulsion to ease her concerns in what was an utterly traumatic experience for the first-time mother.

After what seemed like an eternity for Ellen, she gave one final push and the next thing she heard was the squeal of a baby filling the room. The doctor cut the cord, wrapped up the baby with a far from soft blanket and, without a word, handed it to Sister Francis. Ellen felt this innate desire to cuddle the baby and, in what was a rare external sign of empathy, Sister Francis said to Ellen, 'That was a tough labour. Well done on getting through it. Would you like to hold your baby?'

Although clearly exhausted from the experience, Ellen nodded and reached out to grab the baby. She then asked, 'What is it?'

The doctor finally uttered his only words directly to Ellen, albeit continuing to avoid eye contact with her. 'A girl.'

Ellen cuddled the baby and immediately called her Deirdre, after her mother Dee. She was given thirty minutes to be alone with her new baby, with only water and dry toast on offer, such was the basic nature of this place. Her life had changed utterly in the five or six hours in that room and she quietly talked to Deirdre for that half hour.

'I love you very much. No matter what happens, you'll always be my daughter and we'll get through this. I'll always be there for you.'

Ellen had no idea if she could fulfil those promises and

Newborn

knew that her baby couldn't understand a word she was saying, but she felt compelled to say it – more to utter the words and to steel herself for the undoubted fight to keep both her baby and her life in Dublin. Whilst the physical soreness of labour somewhat eased during the hours afterwards, this was replaced with an aching pain as to whether she'd any control over her situation.

Dee was relieved to hear that her daughter and new granddaughter were safe and well, but, from the day Deirdre was brought into No. 12, she went out less than normal, to avoid the stares and whispers from her neighbours. Although living under the same roof, she initially sought to avoid bonding with Deirdre and spent more time in her bedroom, the parlour or any other place in their small house so that she didn't do what is only natural in enjoying the little things that a new baby does to entertain her carers.

For Ellen, everything was new. She instantly bonded with Deirdre and took to motherhood exceptionally well, especially so under such difficult circumstances. On the first night in No. 12, with Ellen in her bed and Deirdre in the small crib, the baby let out that newborn yelp at 3 a.m. – Ellen, although tired from the delivery two days before, sprang up and delicately cradled Deirdre as she fed her some milk. It was a balmy mid-summer night in Dublin and, as Ellen sat up in the bed to feed her baby, she whispered calm sounds to Deirdre. It took about ninety minutes to feed and change her, but it all felt so natural to Ellen. She understood that there would be challenging days ahead, but right at that moment, it didn't seem to matter that Joe had left her in the lurch or that this baby wouldn't have the normal two-family support in her early years – all that was important was that each feed went well, that Deirdre had enough clothes in those first few weeks and that Mum and newborn had that vital time to bond.

When Deirdre was about a week old, due to a mild bit of jaundice, she wasn't feeding as well as Ellen would have liked. She worried she was doing it all wrong and didn't feel she could ask her mother for guidance or to receive assurance that this was all normal in a baby's first days and weeks. After a couple of days of things not quite going to plan, Deirdre latched on, took a big feed and was alert being changed afterwards. Ellen lifted Deirdre off the makeshift changing mat, and hugged her with all the love and tenderness of a first-time mother. 'Aren't you just the best, my little baba?' Ellen quietly whispered into Deirdre's ear, so proud of her baby. Notwithstanding the 'shame' that the arrival of this baby had brought on the O'Connell family, Ellen felt quite the opposite – she was bursting with pride at every little milestone that Deirdre took in those early weeks and it hurt her that she couldn't openly share those feelings with her family. Deirdre was, in many eyes, a dirty secret, but that didn't stop Ellen from taking her out for short strolls in a hand-me-down Silver Cross pram two or three times per week. Her neighbours generally gave her a wide berth, as if illegitimacy was a disease one could catch by having a casual conversation in the baby's presence, but Ellen's true friends, including Mabel, would make sure to call by regularly to provide some sense of normality.

After three months, Ellen knew she had to get back to work, both to ensure she still had a job and to keep money coming into the house, as the only other household income

Newborn

was Uncle Peter and Dee's pensions. 'Ma, is there any chance that you could look after Deirdre if I go back to work next month?' Ellen knew that her mother was finding it extremely challenging to have this baby in the house, but she hoped that Dee could see a way to helping her out.

'Ellen, I'll help you out up to Christmas,' Dee said, which was two months hence, 'but I don't think this is a permanent solution. We have Bridget to think about also.' Bridget was her granddaughter who, aged nine by now, was staying over in the house on a regular basis such was the predicament in her own home, with poverty leading to a challenging environment in which to raise five children.

'Thanks, Ma. Bridget is like a daughter to me and we'll figure out a way to support her,' said Ellen, hugely relieved that, for the time being, her mother would mind Deirdre and allow her to get back to her seamstress work and bring much-needed money into the house.

Chapter Twelve

Intervention

It was early November 1945 and with Deirdre almost four months old, Ellen returned to her job with the local dressmaker and Dee was tasked with looking after the baby. Whilst Dee had initially distanced herself from Deirdre, she couldn't help her natural maternal instincts from kicking in and, despite the illegitimate status of this baby, she began to feel quite close to her granddaughter during that childminding period. Despite being almost seventy-two, Dee still had quite an amount of energy and she managed, in those initial months, to mind the baby, make meals for everyone and keep the house relatively tidy. Ellen understood how difficult the whole situation was for her mother and fully appreciated the sacrifices Dee was making for her.

However, as the calendar turned into 1946, the State, through the district nurse and a representative of the National Society for the Prevention of Cruelty to Children (NSPCC), began to express an interest in Deirdre's wellbeing. Her illegitimacy was known to authorities and the NSPCC were particularly focused on how the family were managing to mind the baby, given that Ellen had to go to work each day, her niece was effectively living in the same house and Dee

Intervention

and Peter were getting on in age. On a number of occasions that year, the NSPCC called and Ellen would be forced to answer numerous questions about Deirdre's welfare. On one such occasion, the visiting inspector articulated that it was her opinion that Deirdre would be better off being taken from the home and raised in an orphanage. Naturally, Ellen resisted this idea and Dee, who by that time had developed a strong bond with Deirdre, fully supported her daughter and the inspector was ushered out.

Although Dee didn't agree with the NSPCC's perception of Deirdre's upbringing, her Catholic faith was being tested to the limit by the raising of an illegitimate child in the house. The initial two months of childminding had turned into twelve months and the workload had begun to take its toll on Dee's health. 'Ellen, I'm not sure how long we can keep this situation going. I'm not as energetic as I was and Deirdre's a handful.' Deirdre was fifteen months by then and, having mastered walking, was seeking to investigate all parts of No. 12 at every opportunity.

'I know, Ma. I appreciate everything you've done and we'll figure out a way in the new year.'

Dee managed to get to Christmas 1946 in one piece and the best gift Deirdre received was a small grey teddy that Dee gave her. It took pride of place in Deirdre's cot as she fell asleep every night and was never far away from her as she toddled around the house each day.

However, by February 1947, Dee's health had deteriorated. A visit by Dr Smith to the house, and a subsequent battery of tests in hospital, had confirmed that she was suffering from a serious stomach ulcer. She'd lost weight, had a constant burning pain in her abdomen and, over the next few months, would intermittently spend time in hospital. When at home, she was generally bedridden and unable to look after the house.

Ellen was naturally very worried for her mother, but this situation also presented her with logistical difficulties in ensuring that Deirdre was well looked after. During those bouts of illness for Dee, Ellen would juggle work and also enlisted neighbours to mind Deirdre on an ad hoc basis – once again, the stigma of illegitimacy meant that no neighbour would be willing to take on minding Deirdre long-term, so Ellen managed the situation on a day-to-day basis.

In June 1947, Dee was admitted to hospital after vomiting blood on a number of occasions. Through one of the neighbours, the State authorities became aware of Deirdre's precarious childminding situation and the NSPCC called by No. 12 on the evening of 24 June. The inspector, by the name of Annie Wogan, sat down with Ellen and sought to understand how she was managing to mind her toddler daughter, support her eleven-year-old niece and ageing uncle, and make regular hospital visits to see her mother whilst trying to hold down a full-time job.

Ellen broke down. 'I'm trying my best, but it's very difficult when nobody wants to help this poor child.' Ellen nodded to Deirdre's illegitimacy being a significant stumbling block to neighbours, friends and family being willing to offer childminding help.

'I understand your situation, but we have a concern that Deirdre will suffer without a permanent intervention,' said the inspector, as she sought to ensure Ellen understood the

Intervention

gravity of the situation. 'You're a good mother, but something has to give unless your mother recovers.'

Following that house call, and unbeknown to Ellen, the inspector issued a report to the Metropolitan Children's Court expressing her concerns over Deirdre's welfare and saying that, given the child's illegitimate status, it would be in Deirdre's best interests to remove her from the home and place her in an industrial school if her grandmother passed away.

This spectre of the baby being removed from the home had always been in the background, but Dee's actions since 1945 had allowed Ellen to raise her child in No. 12. Now that Dee was incapacitated, the institutions of State were circling around to seek to break the mother-daughter bond. Ostensibly, those institutions were acting in the best interests of the child, but illegitimacy gave them a reason to force home their wish for such children to be banished from their communities and families.

Ellen visited Dee in hospital in early July 1947 and it was clear that her mother was in her final days of life. Ellen was heartbroken that she was losing Dee. Although they'd had many disagreements from the time Ellen fell pregnant, Dee was an emotional and physical support for Ellen all along the journey and it frightened her that she mightn't be able to cope without her mother.

Sadly, on 9 July 1947, on Deirdre's second birthday, Dee passed away from an ulcerated stomach in Sir Patrick Dun's Hospital on Grand Canal Street. Once again, in such difficult times, the local community rallied around and were a great help to Ellen. She did wonder where those same people had been when Deirdre arrived and in the two years since, but such an obvious dichotomy in behaviour was not that uncommon. Dee was buried in Mount Jerome Cemetery with her husband and daughters and, following the burial, Ellen returned to No. 12 uncertain as to how things might unfold for her and Deirdre.

Following submission of the report to the Court by the NSPCC and only one week after Dee's passing, Ellen received a summons to the District Court for a sitting seven days hence. Ellen could read perfectly, but she didn't fully understand the language in the summons and sought assistance from the local solicitor. It turned out that the summons alleged that Ellen did not have the capacity to 'exercise proper guardianship' over her daughter given her mother's recent death and the other obligations Ellen had in relation to her uncle and niece. The Court was now seeking to take Deirdre into the care of an industrial school. Ellen was distraught, with numerous thoughts running through her scrambled mind. 'How can they do this to me? Is there a better solution? Why are they seeking to split us up?' Given the hand to mouth nature of her life, Ellen had no money to spend on solicitors, nobody to turn to for help and, once again, felt the situation was entirely out of her control.

A week later, Ellen was sitting in the Metropolitan Children's Court in Dublin Castle listening to so-called learned people telling each other that they knew best for a two-year-old girl that they'd never met.

'It is evident from this report that Miss O'Connell doesn't have the ability to properly look after her illegitimate child,' said the barrister acting for the NSPCC.

Intervention

Such was the strength of the institutions at the time, Ellen was powerless, frozen and unable to mount a defence to the machinery of State ordering that Deirdre be brought to an industrial school in Newtownforbes, Co. Longford the following day, where she would be 'detained' until her sixteenth birthday. As with the summons, the Court Order stated that Ellen was unable to exercise proper guardianship, which, in this scenario, was Court speak for issues of poverty leading to the need for this illegitimate child to be removed from the family home.

Ellen left the Court in tears and made her way back home to spend her last bit of time with Deirdre. 'Uncle Peter, how can this be happening to us?'

'I know, Ellen, but the Court knows best. Deirdre will be well looked after by the nuns,' replied Peter. 'If you get married, you might be able to take her out of the home.'

As at numerous other times since Ellen found out she was pregnant, marriage was at the heart of everything and, on that evening, that sacrament seemed further away than it had ever been. As she was putting Deirdre to bed for a final time in No. 12 that night, she cuddled her tight and quietly repeated, 'I love you, Deirdre,' until her daughter fell asleep. Ellen suffered another restless night and awoke early to prepare to hand over Deirdre to the authorities.

On the morning of 24 July 1947, Ellen packed as many of Deirdre's clothes as possible into a suitcase and made her way to the NSPCC's offices on Molesworth Street. Such was the shock at what Ellen was experiencing, she just put one foot in front of the other, her emotions frozen, as she walked through the doors of the office and into a waiting room off

Miss, Say Goodbye to Your Daughter

the ground floor hallway. She sat down on one of the chairs and, as Deirdre sat on her lap, Ellen wrapped her arms around her daughter's waist and hugged her tight, whilst Deirdre held on to the grey teddy that Dee had gifted her the previous Christmas. Although Deirdre was wholly unaware of her fate, she stayed entirely silent for the ten or so minutes they both waited in the room – it was as if she'd picked up on the significance of the moment without any understanding of what it all meant.

Then, the door swung open and in walked the same inspector who had visited No. 12 a month earlier and a nun from Newtownforbes, Sister Michael, who introduced herself to Ellen and then got down on her hunkers to say hi to Deirdre. 'Hi Deirdre, I'm Sister Michael. I'm bringing you on the train to the home.' Deirdre had no idea what was going on and gave her mother a quizzical look, with Ellen trying not to make eye contact in case her emotions broke.

After a few minutes of checking forms, the inspector asked Ellen to stand up and place her daughter back down on the chair. In a matter of fact way, she then uttered six words that would haunt Ellen, 'Miss, say goodbye to your daughter,' as the inspector ushered Ellen towards the door.

Ellen blew a final kiss to Deirdre and the only words she could come out with was to repeat her mantra from the previous night as Deirdre fell asleep, 'I love you, Deirdre,' as she slowly backed out of the room. As she turned into the hallway and lost sight of Deirdre, she could hear her daughter calling out, 'Mammy, Mammy, Mammy,' amidst the two-year-old's frightened tears and screams. Ellen uncontrollably wept, as she was helped out of the office. She didn't remember

Intervention

anything from that walk back to No. 12, but, thankfully, was met by Peter in the hallway after he heard the front door latch open – he hugged Ellen tight, but she couldn't find the energy to describe how heartbroken she was.

'Ellen, this is best for both of you and Deirdre will know that you love her very much,' said Peter, trying to soothe the pain that Ellen was feeling as she sat on the sofa staring into space, her slumped shoulders physically manifesting the depth of sadness that was engulfing her every fibre.

Following Ellen's forced departure from the NSPCC offices, Sister Michael and Deirdre were driven by the inspector to Amiens Street Station, the very same station that saw Joe's hastened exit from Dublin thirty months earlier. From the moment Ellen left the room, Deirdre had continually screamed, cried and wept. She had no comprehension of what was going on and what life was ahead of her when the train approached its destination in Longford.

Chapter Thirteen

Newtownforbes

The train pulled into Newtownforbes station. This was a village situated five miles north-west of Longford Town, with a population of less than 500. It was a typical country village with two public houses, grocers, a Catholic church and its own train station on the Dublin to Sligo line.

Known as Our Lady of Succour Industrial School, Newtownforbes, the home was established in 1869 and was run by the Congregation of the Sisters of Mercy. Until 1942, the industrial school was an internal primary school, but, in that year, the primary school was closed and the industrial school children, from then on, attended the external national school, also run by the Sisters of Mercy. At the time of Deirdre's entry to this institution, approximately 120 children were in residence, with the vast majority committed through the courts. The main reasons for committal of children included poverty, death of a parent or being an illegitimate child. Under the court order, Our Lady of Succour Industrial School would operate 'in loco parentis' in all respects in the care of Deirdre.

As Sister Michael and Deirdre stepped off the train, they

were greeted by Reverend Mother Gregory, or 'RMG', as she was known behind her back. RMG was a giant of a woman. Most nuns were diminutive in stature and seemingly feeble, but RMG stood exceptionally tall and was ten inches over Sister Michael. She had a booming voice that reverberated around the small train station and her face was etched with years of experience and domination. RMG had been head of this orphanage and the adjacent convent for ten years and she ruled the place in her own way. Her upbringing was typically rural and she had learnt from her mother that to gain respect, the only way was to dictate to those around you. She could see that Deirdre was still very upset, but she had no regard for those feelings. As if she was speaking to an adult, she said, 'I don't want any tears. Tears are for the weak.' This was RMG's attempt to dominate her new detainee and this did nothing to help calm Deirdre.

Deirdre, Sister Michael and RMG then took the five-minute walk to the orphanage. Relative to the small houses in the Liberties, the home was gargantuan and was set on significant land that had been gifted by Lord Granard in the previous century. Before they made it inside, a couple of young girls, aged five or six, were walking from an outside shed towards the main building. 'Good evening, Reverend Mother,' they chimed in unison.

'Say hello to Deirdre,' replied RMG.

The girls smiled and said hi to Deirdre, who was gripping Sister Michael's hand tightly. These girls were used to new babies and children arriving and neither batted an eyelid as they went about their business.

Despite it being a sunny July day, the warmth hadn't

permeated the thick walls of the home and everyone could see their own breath as they stood in the hallway of the main house. Sister Michael then brought Deirdre upstairs and into a room, which housed four single beds, none of which matched, four small side lockers and a sink in the corner. The beds were made up and Deirdre was brought over to the one bed that had no belongings on its side locker. Sister Michael placed Deirdre's suitcase on the bed, quickly unpacked the contents into the side locker and then brought Deirdre down for dinner.

It was 5 p.m. and, as Deirdre was being walked down the stairs, there was a buzz of noise in a room to the left of the stairs. This was the dining hall – a space that could accommodate about one hundred people. It was in full swing, with young children and babies being fed. The hall had vast high ceilings, ornate cornicing and two large chandeliers hanging at opposite ends of the room. The stained oak floors were laid out in parquet fashion and the wooden tables and chairs were basic, but functional. Sister Michael sat Deirdre down at the end of one long table and went to get her some food. Beef stew, with spuds on the side, was on the menu and Sister Michael helped Deirdre to eat her first Newtownforbes meal – hunger had kicked in and this comfort food provided Deirdre with some solace, which stemmed the flow of tears for that short time. There were five or six nuns helping service that night and they carried themselves with an air of empathy that was a counterbalance to the harsh and intimidating nature of RMG.

Back in Dublin, Ellen spent the rest of the day and evening in a daze. In the space of two weeks, she'd lost her mother

Newtownforbes

and had her daughter taken away. Her grief for both events had taken full control of her body and not a morsel passed her mouth after she came home from Molesworth Street. She went upstairs and, as she was getting ready for bed, looked in the bedroom mirror. What she saw was a broken thirty-two year old woman, with tears streaming down her face. In Newtownforbes three hours earlier, Deirdre was preparing for her first night in 'detention', and, after she stepped onto a wooden box in front of the sink, one of the nuns brushed her teeth. She looked at herself in the cracked mirror above the chipped porcelain sink – tears were similarly flowing for Deirdre, as she had no sense or understanding of what had led to her being brought to this place. As mother and daughter separately lay down to sleep that night, both wept quietly to themselves, with no idea when they might next see each other.

Chapter Fourteen

Growing Up

Aged two years, Deirdre Mary O'Connell, born on 9 July 1945 to Ellen O'Connell, with no father named on her birth certificate, was, in essence, on her own, being raised by a group of nuns that would never themselves experience the joy of becoming mothers. In those first two years of life in Ebenezer Road, Deirdre was showered with affection by Ellen and her formative mind, to that point, experienced only unconditional love. In the early months in Newtownforbes, Deirdre didn't have the ability to understand what had happened to her. She cried herself to sleep most nights and it took her about three months to settle down and make a few friends amongst her fellow 'inmates'.

For Ellen, those initial months were harrowing, as she was not permitted any contact with Deirdre – her only way of communication were a few letters she wrote to RMG, inquiring after Deirdre's wellbeing and how she'd settled into the home. She received short replies to those letters and was comforted, to a limited extent, to know that Deirdre had developed a few friendships with some other girls in the home. How her own community and the institutions of State could see the physical separation of mother and daughter as an acceptable solution

Growing Up

to her predicament was lost on Ellen and, as Christmas 1947 approached, the only thing that kept her going were visits to Newtownforbes every second month, an arrangement that was finally put in place by December of that year.

Without fail, on the last Sunday of alternate months, Ellen would walk from Ebenezer Road to Amiens Street Station, get the early morning Sligo train to Newtownforbes and then take the short walk to the home to see Deirdre. On the first visits, her daughter would play strange with Ellen, but, after a short while, Deirdre would warm up and, for those few short hours, it was like this mother and daughter were inseparable. On one occasion in the first year of their separation, Ellen arrived with a small wooden jigsaw for Deirdre. Deirdre was so infatuated with making the jigsaw, then breaking it up and starting over again, that she hardly noticed Ellen for the entire time they were together. Ellen didn't mind one bit, as this was quality time where a mother and daughter were just comfortable with each other.

However, each visit ended with one of the nuns delivering those very same six words that were uttered in the NSPCC offices, 'Miss, say goodbye to your daughter.' On the train home, the words would spin around Ellen's head like perpetual punishment for the same 'mistake' she and Joe had made back in 1944. Ellen would similarly wonder what long-term impact those parting words would have on her daughter and it was often about a month after each visit that Ellen would hit her low point – she'd think '… it's four weeks since Deirdre has seen me … maybe she'll have forgotten me in another four weeks … maybe she thinks I'm never coming back … if only I could visit every week or even every month.' Ellen was wracked with guilt, sadness and separation anxiety. Three years earlier when Joe abandoned her just before the wedding, she had reconciled herself to bury thoughts on how she had got into this situation and the guilt she felt about her daughter's predicament only pushed those memories further away from her consciousness.

Given the age at which she was admitted to Newtownforbes, Deirdre was starting to form early life relationships with those around her, but there was no certainty that those people, children or nuns, would be around long enough for her to get the most out of those interactions. There were certain nuns who would try and have one-on-one time with each child to develop their overall personalities – however, some of the nuns were transitory and might only be around for six or so months and, just when Deirdre was establishing a bond with a particular nun, they'd be sent to another convent to carry on their pastoral development.

Then there were the other children. The slightly older girls took it upon themselves to look after the younger ones and Deirdre established a sisterly relationship with one of the girls, Áine. Áine's mother, also without a husband, was from north inner-city Dublin – her daughter was in Newtownforbes for over four years and was approaching her fifth birthday. Although there were two years between herself and Deirdre, Áine took a shine to her younger friend and enjoyed the way Deirdre would seek to push the boundaries with the nuns. An example of that was when the girls weren't allowed play in the winter snow one day and Deirdre successfully pestered one of the nuns to allow them play for fifteen minutes outside.

Both girls were, in the main, well behaved, but there was

Growing Up

one time when RMG asked Áine to go into the hen shed and collect some eggs. Áine asked Deirdre to accompany her and, given that they had a combined age of eight by then, this was destined for trouble. Thirty minutes later, little Deirdre walked back into the house with bird feathers in her hair, a smashed egg in her hand and Áine trailed behind trying to look innocent – the girls were just doing what children do, but were marked out from that point in the eyes of RMG.

Then, before Áine turned six, her mother called Newtownforbes to say that she was getting married and that she'd be collecting her daughter the following week. It was a rare occurrence for a birth mother to retrieve a child from an institution such as Newtownforbes and, as if to land one final 'punishment' on the child before being reunited with her mother, RMG never divulged to Áine that she was being 'released'. This meant that Áine and Deirdre never said a proper goodbye and this hurt Deirdre deeply when she learned the truth. Aged four at that time, this made her feel that she was abandoned by her best friend, as if Áine didn't care enough to say goodbye and, subsequently, made Deirdre wary of developing deep friendships in the home.

There was one visit from Ellen that also caused Deirdre significant distress. As usual, Ellen arrived in Newtownforbes around noon for her bi-monthly visit and Deirdre, then almost five, jumped off her seat when she saw her mother and gave her a beautiful, innocent and heart-warming embrace. 'I love you, Deirdre,' said Ellen.

Deirdre responded, 'Love you, Mammy.' Like any child of that age, Deirdre noticed everything and she spotted her mother placing a wrapped package at the door to the room as they ran to hug each other. 'What's in the box, Mammy?' she asked inquisitively.

'Just a little present for your birthday.' It would be Deirdre's fifth birthday three weeks hence, but given the stringent timing of visits, this was the last time Ellen would see Deirdre before that birthday.

'Thanks, Mammy, can I open it?' implored Deirdre, beaming with a broad smile. Ellen looked at the nun who was chaperoning the visit and the nun smiled.

'Of course you can,' replied Ellen, sensing that Deirdre's excitement couldn't have withstood a rejection to that question. Deirdre bounded over to where the present sat and, in an unrefined manner, ripped open the wrapping and her excitement hit new levels on seeing that her mother had given her a wooden doll's house, with all the internal bits and bobs. Deirdre was over the moon and immediately ran back to Ellen to give her another hug. It warmed Ellen's heart and that moment would make up for the fact that she wouldn't see Deirdre on her actual birthday. Deirdre then spent the rest of the visit playing with the house in a way only young girls can. Ellen got down on the floor to share in the fun and, once again, there were mother and daughter just doing normal things with each other. But then, at around 4 p.m., those six words were repeated by the nun and, after one final embrace, Ellen left the room, with Deirdre briefly looking up from her doll's house to smile and wave goodbye.

It was never easy for Ellen on the train back to Dublin, but at least, this time, she was comforted knowing that Deirdre loved the present. What Ellen didn't know was that immediately after she left Newtownforbes, RMG came into the room and,

Growing Up

without a moment's hesitation, directed the chaperoning nun to take the doll's house away from Deirdre. Deirdre was distraught – not only had her mother disappeared again after only four hours together, but the present of a doll's house that she longed for would never be seen again.

Five-year-olds can't keep secrets and Ellen found out the next time she was down. On hearing this, Ellen, leaving Deirdre back in the visitation room, knocked on RMG's office, which was located on the first floor of the building overlooking the front driveway. After a few seconds, she heard, 'Enter,' from within, as RMG beckoned the caller into the room. Ellen slowly opened the creaky old wooden door and saw RMG sitting behind her large, solid teak desk, facing away, as she observed a delivery truck making its way to the side of the building. The room was vast, with a separate seated area to the left and two old paintings adorning the wooden clad walls. RMG swivelled around in her chair and stood up, knowing that her physical presence in front of someone the size of Ellen could influence the direction of the conversation.

'I'm Deirdre O'Connell's mother,' said Ellen, hoping to get her complaint in before RMG had a chance to take control.

'I know who you are. Is there a problem?' said RMG, her voice echoing around the room.

'Yes, there is a problem. I gave my daughter a doll's house for her birthday and I hear that the present was taken away from her immediately after I left the home,' answered Ellen. 'She's only five and doesn't understand why this happened.'

'It's simple, Miss O'Connell. Two reasons. Firstly, a present such as this will make the other girls jealous and will cause more harm to your daughter than good. Secondly, there is not enough space in this home for gifts that big,' said RMG, leaving precious little room for debate with Ellen. 'Those are the rules and, so long as your daughter is with us, she will play by them.'

The discussion went around in circles for another couple of minutes and Ellen decided to leave the room before she said something she regretted. She couldn't believe the callous way in which RMG managed the situation and she longed for the day when Deirdre could be brought home to Dublin – that day was no closer and it gnawed away at Ellen, as she could see that her growing child could soon begin to resent her mother for the situation she was in.

As Deirdre grew up in Newtownforbes, a few things were noteworthy:

- The lack of males around the home meant that none of the children had a father figure to guide and influence their personalities. On some occasions, the local parish priest would visit, which was usually accompanied by the nuns falling over themselves to look after him, stifling any ability for the priest to get to know the girls.

- At the time, Deirdre shared a dormitory style room with up to seven other girls. There was a sink in the corner of the room where the girls could brush their teeth and wash their faces, but privacy was at a premium. As a result of this set up, Deirdre perfected the art of getting changed in jig time and all in the 'privacy' of her own bed.

- Despite her cold and callous manner, RMG understood

Growing Up

the importance of education. The children in her care were educated in the local school, sometimes in classes of girls from three or four different age groups. RMG knew that a good primary school experience for 'her girls' would give them a foundation to go forward with whatever life brought them. Deirdre herself enjoyed getting out of the home to go to school and even got to know some of the village girls, although visits to those girls' houses were forbidden by the villagers – the illegitimacy and poverty brands on Deirdre and her friends from Newtownforbes would deny them the simple pleasures of playing with schoolfriends. Deirdre had a wonderful teacher when she was six, Sister Patrick, who taught her the usual reading, writing and arithmetic. She also introduced the basics of sewing and knitting – those skills meant that Deirdre had something very specific in common with her mother, who'd continued her work as a seamstress in the years since Deirdre's arrival in the home.

In the nature versus nurture debate on a child's upbringing, it was clear that Deirdre's nurturing in those formative years was radically different from other children of her age. The absence of a father figure, the lack of day-to-day emotional connection with a consistent carer and the in-and-out nature of her peer relationships in the home were all influencing Deirdre's character.

Chapter Fifteen

Rosie

One figure would dominate Deirdre's memory from her time in the home – a young nun by the name of Rose Doherty, known as Sister Agnes in Newtownforbes. Sister Agnes, or Sister Rosie, as she liked to be called by her 'favourite' girls, arrived to Newtownforbes in 1952, aged twenty-five and in her infancy with the Sisters of Mercy. Rose was a Derry girl from the Bogside, a staunchly Catholic part of the city situated outside of the city walls. Rose's upbringing was normal enough for its time and she was born into the new state of Northern Ireland following partition of the island of Ireland in 1921. Being the eldest of five children, she was helper in chief to her mother in looking after the house whilst her father worked in various jobs. This was never a chore for her and she loved doing things with her mother, be it making dinner or tidying the house. However, one thing in her childhood that set her on the path to a vocation was seeing the treatment of Catholics by certain Protestant-run employers in the city. Her father was let go from a job in the local factory when Rose was fifteen, ostensibly for the quality of his work, but more likely because the factory owner wanted to replace him with a

Rosie

Protestant, with such sectarianism visible on both sides of the religious divide. After that incident, Rose overheard her parents talking and it was clear that several of her father's peers had suffered similar fates in other Protestant-run businesses. Although having a strong Catholic faith, Rose saw no difference between Catholics and Protestants. How her father was affected by the subsequent six months of unemployment struck her as being unfair and she vowed that, throughout her life and in whatever job she ended up in, she would stand up for those unable to defend themselves. When she chose her vocation and decided to become a nun, she had the clear objective that she would, as much as possible, work with children and particularly those children that had been dealt a more challenging hand than others. Newtownforbes was Rose's first such assignment and her arrival dovetailed with Deirdre's development as a child.

Deirdre walked into the dining room for lunch one day and immediately noticed a new nun doling out the food. Deirdre saw her smiling face and the way she engaged with every one of the children. When Deirdre arrived up to get her food, Rose smiled and gave Deirdre a little wink – it was touches like this that meant so much to all the children, especially those that were slightly older and craved emotional connection. RMG stood up when the children were seated and introduced Rose to everyone – she got the Sister Agnes title, but Deirdre and some of the other children would soon be allowed to privately call her by her more casual name. After that day, Deirdre had many interactions with Rose and the two became quite close – so much so that RMG warned Rose not to be too engaged with any of the children. This was predominantly for the children's benefit, as vulnerable girls, such as Deirdre, were longing for more permanent connections and, should Rose be relocated to another convent or home, those children would again be victims of the system. Rose listened carefully to what RMG was saying, but wasn't sure if she could quell her innate desire to connect with those around her.

One specific incident stood out to Deirdre throughout her interaction with Rose. It was a Sunday morning and one of the younger girls, aged three, had received a visit from her mother the previous day. Kathleen was the girl's name and she had struggled to contain her emotions since the visit – word spread that morning that she was crying 'like a baby' all night. A couple of the older girls were calling her a 'cry baby' and this made a delicate situation even worse.

Whilst giving out breakfast to the girls, Rose overheard some of the name calling and, once all the girls were seated, Rose asked RMG if she could say a few words. 'Girls, you're all here for different reasons and some of you are coping with it better than others. For those coping, I'd ask that you look out for those less fortunate than you. For those struggling, and I know you all experience this at different times, we're here to listen to you and we can help.' It was a short few words that brought those older girls back into line, but in a softer and less authoritarian way than RMG would espouse.

After a few minutes, Rose made a beeline for Kathleen and spent most of the day with her, playing and talking. Even though Deirdre was only six at the time, she carefully observed how Rose picked up on the issue early on, dealt with it in a calm way with the group, then focused in on the individual with acutest need and gave up as much of her time as necessary to ameliorate the situation. This made quite the impression on young Deirdre.

During Ellen's visits to the home after Rose's arrival, this nun chaperoned on several occasions. With Deirdre often playing on the ground or at a table, Ellen had numerous chats with Rose – they got on well and it was clear to Ellen that Rose and Deirdre had become quite close. Ellen felt a touch of jealousy of that relationship, given that she herself couldn't have that day-to-day interaction with Deirdre, but it gave her comfort for the train trip home that Rose was looking out for her daughter. Ellen also noticed how Deirdre was keeping an eye on the younger girls. During one visit, Deirdre was asked by Rose to walk with Ellen to the dining room to get a cup of tea. As mother and daughter walked between the visitation room and the dining room, a four-year-old girl passed by. Deirdre stopped the girl and said that her shoelace was undone and that she might trip up if she didn't attend to it. It was only a little touch, but Ellen could see, by the interaction between these girls, that there was mutual respect and, with the way they giggled at each other, a bit of fun also between them. In that short moment, Ellen realised that her daughter was growing up rapidly and knew it was imperative that she didn't spend any longer in the home than absolutely necessary.

Chapter Sixteen

Second Chance

It was 1952. Deirdre was seven and, despite everything, was doing well in Newtownforbes and in the school she attended in the village. Although not overburdened with thoughts of what might have been, Deirdre would sometimes, when falling asleep in the dormitory, think of what it would be like to be brought back into her mother's home in Dublin. Although young in years, she often thought of what this first period of life could have been like. 'Who is my father? What if I was adopted years ago? Would I have sisters or brothers? Could I fit back into a normal home?' were some of the questions that plagued her as her eyes closed at night. However, someone of Deirdre's age didn't have the experience of time to understand the reasons for her predicament. She often wanted to ask Ellen about why she was in the home, but she would rather enjoy the moments they had together than spoil them by pushing her mother to listen to such emotive questions.

Back in Dublin, Ellen was putting in as much time as she could with the dressmaker to have enough money to pay for the visits to Newtownforbes, for clothes and small gifts for Deirdre and to provide enough to keep life ticking over in

Second Chance

No. 12 with her Uncle Peter. Since the abandoned wedding and Deirdre being placed in the home, it was rare that Ellen would go out with her friends – on the times she did go out, they would generally sit in the snug part of a pub or go to the cinema. Ellen never sought out another man, as the shame of her secret in Newtownforbes wasn't something she felt she could share with anyone.

It was August 1952 and Ellen reluctantly agreed to go to one of the local pubs on Leonard's Corner for a few drinks on a Saturday evening. Ellen got ready for the night, Mabel called to the house and off went the two of them to meet another friend. When they arrived in the pub, it was busy enough, but Mabel managed to steal a few stools from other tables and the three women sat down with their drinks. After thirty minutes or so, a group of men arrived into the pub and Ellen spotted one of them – a tall man by Ellen's standards, probably early forties, clean shaven, well dressed with wispy thin greying hair. It was his smile that she noticed first and, being the only single lady in her group, she interrupted the other two to get them to notice that a group of men had entered the pub. Ellen was acutely aware that she had made the first move with Joe and it hadn't gone to plan after that, so she was not about to walk over and talk to this man. He could be married, although she couldn't see a wedding ring, he might think she was too small for him and he mightn't want to chat to a woman who had an illegitimate child in care. Over the years since Deirdre had arrived, Ellen's confidence in these types of situations had significantly eroded to the extent that she never thought any man would want her given those legacy issues.

However, to her surprise and delight, after another few minutes, she looked up at the group of men, noticed that 'her' man was looking at her and they briefly exchanged a smile. After what seemed like an eternity, he came over and introduced himself. 'Hello. I'm Matty Kelly and I'm from Galway,' he said, in what sounded like a well-rehearsed intro and a very specific reference to his West of Ireland roots.

'Hello, I'm Ellen O'Connell and I'm from Dublin,' said Ellen, trying to mirror his opening salvo.

'Was he up for a Gaelic match or something? Did he live up here? Will we be able to understand each other given the accents?' she thought to herself, as she was intrigued about what brought him to Dublin. They were both a bit shy at first, but, after a short while, got the conversation going.

'What has you up in the big smoke?' asked Ellen.

'I moved up from a village in Galway, Carnmore, five years ago now. I work on the railways and drive the odd lorry, when I can,' replied Matty. He also shared that he lived in a flat off South Circular Road and then introduced his friends to Ellen's group. Ellen liked his laidback nature, that he seemed comfortable with who he was and wasn't trying to be sophisticated. The enlarged group ended up having a nice night and even Mabel managed to stay out past her self-imposed curfew. Matty and Ellen gave each other their addresses, but no date was set for their next meet-up.

Three days later, Matty knocked at No. 12. Uncle Peter answered and, leaving him at the front door, he went back in to impart the news of a male visitor to Ellen. After checking her hair in the living room mirror, Ellen went to the front door and greeted Matty with a demure smile. She brought

Second Chance

him into the parlour, offered him tea and a scone, which he duly accepted, and they had a nice hour of chatting about their jobs and a little bit about their respective lives in Dublin and Galway.

Matty noticed a picture of a young girl on the mantelpiece and he felt compelled to ask who it was.

'That's a lovely picture. Is that you as a child?'

Ellen hadn't thought she'd have to address the elephant in the room so soon. Should she lie and say it was a friend's daughter or should she just be honest? Ellen's personality was to always be up front and straight, but the many knocks she'd taken since falling pregnant made her more guarded than her younger self. However, she felt that connection with Matty three nights earlier and went with her gut.

'That's my daughter, Deirdre. She's in an orphanage since she was two years old.' May as well be hung for a sheep as a lamb, thought Ellen.

Without any hesitation, Matty responded, 'That must be very difficult for you both, but hopefully, someday, you'll be back together again.' Matty had no idea if the father had passed away, but his sense was that there was a challenging story beneath Ellen's swan like exterior.

'I could write a book Matty, but no one would read it,' said Ellen, trying to make light of everything.

'I'd like to read that book, Ellen,' responded Matty. 'I'd love to meet her at some stage, God willing.'

Ellen was astounded at how Matty resisted the temptation to ask the obvious questions, but instead chose to empathise and look forward. Ellen felt the tingle of love immediately – not because she wanted security for herself and her daughter, but because of who Matty was and how he carried himself. That night ended with a peck on the cheek and Ellen felt thirty again, like the clouds were lifting and that good, maybe even great, days lay ahead for her. But experience told her not to get carried away after that one evening together.

Over the succeeding weeks and months, Matty and Ellen grew closer and closer to the point that Matty asked her for her hand in marriage in the Phoenix Park on a windy February day in 1953, to which she emphatically said yes. Ellen had fallen head over heels in love with Matty – he was a simple man in many ways, but understood that circumstances had dealt Ellen a tough hand over the years and he wanted to play a part in allowing the natural Ellen to shine through, the one that he had smiled over at in that pub a few months earlier. Before the proposal, Matty called to Uncle Peter when Ellen was at work and asked for his niece's hand in marriage. Peter really enjoyed chatting to Matty over the preceding months and was delighted to see Ellen beaming again, like she used to. Peter, knowing that Matty was aware of Deirdre, took that opportunity to broach the subject of whether Matty would accept her as his own.

'Of course I will,' was the resounding answer from Matty. 'I want to spend the rest of my days with Ellen. Deirdre is a fundamental part of who she is,' continued Matty.

So, without question from him, they came as a pair and he'd be delighted to adopt Deirdre if that was what it took to bring her back from Newtownforbes.

Peter was delighted and, when Ellen and Matty arrived back to No. 12 to share their news, he had three bottles of Guinness cooling in the back yard for the occasion.

Second Chance

To Ellen, this proposal and impending marriage felt so different from the 1944 shotgun wedding arrangements with Joe – she had no idea of how Joe's life had played out since he left Dublin, but spared a thought that he might have found some happiness along his journey.

From Matty's perspective, he imparted the engagement news to his family in Carnmore and Galway City and knew he risked being ostracised by his Galway clan for taking on this situation. However, his love for Ellen ran deep and he never second guessed his decision of the heart to marry into this pre-made family.

Ellen and Matty were married two months later, on 6 April 1953 – a low-key affair, but a happy day for these two lovers and, also, for Uncle Peter, who knew that Dee would have loved to meet Matty and see how happy he made Ellen. Back in Newtownforbes, Deirdre was unaware of Matty or the marriage.

Although both Ellen and Matty hoped for a quick decision from the Court to allow them to bring Deirdre back from Newtownforbes, it took the best part of two years for Matty's adoption of Deirdre to be formalised, but on Saturday 5 February 1955, Ellen was on the train to Newtownforbes to bring her 'baby' home. Although the long wait to formalise documentation was an unfair delaying of what was right for Deirdre, Ellen couldn't believe how things were playing out and she said a few prayers on the train trip to make sure nothing went wrong.

When she got to the home, she was shown into the visitation room and there was Deirdre, sitting and waiting to give her mother a hug, unaware of the reason for her mother's visit being a day earlier than normal.

Ellen ran towards Deirdre and they met in the middle of the room with a huge embrace that even made Sister Rose sit up and take notice. 'Deirdre, I've news for ya.'

'Mammy, what is it?' exclaimed Deirdre, trying to anticipate what was to come.

'You're coming home, Deirdre, you're coming home!'

The uncontrollably loud squeal of a nine-year-old girl could be heard on the other side of Newtownforbes. Deirdre had hoped, but never expected, that this day would come, but she was now full of questions.

'When do we leave? Where will we live? Is this forever? Can I say goodbye to my friends?' Ellen tried to answer as many questions as possible, but each answer led to several more questions from an increasingly excitable young girl.

As was customary in the home, Deirdre was denied the opportunity to say goodbye to her friends. Áine was long gone, but there were plenty of other girls that Deirdre would have liked to see just one more time. However, RMG's rules were simple – no goodbyes to the other children, end of story. This saddened Deirdre a little bit, but that feeling was far outweighed by the enthusiasm she felt for what lay ahead.

As Rose was chaperoning that day, it gave her and Deirdre a few minutes to chat and say their goodbyes – their strong bond, which was always evident, was all on show for the next fifteen minutes, and at one stage, Rose, Deirdre and Ellen were all in tears. 'My girl, you're a wonderful child and I know amazing things await you in the big world. Be good for your beautiful mother and always look out for the weak ones,' said Rose. Little did Ellen know when she placed Deirdre in the

Second Chance

care of this home that her then two-year-old daughter would blossom into a sweet nine-year-old girl that interacted with adults in an honest and loving way.

'I love you, Rosie,' said Deirdre, dropping all naming protocols.

By then, Rose was choked up and all she could say was, 'All my love, my little butterfly. Go fly! Go fly!'

And with that, Ellen and Deirdre said their goodbyes to Rose, took the walk to the train station and were homeward bound. As the train passed Maynooth, and with less than an hour to go to Amiens Street Station, Ellen chose to impart the news about Matty, the marriage and the adoption. 'Deirdre, I've more news for ya. I'm married and your new father will be at the station waiting for us. Your name is now Deirdre Kelly.'

To Ellen's surprise, and in an example of the resilience that Deirdre built up in her time in Newtownforbes, she took the news in her stride and wanted to know more. 'What's his name? What's he like? Where will we live?'

Ellen gave Deirdre her best description of Matty, but Deirdre was too excited to take it all in. When they alighted the train in Amiens Street, Matty was there waiting for them. A stark contrast to that very same platform when Deirdre boarded the train, with Sister Michael, in July 1947. Everyone was crying, but happy tears this time. Matty gave his new daughter a special hug, but it was quite awkward, at that moment, for both, given they were now inextricably linked, but had never met before. As a treat on the way home, they picked up fish and chips for everyone.

Deirdre couldn't believe what the last few hours had

brought, but she spared a thought for the Newtownforbes girls that she had left behind and hoped that each one of them would find their own piece of happiness in the years to come. She certainly felt very lucky and it was obvious, from the smiles around the kitchen table in No. 12 Ebenezer Road that night, that everyone shared that feeling. Ellen's niece, Bridget, had, by this time, moved out, but Uncle Peter was still part of the furniture. As he ate his fish supper, he sat back and happily observed this new family getting to know each other.

Chapter Seventeen

Father Figure

Deirdre, Ellen and Matty woke the next morning with optimism in their hearts and the rest of their lives ahead of them. Deirdre was in her new bed and, for the first time in her memory, she didn't have six or seven other girls in the room with her. She was now in her own room – more of a box room that could only fit a single bed, but that didn't matter to Deirdre. It was privacy for the first time ever and, over the years to come, she would treasure those moments before sleep when she could just be in her own company, with her own thoughts – staring at the ceiling in absolute silence was an experience in itself.

In the bedroom at the front of the house were Ellen and Matty – this was a bigger room with a double bed, wardrobe in the corner and a window that overlooked the small front garden. Decorated with plain wallpaper, it was a basic room, but had everything they needed. They were very much still enjoying the flushes of romance and, on those rare mornings where time stood still, they would lie there holding hands, not talking, but just enjoying being together. Ellen woke relatively early that morning and, after taking a few seconds to realise what had happened the previous day, crept out of bed, out into the landing and snuck a peek into her daughter's new room, just to make sure that Deirdre was actually in the house. What she saw was a little girl asleep but hugging the same teddy that Dee gave her for the Christmas before she went into the home – it survived Deirdre's time in Newtownforbes and, apart from Ellen's regular visits, was the only constant comfort to Deirdre throughout that period. Ellen then got back into the bed, with Matty still sleeping, and lay back and said a little prayer of thanks for how her life had turned 180 degrees because of that night out with Mabel over two years before. Another fork moment in life, she thought, but, this time, her chosen path was so positive that she could hardly fathom it.

After a while lying in bed, Ellen got up and went downstairs and prepared some breakfast for all in the house. To make that first morning extra special, Ellen prepared a traditional cooked breakfast, including sausages, rashers, pudding and fried eggs. But, before serving, she went upstairs to wake Deirdre. As she walked into the room, Deirdre's eyes popped open and after a few hazy moments, she came to, smiled and then hugged her mother. Although she was only nine, Deirdre knew that her life had changed immeasurably the previous day and almost wanted time to freeze to protect her new-found happiness.

'Morning, dear. Did ya sleep well?' inquired Ellen.

'Yes Mammy. The bed is so comfortable. I could lie here forever.'

'Well, you can forget about that,' said Ellen with a grin on her face. 'There's some food downstairs for everyone and we're then going on that walk your father promised you.'

Father Figure

Ellen got some clothes out of the small chest of drawers in the room and left them at the bottom of the bed for Deirdre. 'Deirdre, these are your good Sunday clothes. Will you get dressed and come down as soon as you can?' Ellen wanted her returning daughter to be in full Sunday splendour as they walked around the neighbourhood.

Ellen then left the room and Deirdre immediately inspected her new clothes. New vest, knickers and socks, but what was most interesting was the floral print dress. Ellen had used some spare material from the dressmaker's and made up this 'all out' Sunday dress for her daughter – she wanted to make a statement that morning and Deirdre was delighted to have such a lovely garment. As a nod to how Newtownforbes had conditioned her, Deirdre grabbed the clothes and changed quickly whilst still under the bedsheets.

She then walked slowly downstairs and opened the living room door, where she could hear all her new housemates chatting. The smell of freshly cooked bacon and sausages filled the house and Deirdre couldn't believe how much food was on the table. In her previous life, food was a luxury. There was no prospect of seconds in Newtownforbes and Deirdre, only a few months earlier, had mentioned to Ellen that she was sometimes hungry falling asleep in the home, a sign that she was going through a growth spurt. Although means were modest in No. 12, from that day forward, Ellen was keen to ensure that Deirdre would never go to bed hungry and would not want for anything. Deirdre helped herself to some sausages, rashers, one sunny side up fried egg and a couple of half slices of white bread, which she used to dip into the egg yolk. On that morning, Deirdre said very little as she played herself into her new life, but she was taking in every interaction between her mother, father and granduncle. She was particularly interested in how Matty and Peter talked, the depth of their voices, how they spoke firmly, with confidence and humour. Given the lack of male characters in Deirdre's life to that point, she was particularly focused on how different the male and female tones of voice were.

'Peter, do you think we can beat the English next Saturday?' asked Matty, as he thought about his country's chances against the 'old enemy' in the Five Nations Rugby Championship.

'I wouldn't be sure Matty,' Peter said, hedging his bets, 'apparently we weren't great last time out.' He was referencing the home defeat to France a few weeks earlier.

After breakfast was finished, and Deirdre helped Ellen with the dishes, the newly united Kelly family headed for that walk around the community. For almost two hours, they covered South Circular Road to Kelly's Corner, Camden Street down to Kevin Street, Clanbrassil Street, Patrick Street, Thomas Street, Meath Street, past Oscar Square and back to No. 12. For a girl whose longest walk before that was probably half an hour, Deirdre was exhausted when they got home. She went upstairs to take a rest on the bed and, although tired, she loved the look of her new neighbourhood. The shops, the people, the Dublin accents, the smells, the different types of houses – it was an assault on the senses for this little girl, but she was soaking it all up and couldn't wait for the next trip out.

On that Sunday evening, the family went to their first mass together, a special vigil mass for the upcoming retreat

Father Figure

week. Although Deirdre was oblivious, the importance of this religious ritual wasn't lost on Ellen and Matty, as it would be their first 'formal' trip out in public as a family. Despite the knocks over recent years, Ellen was a proud person. She would try and look her best when out, but made sure that everyone looked the part that evening. She asked Matty to wear his suit and she herself was wearing her best outfit, a tea length wine dress with long sleeves, complemented by matching heeled shoes. At about 5.50 p.m., they were ready and Ellen opened the front door. It was a calm but chilly February evening and, as they stepped onto the path, the next-door neighbours opened their door. It was Marty and Helen, who had been Ellen's neighbours for the past twenty years.

Helen was well aware who Deirdre was, but still desired to stir the pot. 'Good evening. Who do we have here, Ellen?'

Ellen was a bit unnerved at suddenly being forced to answer a question about Deirdre before she even set foot on the street. But, after a taking a couple of seconds to steady herself, she confidently responded.

'Evening, Helen, evening, Marty. This is our daughter, Deirdre.'

'Nice to meet ya, Deirdre,' responded Helen. 'I remember when ya were only a toots ... before ya went.'

That last comment was unsubtly designed to remind Ellen that everyone knew that Deirdre was somehow tainted. Deirdre didn't pick up on this, but did notice over the coming weeks that people tended to stare at her, particularly those neighbours on Ebenezer Road who felt they knew what had happened over the preceding number of years. Despite the situation being regularised, they didn't seem to want Ellen to think that everything was forgotten.

In any event, Ellen, Matty and Deirdre headed for Donore Avenue Church and took a seat about halfway back from the altar.

When it was time for Holy Communion, all three of them walked along the pew to the left and out into the aisle to queue up with the other parishioners, in a line of people that Fr McHugh was serving. When they reached the top, Ellen ushered Deirdre to take her communion first – Deirdre was well versed on the protocol, having made her First Holy Communion a couple of years earlier in Newtownforbes. Fr McHugh saw this girl in front of him and, following a glance at Ellen, he quickly gathered who Deirdre was. His only words were, 'Body of Christ,' to which Deirdre responded, 'Amen,' but it was the priest's body language that made Ellen angry. From the first moment that Fr McHugh had laid eyes on a then pregnant Ellen, he had never hidden his disdain for her, but he was now reflecting that feeling onto her innocent daughter.

The following weekend, all three went to Sunday morning mass together. After coming home, Matty went into the living room and sat down to read a paper he had picked up at the shop on the way back from the church – the *Connacht Sentinel*. This was a weekly publication that relayed news focused almost exclusively on the Connacht area, primarily being Galway and Mayo, but also including the other provincial counties of Roscommon, Sligo and Leitrim.

After an hour or so, he put the paper down and opened up a conversation with Deirdre, who was sitting on the sofa

Father Figure

in the living room. 'Deirdre, let me tell you about where I'm from,' he said, his deep voice reverberating around the house.

'Yes please, Daddy,' replied Deirdre, who was already calling him by the more affectionate term than his name.

'I'm from a small village east of Galway City. I'm the youngest of six children and you have loads of cousins all over Ireland. I'll bring you down there in the summer,' said Matty, with the love for his home place written all over his face. Above everything else, Matty was a Connacht man, a man with country in his veins, who, when younger, enjoyed nothing more than a roadside chat with a neighbour to catch up on the latest news.

'What's the village like, Daddy?' inquired Deirdre, who was already looking forward to a visit that summer.

'It's a small village, with one shop, a pub, our all-important GAA club and a church. Typical Galway – small fields with stone walls and plenty of sheep,' said Matty, settling into this first meaningful conversation with his new daughter.

Deirdre was lapping up every word. 'Did you play GAA?' she asked, in what was a fortuitous question to ask Matty, who loved hurling, an Irish sport played with sticks and ball, known as a hurl and a sliotar.

'I played hurling for the club. We made the county final a few years ago, but we lost. It's hard for a club like Carnmore to rival the bigger clubs around Galway, but some year we'll do it,' said Matty, his pride for that club evident with each of his words.

After giving up hurling following that county final, Matty had wanted to move to try and make his living in a big city and he chose Dublin. However, from that point on, he would follow how his club and county performed, both in hurling and Gaelic football, as keenly as he followed politics and he took immense pride when any Galway performance was noted on the national stage. He would go on to attend a few All-Ireland Finals featuring his native county and, if the game went against the Tribesman, he wouldn't be bitter. Instead, he would note, 'Emigration is destroying the stream of talent from the minor to the senior ranks.' He felt the minor game was a better comparator for those counties plagued with their young being forced to leave their local areas.

Although it took a few more weeks to get fully used to each other, Deirdre adored this new male influence in her life. Peter was getting old and didn't have enough energy to chase after a child in the house, but Matty, on the other hand, still had some level of fitness and was re-energised by the infectious fun that Deirdre brought with her. The two of them would often head for walks around the area, where Matty would stop to chat with the neighbours in the same way as he would have done in years gone by in Carnmore. Flat cap and blazer on, one arm on the fence and one leg tucked behind the other, he could have stood there chatting all day and he always had some story or other to share. If the story was a funny one, he'd get towards the end of it, then start laughing so that the punchline was a mix of laughs and words and it was hard to figure out how the story finished. Deirdre just loved listening to his voice, his Galway lilt and how the neighbours would engage with him – Matty was becoming quite the local character, with neighbours crossing the road to chat to him. Those very same neighbours that twitched the curtains and wagged the tongues in years gone

Father Figure

by after Ellen's scandal were going out of their way to chat to the 'new' family in the area and would look affectionately at Deirdre and Matty strolling down the road hand in hand without a care in the world.

In terms of parenting styles, Ellen, who, by now, had given up physically working in the dressmaker's premises, but instead invested in a Pfaff sewing machine and was 'working from home', was a typical Irish mother that ensured that the needs of her family were always looked after. Given the non-standard start to their relationship, Ellen was protective of Deirdre and always on the lookout for those that might try and brand her daughter due to that beginning in life – however, she was still strict and expected Deirdre to pull her weight in the house and be respectful of her family and those in the community. Matty had a different approach – he would let Ellen look after day-to-day matters and would only get involved if he felt Deirdre was taking significant liberties. This happened rarely, so that allowed father and daughter to get on with the bonding that they'd missed out on for the first nine years of her life. Given that approach, Deirdre always knew when she had crossed the line, as she'd be on the receiving end of a Galway bark, with that usually doing the trick and Deirdre immediately apologising.

There was one time when Deirdre was eleven and, not for the first time, she spilled milk all over the kitchen floor. Ellen, normally calm, snapped at her daughter for being so careless, with Matty then hearing a tutting from Deirdre and seeing a hint of an eyeroll from his little girl. He hit the roof. 'I heard and saw that, Deirdre. Your mother works herself to the bone so that we have everything we need. Have some respect, girly,' he shouted.

Deirdre quietly went about tidying up and then disappeared upstairs in tears. She came down about fifteen minutes later, full of apologies to Ellen and Matty.

'So you should be,' said Matty, who then diffused the tension by giving her one of his bear hugs.

All was fine again, but Deirdre knew that she had to row in with how the house was run and she would then get way more in return from her parents.

When Deirdre came to Dublin, she went into fourth class in Weaver Square Primary School and one of the things Matty enjoyed doing was helping her with her homework. She received a reasonable standard of first stage primary education in Newtownforbes and was good at her writing. Sums were not her strongest suit and Matty used to come up with creative ways to try and teach her fractions. 'Now, Deirdre, if we cut up this apple tart into twelve slices and we move two slices onto another plate, what fraction of the tart is on the new plate?' Deirdre was a bit lost, but enjoyed tucking into one-sixth of the tart afterwards, to Ellen's annoyance.

In her first couple of years back in No. 12, Matty and Ellen would take it in turns each night to read Deirdre a story. Ellen would stick to the story in the book in front of her, whereas Deirdre had no idea in which direction Matty might bring a story on any given night. He would often just drop the book and say, 'Let me tell ya a story from Galway,' delivered in his unique accent. The story could involve GAA, gun running, sheep or pretty much anything, and it was rare that those stories bore any resemblance to the fairy tales in the book beside the bed. Deirdre would hang on every word and would

Father Figure

look back afterwards and giggle to herself at how madcap her father was. At those moments, she wasn't connecting the dots and saying to herself that this was the missing piece of her jigsaw, but she did have an understanding that this father figure was a dimension that she didn't have access to in her previous life – and she so loved that extra dimension.

Chapter Eighteen

Sisters

Deirdre was in sixth class, her final year of primary school. In her first year after returning from the home, her past and her unusual accent, which was a mix of Dublin from Ellen and country from Longford, made her stand out and this led a few children making fun of her. They didn't mean any harm, just young children picking out a peer who was marginally different from the pack. This did affect Deirdre and she became self-conscious, never wanting to be front and centre. However, in general, her school years in Dublin were great fun and she had a lovely group of friends from her class and around the neighbourhood. At the same time, Deirdre's personality was developing, which, at its heart, had a caring streak for those less fortunate, something which Sister Rose had impressed upon her in the home. She hated to see poverty-stricken people begging on the street and would nudge Ellen to part with a penny or two in those circumstances. Her education was going reasonably well, with some improvement in sums, but a penchant for the written word.

Deirdre knew from her past that 'what you have, you hold' and not to be always looking for something better

Sisters

down the road. But one thing she longed for, especially since leaving the home, was to have a baby sister or brother. In those days in the home, she thoroughly enjoyed looking after and guiding the younger ones and, given that she was eleven, she would have loved a younger sibling to share things with.

In October 1956, she noticed that Ellen was putting on a little bit of weight and that her father appeared to be doing a little more around the house over the preceding weeks. One day, while sitting in the living room, she was staring straight at Ellen through the scullery door as her mother looked up.

'What'ya looking at, Deirdre?' inquired Ellen.

Deirdre immediately looked away and said, 'Nothing.'

Ellen then came into the living room and Deirdre didn't know where to look.

'Were ya looking at me tummy?'

Reluctantly, Deirdre nodded and Ellen grabbed her hand and placed it on her stomach. 'Well, you're going to be a big sister!' exclaimed Ellen, to which Deirdre responded with a series of yelps and squeals, hugs and laughter. Deirdre couldn't believe it. Her mother and father were forty-two and forty-six respectively by then, which was not young by childbearing standards, and Deirdre had thought this day may never come.

The next few months went by quickly, as Ellen grew larger and Matty's expectant father smile similarly increased. On 9 February 1957, a seven pounds six ounces baby girl, by the name of Geraldine Rose Kelly, was delivered in the same Coombe Hospital that Deirdre had been born in. When Deirdre heard that she had a baby sister, her joy was unbridled. Although she would have accepted a baby brother, there was a symmetry in her mind to those younger girls in the home and now having a baby sister to dote over. When Ellen arrived home from hospital and placed Ger, as she would become known, in the same Moses basket that Deirdre had slept in almost twelve years earlier, Deirdre would just sit beside the basket looking at this real life bundle of joy, listening out for any little gurgle from the baby. Many older brothers or sisters have a natural sense of jealousy when younger siblings arrive, but Deirdre, given her age, was mature enough to be simply excited by this new being.

Deirdre was a great help to Ellen in those early weeks and months with feeding, changing and making dinners, and once Ger could sit on the floor, there next to her would be her sister playing and joking with the baby. One Sunday evening that summer, Ger was parked on the floor propped up by cushions, with Deirdre sitting beside her holding her hand, making faces and cooing at her new best friend. Matty was sitting on his favourite armchair listening to the wireless, in the same way as Mick did all those years ago, and Ellen was sitting on the other side doing some knitting. Matty looked up and met Ellen's eyes across the scene of their two children on the floor. They both smiled and Matty just winked.

Over the next few years, all members of the Kelly household were busy in their own way. Matty continued to work on the railways, with lorry driving on the side, and was bringing a reasonable sum into the house to provide a good life for his family. He was hard working and had a traditional belief that a husband and father should strive to provide for the family. Ellen was busy looking after Ger and accepted limited amounts of dressmaking work that she could do on the Pfaff

Sisters

at home. Deirdre progressed into secondary school and was continuing to show plenty of ability with creative writing. With her developing personality also came a questioning of her Catholic faith, which was tested thoroughly during her time in the home and the way in which the Reverend Mother exercised Catholic doctrines.

One day after she turned fourteen, Deirdre broached with her parents her desire to stop going to mass. 'Mammy and Daddy, I don't want to go to mass anymore. I don't have a connection to what the priests are saying.'

This request was evidence that Deirdre was asserting herself, but was met with resistance, mostly from Matty who felt that this was a red line in his house. Ellen, on the other hand, and despite her own strong faith, had witnessed the sharp end of how the Church dealt with challenging situations and ultimately persuaded Matty to let Deirdre find her own path on that issue, notwithstanding that neighbours would talk about their daughter's abandoning of the Church.

From that point, Deirdre avoided the usual Sunday mass routine, which was replaced by a commitment to hoover the house from top to bottom and to look after Ger for that hour on a Sunday – this was a fair compromise from Deirdre's perspective, although Matty still questioned the change. 'Where has my little girl gone?' he thought to himself. She was still there, but just finding her own way in the world.

With Deirdre's progression to secondary school, her gang of friends changed. There was Nuala, who was bright, articulate, but not focused, Eileen, who had a propensity for finding mischief from the most innocent of situations and Nicola, who wasn't the sharpest knife in the drawer when it came to academics, but could buy and sell the other three. They were an eclectic group, but they always found something to chat about to while away those breaks during the school day or weekends.

One girl not in their core group was Grace – she lived in the neighbourhood from a family of four and, to Deirdre, Grace was the epitome of everything she wasn't. She was elegant for her age, carried herself well with teachers in school, was articulate on any point of the day and, most importantly of all to Deirdre, Grace had a 'normal' family. As Deirdre grew into a teenager, she increasingly questioned to herself what happened to her childhood and who her biological father was. Grace's seemingly perfect life was one that Deirdre wanted and to be that type of person.

Those thoughts of a better life did not mean that Deirdre was bitter about her early years. She loved her parents dearly, and appreciated the sacrifices, both financially and emotionally, they made for her. She was never looking to replace Matty in her life, but felt that the missing biological piece of her jigsaw was important in understanding why she was the way she was.

However, any attempt by Deirdre to bring up the past was never mentioned in front of Matty – she had too much respect for his role in rehabilitating the family to put him in that position. Instead, she would subtly try to squeeze out some information from Ellen, but was either totally ignored, too subtle to get any engagement or was met with a brick wall. However, one day stood out. It was late 1960 and Ellen was busy in the scullery making one of her infamous Christmas puddings, full of a lethal cocktail of all sorts of

Sisters

food ingredients and, most importantly, spirits. As ever, Deirdre was by her side helping in any way she could and Ger was in the living room on the floor playing with some second-hand toys handed down by one of the neighbours. As Ellen was tidying the kitchen, Deirdre sidled up to her and, in a less than subtle attempt to broach the subject, opened with, 'Mammy, I just don't understand what happened when I was young.'

'What are ya on about, Deirdre?' snapped Ellen, clearly knowing where Deirdre wanted to bring the conversation.

'I don't know why my father didn't want to know me. Did he not love me?' Deirdre brought emotion straight into the conversation in an attempt to prise some information from Ellen, which had not been forthcoming to that point.

Ellen jumped straight back at her. 'Your Daddy goes out every day to put food on this table,' she said as she pointed at the little table in the scullery and then to the empty living room chair that Matty occupied after a day's graft, 'and he's the only father you need to know about.'

This wasn't the first time Ellen had reacted badly to this line of questioning and Deirdre could see that her mother didn't have the ability to discuss the events that led to her being deposited in the home.

However, Deirdre was surprised by the ferocity of Ellen's words. By then, she was backing into the living room, saying with tears in her eyes, 'I know it's difficult for you, but it's difficult for me too. I just want the truth and, someday, I'll find it. You can't stop me.'

Ellen was incensed and sharply responded to what she deemed a mutiny. 'While you're living in this house, young lady, you'll do as you're told. I've nothing more to say, full stop! Now, bring your sister up for a wash before I get the tea ready.'

Even though that conversation had Ellen in a rage, she knew that she needed to calm everything before Matty arrived home from work. If there was tension, he would want to know what had happened and, if the topic of Deirdre's biological father came up again, he would shut it down with even more anger than Ellen had just shown in the scullery. After doing some preparation for tea, she went upstairs where Deirdre and Ger were chatting to each other in their bedroom.

Ellen asked Deirdre into the front bedroom and made the first move. 'I know you want to know about that man, but he will never be part of your life. He worked as a butcher, but left us and Dublin when the going got tough. That's all I can tell you.'

As she took in those rare nuggets of information, Deirdre responded, 'Mammy, I'm not trying to hurt you. You know I love you both and Ger.'

'I know. You're a good girl, but your family is right under this roof and that's that!' said Ellen, trying to put an end to this part of their collective past. She continued, 'We all have our crosses to bear, Deirdre. This is yours,' in a reference to Jesus carrying the cross to his own crucifixion.

Deirdre didn't appreciate a religious reference at that moment, but chose to let it lie given her mother's continuing strong devotion to the Catholic Church and the fact that she had garnered some information on her biological father. On the flip side, Ellen found it almost impossible to re-open those old wounds about the past, having pushed those memories so deep over the years.

'Yes, Mammy, let's make sure Daddy has a nice tea,' said Deirdre, as she chose to move on from the argument.

As the early months of 1961 passed along, the wintry showers were replaced with a warming sun and, although the Liberties wasn't known for its greenery, some of the scant trees were sprouting pink, blue and pale white blossoms. Deirdre, however, had another focus on her mind – the upcoming Group Certificate exams in Rathmines College. In secondary school education in Ireland, at that time, there were three levels of State exams – the Group Certificate after two or three years of school, then the Intermediate Certificate and, finally, the Leaving Certificate, after which the select few that made it that far had the opportunity, subject to results and means, to enter tertiary education, possibly to a university. However, given that secondary school education was not free at that time, the Group Certificate was the height of educational achievement for many. It was important that one did a reasonable set of exams at that stage to set up the possibility of securing employment, be it a trade apprenticeship for a boy or a job as a typist for a girl, to give two examples.

Deirdre always took pride in her schoolwork and wanted to give this set of exams as good a go as possible – however, she lacked the confidence and self-belief in her abilities and prepared for the worst when sitting the exams that May, when she was yet to turn sixteen. Although not an A student in her primary and early years of secondary school, she received good grades in the Group Cert and there was much excitement in No. 12 on results day. Matty, who had left school after primary, was ever so proud of little Deirdre and a big hug was the order of the day. Ellen, always a bit more reserved with her emotions than Matty, gave Deirdre a simple well done and a small hug to mark that milestone.

With the Group Cert out of the way, there came one of those forks in the road for Deirdre. 'Should I continue with school and take on the Inter Cert or leave school and seek out a job?' she thought to herself. Matty, having always had a good paying job despite leaving school at twelve, was happy for Deirdre to take flight into the workforce, but Ellen was more circumspect and thought Deirdre should think long and hard about it. However, the key deciding factor, and one that Matty and Ellen agreed on, was that education costs and work pays. It would be a significant help to the household if Deirdre got out into the workforce and brought some money home, rather than being an effective drain on their limited resources.

At decision times such as this, one looked around at what peers were doing and Deirdre's other three close friends decided to leave school. Two took up jobs working in local shops and the other landed a coveted office job. Grace, from Donore Road, stayed on in secondary school with a reasonable cohort of Deirdre's other classmates – she excelled in exams and deserved the chance to better herself. Deirdre always looked to her as someone to aim for, maybe emulate, but with that fork in the road right in front of her and Grace walking down the education route, Deirdre made the choice of the workforce.

It was probably not really a choice and perhaps the inevitable consequence of coming from a family of limited means, but Deirdre felt comfortable with her decision, especially as the stifling formality of education was not something she felt comfortable with since returning from the home. However, if Deirdre was being truthful to herself, the insecurities spawned from those years in the home created a fear of failure and leaving school had the bonus of not having to sit formal exams that, in the deepest part of her mind, she felt were beyond her capabilities. So, six short years after returning from the home, Deirdre brought an end to her education – all in all, she was broadly smiling at the prospect of putting away the books and seeking to learn by experience.

Chapter Nineteen

---*---

School of Life

The Group Cert focused less on the broad range of subjects at Inter or Leaving Cert level and more on vocational skills that would be useful in the workforce. Subjects such as woodwork and metalwork were taken by the boys and Deirdre's attention gravitated towards typing and shorthand. By the end of her school years, Deirdre was good at typing, with a speed of around forty words per minute on an old-fashioned manual 'QWERTY' typewriter. She was able to touch type and sought to entertain her friends by typing a full paragraph blindfolded. Deirdre was simply at home in front of this clunky bit of machinery and, once the decision to enter the workforce was taken, it was an obvious choice for her to try and find a starting job as a typist.

A young girl, aged sixteen, from the Liberties didn't have many strings to pull to get such a job, but Deirdre got lucky when a schoolfriend, Dolores, landed an administrative assistant job in Spicers, a paper company, towards the end of summer 1961. In her second week in the job, Dolores struck up a conversation with a fellow employee whilst on a cigarette break and heard that they were looking for a junior in the typist pool. Dolores then called into Deirdre straight

School of Life

after work that day and, after a short interview and typing test that Deirdre passed with flying colours, she was asked to start in the office the following Monday.

On the day before starting, Matty and Ellen sat down with Deirdre. 'Have ya got your outfit ready for tomorrow?' asked Ellen, as if Deirdre was a young child.

'Yes, Mammy, I've everything ready,' replied Deirdre.

'Are you nervous?' inquired Matty.

'A bit,' replied Deirdre, suddenly questioning her ability to talk to adults in the office, wondering how they'd look at this young, petite sixteen-year-old and second guessing whether she was that good a typist. That lack of confidence was coming to the fore on the day before she was venturing into the working world.

'Deirdre, I know ya can do anything you want to do. You've achieved so much already and tomorrow is the start of the next part of your life. I know you're nervous, but we're always here for ya and we know you'll be great,' said Ellen, with the standard motivational speech for a fledgling child entering something new. Nonetheless, Deirdre appreciated the show of support.

As they arrived at Spicers' offices in Henry Street, on the north side of the city, Dolores opened the front door, introduced Deirdre to the receptionist and headed upstairs. The office was two connected three-storey over-basement Georgian buildings, with a rabbit warren of small offices inside. As she waited for someone to come down to meet her, Deirdre's stomach churned. She had kept the conversation light on the walk to the office, but now she was on her own. As she was considering turning on her heels, a young lady, aged eighteen or nineteen, came down to the reception room.

'Are you the new typist? Deirdre, isn't it? I'm Maureen. I'll be working with you.'

Deirdre just nodded and, without letting her get into the conversation, Maureen continued. 'I heard from Jack that you're quite the typist. Now, don't be going too fast to show us all up,' laughed Maureen.

Deirdre got the joke, but half wondered whether Maureen was actually asking her to slow down her typing. This was the issue with sixteen-year-olds hitting the workforce and not being up to speed with office banter, but it wouldn't take long for Deirdre to be able to throw out her own bit of slagging of her fellow girls in the 'pool'. In those days, all documents, ranging from letters to customers, letters to suppliers, orders, invoices, internal office memos, etc., were created on a typewriter. The higher ups would ask one of the typists to come into their office, dictate the document they'd need to have typed and off the typists would go to create the document. Shorthand was the way of noting the request and each higher up had a different style of dictation. This made for a lot of inefficiencies, but at least provided jobs for young ladies, never men.

Maureen showed Deirdre up to the office where the typists sat. It was a basic set-up, with six desks lined in two rows of three facing each other. Each desk had a manual typewriter and plenty of paper to feed into it. Maureen ushered Deirdre to the spare desk, but not before introducing her to the other four typists that were already in situ that Monday morning. Deirdre was the youngest by two years, but all the girls were initially very welcoming to the new recruit – some bitching followed, but never to such an extent that she didn't enjoy coming to work. Deirdre was then shown around the office, to where the all-important stationery was kept, where to make tea and eat her lunch and she was introduced to some more people in the office. A few things Deirdre noticed immediately about the higher ups – they were mostly male, all a good bit older than the typist pool and there was an air of superiority in the way they talked to their female colleagues. Deirdre, even at her young age, felt that there was an unnatural barrier between the male higher ups and the female assistants and that surely there was a place for females at the top table in any office.

After being shown how this specific brand of typewriter worked, Deirdre was asked to re-type a letter to see what her skill level was and to see whether she could get used to typing at speed and under pressure. She passed the test comfortably, as this slightly awkward and nervous sixteen-year-old eased into work life. Maureen repeated the 'slow down and don't show us up' joke and everyone, including Deirdre, had a good laugh. She immediately felt like one of the gang.

Then, after she had spent an hour or so practising her typing, one of the higher ups, a middle-aged, balding man with a classic combover and thick-rimmed black glasses by the name of Mr Duignan, came into the typist pool office and abruptly called for one of them to follow him into his office for some dictation. All the girls looked at Deirdre, as they metaphorically pushed her in his direction. Deirdre reluctantly stood up and followed Mr Duignan – he then turned around and, noticing that she didn't have the necessary with her, barked, 'Bring your pen and notepad. How else do you expect to take notes? Can you memorise it?'

Miss, Say Goodbye to Your Daughter

To Mr Duignan, who was always referred to by his formal name, Deirdre was just another typist – he wasn't great with names, didn't have a clue that this was Deirdre's first day in Spicers and wasn't taking the time to educate her on how to do the job. This was a baptism of fire and Deirdre was visibly shaking as she sat down opposite his desk.

Mr Duignan then dictated a letter for the next three minutes almost without taking a breath, with Deirdre scribbling down what he was saying in the bit of shorthand she had picked up for the Group Cert. He never repeated anything he said, then asked her to get the letter typed up as soon as possible and dismissed her from his office.

Deirdre ran out the door and back to her desk and thought to herself, 'What just happened? How am I supposed to pick everything up on my first morning?'

Maureen observed how frazzled Deirdre was when she returned to the room and knew that Mr Duignan was well known for talking too fast, having zero patience and expecting perfection, so she felt that her new colleague needed some help. She got up and went over to Deirdre, who by then was pale and barely knew how to put paper into the typewriter.

'Don't mind him. He's mad as a box of frogs. I don't think he knows half of what he says. Let's look at your notes.'

For the next thirty minutes, Deirdre and Maureen cobbled together a version of the letter that was close to the spirit of what Mr Duignan was prattling on about in his office. Deirdre then got up and walked to his office door. She gave a gentle rap on the door, and he beckoned her in as if she was his servant.

'Yes, Miss, have you got that letter with you?'

'Yes, Mr Duignan. Here it is.'

School of Life

Mr Duignan went through it, got his red pen out and, to her relief, didn't rip it completely apart.

'Not bad, Miss …?' he said, seeking her surname.

'Miss Kelly, Deirdre Kelly, sir,' replied Deirdre, as if she was addressing her master.

'Keep up the good work, but always know your place in here,' said Mr Duignan with a blend of empathy and contempt for the sort that occupied the typist pool. Deirdre thanked him, re-typed the letter, but wondered what he meant by his final comment.

After a few weeks in the job, Deirdre was getting used to the hustle and bustle of office life and, on one quiet Friday afternoon, she took the opportunity to ask Maureen what Mr Duignan might have meant by that comment about knowing her place.

'Don't worry about that. Mr Duignan's from another era and can't understand why women are allowed in the office. Let him try to type up his own letters and then see him change his tune,' chortled Maureen. She continued, 'I've met his wife and he's as henpecked as it comes. He comes into the office to get away from her and likes to be the boss in here. He's harmless.'

Deirdre, being sixteen, was trying to get to grips with office politics and it reminded her somewhat of the chain of command amongst the nuns in the home. If one nun spoke above her station, there were sanctions from the next level up and everyone needed to know their place. The office had a similar hierarchy, but with men generally in the top ranks and women in supporting roles. This irked her and she asked Maureen whether any women tried to move up and out of the typist and administrative pools to get a more important role.

Maureen, being happy in her role and not wanting to rock the boat, simply replied, 'That's the way it is, girl. Maybe not fair, but that's our lot.'

Deirdre thought to herself that such inequality surely should be challenged, but, given that she was only in the workforce a wet week, that wasn't the time to champion women's rights.

Over the next two years, Deirdre took on different roles, mainly with typing, filing and general secretarial work at its core. As she was short on academic qualifications, the opportunity to break through the glass ceiling in those early years was limited. Her clear talents at typing and organisation were well respected by her peers, but the higher ups never sought to champion her to make it out of administration. Despite her positive and effervescent personality in the workplace, Deirdre continued to battle with self-belief and this held her back in those jobs. Her fear of failure meant she didn't seek to step outside the comfort zone enough and would see some of her female counterparts progress beyond the level she was at – on the face of it, this seemed unfair to her, but she knew that her inner fears played a part in that.

From a personal and family side during those early work years, she solidified her relationship with those in No. 12, albeit one didn't need to scratch the surface too deeply to get at the biological father issue. It wasn't that Deirdre wanted to go and hunt this man down, but she was keen to seek more scraps of information from her mother that would provide some clues as to his background, personality and looks, and the continued silence on the issue was beginning to prey on

School of Life

Deirdre's mind. The happy person that arrived back from the home in 1955 was replaced with a person that thought about social issues of the day, but also of issues that affected her day-to-day life. With that maturing came a quasi-philosophical questioning of why things were the way they were and why she was the way she was – her burgeoning brain, matched with a broadening life experience, made her often lie awake at night wondering what might have been.

On the social side of things, Deirdre had plenty of friends and was a regular in the dance halls on the southside of the city. She loved to dance and immersed herself in the new type of music that emerged from America in the late 1950s. Little Richard, Chuck Berry and Jerry Lee Lewis were prime examples and she enjoyed the faster beat – any opportunity to strut her stuff on the dance floor was taken on with full passion and it was in those moments that she forgot the self-doubts, simply brimmed with confidence and just went for it.

Chapter Twenty

Johnny B. Goode

It was October 1963. It was four months on from those historic few days that changed Ireland when John Fitzgerald Kennedy, the 35th President of America, visited his ancestors' homeland and uttered poignant words on the quayside in his great-grandfather's hometown of New Ross, Co. Wexford:

> When my great-grandfather left here to become a cooper in East Boston, he carried nothing with him except two things. A strong religious faith and a strong desire for liberty. And I'm glad to say that all of his great-grandchildren have valued that inheritance.

Far from the 'land of the free and home of the brave', a twenty-year-old man was getting ready to go out to a dance hall on Dublin's northside. John O'Neill, who lived with his parents and five sisters in a two-bed house on Clonliffe Avenue, Ballybough, in the shadow of Croke Park, didn't have any personal space at home and enjoyed those one or two nights a week when he got out with his friends. John was a bright, well-spoken but shy young man who suffered more than most from being brought up in a house full of women.

Johonny B. Goode

Having received a scholarship to O'Connell's secondary school in nearby Richmond Street North, he completed his Leaving Cert and secured a place in the Diploma in Public Administration in University College Dublin (UCD), whilst working by day in CIÉ, the national transport company. Following the diploma, he took up a place in Night Commerce, but, after a few months, he decided that it was not for him and, instead, focused on his career with CIÉ.

That Sunday evening, John and a few friends agreed to go to O'Lehane Hall for the weekly dance. This dance hall was owned and operated by one of the trade unions and was located on Cavendish Row opposite the Gate Theatre near the top of Dublin's premier thoroughfare, O'Connell Street. As with many dances at the time, this one was run by a religious order, in this case the Legion of Mary. Given the religious connection, it was a strictly no alcohol event, not that it mattered to John as he didn't take a drink.

He got dressed up in his going out suit and on his way out the door received the usual 'Enjoy yourself,' and 'Don't be late home,' comments from his parents. He met up with his friends in one of the local pubs. They had a quick drink and then made their way to the dance. With John's boyish looks and curly mop of hair, he was often questioned about whether he was young enough to be out without his parents, but the doormen knew him from previous dances, so waved him through.

As was still tradition at dances, the men went to one side of the hall, so John and his friends trooped over to the makeshift bar to get some drinks and then went to their side of the hall to see if any new girls were on the scene. Given his timid nature, John would rarely ask ladies to dance and was more interested in taking in the live music. A fan of the new style of rock'n'roll, he enjoyed listening to the band belting out some of the classic and modern hits.

Meanwhile, back in Ebenezer Road earlier that evening, Deirdre, three months on from her eighteenth birthday, was getting dressed up to go out with her friends. When going for a proper night out and taking in a dance, she and her friends used to go to the Mount Pleasant in Ranelagh, about thirty minutes' walk from the Liberties. On that Sunday night, the Mount Pleasant postponed their event, so Deirdre and her friends agreed to venture northside and go to the dance in O'Lehane Hall. That night, Deirdre opted for a full-length dress, hair down and some light make-up on. She thoroughly enjoyed getting ready and, with the help of her six-year-old sister, preparations would begin around 5 p.m. for a 7 p.m. departure.

Deirdre and her friends arrived at the dance hall at 8 p.m. and the place was buzzing – although the floor had some space for those willing to do some dancing, the standing and seating area were jam packed both for the men and women. Deirdre was asked for a few dances, which she duly accepted, but none of the men got her excited.

By coincidence, Deirdre's old classmate and neighbour Grace was also at the dance. Since they had been in class together, Deirdre understood that Grace had completed her Leaving Cert and obtained a place in UCD, studying Economics and History. Although their paths crossed the odd time given the social circles with which they mixed, Deirdre and Grace never engaged in conversation.

On this occasion, Deirdre observed Grace's ever elegant

Johonny B. Goode

looks, style and the ease with which she would carry herself. She was never short of male admirers and certainly captured the attention of the room when she stepped onto the dance floor.

As if it was a throwback to nineteen years earlier and Ellen and Joe's first dance, it came to Ladies' Choice and the lead singer of the band declared that the song would be Chuck Berry's 1958 mega-hit Johnny B. Goode. When Deirdre heard the name of the song, she threw caution to the wind and went over to the men's side of the floor to ask one of them to dance. She had no particular man in mind, but through a crowd, she spotted this young looking fella standing against the wall near the bar area – it was John O'Neill. He was taking in the start of the song, tapping his feet to the first few beats, but then looked away from the band and saw Deirdre coming towards him. He presumed she was either lost or in search of another lad. To his complete surprise, she made a beeline to him and asked him to dance. Of course he said yes, and the next three minutes were a complete blur for him.

Deirdre grabbed his hand and, as if they'd choreographed it in advance, they both started jiving to the song, a dance style that was frowned upon by the organisers of this event. The normally self-doubting Deirdre and the ever bashful John were jiving as if they'd known and danced with each other for years, so much so that the rest of the dance floor created a circle around them, egging them on to even greater heights with their moves. They were captivated with each other and caught up in the moment, with the gang around them clapping and cheering as the last note played from the band. John didn't know what had just happened, but he knew that this whirlwind of a young lady was stunningly beautiful, with her happy demeanour, deep brown eyes and great sense of style, and he had to know more. Deirdre was very impressed with John's moves after what he had just displayed on the floor.

As they made their way to the side of the dance floor, one of the organisers made it clear to them that jiving was strictly prohibited and that they were both banned from the dance hall for the next four weeks. Not only did John have the thrill of his life for that dance, but the young man who had been Mr Goodietwoshoes up to that point in his life had managed to be banned for a month. 'Where did that come from?' he asked himself.

As they found a quieter place to talk, John opened the conversation. 'Wow, that was some dance. Thanks for asking me. I'm John, John O'Neill. What's your name?'

'I'm Deirdre O'Connell. You're some mover,' she replied, keen to keep chatting after what she'd just experienced on the dance floor. However, a man of few words doesn't change stripes in five minutes and he found it difficult to keep the conversation flowing initially. Deirdre filled the gaps and, not wanting to let the moment go, John plucked up the courage to ask her out.

'Eh, would you like to go on a date ... go out with me sometime?' inquired John, expecting to be rebuffed.

'Absolutely, John. I'd be delighted,' replied Deirdre.

After a bit more chit chat, they agreed to meet outside Clery's Department Store on O'Connell Street the following Sunday at 7 p.m.

John, being an excellent timekeeper, turned up to the

Johonny B. Goode

agreed meeting point, outside Clery's on O'Connell Street, at five minutes to the hour, just in case Deirdre was early. He needn't have bothered. Deirdre was always a bit of a last-minute merchant and that day was no different. Even though she was looking forward to seeing John again, there were always one or two things out of place that needed a last-minute fix – so inevitably, she ran late. To her family and friends, she always looked great, but her self-esteem was less than it ought to be and this led to constant checking and re-checking in the mirror. She could have turned up in a bin bag with rollers in her hair and John would have been awestruck.

By 7.15 p.m., John was getting a little chilly on that late October evening, but then he caught sight of a lady walking slowly, but with poise and elegance, in his direction – she was wearing an ankle length royal blue dress under a sand coloured jacket and a matching clutch purse, with her hair up, which made John have a double take as she approached. At the dance hall the previous Sunday, she had her hair down and with a soft curl effect, but for this date, the hair was done in a form of upstyle, with plenty of hairspray to keep it in place notwithstanding the quickening breeze.

'Hi, Deirdre. Jaysus, you look fantastic,' he said with a strong hint of his Ballybough roots.

'Hi, John, you don't look too bad yourself.'

Given where they were meeting, John thought it would be a good idea to head to the cinema for this first date and he secured black market tickets for the Savoy Cinema. They enjoyed the 'B' and 'A' shows and then thought about where to go afterwards.

'Will we go to the Paradiso? It should have a bit of

buzz.' This was a late night restaurant and piano bar on Westmoreland Street above a building society.

'Sounds good,' replied Deirdre, willing to let John make the first decisions in this embryonic relationship. 'I hear they serve a nice pint there,' continued Deirdre.

'Do you drink Guinness?' asked John, wondering what would a mannerly well-spoken eighteen-year-old girl be doing drinking pints of Guinness.

'No way, hate the stuff,' answered Deirdre with a loud chuckle.

'I don't drink myself,' said John, trying to sound refined and controlled in the presence of this beauty.

'Sure we'll change that soon enough,' laughed Deirdre, in her first hint that she was keen to get to know John.

The chat between them went reasonably well, with no awkward silences, and John enjoyed that he wasn't having to make up conversation, with Deirdre well able to share a titbit of information or anecdote to keep it flowing.

'What did you make of JFK and the visit?' queried Deirdre.

It was a fortuitous question to ask someone with a keen interest in history and politics and a brain to match that interest. John's eyes lit up immediately as he knew he could talk about JFK and his almost three years as President without pausing to think.

'It was quite the spectacle and he clearly enjoys his Irish roots. I wonder how much the visit was to do with his re-election campaign for next year and securing the Irish and Catholic vote?'

At this point, Deirdre realised that John was way up the

Johonny B. Goode

curve on this topic and she needed to up her game for their next political discussion.

'I have to say, I'll never forget what it felt like this time last year with Cuba and the missiles,' said John, inviting a wider discussion of Cold War politics.

John recalled going for a haircut in October 1962 and the only discussion in the barber's was not if but when a nuclear strike from the USA or the Soviet Union would commence in response to the latter installing nuclear missiles on the communist-run island of Cuba. He recounted how quiet the roads were, as if Armageddon had already kicked in. Deirdre was only seventeen at the time of that crisis and remembered Matty listening to the wireless and muttering something about it getting serious, but didn't have any other threads to go on.

'I remember my dad telling me something about it, but sure I was only seventeen,' said Deirdre, trying to subtly divert the conversation away from 'end of the world' topics.

John took the hint and they both talked a bit about their work, interests, family, friends and love of music and dancing.

The night went well and, despite it being in the opposite direction to his home, John walked Deirdre to No. 12 – they said their goodbyes and agreed to meet up the following Saturday with a group of their respective friends.

Two weeks later, they shared their first kiss and, with that, they were both in their first serious relationship.

Everyone of that era knew where they were when news filtered through of JFK's assassination in Dallas, Texas on 22 November 1963. It was a Friday and John and Deirdre agreed to meet at Madigan's Pub on O'Connell Street. They met at

7 p.m. and, unbeknown to them, JFK had been shot thirty minutes earlier as his motorcade travelled through Dallas.

As they sat and sipped their second drinks, word filtered through the pub about what had happened Stateside and what struck them on their way home that night was the sight of people openly displaying emotion and shock on the streets. JFK's oratorical skills had captured both the American and Irish people and his words hit home with the Irish that they could dream of achieving anything, especially if the great-grandson of a poverty-stricken, famine-ravaged Irish immigrant could ascend to the highest office in the Land of the Free. Now that light was extinguished and all thoughts were with the American people and their fallen president.

As their relationship continued to develop, John realised three things: (i) he'd fallen for this little fire-cracker; (ii) he'd have to overcome some of his social awkwardness if he was to keep up with her; and (iii) although she had let him decide the destination of that first date, she had asserted herself since then and he'd have to accept being the passenger in this relationship.

Many men, particularly in that era, wouldn't be able to accept being anywhere but the driving seat, but John was different. He enjoyed not knowing what was around the corner, what mad idea Deirdre would have on any given night and knew, that if it was up to him, he'd stay on the well-trodden path of life. However, Deirdre was keen on going off-piste and he knew she'd test the boundaries, but not be reckless. In a way, this was the perfect combination of one person pushing the limits and the other ensuring those limits weren't pushed too far.

However, after two years dating, Deirdre, aged twenty by then, felt the need to take some time away from John. Deirdre

Johonny B. Goode

was open to change more so than John and was evolving from the person that jived with all her passion in O'Lehane Hall two years earlier. It wasn't a complete split in that they would still see each other regularly due to common friends, but their love was on hold.

John felt very low about the break-up. He wasn't thinking of marriage or happy ever after, but just so enjoyed her bubbly approach to life contrasting with her vulnerability and self-deprecation. In his eyes, she was the perfect package, but he had to try to come to terms with what he still hoped would be a temporary split. She had confided in him about her past and, given this was a closely guarded secret, he hoped that she had someone else to talk to when she felt low about those times.

John got back to a steadier social life and, through his work in CIÉ and subsequently RTÉ, he had made some good friends that would look after him as he came to terms with the split. He would never find another woman after that, nor would he seek one – he knew that Deirdre was a one-off and he was giving her the time to realise that he was also a unique catch.

It didn't take long. After about twelve months apart, their respective groups of friends were at the same dance and they spotted each other across the floor. At this dance, jiving was on the menu and, when a rock'n'roll song came on, for posterity, John walked over and asked Deirdre to dance. She said yes and it was like they were back in O'Lehane Hall with a crowd around them cheering their every move. John felt all the same feelings that were put on ice twelve months earlier and, to his surprise, Deirdre whispered in his ear afterwards, 'There's no one quite like you.'

Miss, Say Goodbye to Your Daughter

To which he responded, 'Who's talking, Miss Kelly?' And with that, they were back together and their time apart, whilst a struggle more so for John, turned out to have been just what was needed to make sure they had the chemistry to try to make it work long-term. And then, there was Giorgio …

Chapter Twenty-one

Giorgio

It was the mid-sixties. It was a few years before the era of love and peace was ushered in at Woodstock, but the seeds were being sewn for that time. The Beatles were in their pomp and this new wave of rock music was taking control. Gone were the days of ballads and polite crowds clapping their music heroes – in its place were mobs of people lauding their favourite musicians and fans fainting at the sight of a famous rock star. It was three years since the Beatles had played their one and only gig in Ireland, at the Adelphi Cinema on Middle Abbey Street, when John Lennon famously declared to a frenzied crowd, 'We're all Irish!' At the time, Liverpool, home of the Fab Four, had the highest Irish-born population after Dublin, Cork and Belfast. A sign, if ever one was needed, that Ireland was still suffering under post-war austerity, with emigration the only route for many of its young.

Deirdre, was working in NCR on South Circular Road near Saint James's Hospital and, although she was not quite reaching her potential from a career perspective, she was well respected in the office and in demand from the higher ups to carry out whatever administrative duties were required.

Notwithstanding her performance in the workplace, Deirdre continued to struggle with her confidence and found it difficult to play office politics – she was a straight talker and wasn't bothered with playing games to advantage herself over her colleagues. She had made some great friends through her various jobs to date and now, aged twenty-one, was planning a two-week summer trip abroad. Given how tight money was at the time, most holidays were taken in Ireland, but what was becoming increasingly popular in the 1960s was a trip to the 'sun'. Ireland was not known for its weather and trips to Spain, Italy and France were seen as an ideal opportunity to get away for a couple of weeks and soak up the guaranteed summer sun. Although relatively pale by nature, as most Irish people are, Deirdre had a penchant for sunbathing – whenever a warm day arrived in Dublin, she would be seen in the back garden of No. 12, lying back on the Kelly version of a deck chair, dressed in nothing more than a bikini, and taking in whatever rays were on offer.

With the advent of foreign holidays, Deirdre and three friends planned a fortnight getaway to Italy and, in the run-up to the trip, Deirdre couldn't have been more excited. This would be her first flight and she couldn't believe that she'd be seeing a new country, having only been off the island of Ireland once in her life, when the Kelly family headed to the Isle of Man for a week three years earlier.

Neither Deirdre nor her friends spoke any Italian, but that didn't put them off. 'Sure the Italians must speak English,' they thought to themselves.

Deirdre and John were still on their break in September 1966, as Deirdre headed to Dublin airport, and she thought

Giorgio

of the possibility of meeting a man, maybe an Italian man, on this holiday – always up for an adventure.

When Deirdre and her friends arrived in Rimini on the Adriatic coast of Italy, it was clear that European sun holidays were only in their infancy. The beach was stunningly beautiful, with soft fine white sand and azure blue waters, but the actual town was like a work-in-progress, with construction ongoing at almost every corner. However, the weather was fantastic and the gang spent most of their days at the beach, alternating between sunbathing on the sand in their skimpy bikinis and having a dip in the warm Adriatic Sea.

At night, the town came alive – as with most Latin cultures, it was customary for nights to start late and end very late. This town was no different and it wasn't until the sun was well on the way to the other side of the planet that the locals, and their transient visitors, would converge on the bars and clubs.

On the fourth night of the holiday, Deirdre and her friends had a quick bite to eat in one of the town's many trattorias and had a few drinks whilst sitting outside a nearby bar. The air was balmy and the ladies were wearing light summer dresses that fluttered in the gentle warm sea breeze. Although Irish people long for sallow skin, it's quite the opposite in Italy, where pale and unblemished skin is seen as pure and highly desirable. Hence, Deirdre and the gang were already attracting the interest of the local lads, who thoroughly enjoyed the infusion of energy brought by that summer's crop of visitors.

On that night, a group of four Italian men were drinking

Miss, Say Goodbye to Your Daughter

in the bar. One of them caught sight of Deirdre and was smitten at first glance. Deirdre looked up at the group of lads and saw this man looking at her – she immediately looked back at her group, then took another glance up, then back down to her friends and then let out a nervous giggle.

Her friends knew what was happening and it wasn't long before the lads came out onto the terrace to chat to this group of Irish innocents abroad. Their English was basic, the girls' Italian, after four days, was even less than that, so conversation between the eight of them was more by way of hand gestures and both sides attempting to talk their own language, but with an accent from the other country.

It made for a hilarious evening, but there was no doubt that the lad who had looked over at Deirdre earlier only had eyes for her. His name was Giorgio Albertini, he was in his late twenties and a pharmacist. If he was in Ireland, he would be described as suave, sophisticated and, most definitely, swarthy. His hair was jet black and parted to one side, with a little bit of length at the back and sides – the look gave him a hint of old-style Hollywood.

Deirdre had never seen such a man before and, despite not being able to understand each other, there was definitely mutual physical attraction.

The groups interacted for the next few hours and at 3 a.m. they said their goodbyes. With a few more hand gestures and a bit of writing times on beer mats, both parties agreed to meet up again the following night at the same bar.

As Deirdre got ready to go out that night, one of her friends, Jane, said, 'Giorgio was keen as mustard last night. Just be careful, as we don't know them and we've no idea

Giorgio

what they're talking about.' Jane was just looking out for her good friend and Deirdre appreciated the few words.

'He's gorgeous. I better brush up on my Italian,' said Deirdre, as her heart jumped with anticipation at meeting up with him later that night.

As agreed, both groups came to the bar around 11 p.m. and, after an initial awkward pause, Giorgio made his way over to Deirdre and they spent the next few hours half-talking, mostly laughing and having a few drinks to loosen the mood.

As the bar was closing, Giorgio intimated that he'd walk Deirdre back to the apartment. By then, and despite the earlier warnings to her friend, Jane had hooked up with one of Giorgio's friends, Matteo, and they were smooching behind a beachside tree.

Giorgio and Deirdre walked the ten minutes towards the apartment, holding hands, but still unable to properly talk. The common language of love was in the air, but neither had a clue how to properly communicate that specific language. In any event, outside the apartment, Giorgio gave Deirdre a passionate kiss, which was well received. The holiday romance would continue in that vein for the next week – quite innocent, but Deirdre really enjoyed the uniqueness of this place, the culture, the food, the people and having a lad such as Giorgio showering her with attention gave her a great boost of confidence.

On the day Deirdre and her friends were leaving, Giorgio and Matteo came to the apartment – they'd organised a minibus driver to bring the ladies to the airport. Giorgio and Deirdre were embracing outside the apartment, Jane and

Matteo were kissing like the world was ending outside the bus, with the other two Irish ladies sitting on the bus, looking at their watches and wondering would they make it to the airport in time for their flight.

After a few minutes, Giorgio and Deirdre said their goodbyes. '*Arrivederci amore mio. Sei così bella.*'

Deirdre had no idea what he was saying but was sure he was simply saying goodbye. Although she really enjoyed the attention he had given her over the previous week, she was happy to be going home, to see her little sister and to get back to normality after two weeks of madness.

All she could muster was, 'See you Giorgio. Be good,' and, after a quick kiss, the bus was on its way to Bologna and the flight back to rainy and cold Dublin.

By the time they got to the airport, her friends had come up with an obvious nickname for Deirdre's holiday beau – 'Gorgeous George' – how they laughed on the flight home, as they recounted the multitude of stories from the preceding two weeks.

Two months later, it was November 1966 and Deirdre and John were reunited following that catch-up dance the previous month. Deirdre was on her way back from work and, as it was a Friday, she stopped off at the local grocer's to pick up some coffee cake. By now, everyone in No. 12, including Ger, who was almost ten and growing up rapidly, loved a bit of coffee cake. Out of her wages each week, Deirdre would always try to get some treat or other on the way home from work and, with this week's tempting treat bagged, she strode quickly up Ebenezer Road in the light drizzle.

She opened the front door, took off her coat and burst into

Giorgio

the living room to show the family what this week's post-tea delectation would be. However, she immediately knew something was wrong when she looked straight at Ellen, who made eyes to her daughter to come into the scullery. Matty was still at work and Ger wasn't sure what was going on.

As Deirdre followed her mother into the scullery, Ellen closed the door and said, 'Some Italian fella is in the parlour. I think he's called George or something like that. What's going on? He's barely any English, but is waiting to see you.'

Ellen looked genuinely worried, as Deirdre hadn't shared any of her holiday exploits with her increasingly conservative mother.

Deirdre didn't know what to think. She had enjoyed the flirtation with Giorgio a couple of months earlier, but hadn't spent any time thinking about him since landing back in Dublin. She was back with John and everything was going well on that front.

'Christ, you mean he's in OUR parlour? Now?' exclaimed Deirdre, in hope that her mother was only joking.

Ellen, mindful of the mess she had ended up in twenty-two years before that, hoped that her eldest daughter wasn't in a similar pickle. 'Tell me you're not in trouble, Deirdre?' asked Ellen, more in hope than expectation.

'Of course not, Mammy. Jaysus, I better go in and see him.'

Roll back about nine hours. Giorgio had saved up some of his hard-earned cash from his job in the pharmacy and was sitting on his first flight from Bologna to Dublin. He had fallen for Deirdre in a big way following that brief romance in Rimini and was hell bent on declaring his love for her.

Miss, Say Goodbye to Your Daughter

In what was a radical decision for a generally sensible man, he felt compelled to get to Dublin to woo this Irish beauty. This was mad on a number of levels, but sense went out the window for Giorgio following those ten days of love in his homeland.

His only issue was that all he knew was Deirdre's full name and that her father worked in public transport. Although he had spent the previous couple of months working on his English, he still only had a basic grasp of the language and his Italian accent was so strong that even those few words were difficult to understand.

When he got to Dublin, he picked up a map from the tourist office at the airport and got the bus into the city. He then made his way to Busáras, Dublin's main intercity bus station, to see if he could find Deirdre's father.

After what seemed an eternity, and some phone calls by the helpful lady at reception, they somehow figured out that Giorgio was looking for Matty's daughter Deirdre and he was given the address of No. 12 Ebenezer Road.

He arrived there around 4 p.m. and, after knocking on the door, there was an east meets west scene of Ellen and Giorgio trying to communicate on the front doorstep, with a few locals looking on wondering what this well dressed, deeply tanned individual was doing in the Liberties.

'Me a Giorgio. Amo Deirdre. She house?' Ellen didn't know where to look or what to do. He could have been a missionary priest returned from Africa for all she knew, but the bronzed Adonis look gave him away. Eventually, after a few minutes of negotiations and broken English conversations, Ellen showed him into the parlour and gave

Giorgio

him some tea and biscuits to keep him content before Deirdre arrived home.

Deirdre made her way to the parlour and slowly opened the door. Giorgio jumped up, went over to hug Deirdre and then gave her a bunch of flowers he had bought in a florist he passed on the way to the house.

'*Ti amo e vorrei che tornassi in Italia con me.*'

Deirdre had no idea what he was saying, but it was clear that Giorgio meant business and was obviously interested in more than just tea and biscuits. What ensued was a pantomime scene in which Giorgio, in pidgin English, declared his undying love for Deirdre, Deirdre tried to get rid of him and Ellen and Ger eavesdropped from the hall.

About thirty minutes later, there was a knock at the front door. Ellen ran to the door immediately, as she guessed who it was. She opened the door to a smiling John – he was taking Deirdre out that night and looking forward to a few drinks after a long week's work.

John was brought directly into the living room and Ellen gave him the lowdown on the scene in the next room, followed by strict instructions. 'Will you look after Deirdre tonight? I'd be worried about that fella. I trust you to make sure nothing happens.'

This all sounded a bit bizarre to John – from the frantic words coming from Ellen, he garnered that his girlfriend had had a holiday romance with this Italian fella, but he was now being asked to effectively 'chaperone' his girlfriend and that man. John was fuming, but trying to do the right thing, agreed to make sure to look after Deirdre. After a few minutes, Deirdre came out of the parlour and into the living room to see John.

'It's not what it seems. Can we all just go out and he'll be on the first flight to Italy tomorrow?'

John was hopping mad at being put in this position, but appreciated that Ellen had implored him to look after Deirdre. The shuttle diplomacy continued, with Deirdre running from the parlour to the living room, trying to see if she could keep John onside, whilst being polite to Giorgio.

'Fine. But we need to talk about this,' responded John after Deirdre's third attempt to get him to come out.

However, more pantomime scenes were to follow. It was agreed that Deirdre, a few friends, John and Giorgio would go out in Dublin, to a club near where Giorgio was staying on Parnell Street. John and Deirdre never got the chance to properly talk about what was happening before they all went out and the night ended up like a farcical sketch: Giorgio still trying to woo Deirdre in broken English, Deirdre trying to deflect, her friends laughing at Giorgio, laughing at John, John trying to stop the wooing – all completely bizarre, but John was getting used to this type of insanity when with Deirdre. However, this was about twenty steps too far on his spectrum of acceptability and he had never been so embarrassed in all his life, with Deirdre's friends effectively mocking him for tolerating the situation.

'Jaysus John, I wouldn't be putting up with this. Are you a man or a mouse?' said one of the friends.

John, being a lover not a fighter, just wanted to get away from the scene entirely. However, Ellen's expressed concern earlier that evening, almost begging John to look after Deirdre, was foremost in his thoughts and he was a man of his word.

Giorgio

After the night out, Giorgio went back to his hotel, alone, and, less than twelve hours later, was in Dublin airport on his way back to Italy, never to be seen in Ireland again. They would laugh about that night over the years, but John always remembered how Ellen turned to him in that time of distress. He felt, from that moment, he was in the inner circle of the Kelly family, but it also gave him an insight into the strength of this mother's protective instinct for her daughter. Ellen had seen difficult times and, notwithstanding the 'crosses to bear' metaphor she spouted at regular intervals over the years, she would rather the cross hadn't been delivered in the first place.

Chapter Twenty-two

April 29th

Now that Giorgio was safely deposited back to Italy, the next couple of years went well for Deirdre and John. John was working in RTÉ, Ireland's state broadcaster, at what was a formative time for television broadcasting in Ireland. He worked in the library, that also covered the archives, which was a treasure trove of knowledge since the foundation of the Irish state. Deirdre was, by that time, working for an insurance practice, still mired in administration.

It was October 1967 and John brought Deirdre for a drive up the Dublin Mountains. It was a still clear evening and, as John pulled the car into a space, they had a perfect view over Dublin, with the city twinkling beneath them and the lights of incoming flights to Dublin airport flashing in the distance.

John turned to Deirdre. 'Deirdre, you know you mean the world to me. I would love it if you'd spend the rest of your life with me.'

Deirdre was excited and delighted in equal measure. 'If you're asking me to marry you, the answer is yes! But tell me you don't have the ring yet?' asked Deirdre. She had no issue with being surprised with the proposal, but she wanted to be

April 29th

the one to pick out her own ring. It was a low-key proposal, but that was exactly how Deirdre liked it – she wouldn't have wanted to be the centre of attention if he proposed in front of friends, family or even strangers.

Before the ring was bought from a jewellery wholesaler on Grafton Street, John wanted to formally ask Matty for his daughter's hand in marriage. Between Ellen and Deirdre, they organised for Matty and John to go to a pub on nearby Clanbrassil Street. John was a nervous wreck as he stood at the bar to get a couple of pints of Guinness. Under Deirdre's tutelage, John had started to have the odd drink.

When he brought the drinks to the table, he sat down and blurted it out rather clumsily. 'Mr Kelly, I'd like to ask you, I mean, ask you and Mrs Kelly, for Deirdre's hand in marriage. Is that all right?'

Matty replied in his typical relaxed and deadpan style, 'If you're looking for my approval to marry Deirdre, you have it. Sláinte.' He lifted his pint and invoked the Irish language version of 'To Your Health' or simply 'Cheers'.

After another pint each, they walked back to No. 12, where it was all smiles – Ellen was delighted for Deirdre and she had a soft spot for 'Johnny', as she was calling him by then. Matty, wearing a broad grin, lifted another pint of Guinness to toast the happy couple – he had a sense of understanding of how Deirdre felt as she came back to the house aged nine and this impending marriage was validation, in his mind, of his decision to adopt her and give her as normal a second half to her childhood as he could.

After the engagement came the planning for the big day. Any wedding brings up tensions, some between the would-be spouses, some between siblings and some between the two families party to this union. This one was no different, but the most challenging issue was whether the day would be subject to the usual religious pomp and ceremony of an Irish wedding. Deirdre hadn't attended church since she was fourteen and was keen to have a relatively low-key event. Part of her thought about the idea of a registry office wedding with John, but neither family would put up with that. The Kellys' first wedding and the O'Neills' only son's big day would not pass with a clinical visit to the Dublin Registrar.

The wedding date was initially fixed for March. However, fate intervened, and the arrival of John's second nephew from his eldest sister meant that the wedding was rescheduled for Tuesday, 29 April 1969. In the final few days before the wedding, there was much emotion, including Ellen remembering to herself her aborted wedding plans with Joe and Deirdre knowing that her biological father wouldn't be present. On the other hand, Deirdre had such a strong bond with Matty and her delight at asking him to give her away on the day was only matched by the pride he felt being asked to take on that role. He had risked his relationship with his own family when he took on Ellen and Deirdre, but he never once thought he had made the wrong decision. Now his little Deirdre was close to flying the nest, a few fatherly words of advice were dispensed.

'Deirdre, I can't believe you'll be married in a few days. Are you nervous?'

'Maybe a little bit, but not about being married. More about the day and being the centre of attention. As you know Daddy, I don't like photos,' replied Deirdre.

April 29th

'Let me tell you something. You're a beautiful girl inside and out. Photos only show what's outside, but we know what's inside there,' he said as he pointed to her heart.

'Ah Daddy, you'll have me in tears. Just make sure you walk fast up that aisle.'

Matty was well known for his meandering gait, but he was under strict instructions from his eldest to practically run up to the altar. On the photo front, Deirdre insisted that there would be no official photographer for the day, meaning the only pictures taken were by family and friends.

In those final few days, No. 12 was a buzz of activity. Ellen was tasked with making all the dresses, including Deirdre's classical white dress, one bridesmaid dress for Jane and two flower girl dresses for Ger and John's youngest sister, Yvonne. On the day before the wedding, Deirdre had a mini-meltdown after she tried to trim a little bit of her hair and went fractionally too far, but Ellen jumped in and sorted it. After that moment, Deirdre took a short walk with Ger to get out of the pressure cooker.

As they walked past Oscar Square, Deirdre caught sight of Grace, her former classmate, at the playground with her nephew and niece. Deirdre had heard that Grace had graduated from UCD a few years earlier and had a job in the civil service – she couldn't help comparing her humdrum administrative career to high-flying Grace. If only she had had the capacity to stay in school for a few more years, maybe she could have been like her. In the few seconds that Grace was in her sight, Deirdre observed that the years had been kind to her that she still carried herself well. 'Maybe, someday, people might say the same about me,' said Deirdre

Miss, Say Goodbye to Your Daughter

to herself. She then turned to Ger, who was a very excited younger sister who couldn't wait for the following day. 'Let's go get an ice-cream.' The two of them went to Black's shop near Donore Avenue Church.

On the morning of the wedding, Deirdre woke early and the waft of bacon was coming up the stairs and into her and Ger's room – Ellen was treating the four of them to a cooked breakfast to line the stomachs for what would be a long day. Deirdre came down and, although words were at a premium around the table, the looks exchanged between parents and eldest daughter were enough to confirm that pride was the order of the day – it was a rocky enough road to this point, but this day was when the 'never give up' human spirit was on full show and they all knew it.

The ceremony was scheduled for 11 a.m. and, after having her hair done, Deirdre went upstairs to get into her dress. By 10.45 a.m., she was ready. As she came out of her room, Matty was making his way from the living room into the hall and to the bottom of the stairs. He looked up to the top of the sixteen steps and there stood a vision.

As Deirdre walked down the stairs and got closer to Matty, his eyes filled up. Both knew this would be an emotional moment, but her radiance and beauty, and the confidence with which she took each step, blew Matty away. Suddenly, the enormity of the fact that this was the last time his daughter would leave this house as a single woman hit Matty. He gave her a big hug and just said, 'Wow, Deirdre, you look simply beautiful.'

Deirdre's dress was stunning. It was a fitted dress, with Mandarin collar, lace trimming and a relatively short train.

April 29th

Deirdre wore a short veil and held a small bouquet of yellow and white flowers.

Deirdre was trying to keep the tears to a minimum for fear of the damage it would do to her make-up, but the significance of the moment was there for all to see. After a few moments of fixing the dress and veil, Ger opened the door and they all stepped into the sunlight. As was tradition in communities such as the Liberties, the neighbours gathered outside the front gate of No. 12 to grab a glimpse of the beautiful bride-to-be and take a few snaps. One of the party took a picture front on of Deirdre linking arms with Matty and his proud wide smile was a picture in itself. Ellen herself, who was more focused on the logistics of the wedding than emotions to that point, had a warm smile on her face and was bursting with happiness for Deirdre, and for John too, who was nervously waiting in Saint Teresa's Church for the arrival of his bride.

A plush car was arranged to bring Deirdre and Matty on the short journey to the church and she gripped his hand white-knuckle style all the way there. As they emerged from the car outside the church, more photos were taken and then came the moment Deirdre was dreading – the walk up the aisle with every eye focused on her, her dress, her hair, her make-up. 'Right Daddy, let's get this done,' she said, as if preparing to face mortal combat. Matty, as relaxed as ever by now, and fitting nicely into the role of father of the bride, linked her arm into his and held her hand as they started the journey up the aisle. With her petite stature, Deirdre looked fantastic in anything she wore, but her mother had gone above and beyond when she created the dress. There were gasps from the guests as father and daughter made their way up the

Miss, Say Goodbye to Your Daughter

aisle and, after what seemed like an eternity to Deirdre, they got to the top. John turned around and, with emotion all over his face, shook Matty's hand firmly and then took his fiancée up to the altar to meet the then parish priest, Fr Conlon. John looked like the cat that got the cream – he'd no idea how he managed to snaffle this woman and knew that this adventure was only really beginning.

They were both ecstatic as they exchanged vows, shared a kiss and turned around to the cheers of their guests. It reminded them both of the cheers they had received after that first dance in O'Lehane Hall and this wedding day was a wonderful bookend to that first encounter.

The wedding reception, held in the Camelot Hotel, Coolock, was a usual Irish affair – a mix of family feuds, some drunken guests, even some guests who weren't invited but came along as they thought the invitation was lost in the post. The speeches were short, the craic was mighty and the music went on until late in the night. As was tradition, the wedding couple left the reception relatively early to go on honeymoon – Deirdre and John had booked to go to Mallorca.

On the day after they arrived, they got chatting to another honeymoon couple from the south coast of England – they buddied up for the rest of their time there and, as with all things Deirdre, got up to mischief. One night, Deirdre decided to have a different drink in each bar they went into in Palma, which turned into a pub crawl for about eight hours. They staggered back to the hotel room around 3 a.m. and legend has it that the bathroom had to be re-decorated after Deirdre paid a visit in the middle of the night. Of course, John was more sensible than that, but he couldn't help but

April 29th

admire Deirdre's ability to get into situations, then dust herself down and get ready for the next adventure.

Later that year, Deirdre and John moved into a new house in Shankill, Co. Dublin and, more importantly, just before their first married Christmas, announced they were expecting a baby the following summer. The expectant first-time parents were so excited about this news, but Ellen and Matty were also overjoyed at the prospect of being grandparents – they would be fifty-five and fifty-nine respectively when the baby arrived and both felt they had plenty of energy to chase a nipper around. Ger was also over the moon at becoming an aunt at the relatively young age of thirteen. 1969 was quite the year and Deirdre and John toasted the future in their new home on New Year's Eve – for once, a quiet evening in was preferred to a raucous night in town.

Chapter Twenty-three

Family

Apart from second trimester tiredness, the pregnancy went by relatively smoothly and, on the morning of 9 June 1970, Deirdre turned to John. 'John, I think the baby is coming. I can feel contractions.'

'Jaysus, Deirdre, what'll we do?' John, known for being relatively calm under pressure, suddenly went into a headless chicken routine. He forgot where the car keys were, where his coat was, where the front door was – he was running frenetically around the house, whilst Deirdre just stood there waiting for him to regain his composure.

Eventually, some sense returned and they jumped in the car – then John realised he had left her suitcase in the hall. He jumped back out of the car, grabbed the suitcase and got back into the car. He drove like a man possessed to the Coombe Hospital on Cork Street, only a short walk from Ebenezer Road, and, when they got there, John rushed around to help Deirdre out of the passenger seat. He then went to the boot of the car to retrieve the suitcase only to realise that he couldn't open it – it was jammed and, electing to leave it for the moment, he walked into the hospital to check Deirdre in.

John was then banished from the delivery area – in

Family

those days, fathers were not welcome to see the arrival of their children and would generally find out by telephone. In John's case, he returned to the car and brought it to a local garage, who were able to jemmy the boot open so that John could bring the suitcase to the hospital. He then went over to Ballybough to await news of the next generation.

After a mammoth thirty-six hours in labour, Andrew John O'Neill was delivered safely – he weighed seven pounds ten ounces and, after news filtered through to Ballybough, John was so happy to hear of the safe arrival of his new son. He made his way across to the Coombe to be united with Deirdre and baby Andrew, but not before he called by No. 12.

'Mr and Mrs Kelly, you're grandparents to a little boy, Andrew. They're both doing great, but Deirdre's a bit tired after a long labour,' said John.

'Ah Johnny, we're delighted for both of you and can't wait to meet him. Give them both a big hug from us.' said Ellen, after which she gave John a maternal hug.

Matty was grinning from ear to ear and promised to wet the baby's head with John over the next few days. A truly happy day, albeit the new mum was exhausted and couldn't imagine having any more children after that experience.

The next few years were more challenging for the O'Neill family. Some money troubles, predominantly brought about by John trying to keep up with the Joneses and ultimately overspending behind Deirdre's back, meant that they were forced to sell the Shankill House and rent a bedsit for a while, resulting in Andrew having to stay with Ellen and Matty for the best part of a year. The parallels between Andrew's start to life and the early years endured by Deirdre in Newtownforbes were obvious, if a little unfair, but, whilst Ellen and Matty loved having their only grandchild in the house with them and created an indelible bond with him during that period, Deirdre and John were suffering with guilt for not being able to live with their first child for a period when he was so young.

With John being the breadwinner for the family, he felt very low for letting down Deirdre and Andrew and not being able to give them the life he felt they deserved. But Deirdre was greatly affected on two levels by these events. Firstly, the guilt of having to place her only child in the temporary care of others brought her mind straight back to those days in Newtownforbes, when she herself was the child abandoned – she had many sleepless nights thinking about how history could be repeating itself and what she could do to get out of this predicament. Secondly, she felt let down by John and his reckless overspending – if she couldn't have full trust in him, then what did she have? Although she was not in possession of the full facts, it resurrected thoughts of her biological father and his apparent disregard for his unborn child. 'What have I done to deserve this treatment from those meant to protect me?' she thought to herself. Those 'slings and arrows' of life were creating turmoil for Deirdre and she wasn't sure if she had the courage to get to the far side of those issues.

A turning point came when John returned to their bedsit following a visit to his own parents in Ballybough. He was fuming, as his parents knew the issues he and Deirdre were experiencing but they never once asked him how he was. It wasn't that they didn't care, but, for some reason, they couldn't find the words to offer support to their only son at his time of need. 'Deirdre, I know you're the victim in this,

Family

but I'm really struggling. Without knowing that we're in this together, I don't think anyone else has my back,' said John, with an air of despondency that Deirdre hadn't witnessed from him before.

In survival mode to that point, it clicked with her that John was also having great difficulty coming to terms with his separation from Andrew. 'John, you've hurt me a lot, but I know you're feeling it too. If we can rely on each other, then we have something,' said Deirdre, empathising with John's emotions. That realisation enabled them, over the succeeding period, to discuss their respective feelings more fully and they jointly sought a way to navigate those troubled times.

After they got back on their feet financially, John, Deirdre and Andrew moved to a house in a suburb in southwest Dublin, Tallaght. At that time, Tallaght was long on houses and short on everything else, including shops and buses. Every morning, John would head for work, taking their only car and leaving behind Deirdre and Andrew. Deirdre gave up her work to look after Andrew and felt trapped in their house in Old Bawn, with her only release being a walk to the local shop with Andrew in his buggy. It was a reasonably bare existence for the O'Neill family in those early years and John could sense that Deirdre's spark and adventurous personality were waning. Then, in early 1973, came more news that would either lift Deirdre's spirits or push her deeper into the hole that this form of living was causing – she was pregnant and their second child was due that August.

On 9 August 1973, Deirdre and John took delivery of

Miss, Say Goodbye to Your Daughter

Stephen Matthew O'Neill – the middle name being out of respect for Matty. Despite the challenges of the previous few years, Deirdre and John were over the moon with the safe arrival of No. 2.

To her friends and family, Deirdre did her best to put on a brave front, but behind closed doors, it was obvious to John that the combination of two young children and living in an area so underserved by public amenities was having a significant impact on her. John vowed to double down and figure out a way in which they could move to a better area. 'I know it's only words, but I will get us away from this area. I promise you that,' said John, knowing that this was not the existence either of them wanted for their fledgling family.

Then, in 1974, there were two significant and positive changes for the family. In April, they sold the house in Tallaght and moved to a new estate called Clonard, between Dundrum and Sandyford villages, in south Dublin. No. 23 Clonard Heights, a typical 1970s semi-detached four-bed house, would become the 'real' O'Neill family home and this move was matched by the news that John was changing jobs and getting an effective promotion. He was joining the ESB, the semi-state entity charged with electricity generation and distribution in Ireland, which meant more money coming into the house just when they needed it most. As Clonard was a new estate, pretty much every house was bought by young families, which led to an endless supply of children for Andrew and Stephen to play with. Coupled with a large park less than five minutes' walk from the house, it made for a superb place to bring up children and there were also Dundrum and Stillorgan shopping centres close by. There

Family

was an abundance of schools to choose from, which wasn't lost on Deirdre and John as they both placed huge importance on the nature and longevity of education, something which neither of them quite got right in their younger years.

From those early years in Clonard, one day stood out to Deirdre more than any other. It was a normal day in winter 1974. John went to work and Deirdre dropped Andrew to school in Dundrum, where he was in junior infants. She was looking after Stephen at home, when the doorbell rang followed by what seemed a panicked knock on the door. Deirdre dashed to the front door and, when she opened it, it was a neighbour from around the corner, Daphne, with her baby son, Colin, in her arms. Daphne was in tears and Deirdre was struggling to understand what was wrong. 'I can't do it, I can't do it anymore,' was all that she could make out, as Daphne shook uncontrollably. Deirdre helped Daphne into the kitchen.

'What's wrong, Daphne?'

Daphne and her husband Gerry moved into Clonard a few months before Deirdre and John and both young mothers hit it off when they bumped into each other in Ballawley Park over the summer of 1974. In those early months in Clonard, they'd regularly share morning teas and a couple of fags.

Daphne opened up to Deirdre that she was struggling with 'baby blues', albeit her male GP was reluctant to formally diagnose post-natal depression and adopted a 'pull yourself together' approach to her condition. Deirdre kept a close eye on her friend over the next few months and thought she was showing positive signs.

Daphne was still in a state of panic as Deirdre handed

her a cup of tea to calm her nerves. Her hand was shaking uncontrollably. 'They're going to take him away from me ... the doctor doesn't believe me ... they can't do it ... he's everything to me!'

'We won't let that happen, Daphne. I know what a great mother you are,' said Deirdre in an affirmative tone.

Daphne replied, 'Social Services are calling this morning ... I'm afraid they think I'm a useless mother ... they can't take him from me ... I can't get in touch with Gerry!'

Unfortunately, Gerry couldn't be contacted, as his work as a quantity surveyor meant he was on some building site or other. It was up to Deirdre to try and help her friend. Daphne was clearly in a frenzy and Deirdre had no idea if her thoughts on why Social Services were calling were an over the top reaction to a system surely designed to protect the integrity of the family, or was there something real behind her concerns.

On their almost daily catch-ups since they moved into Clonard, Daphne articulated that herself and Gerry had found it difficult to have a baby and maybe that naturally strong desire to have children caused Daphne to be more anxious with her newborn. Or possibly, Daphne was suffering from symptoms common to first-time mothers of feeling like they're failures and without any supportive state institutions to turn to for help in those days. In the six months since they first met, Deirdre and John remarked to themselves that Daphne and Gerry were the most genuine, down-to-earth couple you could ever wish to meet, simply adored their baby and made for a beautiful family on walks the three of them would take.

Family

Deirdre's protective instinct, something that was simmering since her days looking out for the younger ones in Newtownforbes, kicked in. Over the next two hours, she shuttled between phone calls to various authorities and the kitchen soothing Daphne. It turned out that the doctor recommended to Social Services that they visit the house, talk to Daphne and Gerry, and then decide on the best course of action, which could range from regular visits from the district nurse to the child being temporarily taken into care, with that extreme scenario being a rarity. None of this was articulated to Daphne in those direct conversations with her GP, but her maternal instinct kicked in and she was right to be concerned about what the doctor might do.

At lunchtime, the district nurse called to the O'Neill house, chatted to Daphne and shared her concerns with Deirdre. Ultimately, Social Services recommended that the family unit be kept intact and, against the recommendation of the local GP, Daphne was prescribed with anti-depressants for a short period and never looked back.

After the maelstrom of the preceding three hours, Deirdre walked to Dundrum to pick Andrew up from school. She put on a calm face for her eldest, but when she got home, a flood of emotions hit her. The risk, even if remote, of Daphne and Gerry losing their child dredged up memories for Deirdre of the sense of rejection she felt at times in Newtownforbes, but it also gave her an insight into what must have been going through Ellen's mind as she handed her two-year-old child into care, with nobody to turn to for advice and very few shoulders to cry on. 'Why did I have to live in the home for so long? Why could I only see my mother a few times a year? Why are mothers forced to give up their children?' were all questions racing around Deirdre's head. Then she thought of how lucky she was to be taken out of that home and brought back to a loving house in Dublin, where she had the opportunity to become a big sister to Ger. There were so many conflicting emotions in Deirdre's head and what happened in Clonard Heights that day showed her that those feelings were always close to the surface.

Later that afternoon, she sat down on the sofa, closed her eyes and the depth of sadness she felt was difficult to take. Sadness for what her mother was forced to endure, sadness for what was denied to her during the first part of her life and, still, she had no real answers as to why it all happened. The left side of her brain steeled herself to call down to Ebenezer Road and try and force some more details from Ellen, but the other side of her mind empathised with her mother – this conflict was enough to have Deirdre weeping sorrowfully as the afternoon hours passed by. Her thoughts that the ordeal that Daphne just went through could easily have been avoided through institutions that should have put the mother at the heart of their care were reflected back to how Ellen was treated by similar institutions almost thirty years earlier.

When John came home from work that evening, he walked in and was greeted by Andrew with his cheeky happy smile. However, he noticed that Deirdre wasn't in the living room with the two boys. He went into the kitchen and there she was sobbing at the table. When he got to the bottom of what was wrong, he was the one soothing her like she had done for Daphne a few hours earlier. 'It's all right, Deirdre, you did your best for Daphne and she'll have appreciated it,'

Family

said John, trying to empathise with the emotions his wife was experiencing.

Deirdre felt such a strong urge to help her friend in her hour of need, but it clearly took its toll. As Deirdre lay down to sleep that night, she could only imagine the torment that was going through Daphne's head and, although Deirdre was not one to pray, she said to herself that she hoped Daphne and Gerry would get through this difficult period and maybe, in time, could have more children.

Less than twelve months later, Daphne and Gerry had a baby girl and were blessed with two more sons over the succeeding five years. Daphne and Gerry made great parents to their four children, who were brought up in a loving house by two of the nicest people Deirdre and John ever met, two people that had the bravery to grow their family despite the challenging period with their firstborn. Although they were different kinds of people, Daphne, the country girl with traditional ways, and Deirdre, the city slicker with modern views on all topics, these two mothers shared the difficult memory of that day and had a permanent bond after that.

As regards the conflict of head and heart on whether she should push Ellen for more information on her biological father, in this instance, Deirdre opted to hold fire. She discussed her desire to have more information with John and, with his open and modern approach to life, he was on the side of probing her mother. Although Deirdre couldn't quite articulate it to John, that need for information was balanced by a fear of what she might discover if she found out who her father was. 'Is he still alive? If he is, will he reject me like he did before I was even born?' were the type of questions she had. Brought about by those negative feelings of self that were engendered by almost eight years in the home, the fear of rejection was an almost overwhelming emotion in Deirdre's head and she felt she couldn't face the risk of being abandoned once again by her biological father.

For the O'Neill family, summer holidays were vitally important to spend time with each other and to experience something different – for Andrew and Stephen, those holidays were a thrill ride. Deirdre and John believed in the 'Drive Drive' holiday concept and stories of those summer adventures were countless:

- In 1979, there were two weeks in Donegal and Sligo. The last part of the holiday was in Mullaghmore, Co. Sligo at the same time that Queen Elizabeth's cousin, Lord Louis Mountbatten, was assassinated off the coast of that seaside village. It was a horrific incident, with responsibility ultimately claimed by the IRA, a pro-united Ireland terrorist organisation. This unusual end to the holiday gave Andrew and Stephen a sense of what might be to come.

- In 1980 and 1981, Deirdre and John decided to get more exotic and the family holiday was more of a 'Ferry Drive' to the 'Continent' for driving trips around Europe. 1981 was an extended three-week holiday, which essentially involved a ten-day road trip for one or two nights by the Adriatic Sea and then ten days driving back to Ireland. The highlight was an attempt to get behind the Iron Curtain after Deirdre convinced border guards to let the boys walk

Family

one hundred metres into Czechoslovakia.

- In 1982, they had an actual 'Fly Drive' holiday to Canada and the US for John's sister's wedding. This was a complete change for the boys, with highlights being the wedding day, the boys playing Atari with their Canadian cousins and a day trip into Manhattan to meet one of John's cousins – a complete eye opener for the O'Neill family, which ended with a late night stop at Tommy Makem's traditional Irish bar on East 57th Street.

- In 1986, a 'business trip' for John to Silicon Valley, California was combined with the family holiday. Although John's job was covering some of the cost of the holiday, Deirdre wanted to do her bit to contribute. She spent June and July that year knitting mohair multi-coloured jumpers and packed one suitcase full of them for the trip. Then, on the second day of the holiday, the family were loaded into the car and drove to the affluent village of Burlingame. Deirdre found a craft shop on the main street and, thirty minutes later, she came out with a fistful of dollars, having sold the job lot of jumpers to the shop owner. Deirdre was delighted to have some cash to splash on the holiday and demonstrated her ingenuity at creating something from nothing.

They were great times for the O'Neill family that provided memories for the boys and their parents, to be treasured and recounted for decades to come.

Chapter Twenty-four

Das Kapital

Das Kapital is a foundational theoretical text in materialist philosophy, economics and politics by Karl Marx. In summary, the book calls into question the motivations behind capitalism and theorises a better way of operating an economy based around the principles of collectivism and the strength of the labour class. Parts of Marxist theories were the foundation stones for communism, as practised by Russia following the 1917 Revolution.

Deirdre had never read the entire text of that book, but her background in the home gave her a socialist leaning, a desire to see the underprivileged and labour classes treated in a fairer way. Essentially, she believed in a more equitable wealth distribution than was the case under an unfettered market economy. Going back sixty years or so, and before Ireland secured its independence from Britain, the 1913 Lockout, led by Big Jim Larkin, was a general strike called by unions in defence of the labour classes. This strike led to the foundation of the Labour Party, a left-leaning socialist democratic political party, the views of which Deirdre connected with, and, in 1977, she went to a Labour Party public meeting in Sandyford. The purpose of the meeting was

Das Kapital

to discuss the party's opposition to the introduction of a rates system on households. As the speakers went through their rallying calls, Deirdre immediately felt they were speaking her language and she went up afterwards to chat through some of their points. She felt at home in their company and signed up as a member of the party a couple of weeks later.

That started an almost forty-year relationship with the Labour Party, but that didn't mean that Deirdre was taken in by everything that the party espoused. She always called it as she saw it and, at a party conference in the mid-1980s, she was removed from the hall for speaking out against what she believed were overly centrist policies by the party. When she got home from the conference, she recounted the weekend's events to John, with the two boys listening to every word. 'Sure, I had to speak up. Spring has gone too far towards the centre,' said Deirdre bullishly, in reference to then party leader Dick Spring.

John was proud of Deirdre's desire to stand up for what she believed in, no matter the consequences – he could also see the passion she had for those topics and this gave him a sense that she was finding her own feet and had a platform to express her opinions. To the boys, Deirdre was their mother, but, even at that young age, it imbued them with a belief that authority was there to be questioned.

Another example of Deirdre's politicisation was the Campaign for Nuclear Disarmament (CND) movement that she, and the entire family, joined in the early 1980s. At the time, there was an existential threat to humanity through the proliferation of nuclear weapons and, on a trip to London in 1983, she brought the family to meet the Greenham

Common women, who were protesting against US nuclear missiles being stored at a British army base. Deirdre also campaigned vociferously on the pro choice side of the 1983 abortion referendum and on the pro divorce side of the 1986 referendum. Her views were defeated on both of those occasions – however, this only motivated her more towards working to change the system and she was pleased when divorce finally won the support of the Irish people in a second referendum in 1996 and the Eighth Amendment on abortion was repealed in 2018. Deirdre's progressive views were brave and didn't always sit well with some of her family and friends. She often had heated debates with Ellen and Matty on those issues – however, she believed strongly in her core principles of fairness and equality and would stick to those beliefs no matter the consequences.

A spin-off from Deirdre's activeness in the late 1970s and early 1980s was a lobby group called Challenge, which she established to seek changes to the Irish taxation and social welfare system to deal with what Deirdre felt were the lack of supports for stay-at-home parents, predominantly mothers. Deirdre was energised on the topic, but, given that this passion wasn't matched by the hierarchy in the Labour Party, she set up the lobby group and met with several politicians of all hues. She successfully persuaded Mary Robinson, a barrister with a socialist background, and John Kelly, a Fine Gael member of parliament, to take a pro bono case against the State for perceived inequality and discrimination embedded in the tax and social welfare legislation at the time. Ultimately, that case was shelved due to a Commission on Taxation being considered at the time, but, not for the first time, those views finally came into vogue with changes to the tax system, similar to what Deirdre had been advocating, introduced in 2001, some twenty years later.

It was possibly luck that Deirdre's views on topics ranging from abortion and divorce to the tax and welfare system were ultimately adopted by the political middle ground twenty or thirty years later. Society often catches up with progressives eventually. However, Deirdre was a deep thinker and her views were not formed without carefully analysing the pros and cons. When the Irish people voted overwhelmingly to support the right to marriage for same-sex couples in 2015, Deirdre was thrilled – this was not a cause she had specifically fought for thirty years earlier, but, to her, it was another example of her country and people growing up and away from the post-independence Church-dominated era.

From a family perspective, her two children became enthused with politics when Deirdre brought them to Labour Party envelope stuffing nights, to marches against rates and to polling centres to hand out leaflets. It was unusual for children to be interested in politics, but that was the house they were brought up in – a house where views on any topic could be discussed around the kitchen table and where the political or social goings on locally, nationally and internationally were ripe for debate. An example of that was Sunday 11 February 1990. John was cooking the usual roast chicken dinner and Deirdre and the boys were summoned down as the food was being served.

'Change of plan today, kids,' said John, to the surprise of Andrew and Stephen. 'We're having dinner in front of the TV. I want you to see something very special.'

Miss, Say Goodbye to Your Daughter

The boys were intrigued, as they sat down in the lounge. John continued, 'This is the end of Nelson Mandela's long walk to freedom. This is what the black people have been fighting for. We're witnessing history.' The boys knew about apartheid and were tangentially aware that Mandela had been incarcerated for a long time. As the footage unfolded on the TV, the family soaked it in and all were aware that global change was happening right in front of them, especially coming three months after the fall of the Berlin Wall.

For all elections and referenda, Deirdre would pound the streets of the Dublin South constituency. She would often bump into people from her past on the doorsteps, but one of those serendipitous moments occurred during the 1983 abortion referendum. It was in Ardglas, an upmarket scheme of houses near Dundrum Village and generally not seen as either a haven for Labour Party supporters or, in this case, supporters of Deirdre's views on a morally sensitive topic such as abortion. Deirdre elected that night to take one for the team and headed into Ardglas for a solo tilt at converting some of those residents to her way of thinking. She knocked on about ten houses and, to that point, was met with no answer, a polite 'no thank you' to her views or, in one instance, a vehement constituent that felt a pro choice stance would lead to a fundamental breakdown in Irish society. She trudged onto the next house, but was already looking forward to heading to Balally, a housing estate across the road with a reasonable cohort of more liberal constituents. She rang the bell and, to her surprise, a familiar face opened the door – it was Grace, her former classmate from Weaver Square. After a few seconds of her opening spiel, Deirdre recognised her,

Das Kapital

especially from the way she still carried herself, with elegance and poise. However, in self-defence and not wanting to have to re-introduce herself to someone that should know her, Deirdre ploughed on with the pitch only to be rebuffed, but, this time, with respect for this canvasser's perspective. As the door was closing, Deirdre contemplated calling out the past connection to Grace, but chose to just move on to the next house.

That night, after wearing out her shoe leather calling to more than one hundred houses, Deirdre walked into the house with a heavy heart. This was partly due to the negative feedback she was receiving on the doorsteps, which would make it exceptionally difficult for the referendum to be defeated, but also because of a tinge of jealousy towards Grace – she lived in a nicer house, looked prettier, was more elegant and, most probably, had a successful career given her educational background and her starting job in the civil service. The green-eyed monster is not a pleasant trait in anyone, but Deirdre was probably more jealous of the opportunities that were afforded to people like Grace. Deirdre was happy with her family life, but that hankering for the next life challenge was always there. She was also frustrated at her fear of striking up a peer-to-peer conversation with Grace that evening, which was in stark contrast to the personality traits that would push her to passionately rally behind many causes throughout her life. It further highlighted to her that she felt unequal to Grace, and her kind, and this compounded her low self-esteem. She didn't impart any of this to John, but, as they were going to bed, noted that, 'Middle-class Ireland is not yet ready to take on abortion, John, but I'll soldier on.'

Miss, Say Goodbye to Your Daughter

One final connection to the Labour Party was the 1990 Irish presidential campaign. In this election, the two main protagonists were Fianna Fáil's Brian Lenihan, a former Minister for Foreign Affairs, and Austin Currie, a Northern Irish civil rights campaigner nominated by Fine Gael. There was a third candidate, Mary Robinson, whom Deirdre had canvassed about her lobby group some years earlier, nominated by the Labour Party – however, she trailed the other two candidates significantly as the campaign revved up. In a twist of events mid-campaign, Lenihan tripped up in an interview on whether he had sought to influence President Hillery in 1982 on a decision to dissolve parliament. This left a possible route to victory for Mary Robinson, as Austin Currie's campaign had never got out of the blocks. Deirdre campaigned vociferously in her local area and was bolstered by the fact that the candidate was a woman, the first time a woman had contested a presidential election. On Friday 9 November 1990, Mary Robinson was declared victorious and there was a scene in a hotel in Waterford that night, with Deirdre, never known as a singer in her own right, leading a chorus of 'Here's to you, Mrs Robinson.' President Robinson was inaugurated the following month and noted the importance of women in her speech:

> As a woman, I want women who have felt themselves outside history to be written back into history, in the words of Eavan Boland, 'finding a voice where they found a vision'.

Deirdre was beyond happy that, for the first time in the history of the state, a Labour Party candidate had won a

Das Kapital

nationwide election. However, she also understood the importance of a woman being that person and it felt like a watershed moment to her. In many ways it was, but Deirdre also knew that women's rights still had a long way to go and this victory only emboldened her towards that goal.

Deirdre was also well aware of Mary Robinson's tireless work on behalf of unmarried mothers and their illegitimate children, when, in 1974, she sought, with the assistance of her fellow senator John Horgan, to introduce legislation that would treat illegitimate children as equals to those born in wedlock. In her speech to the Irish Senate introducing the Bill, she said:

> Children born out of wedlock are discriminated against in that they do not have succession rights to their father's property; in that their family relationship is not given full recognition and protection, and in that they are burdened with the social stigma implied in being called illegitimate.

Political pragmatism didn't permit that legislation to progress beyond the Senate, but this groundwork and Mary Robinson's role with Cherish, a lobby group for unmarried mothers and their children, ultimately led to the abolition of the status of illegitimacy in 1987.

Deirdre certainly had politics to keep herself busy in those years, but one other 'pastime' entered the equation in the late 1970s and one that would keep Deirdre and John both amused over the years – bridge. In 1979, Deirdre and John decided to take up the card game in a local club in Ballinteer and this would be the 'thing' they would share as a couple for almost forty years. The intricacies of bridge are numerous, but it generally requires two partners who know each other exceptionally well, such that they can read the other's intentions from their bids. John, not surprising given his occupation as a librarian, was conservative and structured in his bidding, so Deirdre could generally read his moves quite well. Deirdre, on the other hand, was a risk taker and could take a flyer bid at times based on gut instinct and based on the bids she was hearing from around the table. This was a dream mix of John ensuring that Deirdre didn't lose the run of herself and Deirdre encouraging John to step out of his comfort zone, much like their relationship since the early 1960s. Bridge gave them a reason to travel and to spend time together away from the family home, as they also arranged numerous bridge trips with friends and acquaintances to places such as England, Spain and Turkey. As a reflection of her low level of self-confidence, Deirdre would never want to know how they were doing during a game, as it might put her off as the evening progressed and she always thought they were doing worse than they were – a strange perception given they often won big competitions and both ultimately progressed to being masters, but another sign that Deirdre didn't have enough self-belief in her talents.

Despite her lack of formal education, politics and bridge gave Deirdre the opportunity to display her natural intellect, but her work life still didn't match up to those highs. Having returned to part-time work in the late 1970s, she worked in accountancy practices, loss adjusters, solicitors and engineering practices. At one stage, she spent around six months without a job, which was not uncommon given the

Das Kapital

deep recession Ireland experienced at the time, but it got to Deirdre that the years were flying by and the possibility to realise her potential was maybe slipping away. John encouraged her to take an assertiveness course, as maybe that would allow her to free herself from the self-doubts that had plagued her since childhood. It didn't instantly solve those deep-seated issues, but the course certainly gave her the perspective that it was up to her to take steps to change her life – nothing was going to land on her plate, so she felt it was now or never.

Chapter Twenty-five

Education

It was spring 1984. Deirdre was thirty-eight years old and still working on a part-time basis, more to keep busy than for the amount of money it was bringing into the house. John had been with the ESB for ten years by then and had a role and a team that he enjoyed – IT was growing in importance across the organisation and he thrived in keeping up his skills compared to the younger employees. One Sunday night, whilst Deirdre and John were in their local, the Coach House in Ballinteer, for a couple of drinks, Deirdre opened up a discussion. 'John, I wonder could I go to college? I might be able to get into something new that is more of a challenge.'

'Do you mean go back to school and do your Leaving?' asked John, pointing out that the basic entry to most colleges was a reasonable Leaving Certificate.

'I really don't think I could go back to school. I've read there's a way in which they let a number of mature students in without the Leaving,' replied Deirdre, as she had seen something about this when on that assertiveness course a couple of years earlier.

'You know I'm right behind you if want to try and do that,' said John, as he was keen that his wife have a go at changing

Education

direction if that was what she wanted. John knew someone in the library in UCD, which was the closest university to where they lived and the college that Deirdre's sister Ger had graduated from a few years earlier, and said he'd ask her to find some information on that access scheme.

A week later, an A4 envelope addressed to John arrived to Clonard Heights with a UCD emblem on it. Before John arrived home, and suspecting that this envelope may relate to her desire to go to college, Deirdre opened it and it contained all the information she needed to apply for mature access to third level without doing a Leaving Cert. UCD required an up to date CV, completion of a standard application form and a cover letter, which called for an explanation as to why the applicant didn't have a Leaving Cert and why, in their opinion, one of the places should be granted to them. Deirdre completed the application herself – John offered help, but she had it under control.

The application was submitted and, about four weeks later, a small envelope arrived, again with the UCD emblem. Deirdre opened it immediately, but, unfortunately, it was a short letter saying that, with regret, they wouldn't be allocating a space to Deirdre. It encouraged her to try again the following year or she could appeal the decision.

When John came home that evening, Deirdre was very down. 'I thought I'd a good chance, but maybe it's not meant to be,' she said with a tone of resignation.

John was having none of it. 'Do you have a copy of the letter you submitted?'

Deirdre had kept a copy and, after a few minutes, she found it and handed it to John. He read it twice and couldn't believe how subdued it was. He had known Deirdre for well over twenty years and she had written various pieces ranging from articles for papers, policy idea pieces for the Labour Party and letters to editors of numerous newspapers on topics of the day – but the letter lacked the passion and creativity he saw in those other writings. He decided to go after it. 'Is there a reason you were so low key in the letter? You didn't mention your work with the Labour Party, the foundation of Challenge, your passion for education access for the underprivileged. I don't believe it!'

There weren't many times in their relationship when Deirdre was stuck for words, but she knew she hadn't given the letter the energy or enthusiasm with which she normally embraced her writing. Slowly, she opened up to John. 'I was afraid that if I gave the process one hundred per cent and failed, it would be another sign that it's not to be ... I was also afraid if I got a place, that I wouldn't deserve it and would fail the exams.' She continued, 'I know it's a poor excuse, but I'm afraid of what might happen if I open myself up to this opportunity.' Deirdre was upset at herself, as she let the voice inside get to her.

But John was having none of it. 'You're capable of anything. There's an appeals process. Let's get working on a cover letter for the appeal.'

Deirdre and John spent the next couple of hours, and a few hours the following evening, writing up a more impassioned cover letter that spoke to Deirdre's achievements since leaving school and why she felt she could achieve anything with a fuller education. She submitted the appeal and, against all odds, received a call from UCD a few days later to say that

Education

her application was accepted and she was welcome to start in college that autumn. More tears, this time of happiness, followed when John came home from work that day – this was another one of those fork moments in life and through focus, passion, energy, unflinching support from her husband and a bit of luck, Deirdre forced herself down a new path and it would be down to her to seize that opportunity with both hands. Carpe Diem.

A few months later, it was one of those typical autumn days, the trees gently swaying in the light breeze and what was left of the year's barely warm sun casting shadows amidst what appeared to Deirdre to be a concrete jungle. It was 8 October 1984 and her first day in university – a day of excitement about who she would meet, what she would do and where this new adventure might lead to over the next few years. As Deirdre approached the Arts Block in UCD's Belfield Campus, she was immediately taken by the youthful and wide-eyed nature of her fellow students, some comfortable with their new surroundings, some feeling their way slowly into their new setting and others, like Deirdre, petrified of how the next few days and weeks would challenge them, a test she felt might be beyond her. She knew that day would be one of those moments she'd look back on in years to come as either 'that' turning point or just another day when she realised her future was pre-ordained.

Deirdre walked up the grey steps to the Arts Block, pulled the late 1960s wooden doors towards her and walked into what would be her second home for the next few years. The first thing that struck Deirdre were the hard surfaces and straight lines, a harshness that made her wonder if this was what Cardinal Newman had in mind as a place to educate the mind, the body and, most importantly, the soul – but, at that moment, she just needed to find Theatre L. 'What's a theatre? Why are they lettered? Oh Jesus, what am I doing here?' said Deirdre to herself. What had her there was simply an unsated desire to learn.

For First Arts, Deirdre picked three subjects, all of which held a strong interest for her:

- Politics, given her membership of the Labour Party and her upbringing by Matty, a fervent Republican;

- Philosophy, as she was always curious about what all of 'this' means; and

- Psychology, as she was keen to know why the mind works the way it does.

After a few false dawns and a couple of questions asked of those young enough to be her children, Deirdre finally found Theatre L for her first lecture, an introduction to Psychology from the head of the faculty. Deirdre took her seat and, although she felt like she was having an out of body experience, she struck up a conversation with some of the young students around her. 'Hi girls. I'm Deirdre O'Neill. What do you make of this place?' she said as she gestured at the vastness of Theatre L.

'I'm Helen and this is Mary. This place is huge. Sure makes a difference from my tiny school in Cork,' replied one of her classmates.

As much as Deirdre was fascinated by her classmates' youth and energy, they were equally inquisitive about why

Education

an 'old' person was in their class. What she had thought would act as a divide between her and the younger folk in the class was actually the conduit to drive deep and lifelong relationships.

The next few weeks went by rapidly, exciting and daunting in equal measure, as Deirdre juggled the educational demands of UCD with having a family at home. She got involved in various societies around the college, including, the Mature Student Society, the 'Wrinklies', and Psych. Soc. During those initial months, Deirdre found that some of her classmates, especially ones that were wide-eyed on that first day, gravitated towards her, particularly the girls – she thought she was maybe a mammy type figure for those that left home for the first time that year or maybe they felt Deirdre had some real world experience that could guide them along – but she too felt a pull towards them and really enjoyed feeding off their vivaciousness. It was a real life symbiotic relationship, one that Newman would be proud of, as those interactions taught them all more on what life was about than any lecture in Theatre L could.

It was after Christmas in 1984 and Deirdre couldn't wait to get back into UCD in January for the second half of her first year, albeit she was dreading the summer exams. Then, out of the blue, John fell very sick – it turned out to be a stomach ulcer. He had emergency surgery a couple of nights later and at least six months recovery lay ahead for him.

Deirdre questioned whether she should throw in the towel in UCD. 'John, I think I'll defer the rest of first year and start again next September, when you're back on your feet.' She felt it wasn't meant to be, she had other priorities and part of her was keen to put off doing those end of year exams.

However, two weeks after falling sick, John got home from hospital, and he was having none of it. 'This is your time and I'll be fine.'

Helped by John being at home for the next six months, Deirdre continued her studies and began to realise that her hunger for more knowledge on Psychology was unbounded. The relationships deepened with those around her in UCD and she sat the exams in May 1985.

It was July 1985 and Deirdre had just become an aunt for the first time when Ger took delivery of her first child, Lauren, having married her college sweetheart, Mark, a year earlier. It was the week of Live Aid, when the world of music united to raise funds for the Ethiopian famine, but Deirdre's focus was solely on her impending First Year Arts results. Deirdre feared the worst, hoped for the best and, in the end, the results went well, all passed with flying colours and Deirdre achieved the required result in Psychology to take on 'Pure Psychology' – she was relieved and delighted in equal measure and it gave her a huge confidence boost heading into second year.

Five years later, Deirdre secured an honours degree in Psychology, a Masters in Clinical Psychology and an M.Sc. in Psychotherapy – all great accolades of her six years in college, but what she most treasured from those days were the people that lived through the experience with her – her family for allowing her the space to take on the adventure, but equally important were those gangs of students that Deirdre laughed and cried with, listened to when they needed a friendly ear and who listened to her when she was

Education

wracked with self-doubt. Those relationships with people from a different generation would persist, and if she had not taken those difficult steps up to the Arts Block on that mild autumnal day in 1984, she would never have been able to discover the art of the possible. Not surprising for a woman that sought to hide from the limelight, she never attended any of her graduations, but took quiet pride when she received her certificates from UCD.

Two relationships with her fellow students stood out. One was with Helen, who Deirdre had chatted to in that first lecture, the daughter of a local politician from Cork, who landed in First Arts in UCD aged eighteen and was a duck out of water during that first year away from her family. Deirdre identified early on that Helen was struggling with integrating into college, sought to include her in various events and meet-ups and they struck up a long lasting friendship. Despite their twenty-one year age difference, they stayed in touch after college and after Helen moved to Waterford for work. Deirdre was like a proud mother at Helen's wedding and both friends were always there for each other when needed.

A second of Deirdre's enduring friendships from her college years was with Brendan – he was nineteen when he joined UCD and got to know Deirdre during second year. Deirdre noticed that he withdrew from the group at various times during the academic year – she sought him out at one stage and he opened up about his struggles with mental health. For the next thirty-plus years, Brendan and Deirdre would meet up and share war stories and it was like unpaid counselling sessions for both friends. These were two examples of the friendships that Deirdre developed from her college years, but there were numerous other relationships formed that marked Deirdre as one of the go-to people when in need of advice and a friendly ear.

Deirdre's career had been administrative work mixed with looking after Andrew and Stephen and the lack of self-belief held her back from moving up the corporate ladder. However, now, armed with three degrees, she had several options that promised a level of self-actualisation – she ultimately chose Psychotherapy. Deirdre set up her own part-time private practice and, for the succeeding twenty-five years, sat with hundreds of clients, listened to their issues, doubts and challenges, and tried to give them some guidance on possible next steps. It wasn't about providing solutions, but more importantly about listening, helping them to mentally declutter and solutions often then became quite apparent. It reminded her of those many conversations she had shared with her classmates in college – best psychotherapy training was in the depth of those chats in the Bar or Restaurant in UCD, when anyone could say anything in a safe environment.

One of Deirdre's toughest but most rewarding stints as a counsellor was with the fledgling Childline helpline for children in distress. Deirdre heard all sorts of problems from children brave enough to call in and desperately tried to engage with them, keep them on the line and allow them the time and space to open up. She often wondered about the nine out of ten children that either didn't have the means to call in or just couldn't bear to tell the truth about their suffering, but consoled herself with the fact that she was providing an outlet for the ten per cent that could call. As she'd drive home after a session, she sometimes thought back to the loneliness

Education

she felt in the home in Longford and knew she benefited from the kindness of people such as Rose. Childline didn't exist back then, but Deirdre was fortunate to have been generally treated well and that she could see her loving mother every other month. Those Childline sessions were draining and, when she got home, she'd need time to clear her mind of the hardship she heard about from some of the children. Deirdre would look at her own children and couldn't help but think how they would feel if they were to experience what deprived boys and girls were having to go through.

Separately, some of Deirdre's most enjoyable stints in her counselling career were in a college environment, including NUI Maynooth, Trinity College and All Hallows College, listening to students who needed a sensitive ear, a gentle prod in one direction or other – not all cases were that simple, but she felt there was no better way to practise her profession than with the younger generation who were generally more open to new ideas than their wrinkly ancestors.

Chapter Twenty-six

1990s

The 1990s were another decade of change, globally, nationally and for the O'Neill family. Within Ireland, the biggest change was brought about by negotiations between Ireland and the UK, moderated by the US, with Bill Clinton, 42nd President, taking an exceptionally deep interest in resolving the Troubles that had plagued the island of Ireland for over twenty-five years. In 1994, the IRA announced a ceasefire and, on Good Friday 1998, a political settlement was agreed that would pave the way for devolved government and shared power in Northern Ireland.

From an O'Neill family perspective, they left Clonard Heights in 1992 and moved into Donnybrook, nearer to Dublin City. It was partly opportunistic, in that depressed house prices meant the possibility of buying a house before the economy got back on its feet, but the move was also motivated by Deirdre needing an office in the house to run her counselling practice, which she had started a year earlier in a rented office in Dundrum. That same year saw Andrew graduate from UCD with an honours degree in Pure Psychology, only five years after Deirdre graduated with the very same degree. The following year would see

1990s

Stephen graduate with an honours degree in Commerce from UCD. Three of the family of four had degrees from UCD and John also secured a master's degree by dissertation in the mid-1980s from Queen's University, Belfast. From humble backgrounds, this family had become highly educated. Andrew would go on to carve out a successful career as an IT analyst and Stephen qualified as a chartered accountant in 1996. Deirdre and John were fiercely proud of both boys and how they'd ploughed their own furrows in life.

The 1990s were quite the time for John and Deirdre from a career perspective. Deirdre continued to develop her psychotherapy and counselling skills, John took early retirement from the ESB and replaced that job with his own business in the provision of library and cataloguing systems, one of which was developed by Andrew, to various institutions in Ireland. It was a fulfilling period for both of them and they also took the time to travel to various new places across the globe. There was a trip to Hong Kong in 1992 to visit Deirdre's sister Ger and her family. By then, they had three children and one on the way, and had moved to Hong Kong for Mark to expand his experience base in orthopaedics, his specialty after completing medical school in the early 1980s.

Their most enjoyable trip was the one to Australia in 1997. Stephen was on a four-month secondment to Brisbane and that was the perfect excuse for Deirdre and John to take their one and only trip Down Under. Their favourite part of the holiday was a few days staying with Deirdre's cousin, Brian, and his wife Sarah, in the suburbs of Melbourne. Brian was Matty's nephew and, along with his brothers and sisters, he had entertained Deirdre on several summer trips to Galway when she was a teenager. That family in Galway, under the keen eye of Matty's sister Brigid, were well aware of Deirdre's adoption by Matty, but always treated Deirdre as simply one of the family. When Deirdre and John arrived in Melbourne, it was like going home, as they chatted about the old times in Dublin and Galway. They were over 10,000 miles from Ireland, but on those few evenings in Melbourne, they could well have been back on the Emerald Isle. Brian and Sarah were very fond of Matty and Ellen and loved recounting a multitude of stories of their visits to No. 12 and how Ellen, particularly, always looked out for them before they left Ireland for foreign shores.

Moving onto the end of the decade, it was October 1999. Deirdre and John were in Clonmany, a small village in the Inishowen Peninsula of Donegal, about fifteen miles as the crow flies from the most northerly point in Ireland, Malin Head, for Stephen's wedding to his fiancée Marie Doherty. Two days earlier, they'd arrived up and had the pleasure of meeting Marie's parents, Margaret and Patrick, for the first time and thoroughly enjoyed the Donegal hospitality with a wonderful pre-wedding meal in the Doherty family home.

The wedding was one of those days that Deirdre and John had been looking forward to for ages and would remember for the rest of their lives. One aspect of the day that was so important to both of them, but particularly Deirdre, was that her parents were there to share their youngest son's big day. Matty was eighty-eight and Ellen eighty-five and getting them up to Donegal was no mean feat. Ger, Mark and their four children, who by then had moved back to the UK, having got the ferry over to Dublin, picked up Ellen and Matty for a seven-hour drive to Donegal. They arrived at the hotel early in the evening the night before the wedding, only for Matty to be ushered king-like to the bar by his Galway nephews for a few pints and whiskey chasers. That led to one of the funniest moments of the weekend, when Ellen came down to the hotel lobby later that night to get Andrew to help lift Matty into bed after he stumbled in the room, due to being a little bit under the influence.

The following morning, the morning of the wedding, Stephen was working the room, chatting to the many guests that had travelled to be there, and he went up to his grandparents. Poor Matty wasn't in great shape.

'Nana and Grandad, how are ya? Did you enjoy last night? That was some crowd in the bar,' said Stephen.

'I'm a bit tired, Stephen, but looking forward to the day,' replied Matty, who looked every day of his eighty-eight years.

Ellen then couldn't resist. 'Ah Matty, you made of fool of yourself last night. You're not twenty-one anymore!'

After a few more minutes chatting, Stephen walked way grinning from ear to ear at how a marriage of forty-six years still boiled down to a wife giving out to her husband for acting the maggot the night before, but he was so chuffed to have them there to share his big day. Matty's health was fine, with a hip replacement a few years before giving him a new lease of life. However, Ellen's health gradually went downhill throughout the 1990s following a COPD diagnosis, which meant she was often on oxygen while at home. But that day they were in great spirits, in more ways than one, and a touching moment was when Stephen gave Ellen a bouquet of flowers during the speeches.

The day itself was a thrill ride for Deirdre and John. As it was a big wedding, it gave them scope to invite plenty of family and friends and they both enjoyed the interaction with everyone, both before and after the ceremony. The wedding ceremony went off like clockwork, which was not surprising with two accountants at the altar. Marie looked stunning as she walked up the aisle with Patrick, who looked like he was on a Sunday stroll, not dissimilar to how Matty had walked with Deirdre on her wedding day thirty years earlier. Another highlight was John doing a slideshow presentation of pictures of Stephen and Marie as children. There was embarrassment for all concerned, but it was a great way to get everyone in on where these lovebirds had come from. Although John was tasked with implementation, Deirdre was the instigator behind the idea.

That day was a fantastic and fitting finale to the decade, the century and the millennium. Deirdre and John had come a long way since they first met in the 1960s, marrying later that decade, the 1970s when they expanded their family, the 1980s when Deirdre focused on her education and the 1990s when their family grew up and they'd time for each other and their respective careers. They had no idea what the advent of the twenty-first century would bring them, but, although they didn't always agree on everything, one thing they shared was a common desire to enjoy the latter part of their lives together.

Chapter Twenty-seven

2002

Roll back forty-seven years and Ellen was giddy with excitement on the train to Newtownforbes as she was about to bring her beautiful daughter back to Dublin. The relationship with her daughter was strong, but there were scars that needed caring for in the years after the homecoming. As with any mother-daughter relationship, there were times during Deirdre's teenage period when she pushed too hard and Ellen would pull her back into line and there were numerous times where the 'father' discussion would rear its head only to be cut down before it grew legs.

Over the intervening years, and as Deirdre faced her own adult challenges, there were flash points between herself and Ellen. There was one time that they came to blows over something reasonably small, when Deirdre was complaining about something going on between herself and John, and Ellen, in no uncertain terms, told her to get on with it. The 'cross to bear' reference was brought up and Deirdre couldn't resist bringing up the past. 'Well, we know one of those crosses you keep mentioning is one you'll never talk about. I've been bearing the cross of your mistake all my life,' Deirdre said, as her emotions took over.

'You've no right to say that. You had a good life and your father and me looked after you as best we could,' replied Ellen, her voice quivering from a mix of anger and sadness at what her daughter had just said.

'Well, if you told me more about what happened, I might understand it more,' said Deirdre, sensing an opportunity to garner more information. On hearing this, Ellen clammed up, which frustrated Deirdre even more. At that time in her life, Deirdre could be like a dog with a bone and she pushed once more. 'Why can't you give me more information? You know it's important to me,' pleaded Deirdre.

Ellen couldn't reply nor make eye contact with her daughter. Matty heard the goings on in the scullery and, like a bull in a china shop, rushed in and told Deirdre to back off and not to talk to her mother with such disrespect.

That was it for Deirdre. She wasn't being disrespectful, she just wanted to know more about her past, information she felt she deserved as 'compensation' for almost eight years in a home. Deirdre walked out, followed by John, and it was five months before the two women would see each other again.

At one stage during the five-month hiatus, John paid a solo visit to Ellen and Matty to try, in his own way, to heal some of the wounds. Dating back to the night with Giorgio, where Ellen had implored him to look after her daughter, John, in some ways, felt more at home in No. 12 than in his own home in Ballybough, and, on that visit, he expressed that sentiment to Ellen and Matty. Although it didn't result in an immediate thawing of relations between mother and daughter, it allowed Ellen to be more open than usual. She reciprocated John's feelings, emotionally expressed that he

2002

was precious to her and Matty and gave him a big hug as he left the house that evening.

Towards the end of that period, Stephen, on a visit to see his grandparents, tried to broach the subject of his grandmother's estrangement from his mother, not to discuss the past, but just to see if there was a way in which the argument could be forgotten and the two women reunite – it was tearing him up that the two most important women in his life at that time weren't talking and it was obvious to him that both wanted to see each other again. But both women were too proud to stand down and present an olive branch. Stephen was met with the all too familiar brick wall and no matter how he tried to open up the discussion, it was shut down firstly by Ellen and then by Matty, supporting his wife unreservedly. That evening, he left Ebenezer Road wondering how the mother-daughter relationship could be repaired, but, after a few more weeks of silence, Deirdre called her mother and the two women chatted as if they'd talked every week for the preceding five months. Those flare-ups would only happen irregularly, but the skeletons of the past were never too far away.

As the years went by, Ellen's COPD illness worsened and she had numerous stints in hospital. By then, Andrew had moved abroad, so Stephen would do his best to pop into the hospital over lunchtimes, but the mainstay visitors were, of course, Matty, who would get the bus to Saint James's Hospital near Rialto no matter what the weather, and Deirdre with John. It was at those times that Deirdre showed how much she cared for her parents, by doing what she could for Ellen and ensuring that Matty was looked after at home.

Miss, Say Goodbye to Your Daughter

With Ger and her family in the UK, it was down to Deirdre to provide that day-to-day support, like Ellen and Matty had supported Deirdre through those childhood years after coming back from the home. Deirdre never thought about it – it was her duty to look after her parents and she enjoyed their company so much.

Ellen had a wicked sense of humour and loved a bit of gossip. On some of the visits to hospital, Ellen would be in flying form about the goings on in the hospital ward. 'Deirdre, wait till I tell you about your wan next door,' said Ellen pointing to the bed next to her, 'She was ranting in the middle of the night about all sorts. I think she has three children and none of them are talking to each other ... probably just waiting for the will!'

With Ellen being hard of hearing, this story was relayed at full volume, with Deirdre trying to shush her mother, which would only rev her up even more in telling the story. It was a comedy show most of the time, but Deirdre was just happy to see her mother in good form, as COPD could be quite a debilitating disease. Matty also recognised that his daughter gradually and almost imperceptibly increased her caring for the two of them over the years and he really appreciated the help she gave.

It was Saturday 16 March 2002 and Stephen and Marie were in Dublin City enjoying the annual SkyFest Saint Patrick's Weekend fireworks display. His mobile rang and it was his Aunt Ger. He pulled back from the crowd so he could hear her voice. 'Hi Stephen ... Mammy's dead ... Daddy just called me.'

Still trying to assimilate what she was talking about, he

2002

said, 'Nana's dead? Oh Jesus, what happened?'

'Daddy said they had a drink together in the parlour. She was in good form. He went back into her an hour later to say goodnight and she was dead.'

'Oh God, we'll go to the house now.'

Ger was very upset and Stephen was in shock. He had only seen them a few days earlier and there was no inkling that Ellen was that unwell. He also knew that he was going to find it difficult to contact Deirdre and John, who were in Spain on holiday and had forgotten to bring their mobile phone.

About thirty minutes later, they arrived at Ebenezer Road. Matty was inconsolable and, as he felt a strong connection to Marie from their respective rural backgrounds, he turned to her. 'What am I going to do without Ellen?' asked Matty.

He wasn't the tallest man in the world, but he was a big presence in any room. On that night, he was a beaten man and it was like the light had gone out. He was completely distraught and Marie and Stephen had no answers for him.

Ellen's body had already been taken into Saint James's Hospital and, about an hour later, the hospital called and explained that someone would have to go in to identify the body for the purposes of the death certificate. Stephen volunteered, as Matty was in no state to leave the house, and he headed off leaving Marie to try and comfort his grandad. He was shown into a hospital room where Ellen's body was laid out. Although it resembled his nana, the mischievous smile no longer graced her wrinkled face – it was at that moment that he realised his nana was gone and it hit him hard.

The following day, Stephen drove out to Dublin airport, as Deirdre and John were due back from Spain. After about an hour of trying to spot his parents, he saw John followed by Deirdre, who was always that bit slower than her husband. He made his way to where they came through Arrivals.

Deirdre spotted her son before John did and immediately knew something was wrong. 'What's wrong? Is it Nana?'

'I'm sorry, Mammy. Nana died suddenly last night.'

Deirdre, and John of course, became quite emotional and the three of them went for a cup of tea in the nearby café.

'I woke this morning and felt something was wrong,' said Deirdre. 'How's Grandad?'

'He's not great. He's a bit lost,' replied Stephen.

Deirdre felt guilty for not being there at her mother's greatest moment of need, but Stephen comforted her by telling her that she had passed peacefully and quickly. Deirdre couldn't believe that this person who had been looking out for her, in her own way, for the past fifty-seven years was gone, but she tried to prepare herself for what was coming, both in terms of her own grief but also trying to help her father cope with his loss.

It was very emotional when Deirdre and John arrived at Ebenezer Road. There were lots of hugs and tears, but there were also some laughs as they recounted stories of Ellen, her sense of humour and the capers she got into.

'Do you remember when we brought Mammy up to Belfast and we bought a record player? To smuggle it down, we put it under Mammy's feet and then piled forty toilet rolls on top. The customs guard didn't know what to think and waved us on, with Mammy grinning away,' said Deirdre, recounting one of the many stories of cross-border smuggling that went on over the years.

2002

Above all, they realised they were blessed to have had Ellen in their lives and, even if she could be stubborn as a mule, she would do anything for her family and would always protect them as best as she could.

Amidst the cloud of grief, Deirdre recalled a conversation she had had with her mother a few years earlier, in which Ellen said she had written a note of instructions for her funeral and burial. Deirdre then went to find the note and, thankfully, after about an hour, discovered it in one of Ellen's handbags. The instructions were clear: requiem mass in the church on the grounds of Our Lady's Hospice, Harold's Cross, dressed in a plain white tunic and, if she pre-deceased Matty, burial with her parents in Mount Jerome Cemetery provided it had sufficient depth for Matty – if not, a fresh plot. Deirdre was pleased that she had found these clear instructions. She knew some of what Ellen wanted, but Matty wasn't convinced – however, once the note was found, he was relieved that everyone could carry out Ellen's last wishes to the letter.

Although she didn't comment on it at the time, but later imparted it to John, Deirdre was disappointed that Ellen didn't leave another note to her with some additional information on her biological father, perhaps just his name. She felt she'd come to terms with the fact that those secrets might go to the grave with Ellen, but she still harboured hope that some information might be forthcoming. Despite searching everywhere in No. 12, there was no note to be found and it was clear to her that, due to those difficult circumstances in the mid-1940s, Ellen had simply buried those memories too deep to ever resurface.

The funeral the following Thursday was a fitting tribute

to Ellen, with Andrew reading out a poem he wrote especially for his nana. He was exceptionally close to Ellen, given his status as first grandchild and the fact that he spent so much time when he was small with her and Matty. Matty himself was very cut up on the day and it was clear to Deirdre and Ger that he was going to need a lot of minding in the weeks and months to come. It wasn't that he couldn't fend for himself, as he had become the main carer as Ellen's health deteriorated over the years. However, a strong man was suddenly frail and he was looking every day of his ninety-one years.

On the funeral day itself, Matty was profusely sweating and Deirdre and Ger felt that the shock may have brought on some illness. They called a doctor a couple of days later and he was diagnosed with pneumonia. The doctor felt it was likely he was sick before Ellen passed away, but the adrenalin of caring for her kept the virus at bay. But, with his defences down, the virus took a grip. He was given an antibiotic, but, after a few more days, was admitted to hospital for some more aggressive treatment.

Despite the doctors doing everything they could, exactly two weeks after Ellen's funeral, Matty lost his fight with pneumonia and, in the space of nineteen days, Deirdre and Ger lost both of their parents. When Ellen passed, Matty's heart broke, his ninety-one-year zest for life fizzled out and it was appropriate that they died so close together. From the night they had met in that Dublin pub, they were rarely out of each other's company. They were well known for having tiffs in public, generally when Matty did something silly, but they were a lovable sweet couple – him with his jelly and ice cream for dessert, her with her dash of blackcurrant in a glass

2002

of Guinness. Matty's funeral day was more upbeat, as family and friends felt it was right that they be reunited so quickly. Stephen gave a eulogy and stressed the importance of their children and grandchildren in the lives of Ellen and Matty. He went on to talk about his grandad's interests. 'As most of you know, Grandad loved the odd bet on a horse race. The Grand National is on today and watch out for one specific horse. "You're Agoodun" might be worth sticking a bet on.'

As they all looked at the race in the pub after the funeral, 'You're Agoodun' finished a respectable seventh place, and everyone agreed the name captured the spirit of Matty – nobody had a bad word to say about him, one of life's good ones.

A sour note for Deirdre on the day was a comment made by one of Matty's relatives along the lines of, 'Wasn't he great to marry Ellen and take you in, despite everything?' reminding Deirdre that a past is never forgotten. She and John let that comment go. She thought to herself of the day that Matty walked her up the aisle – both so proud of each other – that's what mattered to her, not what happened in the distant past. Although the next few months were challenging for Deirdre, she took great comfort from the long and mainly happy lives her parents had lived.

Despite their great ages, Ellen and Matty never got to meet any great-grandchildren. However, about a week before his grandad passed away, Stephen visited him in hospital and, to his surprise, Matty asked him when he and Marie were going to have children. Matty felt it was time for them to start a family and, when Stephen sought to deflect the question, his grandfather put him straight. 'Get on with it!' exclaimed Matty.

Miss, Say Goodbye to Your Daughter

Stephen chuckled at the intensity with which this frail ninety-one-year old man was pushing the agenda, which only egged Matty on further.

'Just do it!' he said like something from a Nike ad.

Stephen got the point and promised to talk to Marie later.

Chapter Twenty-eight

Granny

Deirdre had an ounce more subtlety than her father when it came to the reproductive plans of her two children. Although she and John were looking forward to the day they themselves would become grandparents, they weren't the sort to start asking questions like, 'Anything stirring?'

They wouldn't have to wait long. On 9 July 2003, on what was Deirdre's fifty-eighth birthday, Stephen and Marie asked them over to dinner. Before dinner was served, he said, 'Mammy, I've two presents for you. One you get today, but the other you're going to have to wait about seven months for.'

John detected what was going on, but it took a few seconds for the penny to drop with Deirdre. When it was clarified that Marie was two months pregnant, Deirdre and John were ecstatic, simply on cloud nine.

Deirdre was instantly asking Marie questions about how she was feeling. 'Any morning sickness? Any cravings? Any tiredness?' The usual questions that a mother who has been through it asks.

The baby was due at the end of January 2004 and it was

now 6 February. Unbeknown to Deirdre and John, Marie went into hospital that evening, her waters having broken earlier that morning. Deirdre called the house to check on how Marie was keeping and, when she didn't receive an answer, nor an answer to Stephen's mobile, she became suspicious. On the other side of this situation was Marie, who was lying on a pre-delivery bed, with contractions coming at increasingly regular and more painful intervals. Both Stephen and Marie heard the phone ring at the nurses' station outside the room. 'Yes, she's in here ... she's early stage ... I'd say the baby will arrive in the next twelve hours or so ... thanks,' said the midwife.

'I bet that's your mother,' said Marie, with a tone of frustration, as they'd wanted to keep the news to themselves until the baby arrived.

The midwife then came in. 'That was Daddy's mother,' she said, confirming Marie's suspicions. 'I told her you're early stages, so that should keep her happy for a while,' said the midwife with an air of mischief.

About five hours later, David Matthew O'Neill arrived weighing eight pounds three ounces. Marie and Stephen were instantly besotted with their new baby and, when Stephen called his parents to impart the news, Deirdre was for coming into the hospital, even though it was 2 a.m. The new grandparents were beyond excited to meet their first grandchild and were spotted in a local shopping centre the following day by one of John's sisters – she would later describe them as being like two children on Christmas morning. They came into the hospital that afternoon to see baby David and it was love at first sight.

Granny

Like waiting for a bus for ages and then two arrive, their second grandchild was delivered in Spain three months later, as Andrew, who had moved there a few years earlier, and his partner had their first child, Diego. Over the next eight years, four more grandchildren arrived, three boys named Alex, Tarin and Jiru and their one and only granddaughter, Julia. Each of the grandchildren had their own personalities, their own desires, wants and needs, but Deirdre and John loved each of them for who they were at that moment in time. There's no doubt that Julia Ellen O'Neill had a special place in Deirdre's heart – she always felt a bit outnumbered in the O'Neill house, given its male-dominated nature, and loved the idea of having a granddaughter to dote over, the dresses, the pinks, the hair. One of the presents Deirdre got such pleasure from buying was a large teddy bear dressed in a pink outfit with the words 'Special granddaughter Julia' on the front – to this day, the teddy has pride of place in Julia's bedroom, a reminder of the mutual love between her and her Dublin grandparents. Similar gifts came from the Donegal grandparents and Julia has always known how lucky she is to have developed relationships with all her grandparents.

Babysitting and childminding were a regular job for Deirdre and John after the arrival of their grandchildren. Fitting it in with the busy schedule of trips away and Bridge competitions was always tricky, but Deirdre treasured story time with the grandchildren. Bedtimes can be fraught with small children, but, whilst John was the 'on the floor playing' type of grandad, Deirdre was the carer in the evening that would make sure they all went to bed having had some wind down moments with her. There was one time they were babysitting Stephen's children, when Julia had just turned two, and she was first for bedtime. Deirdre brought her upstairs and did the usual story time followed by teeth brushing. However, when it came to changing Julia into her pyjamas, Deirdre went for a nappy for night-time, even though Julia had been in pants during the day since earlier that week.

The response she got was forthright. 'I not wear that!' Julia said pointing to the nappy, 'I wear big girl pants!'

Deirdre was delighted on two fronts – firstly, she was impressed that her only granddaughter had ditched nappies having just turned two, but, secondly, that this little girl with baby blonde curly hair was having none of it when her granny tried to put on a nappy – Deirdre's strength of character was alive and well in the next generation.

As the grandchildren started to grow up and develop their characters and personalities, Deirdre and John loved to hear about how each of them was getting on in school and sports. Probably because of her background and training as a psychotherapist, Deirdre was acutely aware of the subtleties of their personality traits. Most parents, to some degree, live through the achievements of their children and this is equally true in grandchildren. Reading end of term school reports was always something Deirdre and John enjoyed, less to do with the percentage results and more to do with hearing what teachers thought about their grandchildren's respective personalities and how they behaved with their peers. With the infinite differences between each child, this led to an array of traits that thrilled Deirdre and John. From the strong work ethic of David, the adventurous nature of Diego, the

Granny

mile a minute Alex, the caring side of Julia, the innocent and gentle kindness of Tarin and the earnest and inquisitive side of Jiru, it was each to their own, but this group of six O'Neill offspring were a sight to behold.

Deirdre and John valued regular visits to see their grandchildren, so they could establish that vital bond between the generations. Andrew and Stephen treasured their close and enduring relationships with Ellen and Matty. Deirdre and John were equally keen to ensure this was the case with all their grandchildren. Geography can mitigate against this and, in the case of Andrew's first child, Diego, his early years being brought up in Spain, initially in Madrid and later in the south of the country, made it a bit more challenging for Deirdre and John to see him regularly. In any event, Deirdre and John enjoyed visiting Spain, so they still got to see Diego a lot between 2004 and 2008 and developed a strong bond with him. This thrilled Andrew, as he was keen for this bond to become ingrained in his eldest child. Also, Tarin and Jiru hadn't yet arrived, which meant that Deirdre and John could devote all their attention to Diego during their regular meet-ups.

2008 proved to be a watershed in Deirdre and John's relationship with him, as Andrew and his partner separated that year. After a number of months of separation, Diego's mother moved back to Madrid with him, but, on the plus side, regular access was granted at that time, so Andrew and his parents could see Diego, both in Madrid and for thirty-six hour trips from Madrid to the south of Spain. Although not ideal, such regular access was sufficient to maintain the strong bond between all four of them.

However, the Court process for parental access in Spain is convoluted and significantly favours the mother, almost no matter what the reasons for separation. From 2011, access became more challenging, especially with Andrew living in the south of Spain, Diego in Madrid and visits reduced to eight-hours. By that time, Andrew and his new partner, Prisha, had Tarin, and, for a period, Andrew would commute up to Madrid for the eight hour access window every second weekend, but this was taking its toll on his health. He sought a more flexible access arrangement, which was rejected outright and, eventually, Andrew was forced to call a halt to seeing his son under that arrangement when he moved back to Ireland in 2012. Not only did this mean that he wasn't seeing his eldest son at all, but Deirdre and John also had no access rights.

They went from eight years of developing a strong bond with Diego, through regular trips to Spain, to not seeing him at all – this cut deeply for them and, as the years went by, they realised that Diego would be changing so much that they wondered whether the relationship could ever be rekindled. With no access, either in person or by telephone, Deirdre and John couldn't express the unconditional love they had for this fun-loving, spirited and adventurous soul. This estrangement affected Andrew on two levels, that his own relationship with his eldest son had stalled, but also that there was such a permanent rift between his parents and Diego. This whole situation brought back painful memories for Deirdre and she was drawing parallels with what Diego and Andrew were going through by being separated to what she and Ellen experienced when she was in the home. Also, Deirdre felt that this estrangement from his blood relatives would have a

Granny

permanent and significant impact on Diego – this worried her greatly and led to more sleepless nights.

Chapter Twenty-nine

Illness

It was December 2016 and Deirdre, John, Andrew, his partner Prisha and their two boys were in the south of Spain for a pre-Christmas break in the winter sunshine. They took a day trip to nearby Gibraltar, a place where Andrew and Prisha had once lived. The Rock of Gibraltar dominates that skyline, with the place being hilly and a tough walk for any tourist. However, John knew something was wrong with Deirdre when she was absolutely exhausted from one relatively short walk up a hill that day. She took a break at the top, but it was clear to both of them that there was something not right. Deirdre had also put on a little bit of weight around her tummy – for a naturally slight woman, this didn't feel right, but she put it down to a changed diet in recent years and a marginally more sedentary lifestyle. After the trip, they were back in Dublin for Christmas and, although Deirdre still didn't feel one hundred per cent, the day was a great joy, with five of her six grandchildren running around together.

By this stage, Deirdre and John had bought an apartment in Fuengirola, Spain, and they loved their four to six week post-Christmas trips down there. It broke up the ordinary

Illness

Irish winter and, in January 2017, they flew out as per normal. However, it was clear, after a couple of weeks out there, that there was something seriously wrong with Deirdre's health. Her stomach had bloated further to the point that she almost looked pregnant and, after some protestation with the local doctor, she was admitted to hospital for a series of tests. This went on for a week or so, with incorrect diagnosis after incorrect diagnosis, until Deirdre's eldest niece, Lauren, who was a urologist in the UK, sensed that the fluid retention, which was causing the bloating, could well be a sign of cancer in Deirdre's body. Finally, one of the doctors commissioned a test on the fluid, which confirmed the presence of a cancerous marker at an exceptionally high level. After a few more days, they both received the devastating news that Deirdre had ovarian cancer, known as the 'hidden cancer' as it only presents when it's far progressed.

Although John had suspected there was something seriously wrong for quite a few months, this news came out of the blue for Andrew and Stephen, who were both back in Dublin and felt helpless as Deirdre was in a hospital in Spain, with nurses and doctors that only had limited English.

After a bit of back and forth, it was agreed that Deirdre would come home and a consultation with a specialist in ovarian cancer was lined up. They arrived home and Stephen, who picked them up from the airport, was shocked at her appearance – she had gone from a reasonably fresh looking seventy-one-year old pre-Christmas to an old and frail woman being pushed in a wheelchair six weeks later.

The following Monday, Deirdre received the diagnosis that she had Stage 3C ovarian cancer, which meant that cancerous cells had spread to lymph nodes in the abdomen. On a quick internet search, it was clear to John, Andrew and Stephen that the survival rate beyond five years was less than forty per cent. At the consultation, Deirdre and John asked what the prognosis was and the oncologist indicated that this was likely to be terminal, with an expected lifespan of eighteen months to five years. However, John picked up from her tone that she thought it might be closer to the lower end of that range. On hearing the diagnosis and subsequent prognosis, Stephen left work early that afternoon and went up to Dundrum to be with his parents. It was a cold, wet and miserable February day and, as he stepped into the apartment, the air was cold, in a way that Stephen had experienced when he returned to his parents' house after his grandad's funeral some fifteen years earlier – the feeling that death was near. Deirdre and John were visibly shaken by the news, but both were resolute that there were a number of treatment options and they were up for the fight that was coming down the tracks.

When Stephen left, John sought to reassure Deirdre. 'I'm with you every step of the way, Deirdre. We'll beat this together.'

Deirdre and John's relationship since that first meeting in O'Lehane Hall had had its ups and downs, but there were far more good times than bad. John supported Deirdre as she embarked on the life-changing experience of a college education and Deirdre supported John when he became frustrated with his job in the ESB. They were an inseparable pair, genuinely enjoying each other's company, and John particularly loved Deirdre's never-ending inquisitive nature

Illness

and the desire to learn why things were the way they were. As their respective heads would hit the pillow on a random night, he would dread the words, 'Did you ever wonder why this or that is the way it is …?' A deliberately open question that John couldn't avoid – either he ignored the question and incurred her wrath or he engages – either way, sleep would be on hold for a while.

'Thanks, John. I know you're there for me. I'm scared.' They embraced and John reassured her that they'd face every step together, no matter what happened. It meant everything to Deirdre to know that she had her life partner there to meet each challenge. For John, he was also scared for how Deirdre would take to the treatment and his mind was also wandering to what would happen if the treatment didn't work as planned.

Something that focused Deirdre's mind amidst this sad news was the anniversaries or birthdays coming up that she wanted to be part of: John's seventy-fifth birthday in May 2018, their fiftieth wedding anniversary in April 2019, Stephen and Marie's twentieth wedding anniversary in October 2019 and Andrew's fiftieth birthday in June 2020. These were all vitally important dates in her calendar and she was looking forward to knocking them off over the coming years. Another focus, or more a concern, for Deirdre was how John would cope if she succumbed to the illness. John was self-sufficient in terms of household chores such as cooking and cleaning – Deirdre's six years in UCD in the 1980s had bumped John up in the pecking order of 'servants' in the O'Neill household – so she had no concern in that regard. It was his innate shyness and his follower rather than leader disposition that worried her, that he might be a lost soul.

Miss, Say Goodbye to Your Daughter

Although he was keen that she didn't dwell on these scenarios, John would let her articulate her concerns over the coming months. However, he always reassured her that, if it came to that, he would be fine and that she wasn't to worry about that aspect – her sole focus should be on positively approaching each treatment and knocking over only those hurdles in front of her at that time.

Although she would question treatment options over the coming months, cancer was not something she knew anything about and she placed her trust in the doctors and in John to guide her towards the best decision. In some ways, this was the first step in passing the baton to John – by his own admission, he was a spectator for almost fifty-five years in the relationship and he would rarely get a glimpse of the baton, not to mention being allowed to run with it. In the relay of life, there's a time for everyone to show their abilities and this coming period would be one such time for John.

The weekend after Deirdre's diagnosis, she, John and Stephen were meant to be heading to Exeter to celebrate Ger's sixtieth birthday. For Deirdre and John, the trip was a non-runner, but Stephen flew over to represent the O'Neill family. It was emotional for him that weekend, but being surrounded by such a warm family, one that he thoroughly enjoyed spending time with over the years, made it easier. Also, with Mark and three of their children being doctors, it gave Stephen the chance to ask general questions about this cancer and the treatments coming up for Deirdre.

On that Sunday night, whilst waiting for his flight home, he called Deirdre, who'd been admitted to the hospital for her first bout of chemotherapy the following day. They talked about the weekend in Exeter and about the upcoming treatment and, at the end of the call, he instinctively said, 'Love you', which was not something he would normally have said at the end of a call with Deirdre. Although she was delighted to hear those words, Deirdre began to wonder if she was being given the full picture. Of course, she had the full story, but she worried that maybe the cancer had spread further than had been articulated to her.

The next morning, Andrew and Stephen surprised Deirdre by being with her for that first session of chemo – with Deirdre on steroids, she was hyper and just got on with the treatment. The boys, on the other hand, were finding it difficult to take in what had happened to their mother in such a short space of time.

Over the next three months, Deirdre had six chemotherapy treatments, followed by a full hysterectomy in June, followed by another six chemo sessions over the succeeding three months. Deirdre had always been self-conscious about her appearance, but losing her hair as a result of the treatment didn't bother her. She got a well-fitted wig and boasted about having the hair she always wanted, having had very thin hair all her life. Deirdre recovered well from the hysterectomy surgery, but the chemo took its toll on her body – for cancer, the treatment can be worse than the disease but, in Deirdre's case, it wasn't a choice. The cancer had spread silently for a long period and aggressive treatment was required to give her a fighting chance of life.

In this period, there were good times. Once she received her diagnosis, Deirdre's mission was to make it to her eldest niece's wedding seven months later. It was in the family garden in Exeter and, with the help of John, Andrew and Prisha, she made it over in one piece and was beaming with pride as Lauren walked up the makeshift aisle with Mark and then back down with her new husband Jack. As with any first born, Deirdre had a soft spot for Lauren and was delighted to see her so happy and content – Lauren was a free spirit, much like Deirdre, and the eclectic nature of the day was right in Deirdre's wheelhouse. Given her weakness from the various treatments, she sat back, for once, and enjoyed watching everyone else strut their stuff on the dance floor.

By Christmas 2017, Deirdre felt marginally better and Christmas Day was another family-filled experience – Stephen and Marie hosted everyone and there was lots of love and laughter shared around the kitchen table. Deirdre still took some time out to rest on the sofa, but she loved seeing the grandchildren, especially the small ones, running around with giddy excitement. Her mind did turn to Diego, whom she hadn't seen for over five years, and she hoped he was having a nice Christmas Day and that he was likewise thinking about his Irish family. Since Deirdre's diagnosis, John had reached out to Diego's mother, but to no avail, and Deirdre had come to terms with the fact that she might never see Diego again. At times, this filled her with overwhelming sadness, but she tried to be practical and just got on with it. In Ellen's parlance, just another cross to bear.

Another special memory was in May 2018. It was John's seventy-fifth birthday and he and Deirdre, together with Andrew and Stephen's families, headed for Portlaoise for a night away to celebrate. In many ways, it was a quiet evening, but despite being weak, Deirdre mustered enough energy to

Illness

still be up after midnight. In a lovely part of the night, and with the grandchildren in bed, it was just Deirdre, John, Andrew and Stephen in the lounge, with each recounting some of those bizarre holiday stories from the 1980s. 'Mammy, do you remember when you pushed us over the Czech border, with the border guards looking on with their rifles?' said Andrew, about that attempted trip behind the Iron Curtain.

'Do you remember the red light district in Munich?' said Stephen, reminding the family of the time they all strayed into the dodgy part of town and John covered Stephen's eyes, as he asked why those women were sitting in the windows.

It was almost like they were back in those times, with the 'four musketeers' ready for another real-life adventure. Earlier that night, a group of French people sang 'Happy Birthday' in their native tongue to John and then sent over a round of Irish whiskeys to the O'Neill table. It seemed, wherever the O'Neill family went, fun followed and it gave Deirdre a lift to see her family around her for this occasion. This was the first box ticked on that long list of events she wanted to be at over the coming years.

However, a month earlier, Deirdre and John had received the news they were dreading – the cancer was back and it was growing aggressively. The hysterectomy had removed much of the tumour, but, whilst it was always going to come back, the consultant had hoped this might be years rather than months. This was awful news for Deirdre in that she had put up with the side effects of chemo in the hope that she might get a year or two of life quality before having to go back into treatment. But now, it seemed that she was heading back for more rounds of chemo before her ravaged body had any time to repair.

Deirdre was in and out of hospital over the next few months, mostly for infection control, but she was finding it increasingly difficult to manage pain. She knew that pain was a side effect of both cancer and its treatment, but her normally high threshold was being tested to its limit. Then, in August 2018, Deirdre had a dizzy episode at home, which gravely concerned John – she couldn't articulate herself and she immediately went into hospital.

Chapter Thirty

Acceptance

After she was admitted, Stephen visited Deirdre in hospital. He noticed that the pain was being managed by low dose intravenous morphine and he wondered why this had progressed from oral medicine. He asked John, who simply said that Deirdre's pain levels were too high for oral medication, but it was hoped that an upcoming bout of chemotherapy would reduce the tumours so the pain might lessen to allow moving off morphine. Although he offered to cancel a family holiday, Deirdre and John encouraged Stephen to bring the family to California. In one final visit to the hospital before the holiday, he recalled the O'Neill family trip there in 1986 and promised that he would try and create similar memories for his children to the ones he had. Andrew and his family similarly went on holiday that month to Spain, but Deirdre was insistent that life should go on and that she was in good hands.

During their respective trips, Andrew and Stephen kept in touch with Deirdre and John, but both were increasingly worried at the lack of progress, delays in chemo treatments and John's disposition on those calls. Stephen and family landed from California and he dashed up to the hospital to see Deirdre – he knew that John was to see the consultant on his own earlier that day, which concerned him. He was taken aback at how frail Deirdre had become, but she still had enough fight to give out about her room-mate, in what was a re-run of the times she herself would visit Ellen in hospital.

When Deirdre was having her drip changed, Stephen took the opportunity to get John out of the room so he could find out how his father had got on with the consultant.

'How did you get on with the doctor?' inquired Stephen.

Trying to hold back the tears, John's trembling voice said, 'She said Mammy has only got weeks to live.'

'Weeks? You're joking? Oh, Jesus,' was all Stephen could respond with.

Without saying it to each other, John, Andrew and Stephen had felt for a few weeks that the end game might be coming, but none of them expected it would happen this quickly. Maybe she might make it to Christmas, maybe to their fiftieth wedding anniversary the following April. But when it was starkly put in 'weeks', it was like a thunderbolt.

'Does she know yet?' asked Stephen.

'No, I don't know how to tell her, but I'll have to do it over the next couple of days.'

That was not a conversation John ever wanted to have, but he had promised to always be honest with her and wasn't going to renege now. But first, he wanted to let Andrew and Stephen know and he said he was going to ring Andrew later that evening, who was still in Spain on holiday.

After a few minutes, John and Stephen gathered themselves and, shortly after that, Deirdre received what she thought was good news – she was being moved to a private

Acceptance

ward, but this was standard practice in the hospital for end of life palliative care patients. Later that evening, John imparted the awful news to Andrew, who tried to be pragmatic, but underneath it, was devastated that the parent he had most in common with was entering her final weeks.

The following afternoon, Deirdre and John were talking in the hospital room. 'John, I don't think I'm well enough to have chemo next week. I'm in too much pain and what happens if I can't get the treatment started?'

John had been hoping to stave off the moment he told her about the prognosis until the following day, but his face gave way. He started to cry and Deirdre asked what was wrong.

'Deirdre, I'm afraid there's nothing more they can do.'

Amazingly, Deirdre took it in quickly and responded, 'I thought you might say that. Is this the end?'

As John edged closer to her and they held each other's hands, John replied, 'I'm afraid so, Deirdre. I'm so sorry,' and they both shed some tears.

'How long do I have left?' inquired Deirdre, with a practical sense to try and put specifics around the nebulous thought that all treatments were exhausted.

'They're saying a few weeks,' said John, hardly able to get the words out at that stage.

'It's OK, John. I knew this day was coming. Are you going to be OK?' At the moment Deirdre was told her life would end shortly, her first thought was for John, concerned that he wouldn't cope without her. John couldn't quite believe it, but she re-emphasised that he would now be her focus – when they met in that dance hall fifty-five years before, they never thought it would come to this, but, for both of them,

Miss, Say Goodbye to Your Daughter

they never felt as close as they were at that moment. Rather than being a couple whose ravages of life eat away at the love that once attracted them, and despite the odd hiccup along the journey, their love and respect for each other blossomed as the years went by – they admired each other's traits and the synergistic benefit of being together far outweighed their individual strengths.

As they held hands at that hospital bed, John felt Deirdre's energy and zest for life dissipate ever so slightly, but it was replaced by a zeal to gracefully leave this earth with dignity.

That evening, Stephen and Marie visited the hospital in the knowledge that Deirdre knew her time was coming. The hugs that were banned for the previous eighteen months, for fear of Deirdre catching an infection, were back and the tears weren't far behind. A similar scene ensued a couple of days later when Andrew and Prisha got back from Spain. Deirdre was enjoying the fact that everyone was around her, even if she found it increasingly difficult to stay awake, as the impact of increased pain control kicked in.

On the night she found out her prognosis, Deirdre laid her head on the pillow and, despite her weakness and lethargy, she understandably found it difficult to wind down and sleep. As she closed her eyes, thoughts of the life she had lived came flooding into her mind, ranging from her vague memories of the big return to Ebenezer Road, that first meeting with John, their wedding day, the arrival of her two children, her six grandchildren and the day she received her Bachelor of Arts certificate from UCD. They were overwhelmingly positive moments in her life, but her mind also wandered to what her life could have been like if her biological father had stuck

Acceptance

the course with Ellen. These weren't negative thoughts, but being a deep thinker, she was trying to think through scenarios that may have played out if her fate was different.

Throughout all the years that she had tried to prise information from Ellen, and partly out of respect for the sacrifices her parents made for her, Deirdre never once searched for her biological father – no DNA tests, no private investigations, no Google, Facebook or other searches. That level of respect for her parents was equally matched by a fear that such an investigation may uncover something she'd rather not know about her past. That night in the hospital was the last time that Deirdre's difficult upbringing strayed into her conscious thoughts and she instead focused on enjoying every moment she had left.

A few days after the news, Stephen delivered a short letter to his mother that he had written after finding out that the disease was back the previous April. He felt he couldn't express his thoughts in person and so gave it to John to read after he left the hospital. The note simply expressed his admiration and love for his mother and pointed out that her belief system was alive and well in the next generation. John read it out to her and there were tears, but she was thrilled to hear the positive impact she had had on her children.

If Deirdre was to be granted one last wish, it would be to have the opportunity to talk one last time to Diego and to tell him how much he was loved. About a week into her end of life treatment, Andrew and Stephen managed to get in touch with Diego's mother, such that he called and talked to both Deirdre and John. It was a short call, but long enough for Deirdre to express her love for him and, after the call, she was high as a kite. If her life was to be taken right at that moment, she would have passed peacefully.

Ger made it back from Singapore, where she and Mark had relocated to earlier that year, and Deirdre was delighted to see her. She had feared, with the Singapore move, that she mightn't see Ger again and to have her there in the hospital soothed her greatly. Then came the visits from her four nieces and nephews, who all made the trip over from the UK. Her eldest niece Lauren, whose marriage was such an enjoyable affair for Deirdre the previous year, was seven months pregnant at the time and, knowing that Deirdre most likely wouldn't make it to the birth of that child, she let her aunt feel the baby kicking and quietly told Deirdre that it was a girl and would be called Ruth. Often in Deirdre's life, she felt like an outsider, but this symbolic sharing of the baby news filled her with joy and that goodbye embrace was particularly poignant.

About ten days before she passed, Stephen had the chance to sit down with his mother to chat. The discussion covered issues such as Brexit and Trump. For whatever reason, Stephen brought up Ellen and Matty. 'What do you think Nana and Grandad would make of all of this?'

'They'd be sad, but Nana would probably say "We all have our crosses to bear",' said Deirdre with no small hint of irony. She went on to discuss her relationship with her parents and how Matty cared for her as his own. The topic of the home or her biological father never came up, but Deirdre, ever the philosopher, queried whether any being, human or insect, really matters. 'Do any of us really make a difference?' inquired Deirdre.

The discussion was, by now, getting heavy, which was no

Acceptance

surprise to Stephen, as he knew what his mother could be like when it came to such matters. With an emotional voice, Stephen responded, 'You made a difference for sure. Maybe not on a global scale, but on the community around you, your family, friends, classmates and your clients.' He liked to think she rested easy on hearing those words, but knowing her for over forty years by then, he thought, in her own mind, she had the last word.

There were also moments in those days where Deirdre had solo time with Ger, Andrew and, of course, John. In some ways, it was like the clocks stood still and everyone had sufficient time to just talk, without having to think about something else that needed to be done. In other ways though, time was rushing by and Deirdre was increasingly finding it difficult to articulate her thoughts.

At one stage, John helped Deirdre towards the bathroom in the hospital room. She was very weak and the effort of making it those few steps was enormous. He walked her to the door and then let her have some peace and quiet. After a few minutes, she stood up from the toilet and looked in the mirror. What she saw was an old woman. What she also saw in the reflection was Grace, whom she had, by happenstance, 'bumped into' numerous times over the years since they 'shared' a classroom. That elegant well-educated lady from a stable family background was actually Deirdre all along. Deirdre had labelled herself in a certain way from the moment she left that home in Longford, whilst those around her simply admired her for the person she was, an articulate, bright, passionate, enthusiastic, eccentric and elegant woman. As she looked in the mirror one last time, she accepted how she looked, accepted how she had carried herself throughout her life and walked slowly out of the bathroom. John, unaware of what transpired, walked her back to the bed and helped her in. Although still exceptionally weak, Deirdre was content and ready for what would come next.

On 12 September 2018, at 5 p.m., Deirdre Mary O'Neill passed away peacefully surrounded by her husband John, children Andrew and Stephen and her sister Ger. It was beautifully emotional, with all of them holding her as she took her last breath, talking to her and encouraging her to let go. Everyone in the room knew the importance of that moment, but it didn't help ease the pain of loss.

The funeral ceremony in the packed-out Victorian Chapel of Mount Jerome Cemetery was a wonderful tribute to a lady that touched many during her seventy-three years. There were eulogies from John and Stephen, uplifting music, including Chuck Berry's Johnny B. Goode, a beautiful poem written by Andrew and each of the five grandchildren present had a role to play, including David who linked arms with John to help carry Deirdre into the chapel. This was a life well lived and a person well loved.

Epilogue

From the perspective of twenty-first century pluralist Ireland, in which, as a nation, its people have become increasingly diverse and accepting of so many moral issues ranging from abortion to gay rights to divorce, it's difficult to understand what led to many mothers being banished from their communities or, worse, separated from their babies. Ellen and Deirdre's story is a positive outcome for mother and baby, with many other babies dying prematurely, buried in mass graves with no ceremony or dignity. A multitude of mothers and babies survived the ordeal and remained together, but survival is not what Ireland should have strived for as a nation. Every one of these human beings deserve full redress, maybe not financial at this stage, but recognition by the State and Church of the wrongdoings of the past, that the actions of those institutions were morally wrong. The Irish nation has begun to face up to the consequences of those decisions, but it's often after a time-consuming and emotionally draining tribunal or inquest.

For Ellen and Deirdre, they 'survived' the exceptionally difficult circumstances they were thrown into in the mid-1940s, but their relationship was forever changed from the moment the courts committed Deirdre to the Industrial School of Newtownforbes in 1947. Relationships between parents and their children are naturally fraught with difficulties, as parents strive for perfection, end up with imperfection and simply hope that children eventually appreciate the sacrifices they made to enable their offspring to have greater opportunities in their lives. For Ellen and Deirdre, their relationship would be tested in the same way as any growing child tests the boundaries with their parents, but against a backdrop of short supervised visits every second month for eight of Deirdre's first ten years of life. With that background, it was no wonder there were flashpoints along the journey from their permanent reunion in 1955 to Ellen's sudden death some forty-seven years later.

For Ellen, the events of 1944 through 1947 changed her life utterly and she bore enormous guilt for the first period of her daughter's life. The circumstances Ellen found herself in forced her into a whirlwind of emotions, pressures and decisions – she wasn't in control in those dark moments, but that didn't ease her feeling that she had abandoned Deirdre when she was most vulnerable. She ultimately built up walls around her that not even Matty was fully able to scale. Once the foundations for those walls went in, Ellen added rows of blocks to protect herself to the point that she never felt she could let Deirdre behind to share some of the pain and guilt that she brought to the grave.

For Deirdre, no child should ever have to be brought up by strangers in a clinical institution when, with a bit of help from the State, her own mother would have been able to raise her. As with the extent of Ellen's guilt, it's difficult to

Epilogue

truly understand the emotions that raged through Deirdre, from her early years through to her own death, about the whys, the whos, the hows. Her own mother was the one with some answers and Deirdre was only able to prise morsels of meaningful information from that source.

There's no doubt that many of Deirdre's character traits were formed in Our Lady of Succour, Newtownforbes rather than Ebenezer Road, both positive and negative. Despite her obvious external beauty and elegance, she could never accept her appearance and would, for all her life, shy away from the centre of the room, never wanting her photo to be taken for fear of how it would portray her. It was like every camera that pointed towards her could x-ray, see her emotions from the inside and she couldn't abide people seeing how she really felt.

Deirdre would always stand up for the downtrodden and there's no doubt some of that came from her experiences in Newtownforbes, but it was also partly attributable to how her parents acted towards those less fortunate in the local community. Deirdre would often worry about what might happen, what could happen in any given situation – she would play out multiple scenarios, ad nauseum, and this was partly due to her time in the home, which gave her an 'expect the worst' mentality in many circumstances. People had to earn Deirdre's trust to be accepted into her circle – once in though, it was a treasure trove for those friends. The way Deirdre turned around her life aged thirty-nine, zealously pursuing further education and carving out a successful career caring for others, showed that many people get to where they're meant to be eventually. Deirdre certainly did that, but, for sure, others from the same background were pushed too far down one path to be able to turn it around in later life. Deirdre knew she was one of the lucky ones and often thought of the girls she ran around with in Newtownforbes – who knows the breadth of life experiences they all eventually had and how those experiences would match up if fate hadn't intervened.

Acknowledgements

———✶———

This book could not have been written without the time taken by my dad to recount his understanding of my mother's background, her childhood years and their lives together after meeting in 1963. His patience in talking through the various events of my mother's life was only matched by his dedication to reading version after version of the book and his encouragement every step of the way. I'm also grateful to him for allowing me to bend his ear on various matters unrelated to the book over recent years – always a calming presence who gave me the confidence to believe in myself.

I want to thank my wife and three children for putting up with me wittering on about this book for the past fifteen months and for giving me the space to get through the process. Hopefully, the book will be there for my children as an inspiration to believe that anything is possible with focus, determination and a bit of luck.

I'm also very thankful to my aunt for reading the drafts of the book, encouraging me to keep going and for providing invaluable guidance on my mother's early years.

For engaging with me over various drafts, I'm especially

grateful to Joan Burton, Garrett Fagan, Alan Kealy, Sarah Ó Cinnéide, my brother, Gavin, Stephen Wilson, The Inkwell Group, Design for Writers and Kazoo Independent Publishing Services. Your individual perspectives guided me in so many ways and a heartfelt thanks to you for taking the time to invest in my work of passion.

Finally, to my mother and grandmother for being the two most important female role models in my life and for surviving the ordeal presented to them in the 1940s. My grandmother was a typical Irish granny that would do anything for her grandchildren, with a mischievous smile to boot. I'm forever grateful to my mother for being my moral guiding light and for showing me that you can achieve anything if you bring passion and energy to it, qualities she had in spades.